Dear Reader,

I've often written books about family, the relationship between sisters and brothers. But family isn't only blood and shared ancestors. It's memories and affection, loyalties and frustrations. At its best, family is friendship.

In *Daring to Dream*, I'd like to introduce you to three women of different backgrounds who through circumstances were raised in the same household. They shared childhood, and those loyalties, and the friendship that comes to mean family. They also share a dream inspired by a tragic legend. But each has a separate and personal dream of her own.

For Margo, the housekeeper's daughter, it is to be someone. And when her world falls apart, there is nowhere to go but home. What does a woman do when she's lost everything she thought mattered to her? How does she handle the humiliation of public scandal and financial ruin?

Margo starts from scratch with a new dream, a daring one. With the women who are the sisters of her heart, she works to make that dream a reality, one they can share. Margo's story is one of self-discovery, of risk and reward. And, of course, of love.

The attraction between Joshua Templeton and Margo has simmered since they were children. Acting on that attraction as adults—stubborn, headstrong adults—and learning to accept each other as they are, is another risk, and still another dream. I hope you enjoy sharing it.

Nora Roberts

By Nora Roberts

Homeport	Northern Lights	Black Hills
The Reef	Blue Smoke	The Search
River's End	Montana Sky	Chasing Fire
Carolina Moon	Angels Fall	The Witness
The Villa	High Noon	Whiskey Beach
Midnight Bayou	Divine Evil	The Collector
Three Fates	Tribune	The Liar
Birthright	Sanctuary	The Obsession

The Born In Trilogy:
Born in Fire
Born in Ice
Born in Shame

The Bride Quartet:
Vision in White
Bed of Roses
Savour the Moment
Happy Ever After

The Key Trilogy:
Key of Light
Key of Knowledge
Key of Valour

The Irish Trilogy:
Jewels of the Sun
Tears of the Moon
Heart of the Sea

Three Sisters Island Trilogy:
Dance Upon the Air
Heaven and Earth
Face the Fire

The Sign of Seven Trilogy:
Blood Brothers
The Hollow
The Pagan Stone

Chesapeake Bay Quartet:
Sea Swept
Rising Tides
Inner Harbour
Chesapeake Blue

In the Garden Trilogy:
Blue Dahlia
Black Rose
Red Lily

The Circle Trilogy:
Morrigan's Cross
Dance of the Gods
Valley of Silence

The Dream Trilogy:
Daring to Dream
Holding the Dream
Finding the Dream

The Inn Boonsboro Trilogy:
The Next Always
The Last Boyfriend
The Perfect Hope

The Cousins O'Dwyer Trilogy:
Dark Witch
Shadow Spell
Blood Magick

Many of Nora Roberts' other titles are now available in eBook and
she is the author of the In Death series using the pseudonym J.D. Robb.
For more information please visit
www.noraroberts.com or www.nora-roberts.co.uk

NORA ROBERTS

Daring to Dream

piatkus

PIATKUS

First published in the United States in 1996 by The Berkley Publishing Group
A division of Penguin Group (USA) Inc., New York
First published in Great Britain in 2008 by Piatkus
Reissued in 2008 by Piatkus
This edition published in 2016 by Piatkus

10 9 8 7

A CIP catalogue record for this book
is available from the British Library.

ISBN 978-0-349-41169-9

Data manipulation by Phoenix Photosetting, Chatham, Kent
Printed in Great Britain by Clays Ltd, Elcograf S.p.A.

Papers used by Piatkus are from well-managed forests
and other responsible sources.

MIX
Paper from
responsible sources
FSC® C104740

Piatkus
An imprint of
Little, Brown Book Group
Carmelite House
50 Victoria Embankment
London EC4Y 0DZ

An Hachette UK Company
www.hachette.co.uk

www.piatkus.co.uk

To old friends

Daring to Dream

Prologue

California, 1846

He was never coming back. The war had taken him from her. She felt it, felt his death in the emptiness that had spread through her heart. Felipe was gone. The Americans had killed him—or perhaps his own need to prove himself had done so. But as Seraphina stood on the high, rugged cliffs above the churning Pacific, she knew she had lost him.

Mist swirled around her, but she didn't draw her cloak close. The cold she felt was in the blood, in the bone. It could never be vanquished.

Her love was gone, though she had prayed, though she had spent countless hours on her knees begging the Virgin Mother to intercede, to protect her Felipe after he had marched off to fight the Americans who so badly wanted California.

He had fallen in Santa Fe. The message had come for her father to tell him that his young ward was killed in battle, cut down as he fought to keep the town out of American hands. His body had been buried there, so far away. She would never, never look on his face again, hear his voice, share his dreams.

She had not done as Felipe had asked. She had not sailed back to Spain to wait until California was safe again. Instead, she had hidden her dowry, the gold that would have helped to build their life together—the life they had dreamed of on so many bright days here on these cliffs. Her father would have given her to Felipe when he came back a hero. So Felipe had said as he kissed the tears from her cheeks. They would build a beautiful home, have many children, plant a garden. He had promised he would come back to her and they would begin.

Now he was lost.

Perhaps it was because she had been selfish. She had wanted to stay near Monterey and not put an ocean between them. And when the Americans came, she hid her bride gift, afraid they would take it as they had taken so much else.

Now they had taken everything that mattered. And she grieved, afraid it was her sin that took Felipe from her. She had lied to her father to steal those hours with her love. She had given herself before the marriage was sanctified by God and the Church. More damning, she thought, as she bowed her head against the vicious slap of the wind, she could not repent of her sins. Would not repent them.

There were no dreams left to her. No hope. No love. God had taken Felipe from her. And so, defying sixteen years of religious training, against a lifetime of belief, she lifted her head and cursed God.

And jumped.

One hundred thirty years later, the cliffs were drenched in the golden light of summer. Gulls winged over the sea, turning white breasts to the deep blue water before wheeling off with long, echoing cries. Flowers, sturdy and strong despite their fragile petals, pushed their way through hard ground, struggled toward the sun through thin cracks of rock, and turned the harsh into the fanciful. The wind was as soft as a stroke from a lover's hand. Overhead, the sky was the perfect blue of dreams.

Three young girls sat on the cliffs, pondering the story and the sea. It was a legend they knew well, and each had her own personal image of Seraphina as she had stood in those final despairing moments.

For Laura Templeton, Seraphina was a tragic figure, her face wet with tears, so alone on that windswept height, with a single wildflower clutched in her hand as she fell.

Laura wept for her now, her sad gray eyes looking out to the sea as she wondered what she would have done. For Laura the romance of it was entwined with the tragedy.

To Kate Powell it was all a miserable waste. She frowned into the sunlight, while plucking at stubby wild grass with a narrow hand. The story touched her heart, true, but it was the impulse of it, the mistaken impulse that troubled her. Why end everything when life held so much more?

It had been Margo Sullivan's turn to tell the tale, and she had done so with a rich dramatic flair. As always, she envisioned the night electrified by a storm—raging winds, pelting rain, flashing lightning. The enormous defiance of the gesture both thrilled and troubled her. She would forever see Seraphina with her face lifted high, a curse on her lips as she leapt.

"It was a pretty stupid thing to do for a boy," Kate commented. Her ebony hair was pulled neatly back in a ponytail, leaving her angular face dominated by her large almond-shaped brown eyes.

"She loved him," Laura said simply. Her voice was low, thoughtful. "He was her one true love."

"I don't see why there has to be just one." Margo stretched her long legs. She and Laura were twelve, Kate a year behind them. But already Margo's body had begun to hint at the woman just waking inside. She had breasts and was quite pleased about it. "I'm not going to just have one." Her voice rang with confidence. "I'm going to have hordes."

Kate snorted. She was thin and flat-chested and didn't mind a bit. She had better things to think about than boys. School, baseball, music. "Ever since Billy Leary stuck his tongue down your throat, you've gotten wacky."

"I like boys."

Secure in her femininity, Margo smiled slyly and brushed a hand through her long blond hair. It streamed past her shoulders, thick and wavy and wheat-colored. The minute she'd escaped her mother's eagle eye, she'd tugged it out of the band that Ann Sullivan preferred she tie it back with. Like her body, and her raspy voice, her hair belonged more to a woman than an adolescent girl.

"And they like me." Which was the best part, in Margo's estimation. "But I'll be damned if I'd kill myself over one."

Automatically Laura glanced around to make certain the swear word wasn't overheard. They were alone, of course, and it was blissfully summer. The time of year she loved most. Her gaze lingered on the house crowning the hill behind them. It was her home, her security, and it pleased her just to look at it with its fanciful turrets and high, arching windows, the soft red tiles of the roof baking in the California sun.

Sometimes she thought of it as a castle and herself as a princess. Just lately she had begun to imagine a prince somewhere who would one day ride up and sweep her away into love and marriage and happy-ever-after.

"I only want one," she murmured. "And if something happened to him it would break my heart forever."

"You wouldn't jump off a cliff." Kate's practical nature

4

couldn't conceive it. You might kick yourself for bobbling a routine fly, or bombing a test, but over a boy? Why, it was ridiculous. "You'd have to wait to see what happened next."

She, too, studied the house. Templeton House, her home now. She thought that of the three of them, she was the one who understood what it was to face the worst, and wait. She'd been eight when she lost her parents, had seen her world rip apart and leave her drowning. But the Templetons had taken her in, had loved her, and though she'd only been a second cousin on the unstable Powell branch of the family tree, had given her family. It was always wise to wait.

"I know what I'd do. I'd scream and curse God," Margo decided. She did so now, slipping as easily as a chameleon into a pose of abject suffering. "Then I'd take the dowry and sail around the world, see everything, do everything. Be everything." She stretched up her arms, loving the way the sun stroked her skin.

She loved Templeton House. It was the only home she remembered. She had been only four when her mother left Ireland and came there to work. Though she had always been treated as one of the family, she never forgot that she was a servant's daughter. Her ambition was to be more. Much more.

She knew what her mother wanted for her. A good education, a good job, a good husband. What, Margo wondered, could be more boring? She wasn't going to be her mother— no way was she going to be dried up and alone before she was thirty.

Her mother was young and beautiful, Margo mused. Even if she played both facts down, they were facts nonetheless. Yet she never dated or socialized. And she was so damn strict. Don't do this, Margo, don't do that, she thought with a pout. You're too young for lipstick and eye powder. Worried, always worried that her daughter was too wild, too headstrong, too anxious to rise above her station. Whatever her station was, Margo thought.

She wondered if her father had been wild. Had he been beautiful? And she'd begun to wonder if her mother had had to marry—the way young girls did. She couldn't have married for love, for if she'd loved him, why didn't she ever speak of him? Why didn't she have pictures and mementos and stories of the man she'd married and lost to a storm at sea?

So Margo looked out to sea and thought of her mother. Ann Sullivan was no Seraphina, she reflected. No grief and despair; just turn the page and forget.

Maybe it wasn't so wrong after all. If you didn't let a man mean too much, you wouldn't be too hurt when he went away. But that didn't mean you had to stop living too. Even if you didn't jump off a cliff there were other ways to end life.

If only Mum understood, she thought, then shook her head fiercely and looked back out to sea. She wasn't going to think about that, about how nothing she did or wanted seemed to meet with her mother's approval. It made her feel all churny inside to think of it. So she just wouldn't.

She would think of the places she would someday visit. Of the people she would meet. She'd had tastes of that grandeur living in Templeton House, being a part of the world that the Templetons moved in so naturally. All those fabulous hotels they owned in all those exciting cities. One day she would be a guest in them, gliding through her own suite—like the one in Templeton Monterey, with its staggering two levels and elegant furnishings and flowers everywhere. It had a bed fit for a queen, with a canopy and thick silk-covered pillows.

When she'd said as much to Mr. T., he'd laughed and hugged her and let her bounce on that bed. She would never forget the way it felt to snuggle against those soft, perfumed pillows. Mrs. T. had told her the bed had come from Spain and was two hundred years old.

6

One day she would have beautiful, important things like that bed. Not just to tend them, as her mother did, but to have them. Because when you had them, owned them, you were beautiful and important too.

"When we find Seraphina's dowry, we'll be rich," Margo announced, and Kate snorted again.

"Laura's already rich," she pointed out logically. "And if we find it we'll have to put it in the bank until we're old enough."

"I'll buy anything I want." Margo sat up and wrapped her arms around her knees. "Clothes and jewelry and beautiful things. And a car."

"You're not old enough to drive," Kate pointed out. "I'll invest mine, because Uncle Tommy says it takes money to make money."

"That's boring, Kate." Margo gave Kate's shoulder an affectionate jab. "You're boring. I'll tell you what we'll do with it, we'll take a trip around the world. The three of us. We'll go to London and Paris and Rome. We'll only stay at Templeton hotels because they're the best."

"An endless slumber party," Laura said, getting into the swing of the fantasy. She'd been to London and Paris and Rome, and she thought them beautiful. But nothing anywhere was more beautiful than here, than Templeton House. "We'll stay up all night and dance with only the most handsome men. Then we'll come back to Templeton House and always be together."

"Of course we'll always be together." Margo slung an arm around Laura's shoulders, then Kate's. Their friendship simply *was* to her, without question. "We're best friends, aren't we? We'll always be best friends."

When she heard the roar of an engine, she leapt up and quickly feigned disdain. "That's Josh and one of his creepy friends."

7

"Don't let him see you." Kate tugged hard on Margo's hand. Josh might have been Laura's brother by blood, but emotionally he was every bit Kate's too, which made her disdain very genuine. "He'll just come over and hassle us. He thinks he's such a big shot now that he can drive."

"He's not going to bother with us." Laura rose as well, curious to see who was riding shotgun in the spiffy little convertible. Recognizing the dark, flying hair, she grimaced. "Oh, it's just that hoodlum Michael Fury. I don't know why Josh pals around with him."

"Because he's dangerous." She might have been only twelve, but some females are born able to recognize, and appreciate, a dangerous man. But Margo's eyes were on Josh. She told herself it was because he irritated her—the heir apparent, the perfect golden prince, who continually treated her like a slightly stupid younger sister, when anyone with eyes could see she was almost a woman.

"Hey, brats." With the studied cool of sixteen years, he leaned back in the driver's seat of the idling car. The Eagles' "Hotel California" blasted out of the radio and rocked the breezy summer air. "Looking for Seraphina's gold again?"

"We're just enjoying the sun, and the solitude." But it was Margo who closed the distance, walking slowly, keeping her shoulders back. Josh's eyes were laughing at her beneath a shock of windblown, sun-bronzed hair. Michael Fury's were hidden behind mirrored sunglasses, and she couldn't tell where they looked. She wasn't overly interested, but she leaned against the car and gave him her best smile. "Hello, Michael."

"Yeah," was his reply.

"They're always hanging out on the cliffs," Josh informed his friend. "Like they're going to trip over a bunch of gold doubloons." He sneered at Margo. It was much easier to sneer than to consider, even for a moment, the way she looked in those teeny little shorts. Shit, she was just a kid, and practically

8

his sister, and he was going to fry in hell for sure if he kept having these weird thoughts about her.

"One day we'll find them."

She leaned closer, and he could smell her. She arched a brow, drawing attention to the little mole flirting with the bottom tip of it. Her eyebrows were shades darker than all that pale blond hair. And her breasts, which seemed to grow fuller every time a guy blinked, were clearly outlined under the snug T-shirt. Because his mouth was painfully dry, his voice was sharp and derisive.

"Keep dreaming, duchess. You little girls go back and play. We've got better things to do." He roared away, keeping one eye trained on the rearview mirror.

Margo's woman's heart pounded with confused longing. She tossed back her hair and watched the little car bullet away. It was easy to laugh at the housekeeper's daughter, she thought with bubbling fury. But when she was rich and famous . . .

"One day he'll be sorry he laughed at me."

"You know he doesn't mean it, Margo," Laura soothed.

"No, he's just a male." Kate shrugged. "The definition of an ass."

That made Margo laugh, and together they crossed the road to start up the hill to Templeton House. One day, she thought again. One day.

Chapter One

When she was eighteen, Margo knew exactly what she wanted. She had wanted the same at twelve. Everything. But now she had made up her mind how to go about attaining it. She was going to trade on her looks, her best and perhaps only talent as far as she was concerned. She thought she could act, or at least learn how. It had to be easier than algebra, or English lit, or any of those other stuffy classes in school. But one way or another, she was going to be a star. And she was going to make it on her own.

She'd made the decision the night before. The night before Laura's wedding. Was it selfish of her to be so miserable that Laura was about to be married?

She'd been nearly this miserable when Mr. and Mrs. T. had taken Laura and Josh and Kate to Europe the summer before for an entire month. And she had stayed home because her mother had refused the Templetons' offer to take her along. She'd been desperate to go, she remembered, but none of her pleas, nor any of Laura's and Kate's, had budged Ann Sullivan an inch.

"Not your place to traipse off to Europe and stay in fancy hotels," Mum had said. "The Templetons have been generous enough with you without you expecting more."

So she'd stayed home, earning her keep, as her mother called it, by dusting and polishing and learning to keep a proper house. And she'd been miserable. But that didn't make her selfish, she told herself. It hadn't been as if she hadn't wanted Kate and Laura to have a wonderful time. She'd just ached to be with them.

And it wasn't as if she didn't hope that Laura's marriage would be perfectly wonderful. She just couldn't stand to lose her. Did that make her selfish? She hoped it didn't, because it wasn't just for herself that she was unhappy. It was for Laura too. It was the thought of Laura's tying herself to a man and marriage before she had given herself a chance to live.

Oh, God, Margo wanted to live.

So her bags were already packed. Once Laura flew off on her honeymoon, Margo intended to be on her way to Hollywood.

She would miss Templeton House, and Mr. and Mrs. T., and, oh, she would miss Kate and Laura, even Josh. She would miss her mother, though she knew there would be ugliness between them before the door closed. There had already been so many arguments.

College was the bone of contention between them now. College and Margo's unbending refusal to continue her education. She knew she would die if she had to spend another four years with books and classrooms. And what did she need with college when she'd already decided how she wanted to live her life and make her fortune?

11

Her mother was too busy for arguments now. As house-keeper, Ann Sullivan had wedding reception on her mind. The wedding would be held at church, then all the limousines would stream along Highway 1, like great, glinting white boats, and up the hill to Templeton House.

Already the house was perfect, but she imagined her mother was off somewhere battling with the florist over arrangements. It had to be beyond perfect for Laura's wedding. She knew how much her mother loved Laura, and she didn't resent it. But she did resent that her mother wanted her to be like Laura. And she never could. Didn't want to.

Laura was warm and sweet and perfect. Margo knew she was none of those things. Laura never argued with her mother the way Margo and Ann flew at each other like cats. But then, Laura's life was already so settled and smooth. She never had to worry about her place, or where she would go. She'd already seen Europe, hadn't she? She could live in Templeton House forever if she chose. If she wanted to work, the Templeton hotels were there for her—she could pick her spot.

Margo wasn't like Kate either, so studious and goal-oriented. She wasn't going to dash off to Harvard in a few weeks and work toward a degree so that she could keep books and read tax law. God, how tedious! But that was Kate, who'd rather read the *Wall Street Journal* than pore over the glamorous pictures in *Vogue*, who could discuss, happily, interest rates and capital gains with Mr. T. for hours.

No, she didn't want to be Kate or Laura, as much as she loved them. She wanted to be Margo Sullivan. And she intended to revel in being Margo Sullivan. One day she would have a house as fine as this, she told herself as she came slowly down the main stairs, trailing a hand along the glassy mahogany banister.

The stairs curved in a long, graceful sweep, and high above, like a sunburst, hung a sparkling Waterford chandelier. How many times had she seen it shoot glamorous light onto the glossy white and peacock blue marble tiles of the foyer, sparkle elegance onto the already elegant guests who came to the wonderful parties the Templetons were famous for?

The house always rang with laughter and music at Templeton parties, she remembered, whether guests were seated formally at the long, graceful table in the dining room under twin chandeliers or wandered freely through the rooms, chatting as they sipped champagne or cozied up on a love seat.

She would give wonderful parties one day, and she hoped she would be as warm and entertaining a hostess as Mrs. T. Did such things comes through the blood, she wondered, or could they be learned? If they could be learned, then she would learn.

Her mother had taught her how to arrange flowers just so— the way those gleaming white roses in a tall crystal vase graced the Pembroke table in the foyer. See the way they reflect in the mirror, she thought. Tall and pure with their fanning greens.

Those were the touches that made home, she reminded herself. Flowers and pretty bowls, candlesticks and lovingly polished wood. The smells, the way the light slanted through the windows, the sounds of grand old clocks ticking. It was all that she would remember when she was far away. Not just the archways that allowed one room to flow into another, or the complex and beautiful patterns of mosaics around the tall, wide front door. She would remember the smell of the library after Mr. T. had lighted one of his cigars and the way the room echoed when he laughed.

She'd remember the winter evenings when she and Laura and Kate would curl up on the rug in front of the parlor fire— the rich gleam of the lapis mantel, the feel of the heat on her cheeks, the way Kate would giggle over a game when she was winning.

She'd imagine the fragrances of Mrs. T.'s sitting room. Powders and perfumes and candlewax. And the way Mrs. T. smiled when Margo came in to talk with her. She could always talk to Mrs. T.

Her own room. How the Templetons had let her pick out the new wallpaper when she turned sixteen. And even her mother had smiled and approved of her choice of pale green background splashed with showy white lilies. The hours she'd spent in that room alone, or with Laura and Kate. Talking, talking, talking. Planning. Dreaming.

Am I doing the right thing? she wondered with a quick jolt of panic. How could she bear to leave everything, everyone she knew and loved?

"Posing again, duchess?" Josh stepped into the foyer. He wasn't dressed for the wedding yet, but wore chinos and a cotton shirt. At twenty-two he'd filled out nicely, and his years at Harvard sat comfortably on him.

Margo thought disgustedly that he would look elegant in cardboard. He was still the golden boy, though his face had lost its innocent boyishness. It was shrewd, with his father's gray eyes and his mother's lovely mouth. His hair had darkened to bronze, and a late growth spurt in his last year of high school had shot him to six two.

She wished he was ugly. She wished looks didn't matter. She wished he would look at her, just once, as if she wasn't simply a nuisance.

"I was thinking," she told him, but stayed where she was, on the stairs, with one hand resting casually on the banister. She knew she'd never looked better. Her bridesmaid's dress was the most glorious creation she'd ever owned. That was why she'd dressed early, to enjoy it as long as she possibly could.

Laura had chosen the summer blue to match Margo's eyes, and the silk was as fragile and fluid as water. The long sweep

14

of it highlighted her frankly lush figure, and the long, sheer sleeves showcased her creamy ivory skin.

"Rushing things, aren't you?" He spoke quickly because whenever he looked at her the punch of lust was like a flaming fist in his gut. It had to be only lust because lust was easy. "The wedding's not for two hours."

"It'll take nearly that long to put Laura together. I left her with Mrs. T. I thought they . . . well, they needed a minute or two alone."

"Crying again?"

"Mothers cry on their daughters' wedding day because they know what they're getting into."

He grinned and held out a hand. "You'd make an interesting bride, duchess."

She took his hand. Their fingers had twined hundreds of times over their years together. This was no different. "Is that a compliment?"

"An observation." He led her into the parlor, where silver candlesticks held slim white tapers and sumptuous arrangements of flowers were decked. Jasmine, roses, gardenias. All white on white and heady with scent in the room where sunlight streamed through high, arched windows.

There were silver-framed photos on the mantel. She was there, Margo thought, accepted as part of the family. On the piano sat the Waterford compote that she had recklessly spent her savings on for the Templetons' twenty-fifth anniversary.

She tried to take it in, every piece of it. The soft colors of the Aubusson carpet, the delicate carving on the legs of the Queen Anne chairs, the intricate marquetry on the music cabinet.

"It's so beautiful," she murmured.

"Hmm?" He was busy tearing the foil off a bottle of champagne he'd snatched from the kitchen.

"The house. It's so beautiful."

"Annie's outdone herself," he said, referring to Margo's mother. "Should be a hell of a wedding."

It was his tone that drew her gaze back to him. She knew him so well, every nuance of expression, every subtle tone of voice. "You don't like Peter."

Josh shrugged, uncorked the bottle with an expert press of thumb. "I'm not marrying Ridgeway, Laura is."

She grinned at him. "I can't stand him. Stuffy, superior snot."

He grinned back at her, at ease again. "We usually agree on people, if little else."

Because he hated it, she patted his cheek. "We'd probably agree on more if you didn't enjoy picking on me so much."

"It's my job to pick on you." He snagged her wrist, annoying her. "You'd feel neglected if I didn't."

"You're even more revolting now that you've got a degree from Harvard." She picked up a glass. "At least pretend you're a gentleman. Pour me some." When he studied her, she rolled her eyes. "For Christ's sake, Josh, I'm eighteen. If Laura's old enough to get married to that jerk, I'm old enough to drink champagne."

"One," he said, the dutiful older brother. "I don't want you weaving down the aisle later." He noted with amused frustration that she looked as though she'd been born with a champagne flute in her hands. And men at her feet.

"I suppose we should drink to the bride and groom." She pursed her lips as she studied the bubbles rising so frothily in her glass. "But I'm afraid I'll choke, and I hate to waste this." She winced, lowered the glass. "That's so damn mean. I hate being mean, but I can't seem to help it."

"It's not mean, it's honest." He moved a shoulder. "We might as well be mean and honest together. To Laura, then. I hope to hell she knows what she's doing."

"She loves him." Margo sipped and decided that cham-

16

pagne would be her signature drink. "God knows why, or why she thinks she has to marry him just to sleep with him."

"Nice talk."

"Well, be realistic." She wandered to the garden door, sighed. "Sex is a stupid reason to get married. The fact is, I can't think of a single good one. Of course, Laura isn't marrying Peter just for sex." Impatient, she tapped her fingers against the glass, listened to the ring. "She's too romantic. He's older, more experienced, charming if you like that sort. And of course, he's in the business, so he can slip right into the Templeton empire and reign right here so she can stay at the house, or choose something close by. It's probably perfect for her."

"Don't start crying."

"I'm not, not really." But she was comforted by the hand he laid on her shoulder, and she leaned into him. "I'm just going to miss her so much."

"They'll be back in a month."

"I'm not going to be here." She hadn't meant to say it, not to him, and now she turned quickly. "Don't say anything to anyone. I need to tell everyone myself."

"Tell them what?" He didn't like the clutching feeling in his stomach. "Where the hell are you going?"

"To L.A. Tonight."

Just like her, he mused and shook his head. "What wild hair is this, Margo?"

"It's not a wild hair. I've thought about it a lot." She sipped again, wandered away from him. It was easier to be clear when she couldn't lean on him. "I have to start my life. I can't stay here forever."

"College—"

"That's not for me." Her eyes lit, the cold blue fire at the center of a flame. She was going to take something for herself. And if it was selfish, then by God, so be it. "That's what

17

Mum wants, not what I want. And I can't keep living here, the housekeeper's daughter.''

"Don't be ridiculous." He could brush that off like a stray mote of lint. "You're family."

She couldn't dispute that, and yet . . . "I want to start my life," she said stubbornly. "You've started yours. You're going to law school, Kate's going off to Harvard a full year early, thanks to her busy little brain. Laura's getting married."

Now he had it, and sneered at her. "You're feeling sorry for yourself."

"Maybe I am. What's wrong with that?" She poured more champagne into her glass, defying him. "Why is it such a sin to feel a little self-pity when everyone you care about is doing something they want and you're not? Well, I'm going to do something I want."

"Go to L.A. and what?"

"I'm going to get a job." She sipped again, seeing it, seeing herself, perfectly. Centered in the light of excitement. "I'm going to model. My face is going to be on the cover of every important magazine there is."

She had the face for it, he thought. And the body. They were killers. Criminally stunning. "And that's an ambition?" he said, with a half laugh. "Having your picture taken?"

She lifted her chin and seared him with a look. "I'm going to be rich, and famous, and happy. And I'm going to make it on my own. Mommy and Daddy won't be paying for my life. I won't have a cozy trust fund to bounce on."

His eyes narrowed dangerously. "Don't get bitchy with me, Margo. You don't know what it is to work, to take responsibility, to follow through."

"Oh, and you do? You've never had to worry about anything but snapping your fingers so a servant can buff up the silver platter you're served on."

18

As hurt as he was insulted, he crossed to her. "You've eaten off the same damn platter most of your life."

Her color rose at that, shaming her. "That may be true, but from now on I'm buying my own platters."

"With what?" He cupped her face in tensed fingers. "Your looks? Duchess, beautiful women clog the streets in L.A. They'll gobble you up and spit you out before you know what hit you."

"The hell they will." She jerked her head free. "I'm going to do the gobbling, Joshua Conway Templeton. And no one's going to stop me."

"Why don't you do us all a favor and think for once in your life before you jump into something we'll have to pull you out of? This is a hell of a time to start acting up like this." He set his glass down so he could push his hands into his pockets. "Laura's wedding day, my parents half crazy because they're worried she's too young. Your own mother running around with her eyes all red from crying."

"I'm not going to spoil Laura's wedding day. I'm waiting until after she's left on her honeymoon."

"Oh, that's damn considerate of you." Fuming, he spun around. "Have you thought how Annie's going to feel about this?"

Margo bit hard on her bottom lip. "I can't be what she wants. Why can't anyone understand that?"

"How do you think my parents are going to feel, thinking about you alone in L.A.?"

"You won't make me feel guilty," she murmured, feeling exactly that. "I've made up my mind."

"Goddamn it, Margo." He grabbed her arms, throwing her off-balance so that she toppled against him. In her heels she was eye to eye with him.

Her heart thudded hurtfully against her ribs. She thought— she felt—something was going to happen. Right here. Right

19

now. "Josh." She said it quietly, her voice shaky and hoarse. Her fingers dug into his shoulders, and everything churned inside her, yearning.

The rude clatter on the stairs had them both springing back. When she managed to draw a breath, he was glaring at her. Kate clomped into the room.

"I can't believe I have to wear something like this. I feel like an idiot. Stupid long skirts are impractical and just get in the way." Kate stopped plucking at the elegant silk dress and frowned at Margo and Josh. She thought they looked like two sleek cats about to spring. "Do you two have to fight now? I'm having a crisis. Margo, is this dress supposed to look like this, and if so, why? Is that champagne? Can I have some?"

Josh's gaze remained on Margo's for another humming moment. "I'm taking it up to Laura."

"I just want a sip before— Jeez!" Pouting now, Kate stared as Josh strode out of the room. "What's with him?"

"The same as always. He's an arrogant know-it-all. I just hate him," Margo said between gritted teeth.

"Oh, well, if that's all, let's talk about me. Help." She spread her arms.

"Kate." Margo pressed her fingers to her temples, then sighed. "Kate, you look fabulous. Except for the incredibly bad haircut."

"What are you talking about?" Kate ran her hair through the ruthlessly short black cap. "The hair's the best thing. I barely have to comb it."

"Obviously. Well, we'll cover it up with the hat anyway."

"I wanted to talk about the hat—"

"You're wearing it." Instinctively, Margo held out her champagne to share. "It makes you look very chic, Audrey Hepburnish."

"I'll do it for Laura," Kate muttered, then dropped with little grace onto a chair and swung her silk-draped legs over the arm. "I gotta tell you, Margo, Peter Ridgeway gives me a pain."

"Join the club."

Her thoughts revolved back to Josh. Had he actually been about to kiss her? No, that was ridiculous. More likely he'd been about to shake her like a frustrated boy whose toy wasn't working to his liking. "Kate, don't sit like that, you'll wrinkle the dress."

"Hell." She rose reluctantly, a pretty, coltish girl with over-sized eyes. "I know Uncle Tommy and Aunt Susie aren't happy about all this. They're trying to be because Laura's so happy she's practically sending off radiation. I want to be happy for her, Margo."

"Then we will be." She shook off worries of Josh, of later, of L.A. Now was for Laura. "We have to stand by the people we love, right?"

"Even when they're screwing up." Kate sighed and handed Margo the champagne flute. "I guess we should go up and stand by her then."

They started up the stairs. At the door to Laura's room, they paused, joined hands. "I don't know why I'm so nervous," Kate murmured. "My stomach's jumping."

"Because we're in this together." Margo gave her hand a squeeze. "Just like always."

She opened the door. Laura sat at the vanity, putting the finishing touches on her makeup. In the long white robe she already looked the perfect bride. Her golden hair was swept up, curls falling flirtily around her face. Susan stood behind her, already dressed for the ceremony in a deep-rose gown touched with lace.

"The pearls are old," she said, her voice raw. In the shining mirror framed in carved rosewood, her eyes met her daughter's. "Your Grandmother Templeton's." She handed Laura

21

the lovely eardrops. "She gave them to me on my wedding day. Now they're yours."

"Oh, Mom, I'll start crying again."

"None of that now." Ann Sullivan stepped forward. She looked lovely and restrained in her best navy dress, her deep-blond hair in short, quiet waves. "No swollen eyes on our bride today. You need something borrowed, so I thought . . . you could wear my locket under your gown."

"Oh, Annie." Laura sprang up to hug her. "Thank you. Thank you so much. I'm so happy."

"May you stay half so happy for the rest of your life." Feeling her eyes well, Ann cleared her throat, smoothed the already smooth floral coverlet on Laura's four-poster bed. "I'd best go down and see if Mrs. Williamson is dealing with the caterers."

"Mrs. Williamson is fine." Susan took Ann's hand, knowing their longtime cook could handle the most fussy of caterers. "Ah, here are the ladies-in-waiting now, just in time to dress the bride. And how lovely they look."

"That they do." Ann turned to run a critical eye over her daughter and Kate. "Miss Kate, you could use more lipstick, and Margo, you less."

"We'll have a drink first." Susan picked up the champagne. "Since Josh was thoughtful enough to bring up a bottle."

"We brought along a glass," Kate said, shrewdly omitting they'd already had some. "Just in case."

"Well, I suppose it's an occasion. Just half a glass," Ann warned. "They'll be tippling at the reception if I know these girls."

"I already feel drunk." Laura watched the bubbles rise in her glass. "I want to make the toast, please. To the women in my life. My mother, who's shown me that love makes a marriage bloom. My friend," she said, turning to Ann, "who al-

22

ways, always listened. And my sisters, who gave me the best of families. I love you all so much.''

"That's done it.'' Susan sniffed into her wine. "My mascara's shot again.''

"Mrs. Templeton, ma'am.'' A maid came to the door, all eyes as she peeked in at Laura. Later, she would tell the downstairs staff that it had been like a vision, all those lovely women standing in a room with the sun streaming patterns through fluttering lace curtains. "Old Joe the gardener is arguing with the man who's come to set up the tables and chairs in the garden.''

"I'll see to it,'' Ann began.

"We'll both see to it.'' Susan touched Laura's cheek. "It'll keep me too busy to blubber. Margo and Kate will help you dress, baby. That's how it should be.''

"Don't wrinkle those gowns,'' Ann ordered, then slipped an arm around Susan's shoulders and murmured something quietly as they left the room.

"I don't believe it.'' Margo's smile spread. "Mum was so distracted she left the bottle. Drink up, ladies.''

"Maybe one more,'' Kate decided. "My stomach's so jittery I'm afraid I'll throw up.''

"You do, and I'll kill you.'' Margo recklessly tossed back the champagne. She liked the exotic sensation of it tickling her throat, bubbling through her brain. She wanted to feel just like this for the rest of her life. "Okay, Laura, let's get you into that incredible dress.''

"It's really happening,'' Laura murmured.

"Right. But if you want to change your mind—''

"Change my mind?'' She laughed at Kate as Margo reverently slipped the full-skirted ivory silk gown out of its protective bag. "Are you crazy? This is everything I've ever dreamed of. My wedding day, the beginning of my life with the man I love.'' Eyes misty, she circled as she slipped off

23

the robe. "He's so sweet, so handsome, so kind and patient."

"She means he didn't pressure her to do the big deed," Margo commented.

"He respected the fact that I wanted to wait until our wedding night." Laura's prim expression collapsed into wild glee. "I can't wait."

"I told you it's not that big a deal."

"It will be when you're in love." She stepped carefully into the dress as Margo held it for her. "You weren't in love with Biff."

"No, but I was wildly in lust, which counts for something. I'm not saying it wasn't nice, it was. But I think it takes practice."

"I'll get lots of practice." Laura's bride's heart fluttered at the thought. "As a married woman. Oh, look at me." Stunned, Laura stared at herself in the chevel glass. Yards of ivory silk were sparkling with tiny seed pearls. Romantic sleeves puffed at the shoulders, then tapered to snugness. When Kate and Margo finished attaching the train, Kate arranged it in an artful spill of embroidered silk.

"The veil." Margo blinked back tears. With her advantage of height, she slid the pearl circlet smoothly around the neat bun, then fluffed the yards of tulle. Her oldest friend, she thought as a tear snuck through. The sister of her heart. At a turning point. "Oh, Laura, you look like a princess in a fairy tale. You really do."

"I feel beautiful. I feel absolutely beautiful."

"I know I kept saying it was too fussy." Kate managed a watery smile. "I was wrong. It's perfect. I'm going to get my camera."

"As if there aren't going to be half a million pictures by the time it's over," Margo said when Kate dashed from the room. "I'll go get Mr. T. Then I guess I'll see you in church."

"Yes. Margo, one day I know you and Kate are going to

24

be as happy as I am now. I can't wait to be a part of that.''

"Let's get done with you first." She stopped at the door, turned again, just to look. She was afraid that nothing and no one would ever make her feel whatever it was that put that soft light in Laura's eyes. So, she thought as she quietly closed the door, she would settle for fame and fortune.

She found Mr. T. in his bedroom, muttering curses and fumbling with his formal tie. He looked so dashing in the dove gray morning coat that matched the Templeton eyes. He had broad shoulders a woman could lean on, she thought, and that wonderfully masculine height, which Josh had inherited. He was frowning now as he mumbled to himself, but his face was so perfect, the straight nose and tough chin, the crinkles around his mouth.

A perfect face, she thought as she stepped in. A father's face.

"Mr. T., when are you going to learn how to deal with those ties?''

His frown turned to a grin. "Never, as long as there's a pretty woman around to fuss with it for me.''

Obligingly, she moved over to tidy the mess he'd made of it. "You look so handsome.''

"Nobody's going to give me or any other man a second glance with my girls around. You look more beautiful than a wish, Margo.''

"Wait until you see Laura." She saw the worry flicker into his eyes and kissed his smoothly shaven cheek. "Don't fret, Mr. T.''

"My baby's grown up on me. It's hard to let him take her away from me.''

"He could never do that. No one could. But I know. It's hard for me, too. I've been feeling sorry for myself all day, when I should be happy for her.''

Footsteps sounded in the hall, rushing. Kate with her camera, Margo thought, or a servant hurrying to take care of some last-minute detail. There were always people in Templeton House, she mused, filling it with sound and light and movement. You never felt alone there.

Her heart hitched again at the thought of leaving, of being alone. Yet mixed with the fears was such dizzy anticipation. Like a first sip of champagne, when the rich fizz of it exploded on the tongue. A first kiss, that soft, sultry meeting of lips.

There were so many firsts she yearned to experience.

"Everything's changing, isn't it, Mr. T.?"

"Nothing stays the same forever, however much you'd like it to. In a few weeks you and Kate will be off to college, Josh will be back at law school. Laura will be a wife. Susie and I will be rattling around this house like a bunch of old bones." Which was one of the reasons he and his wife were thinking of relocating to Europe. "The house won't be the same without you."

"The house will always be the same. That's what's so wonderful about it." How could she tell him she was leaving that very night? Running toward something she could see as clearly as her own face in the mirror. "Old Joe will keep on guarding his rosebushes, and Mrs. Williamson will be lording it over everyone in the kitchen. Mum will go on polishing the silver because she doesn't think anyone else can do it properly. Mrs. T. will drag you out to the tennis court every morning and trounce you. You'll be on the phone scheduling meetings or barking orders."

"I never bark," he said with a gleam in his eye.

"You always bark, that's part of your charm." She wanted to weep, for the childhood that had gone so fast though she had thought it would never end. For the part of her life that was behind her now, though she had strained so hard to pull away. For the coward that lived inside her that shrank from telling him she was leaving. "I love you, Mr. T."

26

"Margo." Misreading her, he pressed his lips to her brow. "Before too much longer I'll be walking you down the aisle, giving you to some handsome young man who couldn't possibly be good enough for you."

She made herself laugh, because crying would spoil everything. "I'm not getting married to anyone unless he's exactly like you. Laura's waiting for you." She drew back, reminding herself that this was Laura's father. Not hers. This was Laura's day. Not hers. "I'll go see if the cars are ready."

She hurried downstairs. And there was Josh, staggering in his formal wear, frowning at her as she paused breathlessly. "Don't start on me," she ordered. "Laura's coming down in a minute."

"I'm not going to start on you. But we're going to talk later."

"Fine." She had no intention of talking with him. The minute the last grain of rice was thrown, she would make a quick and quiet exit. She carried the hat she'd brought down from her room to the mirror, instinctively arranging the wide blue brim to the most flattering advantage.

There's my fame, she thought, studying her face. And my fortune. By God, she would make it work. Lifting her chin, she met her own eyes and willed it to begin.

Chapter Two

Ten years later

On the wild, wild cliffs above the restless Pacific, Margo watched the storm build. Black clouds boiled in a black sky, crushing every hint of starlight with their weight and temper. The wind howled like a feral wolf hunting for blood. Needle-bright spears of lightning slashed and snapped and shot the jagged rocks and spewing surf into sharp relief. The witchy scent of ozone stung the air before thunder exploded.

It seemed that her welcome home, even from nature, was not to be a gentle one.

An omen? she wondered, jamming her hands into her jacket pockets to protect them from the biting wind. She could hardly expect anyone at Templeton House to greet her with open arms and joyous smiles. The fatted calf, she thought with a wry smile, will not be served for this prodigal.

She had no right to expect it.

Wearily, she reached up and pulled the pins out of the smooth twist to let her pale blond hair fly free. It felt good, that small liberation, and she tossed the pins over the edge. She remembered quite suddenly that when she'd been a young girl she and her two best friends had thrown flowers over that same ledge.

Flowers for Seraphina, she thought, and nearly smiled. How romantic it had seemed then, the legend of that young girl hurling herself over the edge in grief and despair.

She remembered that Laura had always cried a little and that Kate would solemnly watch the flowers dance toward the sea. But she herself had always felt the thrill of that final flight, the defiance of the gesture, the bold recklessness of it.

Margo was just low enough, just tired enough to admit that looking for thrills, being defiant and embracing recklessness were what had brought her to this miserable point in her life.

Her eyes, a brilliant cornflower blue that the camera loved, were shadowed. She'd retouched her makeup carefully after her plane had landed in Monterey and had checked it again in the back of the cab she'd taken out to Big Sur. Christ knew she was skilled in painting on any image required. Only she would be aware that beneath the expensive cosmetics her cheeks were pale. They were, perhaps, a bit more hollow than they should be, but it was those slashing cheekbones that had boosted her onto the cover of so many magazines.

A good face started with bones, she thought and shivered as the next flash of lightning bolted across the sky. She was fortunate in her bone structure, in the smooth, poreless skin of her Irish ancestors. The Kerry blue eyes, the pale blond hair had undoubtedly been passed on by some ancient Viking conqueror.

Oh, she had a face all right, she mused. It wasn't a matter

29

of vanity to admit it. After all, it and a body built for sinning had been her meal tickets, her pathways to fame and fortune. Full, romantic lips, a small, straight nose, a firm, rounded chin and expressive brows that needed only the slightest bit of darkening and shaping.

She would still have a good face when she was eighty, if she lived that long. It didn't matter that she was washed up, used up, embroiled in a scandal, and bitterly ashamed. She would still turn heads.

A pity she no longer gave a damn.

Turning away from the cliff edge, she peered through the gloom. Across the road and on the crest of the hill she could see the lights of Templeton House, the house that had held so much of her laughter, and so many of her tears. There was only one place to go when you were lost, only one place to run when you had no bridges left to burn.

Margo picked up her flight bag and headed home.

Ann Sullivan had served at Templeton for twenty-four years. One year less than she'd been a widow. She had come, her four-year-old daughter in tow, from Cork to take a position as maid. In those days, Thomas and Susan Templeton had run the house as they ran their hotels. In grand style. Hardly a week would go by without the rooms overflowing with guests and music. There had been a staff of eighteen, to ensure that every detail of the house and grounds was seen to perfectly.

Perfection was a trademark of Templeton, as was luxury, as was warmth. Ann had been taught, and taught well, that fine accommodations were nothing without gracious welcome.

The children, Master Joshua and Missy Laura, had had a nanny who in turn had boasted an assistant. Yet they had been raised by their parents. Ann had always admired the devotion, the discipline, and the care with which the Templetons had reared their family. Although she knew it could, wealth had never outdistanced love in this house.

It had been Mrs. Templeton's suggestion that the girls play together. They were, after all, the same age, and Joshua, being a boy and four years their senior, had little time for them.

Ann would forever be grateful for Mrs. Templeton, not only for the position and the simple kindnesses but for the advantages she had offered Ann's daughter. Margo had never been treated like a servant. Instead, she was treated as the cherished friend of the daughter of the house.

In ten years, Ann had become housekeeper. It was a position she knew she had earned and one she took great pride in. There was no corner of the house she hadn't cleaned with her own hands, no scrap of linen she hadn't washed. Her love for Templeton House was deep and abiding. Perhaps deeper and more abiding than for anything else in her life.

She had stayed on after the Templetons moved to Cannes, after Miss Laura married—too quickly and too rashly, to Ann's mind. She'd stayed after her own daughter ran off to Hollywood, and then to Europe, chasing glitter and glory.

She had never remarried, never considered it. Templeton House was her mate. It stood year after year, solid as the rock on which it was built. It never disappointed her, defied her, questioned her. It never hurt her or asked more than she could give.

As a daughter could, she thought.

Now, as the storm raged outside and rain began to lash like whips against the wide, arching windows, she walked into the kitchen. The slate-blue counters were spotless, earning a nod of approval for the new young maid she had hired. The girl had gone home now, and couldn't see it, but Ann would remember to tell her she'd done well.

How much easier it was, she mused, to earn the affection and respect of staff than it was to earn that of your own child.

Often she thought she'd lost Margo the day the girl had been born. Been born too beautiful, too restless, too bold.

As worried as she was about Margo, after the news had broken, she went about her duties. There was nothing she could do for the girl. She was bitterly aware that there had never been anything she could do for, or about, Margo.

Love hadn't been enough. Though, Ann thought, perhaps she had held too much love back from Margo. It was only because she'd been afraid to give the girl too much, for to give her too much might have made her reach even farther than she had seemed to need to.

And she simply wasn't very demonstrative, Ann told herself with a little shrug. Servants couldn't afford to be, no matter how kind the employer. She understood her place. Why hadn't Margo ever understood hers?

For a moment she leaned on the counter in a rare show of self-indulgence, her eyes squeezed tight against threatening tears. She simply couldn't think of Margo now. The girl was out of her hands, and the house required a final check.

She straightened, breathing deep to balance herself. The floor had been freshly mopped, and the same slate-blue as the counters gleamed in the light. The stove, an aging six-burner, showed no remnants of the dinner it had cooked. And young Jenny had remembered to put fresh water in the daffodils that stood sunnily on the table.

Pleased that her instincts for the new maid had been on target, Ann wandered to the pots of herbs sitting on the windowsill above the sink. A press of her thumb showed her the soil was dry. Watering the window herbs wasn't Jenny's responsibility, she thought, clucking her tongue as she saw to it herself. The cook needed to care for her own. But then, Mrs. Williamson was getting up in years and becoming slightly absentminded with it. Ann often made excuses to remain in the kitchen during meal preparation, just to be certain that Mrs.

Williamson didn't chop off anything important, or start a fire.

Anyone but Miss Laura would have pensioned the woman off by now, Ann mused. But Miss Laura understood that the need to be needed didn't diminish with age. Miss Laura understood Templeton House, and tradition.

It was after ten, and the house was quiet. Her duties for the day were done. Giving the kitchen one last scan, she thought of going into her quarters, brewing some tea in her own little kitchen. Perhaps putting her feet up and watching some foolishness on TV.

Something, anything to keep her mind off her worries.

Wind rattled the windows and made her shudder, made her grateful for the warmth and security of the house. Then the back door opened, letting in rain and wind and biting air. Letting in so much more. Ann felt her heart jolt and stutter in her breast.

"Hello, Mum." The bright, sassy smile was second nature, and nearly reached her eyes as Margo combed a hand through the hair that dripped like wet gold to her waist. "I saw the light—literally," she added with a nervous laugh. "And figuratively."

"You're letting in the wet." It wasn't the first thing that came to Ann's mind, but it was the only practical one. "Close the door, Margo, and hang up that wet jacket."

"I didn't quite beat the rain." Keeping her voice light, Margo shut the storm outside. "I'd forgotten how cold and wet March can be on the central coast." She set her flight bag aside, hung her jacket on the hook by the door, then rubbed her chilled hands together to keep them busy. "You look wonderful. You've changed your hair."

Ann didn't lift a hand to fuss with it in a gesture that might have been natural for another woman. She had no vanity and had often wondered where Margo had come by hers. Margo's father had been a humble man.

"Really, it suits you." Margo tried another smile. Her mother had always been an attractive woman. Her light hair had hardly darkened over the years, and there was little sign of gray in the short, neat wave of it. Her face was lined, true, but not deeply. And though her solemn, unsmiling mouth was unpainted, it was as full and lush as her daughter's.

"We weren't expecting you," Ann said and was sorry her voice was so stiff. But her heart was too full of joy and worry to allow for more.

"No. I thought of calling or sending a wire. Then I . . . I didn't." She took a long breath, wondering why neither of them could cross that short space of tile and touch the other. "You'd have heard."

"We heard things." Off-balance, Ann moved to the stove, put the kettle on to boil. "I'll make tea. You'll be chilled."

"I've seen some of the reports in the paper and on the news." Margo lifted a hand, but her mother's back was so rigid, she let it drop again without making contact. "They're not all true, Mum."

Ann reached for the everyday teapot, heated it with hot water. Inside she was shaking with hurt, with shock. With love. "Not all?"

It was only one more humiliation, Margo told herself. But this was her mother, after all. And she so desperately needed someone to stand by her. "I didn't know what Alain was doing, Mum. He'd managed my career for the past four years, and I never, never knew he was dealing drugs. He never used them, at least not around me. When we were arrested . . . when it all came out . . ." She stopped, sighed as her mother continued to measure out tea. "I've been cleared of all charges. It won't stop the press from speculating, but at least Alain had the decency to tell the authorities I was innocent."

Though even that had been humiliating. Proof of innocence had equaled proof of stupidity.

"You slept with a married man."

Margo opened her mouth, shut it again. No excuse, no explanation would matter, not to her mother. "Yes."

"A married man, with children."

"Guilty," Margo said bitterly. "I'll probably go to hell for it, and I'm paying in this life as well. He embezzled a great deal of my money, destroyed my career, made me an object of pity and ridicule in the tabloid press."

Sorrow stirred inside Ann, but she shut it off. Margo had made her choices. "So you've come back here to hide."

To heal, Margo thought, but hiding wasn't so very far from the truth. "I wanted a few days someplace where I wouldn't be hounded. If you'd rather I go, then—"

Before she could finish, the kitchen door swung open. "What a wild night. Annie, you should—" Laura stopped short. Her quiet gray eyes lighted on Margo's face. She didn't hesitate, didn't merely cross that short span of tile. She leaped across it. "Margo! Oh, Margo, you're home!"

And in that one moment, in that welcoming embrace, she was home.

"She doesn't mean to be so hard on you, Margo," Laura soothed. Calming troubled waters was instinctive to her. She had seen the hurt on the faces of mother and daughter that they seemed blind to. At Margo's shrug, Laura poured the tea that Ann had brewed and Laura had carried up to her own sitting room. "She's been so worried."

"Has she?" Smoking in shallow puffs, Margo brooded. Out the window, there was a garden, she remembered, arbors that dripped with wisteria. And beyond the flowers, the lawns, the neat stone walls, were the cliffs. She listened to Laura's voice, the calming balm of it, and remembered how they had peeked into this room as children, when it had been Mrs. Templeton's domain. How they had dreamed of being fine ladies.

35

Turning, she studied her friend. So quietly lovely, Margo thought. A face meant for drawing rooms, garden parties, and society balls. And that, apparently, had been Laura's destiny.

The curling spill of hair was the color of old gold, styled with studied care to swing at her fragile jaw. The eyes were so clear, so true, everything she felt mirrored in them. Now they were filled with concern, and there was a flush on her cheeks. From excitement, Margo mused, and worry. Emotion always brought either quick color to Laura's cheeks, or drained it.

"Come sit," Laura ordered. "Have some tea. Your hair's damp."

Absently Margo pushed it back so that it cleared her shoulders. "I was down at the cliffs."

Laura glanced toward the windows, where the rain whipped. "In this?"

"I had to build some courage."

But she did sit, took the cup. Margo recognized the everyday Doulton her mother had used. How many times had she nagged Ann into teaching her the names, the patterns, of the china and crystal and silver of Templeton House? And how many times had she dreamed about having pretty things of her own?

Now the cup warmed her chilly hands, and that was enough.

"You look wonderful," she told Laura. "I can't believe it's been nearly a year since I saw you in Rome."

They'd had lunch on the terrace of the owner's suite at Templeton Rome, the city spread beneath them lush with spring. And her life, Margo thought, had been as full of promise as the air, as glittery as the sun.

"I've missed you." Laura reached out, gave Margo's hand a quick squeeze. "We all did."

"How are the girls?"

"Wonderful. Growing. Ali loved the dress you sent her for her birthday from Milan."

"I got her thank-you note, and the pictures. They're beautiful children, Laura. They look so much like you. Ali's got your smile, Kayla has your eyes." She drank tea to wash away the lump in her throat. "Sitting here, the way we used to imagine we would, I can't believe it's not all just a dream." She shook her head quickly before Laura could speak, tapped out the cigarette. "How's Peter?"

"He's fine." A shadow flickered into Laura's eyes, but she lowered her lashes. "He had work to finish up, so he's still at the office. I imagine he'll just stay in town because of the storm." Or because he preferred another bed to the one he shared with his wife. "Did Josh find you in Athens?"

Margo tilted her head. "Josh? Was he in Greece?"

"No, I tracked him down in Italy after we heard—when the news started coming through. He was going to try to clear his schedule and fly out to help."

Margo smiled thinly. "Sending big brother to the rescue, Laura?"

"He's an excellent attorney. When he wants to be. Didn't he find you?"

"I never saw him." Weary, Margo rested her head against the high back of the chair. That dreamlike state remained. It had been barcly a week since her life had tilted and poured out all of her dreams. "It all happened so fast. The Greek authorities boarding Alain's yacht, searching it." She winced as she remembered the shock of being roused out of sleep to find a dozen uniformed Greeks on deck, being ordered to dress, being questioned. "They found all that heroin in the hold."

"The papers said they'd had him under observation for over a year."

"That's one of the facts that saved my idiotic ass. All the surveillance, the evidence they'd gathered, indicated that I was clean." Her nerves still grinding, she tapped another cigarette out of her enameled case, lighted it. "He used me, Laura, finagling a booking here where he could pick up the drugs, another there where he could drop them off. I'd just had a shoot in Turkey. Five miserable days. He was rewarding me with a little cruise of the Greek Isles. A pre-honeymoon. That's what he called it," she added, sending out smoke in a stream. "He was smoothing out all the little hitches on his amicable divorce, and we'd be able to come out in the open with our relationship."

She took a steady breath then as Laura patiently listened. Studying the smoke twisting toward the ceiling, she continued. "Of course, there was never going to be a divorce. His wife was perfectly willing to have him sleep with me as long as I was useful and the money kept coming in."

"I'm sorry, Margo."

"I fell for it, that's the worst of it." She shrugged her shoulders, took one last, deep drag, and crushed the cigarette out. "All the most ridiculous clichés." She couldn't hate Alain for that nearly as much as she hated herself. "We had to keep our affair and our plans out of the press until all the details of his divorce settlement could be worked out. On the outside we would be colleagues, business partners, friends. He would manage my career, use all of his contacts to increase the bookings and my fees. And why not? He'd nailed me some solid commercials in France and Italy. He'd finalized the deal with Bella Donna that shot me to the top of the heap."

"I don't suppose your talent or your looks had anything to do with your being chosen as spokeswoman for the Bella Donna line."

Margo smiled. "I might have gotten it on my own. But I'll never know. I wanted that contract so badly. Not just the money, though I certainly wanted that. But the exposure. Christ, Laura, seeing my own face on billboards, having people stop me on the street for my autograph. Knowing I was

38

doing a really good job for a really good product.''

''The Bella Donna Woman,'' Laura murmured, wanting Margo to smile and mean it. ''Beautiful. Confident. Dangerous. I was so thrilled when I saw the ad in *Vogue*. That's Margo, I thought, my Margo, stretched out on that glossy page looking so stunning in white satin.''

''Selling face cream.''

''Selling beauty,'' Laura corrected firmly. ''And confidence.''

''And danger?''

''Dreams. You should be proud of it.''

''I was.'' She let out a long breath. ''I was so caught up in it all, so thrilled with myself when we started to hit the American market. And so caught up in Alain, all the promises and plans.''

''You believed in him.''

''No.'' At the very least she had that. He had been only one more in the line of men she'd enjoyed, flirted with. And, yes, used. ''I wanted to believe everything he told me. Enough that I let him string me along with that shopworn line about his wife holding up his divorce.'' She smiled thinly. ''Of course, that was fine with me. As long as he was married, he was safe. I wouldn't have married him, Laura, and I've begun to realize it wasn't that I was in love with him so much as I was in love with the life I imagined. Gradually he took over everything, because it was easier for me not to have to bother with details. And while I was dreaming of this glorious future where the two of us would bop around Europe like royalty, he was siphoning off my money, using it to finance his drug operation, using my minor celebrity over there to clear the way, lying to me about his wife.''

She pressed her fingers against her eyes. ''So the upshot is that my reputation is in tatters, my career is a joke, Bella

Donna's dropped me as their spokeswoman, and I'm damned near broke.''

"Everyone who knows you understands you were a victim, Margo.''

"That doesn't make it better, Laura. Being a victim isn't one of the faces I'm comfortable wearing. I just don't have the energy to change it.''

"You'll get past this. You just need time. And right now you need a long, hot bath and a good night's sleep. Let's get you settled in the guest room.'' Laura rose, extended a hand. "Where's your luggage?''

"I'm having it held. I didn't know if I'd be welcome.''

For a moment Laura said nothing, merely stared down until Margo's gaze faltered. "I'm going to forget you said that, because you're tired and feeling beat-up.'' After tucking an arm around Margo's waist, Laura led her from the room. "You haven't asked about Kate.''

Margo blew out a breath. "She's just going to be pissed at me.''

"At the circumstances,'' Laura corrected. "Give her some credit. Is your luggage at the airport?''

"Mmm.'' She was suddenly so tired it was as if she was walking through water.

"I'll take care of it. Get some sleep. We'll talk more tomorrow when you're feeling better.''

"Thanks, Laura.'' She stopped at the threshold of the guest room, leaned against the jamb. "You're always there.''

"That's where friends are.'' Laura kissed her lightly on the cheek. "Always there. Go to bed.''

Margo didn't bother with a nightgown. She left her clothes pooled on the floor where she peeled them off. Naked, she crawled into the bed and dragged the cozy comforter up to her chin.

The wind screamed at the windows, the rain beat impatiently against the glass. From a distance, the sound of the surf roared up and snatched her into dreamless sleep.

She never stirred when Ann slipped into the room, smoothed the blankets, touched her hair. Offered up a quiet prayer.

Chapter Three

"Typical. Lying around in bed until noon."

Margo heard the voice dimly through sleep, recognized it, and groaned. "Oh, Christ, go away, Kate."

"Nice to see you, too." With apparent glee, Kate Powell gave the drape cord an enthusiastic pull and sent sunlight lasering into Margo's eyes.

"I've always hated you." In defense, Margo pulled a pillow over her face. "Go pick on someone else."

"I took the afternoon off just so I could pick on you." In her efficient way, Kate sat on the edge of the bed and snatched the pillow out of Margo's hands. Concern was masked behind an appraising eye. "You don't look half bad."

"For the waking dead," Margo muttered. She pried open one eye, saw Kate's cool, sneering face, and shut it again. "Go away."

"If I go, the coffee goes." Kate rose to pour from the pot she'd set at the foot of the bed. "And the croissants."

"Croissants." After sniffing the air, Margo warily opened both eyes. She was greeted by the sight of Kate breaking flaky bread in two. The steam that poured out smelled like glory. "I must have died in my sleep if you're bringing me breakfast in bed."

"Lunch," Kate corrected and took a hefty bite. When Kate remembered to eat, she liked to eat well. "Laura made me. She had to run out to some committee meeting she couldn't reschedule." Still, Kate lifted the tray. "Sit up. I promised her I'd see that you ate something."

Margo tugged the sheets over her breasts and reached greedily for the coffee. She drank first, felt some of her jet lag recede. Then, sipping slowly, she studied the woman who was briskly adding strawberry jam to a croissant.

Ebony hair cut gamine short accented a honey-toned triangular face. Margo knew the style wasn't for fashion, but for practicality. It was Kate's good luck, she mused, that it suited so perfectly those large, exotic brown eyes and sassily pointed chin. Men would consider the slight overbite undeniably sexy, and Margo had to admit it softened the entire look.

Not that Kate went in for soft, she thought. The trim navy pinstriped suit was all business. Gold accessories were small and tasteful, the Italian pumps practical. Even the perfume, Margo thought as she caught a whiff, stated clearly that this was a serious, professional woman.

The don't-mess-with-me scent, Margo decided and smiled. "You even look like a damn CPA."

"You look like a hedonist."

They grinned foolishly at each other. Neither of them was prepared for Margo's eyes to fill.

"Oh, God, don't do that."

"I'm sorry." Sniffling, Margo rubbed her hands over her

43

eyes. "All this stuff inside me just keeps swinging up and down, back and forth. I'm a fucking mess."

With her own eyes watering, Kate pulled out two tissues. She was a sympathetic crier, particularly where her family was concerned. And though there was no blood between them, Margo was family. Had been family since Kate, eight years old and orphaned, had been taken in and loved by the Templetons.

"Here, blow your nose," she ordered briskly. "Take some deep breaths. Drink your coffee. Just don't cry. You know you'll get me started."

"Laura just opened the door and let me in." Margo mopped at the tears and struggled to level her voice. "Just welcome home, get some sleep."

"What did you think she would do, kick you into the street?"

Margo shook her head. "No, not Laura. This whole ugly mess may bleed over onto her. The press is bound to go for that angle soon. Disgraced celebrity's childhood friendship with prominent socialite."

"That's reaching," Kate said dryly. "Nobody in the States really considers you a celebrity."

Torn between insult and amusement, Margo leaned back. "I'm a very hot name in Europe. Was."

"This is America, pal. The media will toss a little fish like you back in no time."

Margo's lips moved into a pout. "Thanks a lot." She tossed the covers aside and rose. Kate scanned the naked body before reaching for the robe Laura had draped over the footboard.

The centerfold body—lush breasts, tiny waist, sleek hips and long, dangerous legs—hadn't been adversely affected by the scandal. If Kate hadn't known better, she would have said the figure her friend boasted was the result of modern technology rather than the good fairy of genes.

44

"You've lost a little weight. How come you never lose it in your boobs?"

"Satan and I have an understanding. They used to be a part of my job description."

"Used to be?"

Margo shrugged into the robe. It was her own, a long, flowing swirl of ivory silk. Laura had obviously had her luggage delivered. "Most advertisers don't care to have adulterous drug dealers endorsing their products."

Kate's eyes clouded. She wouldn't tolerate anyone talking about Margo that way. Not even Margo. "You were cleared of the drug charges."

"They didn't have any evidence to charge me. That's entirely different." She shrugged, walked to the window to open it to the afternoon breeze. "You've always told me I ask for trouble. I suppose I asked for this."

"That's just bullshit." Incensed, Kate leapt up, began to pace like an angry cat. Her hand automatically dug into her pockets for the always present roll of Tums. Her stomach was already on afterburn. "I can't believe you're taking this lying down. You haven't done anything."

Touched, Margo turned back, started to speak, but Kate was barreling on, popping Tums in her mouth like candy as she stormed the room.

"Sure, you showed poor judgment and an incredible lack of common sense. Obviously you have questionable taste in men, and your lifestyle choices were far from admirable."

"I'm sure I can count on you to testify to that if it should become necessary," Margo muttered.

"But." Kate held up a hand to make her point. "You did nothing illegal, nothing that warrants losing your career. If you want to spend your life posing so people run out and buy some ridiculously overpriced shampoo or skin cream, or in ways that

45

make men lose twenty points of IQ on impact, you can't let this stop you.''

''I know there was moral support in there somewhere,'' Margo said after a moment's thought. ''I just have to weed it out from my poor judgment, questionable taste, and foolish career. Then again, I have to remember that your judgment is always good, your taste perfect, and your career brilliant.''

''That's true.'' There was a flush on Margo's cheeks now and fire in her eyes. Relieved, Kate grinned. ''You look beautiful when you're angry.''

''Oh, shut up.'' Margo marched to the terrace doors, wrenched them open, and strode out onto the wide stone balcony with its mini garden of impatiens and violas.

The weather was clear and fine, one of those unspeakably beautiful days drenched with gilded sunlight, cupped by blue skies, perfumed with flowers. The Templeton estate, Big Sur, stretched out, tumbling gardens and tidy stone walls, graceful ornamental bushes and stately old trees. The pretty stucco stables that were no longer used resembled a tidy cottage off to the south. She could just catch a glint that was the water of the pool, and the fanciful white gazebo beyond it, decked with pretty four-o'clocks.

She'd done some dreaming in that flower-drenched gazebo, she remembered. Imagining herself a fine lady waiting for a devoted and dashing lover.

''Why did I ever want to leave here?''

''I don't know.'' Kate came up behind her, draped an arm over Margo's shoulder. In heels she was still an inch shy of Margo's stacked five ten, but she drew Margo against her and supported her.

''I wanted to be someone. Someone dazzling. I wanted to meet dazzling people, be a part of their world. Me, the housekeeper's daughter, flying off to Rome, sunning on the Riviera, decorating the slopes at Saint Moritz.''

"You've done all those things."

"And more. Why wasn't it ever enough for me, Kate? Why was there always this part of me that wanted one more thing? Just one more thing I could never get a grip on. I could never figure out what it was. Now that I may have lost all the others, I still haven't figured it out."

"You've got time," Kate said quietly. "Remember Seraphina?"

Margo's lips curved a little as she thought of how she had stood on Seraphina's cliff the night before. And of all the lazy days when she and Kate and Laura had talked about the young Spanish girl, the conclusions they'd come to.

"She didn't wait and see." Margo leaned her head against Kate's. "She didn't stop and see what the rest of her life had to offer."

"Here's your chance to wait and see."

"Well." Margo blew out a breath. "As fascinating as that sounds, I might not be able to wait for some of it. I think I may be in some stormy financial waters." She drew back and tried to put on a sunny smile. "I could use your professional help. I figure a woman with an M.B.A. from Harvard can decipher my poorly kept and disorganized books. Want to take a shot?"

Kate leaned back against the rail. The smile didn't fool her for a minute. And she knew if Margo was worried about something as casual as money, it was a desperate time.

"I've got the rest of the day. Get some clothes on, and we'll get started."

Margo knew it was bad. She'd expected it to be bad. But from the way Kate was grumbling and hissing, she understood it was going to be a hell of a lot worse.

After the first hour, she stayed out of Kate's way. It did no good to hang over her shoulder and be snapped at, so she

47

occupied herself by unpacking, carefully hanging dresses that had been carelessly packed into the rosewood armoire, meticulously folding sweaters into the scented drawer of the mirrored bureau.

She answered Kate's occasional questions and tolerated the more than occasional abuse. Desperate gratitude flooded through her when Laura opened the door.

"Sorry I was gone so long. I couldn't—"

"Quiet. I'm trying to perform miracles here."

Margo jerked a thumb at the terrace. "She's working on my books," Margo explained when they were outside. "You can't imagine what she pulled out of her briefcase. This little laptop computer, a calculator I'm sure could run equations for the space shuttle, even a fax."

"She's brilliant." With a sigh, Laura sat down on one of the wrought-iron chairs and slipped out of her shoes. "Templeton would hire her in a heartbeat, but she's very stubborn about not working for family. Bittle and Associates is lucky to have her."

"What is this crap about seaweed?" Kate shouted.

"It's a spa treatment," Margo called back. "I think it's deductible because—"

"Just let me do the thinking. How the hell can you owe fifteen thousand dollars to Valentino? How many outfits can you wear?"

Margo sat down. "It probably wouldn't be smart for me to tell her that was for one cocktail dress."

"I'd say not," Laura agreed. "The kids will be home from school in an hour or so. They always put her in a good mood. We'll have a family dinner to celebrate your homecoming."

"Did you tell Peter I was here?"

"Of course. You know, I think I'll make sure we have champagne chilled."

Before Laura could rise, Margo covered her hand. "He's not pleased with the news."

"Don't be silly. Certainly he's pleased." But she began to twist her wedding ring around her finger, a sure sign of agitation. "He's always glad to see you."

"Laura, it isn't nearly twenty-five years of knowing you that lets me see when you're lying. It's that you're so lousy at it. He doesn't want me here."

Excuses trembled on her tongue, but they were useless. It was true, Laura admitted, lying was a skill she'd never mastered. "This is your home. Peter understands that even if he isn't completely comfortable with the situation. I want you here, Annie wants you here, and the kids are thrilled that you're here. Now I'm not only going to go see about that champagne, I'm going to go bring a bottle up here."

"Good idea." She would have to worry about guilt later. "Maybe it'll help Kate keep me in the black."

"This mortgage is fifteen days overdue," Kate called out. "And you're over the limit on your Visa. Jesus, Margo."

"I'll bring two bottles," Laura decided and kept a smile in place until she'd left Margo's room.

She went to her own, wanting a moment to herself. She'd thought she had gotten over her anger, but she hadn't. It was still there, she realized, high and bitter in her throat. She paced the sitting room to work it off. The sitting room that was becoming more of a sanctuary. She could come here, close herself in with the warm colors and scents, and tell herself that she had correspondence to answer, some little piece of needlework to finish.

But more often she came here to work off an emotion that choked her.

Perhaps she should have expected Peter's reaction, been prepared for it. But she hadn't been. She never seemed to be prepared for Peter's reactions any more. How could it be that after ten years of marriage she didn't seem to know him at all?

She stopped by his office on the way home from her committee meeting on the Summer Ball. She hummed to herself as she took the private elevator up to the penthouse suite of Templeton Monterey. Peter preferred the suite to the executive offices on the hotel's ground level. It was quieter, he said, made it easier to concentrate.

From her days of assisting and learning the business in the nerve center of the sales and reservations offices, she had to agree. Perhaps it separated him from the pulse, from the people, but Peter knew his job.

The sheer beauty of the day, added to the pleasure of having her old friend home again, lifted her mood. With a spring in her step, she crossed the silver-toned carpet to the airy reception area.

"Oh, hello, Mrs. Ridgeway." The receptionist offered a quick smile but continued working and didn't quite meet Laura's eyes. "I think Mr. Ridgeway is in a meeting, but let me just buzz through and let him know you're here."

"I'd appreciate it, Nina. I'll only take a few minutes of his time." She wandered over to the seating area, quietly empty now. The leather seats in navy were new, and as pricey as the antique tables and lamps and the watercolors Peter had commissioned had been. But Laura supposed he'd been right. The offices had needed some sprucing up. Appearances were important in business. Were important to Peter.

But as she gazed through the wide window she wondered how anyone could care about navy leather seats when that awesome view of the coast presented itself.

Just look at how the water rolled, how it stretched to forever. The ice plants were blooming pink, and white gulls veered in, hoping some tourist would offer a treat. See the boats on the bay, bobbing like shiny, expensive toys for men in double-breasted navy blazers and white slacks.

She lost herself in it and nearly forgot to retouch her lipstick and powder before the receptionist told her to go right in.

Peter Ridgeway's office suited the executive director of Templeton Hotels, California. With its carefully selected Louis XIV furnishings, its glorious seascapes and sculptures, it was as erudite and flawlessly executed as the man himself. When he rose from behind the desk, her smile warmed automatically.

He was a beautiful man, bronze and gold and trim in elegant Savile Row. She had fallen in love with that face—its cool blue eyes, firm mouth and jaw—like a princess for a prince in a fairy tale. And, as in a fairy tale, he had swept her off her feet when she'd been barely eighteen. He'd been every-thing she'd dreamed of.

She lifted her mouth for a kiss and received an absent peck on the cheek. "I don't have much time, Laura. I have meetings all day." He remained standing, tilting his head, the faintest line of annoyance marring his brow. "I've told you it's more convenient if you call first to be certain I can see you. My schedule isn't as flexible as yours is."

Her smile faded. "I'm sorry. I wasn't able to talk to you last night, and when I called this morning, you were out, so—"

"I went by the club for a quick nine holes and a steam. I put in a very long night."

"Yes, I know." How are you, Laura? How are the girls? I missed you. She waited a moment, but he said none of those things. "You'll be home tonight?"

"If I'm able to get back to work, I should be able to make it by seven."

"Good. I was hoping you could. We're having a family dinner. Margo's back."

His mouth tightened briefly, but he did stop looking at his watch. "Back?"

"She got in last night. She's so unhappy, Peter. So tired."

"Unhappy? Tired?" His laugh was quick and unamused. "I'm not surprised, after her latest adventure." He recognized the look in his wife's eyes and banked down on his fury. He wasn't a man who cared for displays of temper, even his own. "For God's sake, Laura, you haven't invited her to stay."

"It wasn't a matter of inviting her. It's her home."

It wasn't anger now so much as weariness. He sat, gave a long sigh. "Laura, Margo is the daughter of our housekeeper. That does not make Templeton her home. You can carry childhood loyalties too far."

"No," Laura said quietly. "I don't think you can. She's in trouble, Peter, and whether or not any of it is of her own making isn't the issue. She needs her friends and her family."

"Her name's all over the papers, the news, every bloody tabloid show on the screen. Sex, drugs, name of God."

"She was cleared of the drug charges, Peter, and she certainly isn't the first woman to fall for a married man."

His voice took on the tedious patience that always put her teeth on edge. "That may be true, but 'discretion' isn't a word she seems to be aware of. I can't have her name linked to ours and risk our standing in the community. I don't want her in my house."

That brought Laura's head up and erased any thought of placating him. "It's my parents' house," she tossed back with fury sizzling in every word. "We're there, Peter, because they wanted it to be lived in and loved. I know my mother and father would welcome Margo, and so do I."

"I see." He folded his hands on the desk. "That's a little dig you haven't tried in some time. I live in Templeton House, work for the Templeton empire, and sleep with the Templeton heiress."

When you bother to come home, Laura thought, but held her tongue.

"Whatever I have is due to the Templeton generosity."

"That's certainly not true, Peter. You're your own man, an experienced and successful hotelier. And there's no reason to turn a discussion of Margo into a fight."

Gauging her, he tried a new tack. "It doesn't bother you, Laura, to have a woman with her reputation around our children? Certainly they'll hear gossip, and Allison, at least, is old enough to understand some of it."

The flush rose to her cheeks, then died away. "Margo is Ali's godmother and she's my oldest friend. She's welcome at Templeton as long as I live there, Peter." She straightened her shoulders, looked him dead in the eye. "To use words you'll understand, those terms are nonnegotiable. Dinner's at seven-thirty if you're able to make it."

She strode out and controlled the urge to slam the door.

Now, alone in her room, she fought back the resurging temper. It never did her any good to lose it, only made her feel foolish and guilty. So she would calm herself, put on that smooth false front she was growing so accustomed to wearing.

It was important to remember that Margo needed her. And it was becoming painfully clear that her husband did not.

"Can I try your perfume, Aunt Margo? The one in the pretty gold bottle. Please?"

Margo looked down at Kayla's hopeful face. If they were casting angels, she mused, this one with her soft gray eyes and winking dimples would win the role hands down.

"Just a couple of drops." Margo took the stopper out and dabbed a whisper behind each of Kayla's ears. "A woman doesn't want to be obvious."

"How come?"

"Because mystery is a spice."

"Like pepper?"

Ali, three years superior to Kayla's six years, snorted. But

53

Margo hauled Kayla up on her lap and nuzzled her. "In a manner of speaking. Want a dab, Ali?"

All but salivating over the fascinating bottles and pots on the vanity, Ali tried her best to sound nonchalant. "Maybe, but I don't want what she has."

"Something different, then. Something . . ." Playing it up, Margo waved her hand over this bottle and that. "Bold and daring."

"But not obvious," Kayla chimed in.

"That's a girl. Here we are." Without a thought, Margo sacrificed a few dabs of a two-hundred-dollar-an-ounce scent. It was Bella Donna's new Tigre. She probably had twenty of the gorgeous handblown bottles in her Milan flat. "You're growing up on me," she accused and tugged the gold curls spilling to Ali's shoulders.

"I'm old enough to have my ears pierced, but Daddy won't let me."

"Men just don't understand these things." Because she did, perfectly, she patted Ali's cheek before shifting Kayla on her knee. "Decorating ourselves is a woman's privilege." Giving Ali a bolstering smile in the mirror, she went back to perfecting her makeup. "Your mom'll talk him into it."

"She can't talk him into anything. He never listens."

"He's very busy," Kayla said solemnly. "He has to work and work so we can stand."

"So we won't lose our standing," Ali corrected and rolled her eyes. Kayla didn't understand anything, she thought. Sometimes Mama did, and Aunt Kate always listened, but she had hope, great new hope that her glamorous and mysterious Aunt Margo would understand everything.

"Aunt Margo, are you going to stay now that those bad things happened to you?"

"I don't know." Margo set down her lipstick with a little click.

"I'm glad you came home." Ali wrapped her arms around Margo's neck.

"So am I." The unstable emotions were stirring again. She rose quickly, grabbing each child by the hand. "Let's go down and see if there's anything fun to eat before dinner."

"We're having hors d'oeuvres in the front parlor," Ali said loftily, then giggled. "We hardly ever get to stay up for dinner with hors d'oeuvres."

"Stick with me, kid." She stopped at the top curve of the stairs. "Let's make an entrance. Chins up, eyes bored, stomachs in, fingers trailing carelessly along the banisters."

She was halfway down behind the girls when she saw her mother at the bottom landing. Ann stood with her hands folded, her face solemn.

"Ah, Lady Allison, Lady Kayla, we're honored that you could join us this evening. Refreshments are being served in the front parlor."

Ali inclined her head regally. "Thank you, Miss Annie," she managed before she bolted after her sister.

It wasn't until Margo had reached the bottom that she caught the twinkle in her mother's eyes. For the first time since her return, they smiled easily at each other.

"I'd forgotten how much fun they are."

"Miss Laura is raising angels."

"I was thinking the same thing myself. She's done everything right—everything I haven't. Mum, I'm sorry—"

"We won't talk about it now." But Ann laid a hand briefly over her daughter's on the newel post. "Later—but they're waiting for you now." She started to walk away, then paused. "Margo, Miss Laura needs a friend just now as much as you do. I hope you'll be a good one."

"If something's wrong, tell me."

Ann shook her head. "It's not my place. Just be a good

friend.'' She walked away, leaving Margo to enter the parlor alone.

Ali was already crossing the room, her tongue caught in her teeth, her hands full of a flute of fizzing champagne. ''I poured it for you myself.''

''Well, then, I'll have to drink it.'' She lifted the glass, scanned the room. Laura had Kayla on one hip, and Kate was sampling the finger food arranged on Georgian silver. A sedate fire flickered in the hearth framed by rich lapis. The stunning curved mirror over the mantel tossed back reflections of glossy antiques, delicate porcelain, and rosy light from globe lamps.

''To being home with friends,'' Margo said and sipped.

''Eat some of this mini quiche,'' Kate ordered over a full mouth. ''It's outrageous.''

What the hell, Margo thought, her weight was hardly a burning issue any longer. She took one bite, hummed in pleasure. ''Mrs. Williamson's still a wonder. Lord, she must be eighty by now.''

''Seventy-three last November,'' Laura corrected. ''And she can still whip up the most incredible chocolate soufflé.'' She winked at Kayla. ''Which, rumor has it, is on for tonight.''

''Daddy says Mrs. Williamson should be retired and we should have a French chef like the Barrymores in Carmel.'' Because Margo had, Ali sampled a quiche.

''French chefs are snooty.'' To demonstrate, Margo put a finger under her nose to lift it into the air. ''And they never make jelly tarts with leftover dough for little girls.''

''Did she do that for you, too?'' The image delighted Ali. ''Did she let you flute the edges?''

''Absolutely. I have to admit, your mother was the best at it. According to Mrs. Williamson, I was too impatient, and Kate worried too much about getting it just right, but your mom had a feel. She was the champ jelly tart maker.''

''One of my major accomplishments.'' Margo heard the

edge in Laura's voice and lifted a brow. With a shrug, Laura set Kayla on her feet. "That's a fabulous dress, Margo. Milan or Paris?"

"Milan." If Laura wanted the subject changed, she could oblige. She struck a pose, head tilted, one hand on her hip. The clinging black silk molded itself to her body and stopped daringly short at the thighs. The low square neckline hinted at cleavage, while sheer sleeves journeyed from the curve of her shoulders to wrists where twin diamond bracelets winked. "A little something I picked up from a sassy new designer."

"You'll freeze before the night's over," Kate commented.

"Not when my heart's so warm. Are we waiting for Peter?"

"No," Laura decided on the spot, then buried her annoyance when she caught Ali's worried look. "He was afraid his meetings might run over, so there's no telling when he'll get away. We'll start dinner without him." She took Kayla's hand, then glanced over as Ann came to the doorway.

"I'm sorry, Miss Laura, there's a phone call."

"I'll take it in the library, Annie. Have another glass of champagne," she suggested as she started out. "I won't be long."

Margo and Kate exchanged a look, one that promised they would talk later. Deliberately cheerful, Margo topped off the glasses and launched into a story about gambling in Monte Carlo. When Laura came back, the children were wide-eyed and Kate was shaking her head.

"You're certifiable, Margo. Betting twenty-five thousand on one spin of a little silver ball."

"Hey, I won." She sighed in memory. "That time."

"Was it Daddy?" Ali wanted to know, hurrying over to tug on her mother's hand. "Is he coming?"

"No." Distracted, Laura brushed her fingers over Ali's hair. "It wasn't Daddy, honey." She wasn't so distracted she didn't notice the way her daughter's shoulders drooped. To soothe, she crouched down, smiling. "But it's really good news. Something special."

"What is it? Is it a party?"

"Better." Laura kissed Ali's cheek. "Uncle Josh is coming home."

Margo dropped to the arm of the sofa and found she needed to gulp down the champagne. "Wonderful," she muttered. "Just wonderful."

Chapter Four

Joshua Conway Templeton was a man who did things in his own time, and in his own way. He was driving south from San Francisco because he'd decided not to fly to Monterey from London. He could have excused the detour by pretending that Templeton San Francisco needed a quick study. But his family's landmark hotel ran like a well-wound clock.

The simple fact was that somewhere along the flight he'd decided to buy a car.

And a honey it was, too.

The little Jag roared down Highway 1 like an eager Thoroughbred at the starting gun. It took a wide, sweeping curve at seventy and made him grin.

This was home, this rugged, lonely coast. He had tooled along the spectacular Amalfi Drive in Italy, sped through the fjords of Norway, but not even their heart-stopping beauty could match the sheer drama of Big Sur.

It had more. The glinting beaches and gleaming coves. The cliffs that speared defiantly from savage sea to pristine sky. Brooding forests, the surprise of a stream that cascaded out of a canyon like liquid silver. Then there were miles of tranquillity, broken only by the din of seals, the cold fire of the surf.

Always, the glory of it grabbed at his throat. Wherever he had been, however long he had traveled away, this single spot on the globe pulled at him.

So he was coming home, in his own time and in his own way. Recklessly he tested the Jag on the wild, twisting curves that dropped off to jagged rocks and unforgiving sea. He punched the gas on the straightaway and laughed as the wind rushed over him.

It wasn't hurry that pushed him, but the simple love of speed and chance. He had time, he mused. Plenty of it. And he was going to use it.

He was worried about Laura. There'd been something in his sister's voice on the phone that alerted him. She'd said all the right things. But then, Laura always did. He would do a bit of probing there, he decided.

There was business to see to. He'd been happy enough to leave the California executive offices of Templeton Hotels primarily in Peter's hands. Spreadsheets simply didn't interest Josh. He took an interest in the vineyards, the factories, even in the day-to-day running of a busy five-star hotel, but bottom lines were Peter's concern, not his.

For most of the past decade, he'd enjoyed the freedom of traveling through Europe, spot-checking, overseeing the necessary renovations, revamping policy changes of the family chain. Wineries in France and Italy, olive groves in Greece, orchards in Spain. And, of course, the hotels themselves, which had started it all.

Josh understood and supported the long-held Templeton view that the difference between a hotel and a Templeton was the fact that they served their own wines, used their own oils, their own produce, manufactured their own linens. Templeton products were always offered in Templeton hotels. And part of his job was to see that they were used well.

His title might have been executive vice president, but in essence he was a troubleshooter. Occasionally he handled or supervised the handling of a few of the legal complexities. A man with a Harvard law degree was expected to keep his hand in. Still he preferred people to papers, enjoyed watching a harvest, drinking ouzo with the staff, or closing a new deal over Cristal and beluga at Robuchon in Paris.

It was his charm that was his most valuable asset to Templeton—so his mother said. He did his best not to disappoint her. For despite a careless, somewhat reckless lifestyle, he took his duties to his family and the business seriously. They were one and the same to him.

And as he was thinking of family, even as gravel spit out from under his tires and had the family of four in the sedan he shot past gaping in shock, he thought of Margo.

She would be depressed, he mused. Shattered, penitent, miserable. Not that she didn't deserve to be. His lips curved in something between a smile and a sneer. He'd pulled strings, cashed in markers, and generally executed a wild tap dance to see that she was quickly and completely cleared of any criminal charges in Athens.

After all, Templeton Athens was an old, dignified hotel and, with Templeton Resort Athena, it lured a great deal of money to the country.

There was little he could do about the scandal, or the damage it had done to the career she'd built in Europe. If you could call sending sulky looks into a camera a career.

She'd just have to get over it, he decided, his smile now

tinged with arrogance. And he intended to help her. In his own way.

In an old habit he was hardly aware of, he swung over to the side of the road and brought the car to a screeching halt. There, higher still on the rugged hill, surrounded by trees going lush with spring and trailing vines spilling rich blossoms, was home.

Stone and wood, two of the resources Templeton had profited by, rose out of the rugged earth. The original two-story structure had been built by an ancestor as a country home and stood for more than a hundred twenty-five years, surviving storms, floods, quakes, and time.

Wings had been added by subsequent generations, spearing out here, there, tumbling down to follow the shape of the hill. Twin turrets rose up defiantly —an addition of his father's fancy. Wide wooden decks and sturdy stone terraces shot beneath tall, arched windows, wide glass doors to offer dozens of panoramas.

Flowers and trees were blooming, pink and white and yellow. Spring colors, he thought, fresh and inviting. And the grass was the soft, tender green of beginnings. He loved the way it flowed up out of a rocky base, growing more lush and more tended as it met the house.

The land and the sea were as intricate and as intimate a part of the house as its curving trim and glinting stone.

He loved it for what it was, what it had been, and what it had given him. Knowing Laura watched over it, nurtured it, warmed him.

Pleasure at simply being there had him swinging fast across the road, shooting up the snaking lane carved into the rock, then, in shock, slamming on the brakes to avoid crashing into a high iron gate.

He scowled at it for a moment before the intercom beside his car buzzed on.

"Templeton House. May I help you?"

"What the hell is this? Who put this damn thing up?"

"I— Mr. Joshua?"

Recognizing the voice, he struggled to bank down on his irritation. "Annie, open this ridiculous gate, will you? And unless we're under attack, leave the damn thing open."

"Yes, sir. Welcome home."

What the hell was Laura thinking of? he wondered as the gate swung silently back. Templeton had always been a welcoming place. His friends had roared up that curving lane constantly during his youth—on foot, on bikes, then in cars. The idea of its being closed off, even by something as simple as a gate, spoiled his pleasure in the drive from rugged ground to manicured lawns and gardens.

He swung bad-temperedly around the center island, planted magnificently with hardy spring perennials and nodding daffodils. He left both his keys and his luggage in the car and, jamming his hands in his pockets, mounted the lovely old granite steps to the front terrace.

The main entrance door was recessed, ten feet high and arched, framed by intricately placed mosaics that formed a pattern of trailing purple bougainvillea echoed by the trellises of living blooms spilling over the archway. He'd always thought it was like walking through a garden.

Even as he reached for the door it was swinging open. Laura literally leapt into his arms.

"Welcome home," she said, after she'd rained kisses over his face and made him smile again.

"For a minute I thought you were locking me out." The puzzlement in her eyes made him pinch her chin. An old habit. "What's with the gate?"

"Oh." She flushed a little as she backed up and smoothed her hair. "Peter thought we needed some security."

"Security? All you have to do is climb over a few rocks to skirt around it."

"Well, yes, but . . ." She'd said the same herself, and since it was Josh, she gave up. "It looks secure. And important." She cupped his face in her hands. "So do you. Look important, I mean."

Actually, she thought he looked windblown, dangerous, and annoyed. To soothe, she tucked her arm through his and made admiring noises over the car in the driveway. "Where did you get the new toy?"

"In San Francisco. She drives like a bullet."

"Which explains why you're here a full hour before you were expected. Lucky for you Mrs. Williamson has been slaving all morning in the kitchen preparing all that sweet Master Josh's favorite foods."

"Tell me we're having salmon cakes for lunch and all's forgiven."

"Salmon cakes," Laura confirmed. "Allumettes, asparagus, foie gras, and Black Forest cake. Quite a combination. Come in and tell me all about London. You did come from London, right?"

"Just a quick business trip. I'd been taking a few days off in Portofino."

"Oh, that's right." She moved into the parlor to pour him a glass of the sparkling mineral water that Templeton bottled. The curtains were open, as she preferred them, forming frames around window seats made welcoming with colorful pillows. "That's where I hunted you down when I heard about Margo."

"Um-hmm." He'd already been hard at work on Margo's behalf when Laura had called. But he didn't pass that information along. Instead he gave a sprig of freesia tucked with its fellows into a Meissen vase a careless brush. "So how is she?"

"I talked her into sitting by the pool for a while, to get some sun. Josh, this is so terrible for her. She looked so beaten when she came home. Bella Donna is going to drop her as their spokeswoman. Her contract with them was coming up for renewal, and it's pretty much a given that they'll let her go."

"It's rough." He sat in the wide wing chair nearest the hearth, stretched out his legs. "So maybe she can tout some-one else's face cream."

"You know it's not that easy, Josh. She'd made a mark in Europe endorsing Bella Donna. It was her main source of income, and now it's cut off. If you've paid any attention to the press, you know that the chances of her being offered anything like it here in the States is slim to none."

"So, she'll get a real job."

Loyalty had her jerking up her chin. "You've always been so hard on her."

"Somebody has to." But he knew that arguing about Margo with his sister was useless. Love always blinded Laura. "Okay, sweetie, I'm sorry for what happened to her. The fact is, she got a raw deal, but life's full of them. She's been raking in the lire and francs for the last few years. All she has to do now is sit on her portfolio, lick her wounds, and figure out what comes next."

"I think she's broke."

That shocked him enough to have him setting his glass aside. "What do you mean broke?"

"I mean she asked Kate to look over the figures. Kate hasn't finished yet, but I have a feeling it's bad. Margo knows it's bad."

He couldn't believe it. He'd taken a good long look at the Bella Donna contract himself, and he knew that the salary and benefits should have set her up comfortably for a decade.

Then he let out a sound of disgust. Why couldn't he believe it? They were talking about Margo, after all.

"For Christ's sake, what has she been doing, heaving her money into the Tiber?"

"Well, her lifestyle . . . after all, she's a celebrity over there, and . . ." Wasn't she worried enough without having to explain? Laura wondered. "Hell, Josh, I'm not sure, but I know she had that slime who got her into this mess managing her for the last few years."

"Pinhead," he muttered. "So she comes crawling home, sniveling."

"She did not snivel. I should have expected you to take this line," she went on. "It must be men. None of you have any loyalty or compassion. Peter wanted to toss her out as if—"

"Let him try," Josh murmured with a dangerous glint in his eye. "It's not his house."

Laura opened her mouth, closed it again. If this emotional roller coaster she was stuck on didn't stop soon, she was going to jump. "Peter didn't grow up with Margo the way we did. He isn't attached to her the way we are. He doesn't understand."

"He doesn't have to," Josh said shortly, and rose. "She's out by the pool?"

"Yes. Josh, you're not going out there and start poking at her. She's unhappy enough."

Josh shot her a look. "I'll just go and rub some salt in her wounds, then I think I'll run out and kick some puppies on my way to foreclosing on my quota of widows and orphans."

Laura's lips curved. "Just try to be supportive. We'll have lunch on the south terrace in about half an hour." It would give her time to have his luggage taken upstairs and properly unpacked.

*   *   *

66

Margo knew the moment he stepped off the flagstone path onto the skirt of the pool. She didn't see him, hear him, smell him. Her instincts when it came to Josh went into a sixth sense. When he didn't speak, merely sat on one of the padded lounges on the pool terrace, she continued to swim.

It was too cold to swim, of course. But she'd needed to do something. The water was warm enough. Steam rose from it into the cooler air, and every stroke she took brought her arms into chilly contact with the freshening breeze.

She cut through the water in long, slow strokes and risked a quick glance at him. He was staring off toward the rose garden. Preoccupied, she thought.

He had Laura's eyes, she thought. It always surprised her to see Laura's lovely gray eyes in Josh's face. His were cooler, she thought, more impatient, and often brittlely amused at Margo's expense.

He'd gotten a tan somewhere, she noted as she pivoted and started back across the length of the pool. Just a nice warm hint of color that added another dash of appeal to what was already a sinfully handsome face.

As one who accepted that she'd lucked out in the gene pool, she didn't set much store by simple good looks. It was, after all, just a matter of fate.

Joshua Templeton's fate had been superior.

His hair was shades darker than his sister's. Tawny, Margo imagined was the term. He'd let it grow a bit since the last time they'd run into each other. What was that—three months before in Venice? It flirted with his collar now, the collar of a casual chocolate silk shirt with sleeves rolled up to the elbows.

He had, she recalled, a good, expressive mouth. It could smile charmingly, sneer with infuriating style, and worse, curve in a smile so cold it froze the blood.

The jaw was firm, and thankfully without the beard he'd

sported briefly in his twenties. The nose was straight and faintly aristocratic. Over it all was an aura of success, confidence, and arrogance, all shimmering together with a glint of latent danger.

She hated to admit that there had been a time during her adolescence when she'd been both allured by and frightened of that aura.

She was sure of one thing. He was the last person she would allow to see how badly she was now frightened by the present, and the future. Deliberately she stood in the shallow end. Water slid off her body as she slowly walked to the steps. She was freezing now and would have turned into a chunk of bluing ice before she would have admitted it.

As if she'd just become aware she wasn't alone, she lifted a brow and smiled. Her voice was low, throaty, and just shy of hot. "Well, Josh, the world's much too small."

She was wearing a couple of stingy scraps of sapphire spandex. Her curves were lush, sleek, with skin as smooth as polished marble with the sheen of fine silk. Most men, she knew, took one look at what God had given her and shot straight into fantasy mode.

Josh merely tipped down his Wayfarers and studied her over their top. He noted that she'd lost weight, that that glorious skin of hers was prickled with gooseflesh. In a brotherly fashion he tossed her a towel.

"Your teeth are going to chatter in a minute."

Annoyed, she swung the towel around her neck, fisted her hands. "It's invigorating. Where did you drop in from?"

"Portofino, by way of London."

"Portofino. One of my favorite spots, even if the Templetons don't have a hotel there. Did you stay at the Splendido?"

"Where else?" If she was going to be idiotic enough to stand there and freeze, he'd let her. He crossed his ankles, leaned back.

"The corner suite," she said, remembering. "Where you stand on the terrace and see the bay, the hills, the gardens."

That had been his intention. A couple of days to wind down, to do a little sailing. But he'd been too busy negotiating via phone and fax with the police and politicians in Greece to enjoy the view.

"How did you find Athens?"

He was nearly sorry when he noted her eyes flicker, but her recovery was quick. "Oh, not as accommodating as usual. A little misunderstanding. That's all taken care of. It was annoying, though, having my cruise disrupted."

"I'm sure it was," he murmured. "So inconsiderate of the authorities, too. All that inconvenience over a few pesky kilos of heroin."

She smiled easily. "My thoughts exactly." Negligently, she reached out for the robe she'd slung over the back of a chair. Not even pride was going to hold off the shivering much longer. "I can use the time off, though, a little break from the routine. It's been too long since I've been able to squeeze out any real time to visit with Laura and Kate, and the girls." She belted the robe and nearly sighed with relief. "And you, of course, Josh." Knowing it irritated him, she bent down to pat his cheek. "How long are you going to be in the area?"

He took her wrist, knowing it irritated her, and rose. "As long as it takes."

"Well, then." She always seemed to forget he was four inches taller than she. Until she was faced with that long, rangy build. "It'll be just like old times, won't it? I think I'll go in and get into some dry clothes."

She kissed his cheeks briskly, called *"ciao"* over her shoulder, and strolled down the path toward the house.

Josh watched her go, hating himself for being annoyed that she hadn't been teary and wrecked. Hating himself more, much more, for the undeniable fact that he was, and always had been, in love with her.

It took Margo six tries before she settled on the proper outfit for lunch. The flowing silk tunic and slacks in fragile pink seemed just casual enough while maintaining a certain elegance and style. She accented the outfit with gold door-knocker earrings, a couple of bangle bracelets, and a long braided chain. Shoes added another ten minutes before she was inspired to go barefoot. That would lend an air of insouciance.

She couldn't explain why she was always compelled to impress Josh, or struggle to outdo him. Sibling rivalry seemed too tame and much too ordinary an explanation.

It was true enough that he had teased her unmercifully as a child from his lofty advantage of four years; had tormented her as a teenager; and had, as their paths crossed in adulthood, made her feel foolish, shallow, and irresponsible in turn.

One of the reasons the Bella Donna contract had meant so much to her was that it was a tangible measure of success that she'd been able to flaunt under his disapproving nose. Now she didn't have that any longer. All she had was image—bolstered by the wardrobe and glitters she'd desperately collected over the years.

She could only thank God that she'd gotten out of the mess in Athens before he'd had to come riding in on his white charger to save her. That would have been a humiliation he'd never have let her forget.

It was Laura's laughter she heard first after descending the stairs and wandering toward the south terrace. It made Margo stop. That's what had been missing the past couple of days, she realized. Laura's laughter. She'd been too tangled in her own miseries to notice. However Josh's presence got on her nerves, she had to be grateful—he'd made Laura laugh again.

She was smiling when she stepped out and joined them.

"What's the joke?"

Josh merely leaned back with his water glass and studied her, but Laura reached for her hand. "Josh is always telling me some horrible secret crime he committed when we were kids. I think he does it to terrify me about what Ali and Kayla are pulling off under my nose."

"The girls are angels," Margo said as she sat down at the round glass table under an arbor of sweetly blooming wisteria. "Josh was the devil's spawn." She spread foie gras on a toast point and bit in. "What's the crime?"

"Do you remember that night when you and I went out to Seraphina's cliffs with Matt Bolton and Biff Milard? It was summer, we were just fifteen. Kate wasn't with us because she was a year younger and couldn't date yet."

Margo cast her mind back. "We double-dated with Matt and Biff a lot that summer. Until Biff tried to unhook your bra and you bloodied his nose."

"What?" Josh immediately came to attention. "What do you mean he tried to unhook your bra?"

"I'm sure you've attempted the maneuver once or twice, Josh," Margo said dryly.

"Shut up, Margo. You never told me he'd tried to . . ." His eyes took on a warrior's glint. "What else did he try?"

Laura sighed and decided she was enjoying the salmon cakes more than she'd anticipated. "Nothing worth you flying to Los Angeles to hunt him down and shoot him like a dog for. In any case, if I'd wanted him to unhook my bra, I wouldn't have punched him in the nose, would I? To get back to the story, that was the night we heard Seraphina's ghost."

"Oh, right, I remember."

Margo helped herself to more pâté. It was the Tiffany porcelain lunch service today, she noted. The Monet pattern with its cheerfully bright blue and yellow. And to set it off, a silver vase filled with yellow frangipani from the greenhouse. Her

71

mother's touch, she thought. She'd used the same china, the same flowers when she allowed Margo to have the tea party she'd so longed for on her thirteenth birthday.

Was it, she wondered, her mother's quiet, unspoken way of welcoming?

With a shake, she brought herself back. "We were sitting on the cliffs necking."

"Define necking," Josh demanded.

She only smiled and stole one of the matchstick potatoes from his plate. "There was a full moon, and all this lovely light on the water. The stars were so huge and bright and the sea went on forever. Then we heard her. She was crying."

"Like her heart would break," Laura added. "It was intense, but very soft, like something carried up into the air. We were terrified and thrilled."

"And the guys were so spooked they forgot all about scoring and kept trying to get us back to the car. But we stayed. We could hear this whispering and moaning and crying. Then we heard her speak." Margo shivered remembering it. "In Spanish."

"I had to translate because you'd been too busy painting your nails in class to pay attention to Mrs. Lupez. She said, 'Find my treasure. It waits for love.' "

Even as Margo sighed, Josh was chuckling. "It took me three days to teach Kate how to say that without fumbling it. The kid never had an ear for languages. We nearly fell off the ledge laughing when the two of you started to squeal."

Margo narrowed her eyes. "You and Kate?"

"We planned it for a week." Since she didn't seem that interested, he forked up her salmon cake and transferred it to his own plate. "She was feeling pretty left out when you two started dating. I got the idea when I came across her sulking on the cliffs. Everybody knew you two hung out there with

72

Dumb and Dumber, and I thought it would cheer Kate up." He swallowed and grinned. "It did."

"If Mom and Dad had known you'd taken Kate scrambling down the cliffs to cling to a ledge at night, they'd have murdered you."

"It would have been worth it. It was all you two talked about for weeks after. Margo wanted to call in a psychic."

She winced. "It was just a suggestion."

"You started looking them up in the phone book," Josh reminded her. "And went down to Monterey and bought tarot cards."

"I was experimenting," she began before a laugh bubbled out. "Damn you, Josh, I blew every penny of my spending money that summer on crystals and palm reading when I'd been saving desperately for sapphire studs. It would have served you right if I'd stumbled on the secret of Seraphina's lost dowry."

"Never existed." He pushed his plate away before he ate more and regretted it. In any case, how could a man eat after that hoarse, sexy laugh of hers had driven a spike of lust into his gut?

"Of course it did. She hid it to keep it out of the hands of the invading Americans, then jumped into the sea rather than live without her lover."

Josh sent Margo an affectionately amused glance. "Aren't you past the fairy-tale stage yet? It's a pretty legend, that's all."

"And legends are persistently based on fact. If you weren't so close-minded—"

"Truce." Laura lifted her hands as she rose. "Try not to take any chunks out of each other while I see about dessert."

"I'm not close-minded," he said before his sister had cleared the doors. "I'm rational."

"You never had any soul. You'd think someone who spent

73

as much time in Europe as you, exposed to Rome and Paris and—''

''Some of us work in Europe,'' he interrupted and had the satisfaction of seeing her eyes go dark and dangerous. ''That's just the look you had for that perfume ad,'' he said easily. ''What was that called? Savage.''

''That campaign upped Bella Donna's sales ten percent. That's why what I do is considered work.''

''Right.'' He topped off her water glass. ''So, Margo, did Matt ever try to unhook your bra?''

She was calm, she told herself. She was in control. She lifted the glass, looked Josh dead in the eye. ''I never wore one.'' She watched him frown, watched his gaze wander down. ''In those days,'' she added. Laughing, she rose, stretched. ''Maybe I'm glad you're home after all. I need someone to fight with.''

''Glad to oblige. What's wrong with Laura?''

She looked down. ''You're quick, Josh. You always were. She's worried about me. That might be all, but I'm not sure.''

He'd find out, he thought and nodded as he rose. ''Are you worried about you?''

It surprised her, the gentleness in his voice, the light brush of his knuckles over her jaw. She could lean against him, she realized with a jolt. She could lay her head on that shoulder, close her eyes, and for a moment at least, everything would be all right.

She nearly stepped forward before she decided it would be foolish. ''You're not going to be nice to me, are you?''

''Maybe.'' It might have been the confusion in her eyes, or that sultry scent that wafted from her skin, but he needed to touch. He laid his hands on her shoulders, rubbed while his eyes stayed on hers. ''Do you need help?''

''I—'' She could taste something on her lips, and was baffled that it was anticipation of him. ''I think—''

"Excuse me." With her face carefully blank, Ann stood on the terrace holding a portable phone. Her eyes flickered with something that might have been amusement when Josh dropped his hands as though she'd caught him tearing off her daughter's clothes. "Miss Kate's on the phone for you, Margo."

"Oh." Margo stared down at the phone her mother put in her hand. "Thanks. Um . . . Kate, hi."

"Something wrong? You sound—"

"No, no, nothing at all," Margo interrupted brightly. "And how are you?"

"It's coming on to tax time, pal, how do you think an accountant is? Which is why I just can't get away to come over there. I really want to talk to you, Margo. Can you get over here to my office this afternoon? I can give you some time between three and three-thirty."

"Sure. I suppose. If you—"

"Great. See you."

Margo clicked off the phone. "She's always been one of the champion communicators."

"It's nearly April fifteen. Crunch time."

Margo lifted a brow. He seemed perfectly at ease, she noted. All that tension, all that . . . anticipation must have been her imagination. "That's about what she said. I have to get over to her office. I'd better see if Laura can lend me a car."

"Take mine. It's out front. Keys are in it." He gave her dubious expression a quick, charming smile. "Hell, Margo, who taught you to drive in the first place?"

"You did." Her eyes warmed. "And with uncharacteristic patience."

"That's because I was terrified. Enjoy the drive. And if you put a scratch on her, I'll toss you over Seraphina's cliff."

When she sailed off, he sat down again, calculating that not only would he get her share of cake but he would now have the opportunity to pry out whatever was troubling his sister.

Chapter Five

Kate Powell was consistent, focused, and often inflexible. As Margo strode down the corridor of the second-floor offices of Bittle and Associates with their buzz of activity, ringing phones, and clattering keyboards, she realized this was exactly what Kate had had in mind for herself since childhood. She had, without detour, worked steadily toward it all of her life.

There had been the advanced math courses in high school, which of course she'd aced. Her three terms as class treasurer. The summers and holidays she'd worked in bookkeeping at Templeton Resort to advance her training and on-the-job experience. From there the scholarship to Harvard, her MBA, followed by her refusal, gracious but firm, to take a position in any of the Templeton offices.

No, Margo thought, eyeing the discreet carpet and walls, feeling the jittery tension in the tax-time air. Kate had chosen

Bittle, taken an entry-level position. Her salary would have been higher at a firm in Los Angeles or New York. But she wouldn't have been able to stay close to home.

In that, Kate was also consistent.

So, she'd worked her way up in the firm. Margo didn't know a great deal about accountants other than they were always whining about taxes and shelters and projected earnings, but she understood that Kate was now responsible for several important clients in the old, respected, and—in Margo's opinion—musty firm of Bittle and Associates.

At least all those years of effort had earned her a decent office, Margo mused as she peeked into Kate's door. Though how anyone stood being cooped up in four walls, facing away from the window all day was beyond her. Kate, however, looked contented enough.

Her desk was neat, and that was to be expected. No tchotchkes, no fancy paperweights, no frivolous doodads cluttered its surface. To Kate, Margo knew, clutter was one of the Seven Deadly Sins, along with impulse, disloyalty, and a disorganized checkbook.

A few files were arranged in an orderly stack on the edge of the plain, boxy desk. Dozens of lethally sharp pencils stood in a Lucite holder. A jazzy little computer hummed as Kate rattled the keys.

She'd taken off her navy jacket and hung it over the back of her swivel chair. The sleeves of her crisp white shirt were rolled up in businesslike fashion. She was frowning, a concentration line dug between her brows above the studious horn-rim reading glasses. Though her phone rang busily, it didn't earn a blink of response.

Even as Margo stepped in, Kate held up a single finger, continuing to work the keys one-handed. Then with a grunt she nodded and looked up.

"You're on time for a change. Close the door, will you?

Do you know how many people wait until April's knocking to hunt up their receipts?"

"No."

"Everybody. Have a seat." As Margo took the dung-brown chair across from the desk, Kate rose. She rolled her shoulders, circled her head, murmuring what sounded like "relax." After slipping off her glasses, she tucked the temple into the breast pocket of her shirt so that the glasses hung there like a medal. Then she turned, chose two plain white mugs from a shelf, and reached for the pot on her coffeemaker. "Annie said Josh was home."

"Yeah, he just got in, looking tanned and terrific."

"When did he ever look anything else?" Noting that she'd neglected to open her blinds again, she did so now and let natural light slant into the room to war with the glow of florescents. "I hope he plans to stay a while. I'm not going to have any free time until after the fifteenth." From her desk drawer she took a bottle of Mylanta, uncapped it, and guzzled like a veteran wino with a bottle of Crackling Rose.

"Christ, Kate, how can you do that? It's hideous."

Kate only lifted a brow. "How many cigarettes have you had today, champ?" she said blandly.

"That's hardly the point." Grimacing, Margo watched Kate tuck the bottle back into the drawer. "At least I know I'm slowly killing myself. You should see a doctor, for God's sake. If you'd just learn to relax, try those yoga exercises I told you about—"

"Save it." Kate cut off the lecture in midsentence and checked her practical Timex. She didn't have the time or the inclination to worry about a nervous stomach, certainly not until she finished calculating the realized capital gain and loss summary currently on her screen. "I've got a client due in twenty minutes, and I don't have time to debate our varying addictions." She handed Margo a mug, slid a hip onto the edge of her desk. "Has Peter shown up?"

"I haven't seen him." Margo struggled for a moment, but lecturing Kate had always been a study in frustration. Better, she decided, to concentrate on one friend's problems at a time. "Laura doesn't have much to say about it. Kate, is he living at the hotel?"

"Not officially." Kate started to bite her nails before she studiously stopped herself. Just a matter of willpower, she remembered, and drank coffee instead. "But from the buzz I get, he spends more time there than he does at home."

She moved her shoulders, still working out kinks. Her head was throbbing nastily. Between tax time and the mess her closest friends were in, she welcomed each day with a tension headache.

"Of course, it's a busy time of year for him, too."

Margo smirked. "You never liked him."

Kate smirked right back. "Neither did you."

"Well, if there's trouble in paradise, maybe I can help Laura through it. But if he's just staying away because I'm there, I should leave. I could stay at the resort."

"He missed plenty of bed checks before you rolled back into town. I don't know what to do about it, Margo." She rubbed tired eyes with unpainted fingertips. "She won't really talk about it, and I'm lousy at giving advice on relationships anyway."

"Still seeing that stud CPA down the hall?"

"No." Kate shut her mouth firmly on that. Closed book, she reminded herself. Even if it did still burn. "I don't have time to date. The fact is, as tied up as I am for the next week or so, I'm really glad you're there, with Laura and the kids."

"I'll stay unless it looks like it's complicating things for her." Absently Margo tapped her fingers on the arm of the chair, lovely shell-pink nails bumping against the chair's dull

79

brown. "She's awfully happy to have Josh back. I don't think I realized she was so unhappy until I saw her with him today. Which reminds me . . ." She set the coffee aside. Kate brewed it strong enough to pump iron. "Weren't you worried about risking a haunting by mocking Seraphina's ghost?"

Kate's face went blank. "What?"

"Huddling on a ledge and moaning in bad Spanish about your dowry. Laura and I weren't fooled for a minute."

"What are you . . . Oh. Oh!" As memory flooded back, Kate roared with laughter. It was not the laugh of a thin, serious-minded woman; it boomed straight from the gut, grew deeper in the throat, and tickled Margo into grinning back. "God, I'd forgotten that. Oh, I was so jealous, so *pissed* that you and Laura were dating and Uncle Tommy and Aunt Susan were making me wait another year. I didn't even want to date, but I hated you getting ahead of me." As she spoke, she got up to top off her coffee. "Christ, Josh always had the best and wildest ideas," she added, as she perched on the desk again.

"You're lucky you didn't slip off the ledge and get to meet Seraphina face to face."

"We had ropes." She chuckled into her coffee. "I was scared boneless at first, but I didn't want Josh to think I was lame. You know how he is about a dare."

"Mmm." Margo knew very well. A Templeton never refused a challenge. "Both of you would have been grounded for weeks."

"Yeah, those were the days," Kate said with a wistful smile. "Anyway, I got caught up in the whole thing. Playing Seraphina and listening to the two of you calling out to her was one of the highlights of my life. I can't believe he ratted on me."

"He probably thinks I'm too mature now to pull out your hair." Margo tilted her head and smiled. "I'm not, but you have so little of it to begin with." Then she clasped her hands

80

around her knee. "Well, I know you, and you didn't ask me to come into such professional surroundings to have a giggle over old times. You might as well give it to me."

"All right." It was cowardly, Kate knew, to wish she could postpone the moment. "We can say there's good news and bad news."

"I can use some good."

"You still have your health." At Margo's nervous laugh, Kate set her own mug aside. She wished she had a better way to do this, wished she'd been smart enough or clever enough to find an escape clause for Margo. "Sorry, bad accountant joke. You have to have a pretty good idea that you don't have a hell of a lot else, Margo. Financially, you're fucked."

Margo pressed her lips together, nodded. "Don't soft-pedal it, Kate. I can take it."

Appreciating her, Kate slid off the desk, sat on the arm of Margo's chair, and hugged her. "I put everything in a computer program and printed out a hard copy." And got less than three hours' sleep, thanks to the extra workload. "But I thought you'd get more out of the whole picture if I boiled it down. You've got some choices."

"I don't . . ." She had to pause to level her voice. "I don't want to file bankruptcy. Only as a last resort, Kate. I know it's pride, but—"

Pride Kate understood, enormously well. "I think we can avoid that. But, honey, you're going to have to seriously consider liquidating, and you're going to have to be prepared to take a loss on some of your assets."

"I have assets?" Margo asked hollowly.

"You have the flat in Milan. There isn't a lot of equity, as you only bought it five years ago and your down payment was low. But you can get out what you put in, and with luck, a little more." Because it was personal, Kate didn't need her notes, or the file. She remembered all the details. "You have the Lamborghini, and it's almost paid for. We arrange to sell it, quickly, and you'll save on those exorbitant garage and maintenance fees."

"Okay." She tried not to regret her beautiful flat, lovingly furnished, or the glamorous car she'd adored driving fast in the countryside. There were a great many things she couldn't afford, Margo reminded herself. Top of the list was self-pity. "I'll put them on the market. I suppose I'll have to go over and pack everything up and . . ."

Saying nothing, Kate rose to open a file, not to refresh her memory but to give herself something to do with her hands. She perched her glasses back on her nose. "There's the dead animals."

Sunk in depression, Margo shook her head. "What?"

"Your furs."

"That's such an American attitude," Margo grumbled. "Anyway, I didn't kill those stupid minks."

"Or the sables," Kate said dryly, peering over the tops of her horn-rims. "Sell them and that also saves you cold storage fees. Now your jewelry."

It was an arrow straight to the heart. "Oh, Kate, not my jewelry."

"Toughen up. It's just rocks and minerals." With her free hand she picked up her coffee again, ignoring the faint burning under her breastbone. "The insurance premiums on it are killing you. You can't afford it. And you need the cash to meet your debts. Dressmakers' bills, salon bills. Taxes. Italian taxes are stiff, and you didn't exactly save for a rainy day."

"I had some savings. Alain had been siphoning them off." She realized her fingers were aching and made herself untwist them. "I didn't even know it until last week."

Bastard, Kate thought. But that was then and this was now. "You can prosecute."

"What's the point?" Margo said wearily. "It would just

feed the press.'' Pride again, she thought. It was useless to ask Kate if she could afford a few miserly spoonfuls of pride. ''So, basically I have to give up everything. Everything I have, everything I've worked for, everything I've wanted.''

''Okay.'' Miserable, Kate put the file aside. ''I'm not going to tell you they're just things, Margo. I know they're not. But this is a way out. There are others. You could sell your story to the tabloids, pick up some quick, ready cash.''

''Why don't I just go down to Hollywood and Vine and sell my body? It would be less humiliating.''

''You could go to the Templetons.''

Margo shut her eyes. It shamed her that for a moment, just a moment, she was tempted.

''They'd bail you out,'' Kate said gently. ''Float you until you were on your feet again.''

''I know. I can't do that. After all they've done for me and been to me. Added to that is how it would make my mother feel. I've upset her enough without going begging.''

''I can lend you ten thousand right away. That's what I have liquid,'' Kate said briskly. ''It would put a finger in the dike, and I know that Laura and Josh would plug the other leaks. It wouldn't be begging, and it would be nothing to be ashamed of. Just a loan between friends.''

Margo said nothing for a moment. Touched and ashamed, she stared down at the sapphires and diamonds winking on her hands. ''So I can keep my pride and my furs and diamonds.'' Slowly, Margo shook her head. ''No, I don't think I'm going to be able to keep any of it. But thanks.''

''You'll want to consider this, weigh your options. The offer stays open.'' Kate took the file, proffered it, wished there was more. ''The figures are all there. I calculated the fair market value of the jewelry from the insurance appraisals. I've got the sale value of your car, the flat, and so forth calculated with a ten percent leeway, deducted all the expected fees and taxes. If you decide to liquidate, you'll earn some breathing space. Not a lot, but enough to keep your head above water for a while.''

And then what? Margo thought, but she didn't dare ask. ''Okay. I appreciate you wading through all the mess.''

''That's what I do best.'' Just at that moment, it seemed pitifully little. ''Margo, take a couple of days. Mull it over.''

''I will.'' She rose, then laughed weakly when her knees shivered. ''Christ, I'm shaky.''

''Sit down. I'll get you some water.''

''No.'' Margo held up a hand. ''I really need some air.''

''I'll go with you.''

''No. Thanks, but I need a minute.''

Gently, Kate brushed a hand over Margo's hair. ''Want to kill the messenger?''

''Not right now.'' Instead, she gave Kate a hard, fierce hug. ''I'll be in touch,'' she said and rushed out of the office.

She wanted to be brave. All of her life Margo had yearned for adventure, the glamour and romance of it. She wanted to be one of those carelessly daring women who don't simply follow trends but create them. She had, most of her life, quite deliberately exploited her sense of style, her looks, her sexuality to gain her own ends. Her education had been no more than a necessary phase, something to get through. Unlike Laura or Kate, she had merely put in time in the classroom. What would she need with algebraic formulas or historical facts in her life? It was much more important what they were wearing this season in New York or who the up-and-coming designers were in Milan.

It was, Margo thought as she stood on the windswept cliffs above the sea, pathetic. Her life was pathetic.

Even a month before, she had thought it perfect. Of course, then everything had been streaming along exactly as she wanted. She had a flat in the right part of the city, was recognized and catered to in the right restaurants and boutiques. She had a circle of friends that included the wealthy, the well known, and the wild. She attended fashionable parties, was thrillingly dogged by the press and pursued by men. And, of course, she feigned weariness and ennui over the articles that speculated about her private life.

She had a career that had put her precisely where she had always wanted to be. In the limelight.

Then there was her lover of the moment. The suave, gorgeous older man, as she preferred. French. Married, of course, but that was merely a technicality. An obstacle, again fashionable, that would eventually be overcome. The very fact that they had been forced to keep their affair secret had added a thrill. A thrill that, she realized now, she had so easily mistaken for passion.

Now it was all over.

She hadn't believed she could be any more shocked or frightened than in those first hours after she had been taken into Athens for questioning. The terror of being so alone, so exposed, had bounced her roughly from a privileged world into a dangerous one. And when no one from that carefully selected circle of friends had come to her aid or her defense, she had been forced to stand on her own and reevaluate Margo Sullivan.

But that didn't seem to be enough.

She sat on a rock, absently tugging a woolly white blossom from its slender stem. Laura would know the name of the wildflower, Margo mused. But then, Laura, despite the privileges of birthright, was the wildflower type, whereas Margo was strictly hothouse.

She was ruined.

Somehow it had been easier to handle the possibility of being broke before Kate had put it all in stark black and white.

Possibilities were abstract and changeable. Now it was reality. She was, or soon would be, without a home, without an income. Without a life.

She stared down at the flower in her hand. It was simple, it was stubborn, planting its roots in shallow soil, fighting its way to the sun. Rip off the bloom, another would grow.

She understood now that she'd never had to fight for anything. And she was afraid, deeply afraid, that now that she was uprooted, she would simply wither.

"Waiting for Seraphina?"

Margo continued to study the flower, twirling it as Josh settled on the rock beside her. "No, just waiting."

"Laura took the girls to dance class, so I thought I'd take a walk." Actually, he'd been considering a quick jaunt to the tennis court to work on his serve. But then he saw Margo on the cliffs from his bedroom window. "How's Kate?"

"Busy and efficient. I'd say she's found her Nirvana with Bittle and Associates."

He shuddered. "Scary."

The quick chuckle felt good. Tossing her hair back, she smiled at him. "We're so miserably shallow, Josh. How do we stand ourselves?"

"By never standing still long enough to take a close look. Is that what's got you down, Margo?" He tugged on the hair she'd pulled sleekly back from her face. "Have you been looking too close?"

"That's what happens when you get a mirror shoved in your face."

He slipped her shaded glasses off, narrowed his own eyes. "It's a hell of a face," he said lightly, then tucked the glasses back on her nose. "Do you want to know what I see?"

She pushed off the rock, wandered closer to the edge of the cliff. "I'm not sure I could take another shot today. You've never bothered to sugarcoat what you thought of me."

"Why should I? When a woman looks like you, she collects flattery, tossing the less inventive lines aside like last year's fashions. You're the most beautiful woman I've ever seen." He watched her turn, and though her eyes were hidden, he sensed her surprise. "It's a sinful face, a sinful body. They almost punish a man for wanting them, for wanting you. All that abundant, hot sex with hints of the wild driving it. And you use it without even thinking. A look, a tilt of the head, a gesture. It's a phenomenal, and occasionally cruel, talent you have. But you've heard that before."

"Not exactly," she murmured. She wasn't sure if she was flattered or insulted.

"But most of that's an accident of nature." He rose and walked to stand beside her. "You were born to be a fantasy. Maybe that's all you can manage."

The hurt was so sharp, so sudden she couldn't even gasp. "That's cold, Josh. And just like you."

When she started to whirl away, he took her arm, his grip unexpectedly strong, his voice infuriatingly mild. "I haven't finished."

Bright, bubbling fury spewed inside her. If she could have wrenched away and clawed him, she would have. "Let go of me. I'm sick of you and everyone like you. I'm worth bothering with as long as I fit the mold. The party girl. For a good time, call. But the minute there's trouble it's so easy to say I wasn't anything to begin with. Just a scrabbler, reaching above my station."

He slid his hands down to cuff her wrists, his voice still detestably patient. "Were you?"

"I'm not a damn picture in a magazine. I have feelings and fears and needs. And I don't have to prove anything to anyone but myself."

"Good. Good for you. It's about time you realized that." With an easy strength that both baffled and infuriated her, he

87

simply pulled her back from the cliff and nudged her down on the rock. He kept his grip firm as he crouched in front of her. "You're the one who played with the illusion, Margo, who used it. And you're the one who's going to have to shatter it."

"Don't tell me what I have to do. If you don't take your hands off me—"

"Shut up. Just shut up." He gave her a brisk shake that made her mouth fall open in shock. "You'll have to get used to that, too," he told her. "Being treated like a human being instead of a pampered Barbie doll. Life's finally been tossed in your face, duchess. Deal with it."

"What do you know about life?" Bitterness ached in her throat. "You were born with everything. You never had to struggle for a single thing you wanted, never had to worry if you'd be accepted or loved or wanted back."

He stared at her, grateful for the moment that she couldn't see that he'd spent nearly half of his life worrying that she, the single thing he wanted, would accept him, love him, and want him back. "But we're not talking about me, are we?"

She turned her face, stared hard out to sea. "I don't care what you think of me."

"Fine, but I'm going to tell you anyway. You're a spoiled, careless, and reckless woman who has for a good long time hardly given a thought to anything beyond the moment. Up till now your ambitions have melded nicely with your fantasies. Now you've been given a very rude slap. It'll be interesting to see if you'll be able to draw on your other qualities to pull yourself up again."

"Oh?" she began icily. "I have other qualities?"

He wondered what perverted twist in his makeup caused him to adore that frosty, fuck-you tone of hers. "You come from strong and resilient stock, Margo, a temperament that doesn't take failure lying down." Absently, he lifted her hands

88

and kissed them. "You're loyal and warm and compassionate to those you care for. What you lack in common sense you make up for with humor and charm."

The emotions that swirled inside her threatened to erupt in laughter or tears or screams. She forced them to wither and kept her face as blank and cold as her voice. "That's a fascinating analysis. You'll have to bill me for it. I'm a little short of cash."

"No charge." He drew her to her feet again, brushed at the hair that danced wildly around her face. "Listen, if you need something to tide you over until—"

"Don't you dare offer me money," she interrupted with a snap in her voice. "I'm not some destitute family retainer."

It was his turn to be insulted. "I thought you were a friend."

"Well, keep your money in your numbered Swiss account, friend. I'm perfectly capable of taking care of myself."

"As you like." After a shrug, he held out his hand. "How about a lift back to the house?"

Her lips curved coolly. "How about you stick out your well-manicured thumb?" She strode away, picking her way with careless grace over rocks. Moments later he heard the panther roar of his own car and the skid of tires on pavement.

Christ, he thought with a quick laugh. He was crazy about her.

She was still seething with fury when she marched into the house. Temper carried her well down the central hallway before the sound of voices registered. Calm, reasonable voices. Overly calm, Margo realized at once. Coldly reasonable and bitingly formal.

It made her shudder to think that husband and wife would speak to each other in such lifeless tones. However wrenching it had been, she much preferred the passionate exchange she'd just had with Josh to the kind of studied argument going on between Laura and Peter in the library.

The heavy pocket doors were open, allowing her to step up to the threshold and observe the entire scene. Such a civilized room, Margo thought, with its soaring ceiling, its two levels walled with books and diamond-paned windows. The old Bokhara rug and the smell of leather. A civilized room, she thought again, for a civilized argument.

How perfectly horrible.

"I'm very sorry you feel that way, Peter. I simply can't agree with you."

"The business, the running of Templeton hotels, our place in society, and the media are hardly your fortes, Laura. I would not be in the position I'm in, nor have the responsibilities I have, if your parents and the board of directors didn't value and respect my opinion."

"That's true."

Margo stepped quietly to the doorway. She could see Laura standing in front of the window seat, her hands clasped loosely. There was such temper and distress in her eyes that Margo wondered how Peter could remain oblivious to it.

For himself, Peter was in front of the lovely old Adam fireplace, very lord of the manor with one hand on the mantel and the other wrapped around a Waterford lowball glass gleaming with light and unblended Scotch.

"In this case, however," Laura continued in that same quiet, empty voice, "I don't believe the family would share your concern. Josh certainly doesn't."

Peter let out a hard, dismissive laugh. "Josh is hardly one to worry about reputation. He's more at home flitting off to clubs and rubbing elbows with Eurotrash."

"Be careful." Laura only murmured the warning, but there was force behind it. "You and Josh approach things differently, but you're each an important part of Templeton. My point is that Josh fully supports Margo's remaining at Templeton House as long as she chooses. And, foreseeing this altercation, I contacted my parents this morning. They're delighted Margo is home."

His lips went thin and white at that. Margo would have been pleased by the reaction if his temper hadn't been directed at Laura. "You went behind my back. That's typical of you, isn't it? Running to your parents whenever we disagree."

"I don't run to them, Peter." There was weariness now. As if giving in to it, Laura sat down on the padded window seat. Light streamed in through the lovely arched window at her back, causing her to look fragile, pale, and heartbreakingly beautiful. "And I don't discuss our private problems with them. In this case it was, in your words, business."

"And business is for me to handle." His voice was clipped, all reason with an undertone of carefully controlled impatience. "You only have the house to run and the children to see to. Both of which you're putting in second place to some misguided sense of loyalty."

"No one and nothing comes ahead of my children."

"Really?" A small smile curved his lips as he took a sip of his Scotch. "I don't suppose you found time in your busy and demanding day of manicures and luncheons to watch television? One of the tabloid shows dedicated an entire thirty minutes to your old friend. There was a particularly interesting clip of her sunbathing topless on a yacht. Several of her close friends gave interviews detailing her many affairs and her so-called free-spirited lifestyle. Naturally the show didn't fail to report her connection with Templeton, and her long-standing friendship with Laura Templeton Ridgeway."

Pleased that she didn't respond, he inclined his head. "It included a picture of the two of you, and the children. In addition, a waiter at the country club was happy to tell them how the two of you and an unnamed woman had a giddy champagne lunch by the pool two years ago.''

Laura waited a beat. "Kate's going to be annoyed they didn't get her name." Out of patience, she waved a hand and rose, and he saw that what he had taken for shame was annoyance. "Really, Peter, it's all nonsense. The last time we were on the Riviera you were irritated with me because I was too shy to go French, yet you're condemning Margo because she did. And if any of those people had been her friends, they wouldn't have been chafing to give interviews, which they were paid for, that gossiped about her. And nearly half the women I know get snockered at the club regularly. If we wanted to have a giddy champagne lunch to celebrate being together, it's no one's business.''

"You're not only blind and stubborn, but you're foolish. And this attitude you've developed of late has gone on long enough.''

"Attitude?''

He set his glass on the mantel with a snap. "Questioning me, defying my wishes, neglecting your duties in the community. Margo's presence here is merely an excuse for you to go on behaving badly.''

"I don't need an excuse.''

"Apparently not. I'll put it another way, a clearer way, Laura. As long as that woman lives in this house, I don't.''

"An ultimatum, Peter?" Very slowly, she inclined her head. "I think you might be rudely surprised by my answer to that.''

On impulse, Margo stepped into the room. "Hello, Peter. Don't worry, I'm every bit as thrilled to see you as you are to see me.''

With a brittle smile, she walked over to the decanter. Though she rarely drank anything other than wine, she poured two fingers of Scotch. She wanted something to do with her hands.

"I know I'm interrupting, but I was on my way back to speak to Mum." She took a quick, bracing sip, shuddered it down.

"You seem to be taking your most recent debacle in stride," Peter commented.

"Oh, you know me. Roll with the flow." She gestured widely, rings glittering. "I'm sorry I missed the show you were telling Laura about. I do hope those shots of me sunbathing were flattering. Those long-range lenses can distort, you know." Beaming smiles, she lifted her glass to him. "And you and I understand all about appearances, don't we, Peter?"

He didn't bother to conceal his disdain. She was, as she had always been to him, the housekeeper's inconvenient daughter. "People who eavesdrop on private conversations rarely hear anything flattering."

"Absolutely true." Resolved now, she took a last sip before setting the glass down. "As you'd be aware if you'd ever heard any of my private conversations about you. You can rest easy. I was coming in to tell my mother I have to go back to Milan."

Distress made Laura step forward, step between them. "Margo, there's no need for that."

She took the hand Laura offered, squeezed it. "There is. I left dozens of things hanging. I needed this little breather, but I have to go back and tend to the details."

Ignoring Peter, she gathered Laura close. "I love you, Laura."

"Don't say it like that." Alarmed, Laura drew back, searched Margo's face. "You're coming back."

She gave a careless shrug even as her stomach jittered. "We'll see how the wind blows. But I'll be in touch. I need to talk to Mum before I pack." She gave Laura a last hug before turning toward the door. Not sure if she'd have another chance, she went with impulse again and turned back. She offered Peter her sultriest smile. "One more thing. You're a pompous, egotistical, self-important ass. You weren't good enough for her when she married you, you're still not good enough for her, and you never will be. It must be hell for you knowing that."

As exits went, Margo thought as she glided out, she'd never done better.

"I'm not running away," Margo insisted as she hurriedly packed.

"Aren't you?" With her hands folded at her waist, Ann watched her daughter. Always in a rush, she thought, to get from one place to the next. Never stopping to think.

"I'd stay if I could. I'd rather stay, but—" She tossed a cashmere sweater into her bag. "I just can't."

Out of habit, Ann took the sweater out, folded it neatly, replaced it. "You should take more care with your possessions. And your friends. You're leaving Miss Laura when she needs you."

"I'm leaving to make things easier for her, damn it." Out of patience, Margo tossed her hair over her shoulder. "Can't you ever give me credit for doing something right? She's downstairs right now arguing with Peter because of me. He threatened to leave her if I stay. He doesn't want me here."

"This is Templeton House," Ann said simply.

"And he lives here. Laura is his wife. I'm just—"

"The housekeeper's daughter. Odd, you only remember that when it suits you. I'm asking you to stay and do what you can for her."

Oh, guilt works so well, she thought as she stalked over to wrench a blouse out of the armoire. Like a bell to Pavlov's dog. "I'm a cause of tension in her marriage, an embarrassment. I will not see her torn between me and the man she's been married to for ten years. You know I love her."

94

"Yes." Ann sighed a little. "Yes, I know you do. Loyalty isn't one of your failings, Margo. But I'm telling you she needs you here. Her parents are off in Africa someplace. They know little about what's gone on in this house and little, I suspect, of what's happened to you. They would be here otherwise. But you're here, and you should stay. If you would for once listen to what I say, do as I ask."

"I can't." She sent her mother a thin smile. "Some things don't change. Kate and Josh are here for her. And you," she added. "I have to get out of the way so she can work things out with Peter. If that's what she wants. Though God knows why—" She cut herself off, waved a hand in dismissal. "That's her decision. Mine is to go back to Milan. I have to deal with things there. I have to pick up my life."

"Well, you've made the mess of it, you'll have to clean it up. You'll hurt her by going," she said quietly. And me, Ann thought. Can't you see how it hurts me to see you walk away again?

"I hurt her by staying, too. So either way I'm of no use to her. At least in Milan I can try to put some of my own pieces back together. I need money, I need work."

"You need." Eyes cool, Ann studied her daughter. "Well, then, that naturally comes first. I'll arrange for your cab to the airport."

"Mum." Washed with regret, Margo took a step after her. "I'm trying to do what's right. If it's a mistake, then it's a mistake, but I'm trying to do what I think is best. Try to understand that."

"I only see you're going when you've hardly come home." Ann closed the door behind her, the only good-bye Margo would have.

Chapter Six

Margo had fallen hard for Milan at first sight. She had been dazzled by Paris, awed by Rome, amused by London. But Milan, with its busy streets, impeccable style, and easy panache had won her heart.

Her career had fulfilled her childhood dream of travel, tickled the wanderlust that had always been part of her soul. Yet, in her own way, she had needed roots, a base, a place to call her own.

She had chosen the flat on impulse, because she liked the look of the building, the charming terraces that offered a view of the street and a glimpse of the spearing towers of the Duomo. And because it was a convenient stroll from her door to the elegant shops of the Montenapoliane.

She stood on her terrace now, sipping chilly white wine, watching the late-evening traffic punctuated by the high, double-toned blare of sirens. The sun was setting, gilding the view and making her lonely for someone to share it with.

She had been right to come back. It was perhaps the first selfless thing she'd done in too long to remember. Though Laura had argued until the cab whisked Margo away, and Josh had simply stood eyeing her coolly with an expression that accused her of running, she knew she had done what was best.

Still, doing what was right wasn't always comforting. She was miserably lonely. Fears of the present and the future weren't nearly as difficult to overcome as the isolation.

In the week since her return, she hadn't answered the phone, or returned any of the messages already crowding her machine. Most of them were from reporters or acquaintances hoping for a tidbit of gossip. Mixed among them were a few offers she was afraid she would have to consider.

If she were truly brave and daring, she mused, she'd shimmy into some little black dress and stroll into one of her old haunts to set the room buzzing. Maybe she would before it was done, but for now she had a few more wounds to lick.

Leaving the terrace doors open, she walked into the living area. Other than a few gifts, she'd chosen each and every piece herself. She hadn't wanted a decorator, but had enjoyed the adventure of hunting down every pillow and lamp.

It certainly reflected her taste, she thought with a wry smile. Eclectic. Hell, she corrected—scattered. An antique curio cabinet crowded with Limoges boxes and Steuben glass. The japanned chest that served as coffee table was topped with a huge Waterford compote that was in turn filled with colorful handblown fruit.

There were Tiffany lamps, Art Deco ones, even a Doulton Flambe that featured a seated Buddha and had cost her some ridiculous amount at auction just to sit there and look ugly.

Every room of the two-bedroom flat was crammed with more. Inkwells she'd collected during some passing stage.

Russian boxes, paperweights, vases, bottles—all purchased for no other reason than that they were what she had been acquiring at the time.

Still, it made a lovely, cluttered, and homey place, she thought, as she settled down on the deeply cushioned sofa. The paintings were good. She'd been told she had an eye for art, and the street scenes that lined her walls were clever and lovely and brought the world into her rooms.

Her world. Her rooms. Temporarily, at any rate, Margo thought and lighted a cigarette. But she wasn't going to be able to hide in them for much longer.

Maybe she would take the offer from *Playboy* and drive the wolf back, away from her door. Her eyes narrowed in consideration, she drew in smoke. Why not? Why not sell her pathetic story to the tabloids that called daily to clutter her answering machine tape? Either way, she'd have money again. Either way, she would strip herself naked for the grinning world.

What were those few shreds of pride really doing for her?

Hell, maybe she should shock the civilized world and drag all her furnishings out onto the street for one wild, goes-to-the-highest-bidder bazaar.

Laughing, she envisioned how it would distress her very polite and proper doorman, her elegant neighbors. And how it would delight the ever-hungry press.

So what if she spread herself out on the centerfold of a glossy men's magazine with a couple of strategically placed staples? Who would care if she prostituted her pride to whine about her troubles in a Sunday supplement or supermarket paper?

No one expected any more or any less from her. Perhaps, she thought, tiredly crushing out the cigarette, neither did she.

But to sell her possessions, to publicly barter things for money, that was so . . . middle-class.

Well, something had to be done. The bills were piling up, and she wouldn't have a roof over her head much longer if she didn't pass over considerable lire.

She supposed the logical step would be to find a discreet and reputable jeweler and sell her glitters. It would hold her level until she decided what step to take next. She toyed with the square-cut sapphire on her hand; she didn't have a clue what she had paid for it.

It hardly mattered, did it? she decided. Kate had calculated the worth, and it was what she could get for it now that mattered. She pushed herself up and hurried into the bedroom. After unlocking the safe built into the cedar chest at the foot of her bed, she began pulling out boxes and pouches. In moments, the lamplight beamed on a pile of glittering treasures worthy of Ali Baba's cave.

Dear God, did she really own a dozen watches? What was wrong with her? And what had possessed her to buy that jeweled collar? It looked like something out of *Star Trek*. Marcasite hair combs. She never wore hair combs.

The tension began to ease from her shoulders as she examined, separated, began to make decisions. There were dozens of pieces, she discovered, that she could part with without a qualm. Certainly she would reap enough to keep her head above water until she had time to think.

And clothes.

With manic energy she leapt up, scattering jewelry and dashing to her closet. It was enormous, lined with dresses, suits, jackets. Lucite shelves held shoes, bags. Built-in drawers were packed with scarves and belts. A triple mirror ringed with lights reflected her image as she frantically pushed hangers to and fro.

There were secondhand shops that specialized in designer clothes, she knew. Indeed, she had purchased her first Fendi bag at one in Knightsbridge a lifetime ago. If she could buy from a secondhand shop, then by God, she could sell to one.

She tossed jackets, blouses, skirts, slacks over her arm, rushed out to drop them on the bed, dashed back for more.

She was giggling when the doorbell rang, and she ignored it until the constant buzz cut through what she realized abruptly was the edge of hysteria. It was a struggle to swallow the next bubble of laughter, and for the life of her she couldn't remember the deep breathing exercises from her yoga class.

"Maybe I'm having a breakdown." The sound of her own voice was tight and nervy. The doorbell continued to buzz like a swarm of angry bees. "All right, all right, all right!" she snapped as she stepped over suede boots that had fallen out of her arms. She would face whoever was at the door, get rid of them, and then deal with the latest mess she'd created.

Ready to fight, she yanked the door open and stared. "Josh!" Why, she wondered, was he always the last person she expected to see?

He took a quick survey of the tousled hair, the flushed face, the robe that was slipping off her shoulder. His first jealous thought was that he'd interrupted sex. "I was in the neighborhood."

She folded her arms. "You're checking up on me."

"Laura made me." The charming smile flirted around his mouth, but his eyes were hot. Who the hell was in the flat? Who'd been touching her? "I had a little problem to iron out at Templeton Milan, so I promised her I'd swing by, see how you were." He angled his head. "So, how are you?"

"Tell Laura I'm fine."

"You could tell her yourself if you'd answer the phone occasionally."

"Go away, Josh."

"Thanks, I'd love to come in for a while. No, no," he continued as he nudged by her, "I can't stay long." When she stood firm and left the door open, he shut it himself. "All right, but just one drink."

God, he was gorgeous, she thought. Arrogance fit him as sleekly as his linen shirt. "Maybe I'll call security and have you tossed out."

His quick laugh had her clenching her fists. As he wandered the room, she measured him. In leather bomber jacket and snug jeans, he looked tougher than she would have expected. She wondered if cheerful little Marco, who manned the door, could bite him on the ankle.

"This oil of the Spanish Steps is new since I was here last," he commented, eyeing her painting with mild avarice. "It's not bad. Sixty-five hundred for the French Quarter water-color."

She arched a brow. "You go up five hundred every time you make an offer. I'm still not going to sell it to you."

It belonged in the lobby of Templeton New Orleans. He shrugged off her refusal. He would pry it away from her sooner or later. He picked up a paperweight, icy white shapes swimming inside icy white glass, passed it from hand to hand. He hadn't missed the way she kept glancing back toward the bedroom.

"Something else on your mind, Josh?"

Murder. Mayhem. But he smiled easily. "Hunger. Got anything to eat around here?"

"There's a nice trattoria just down the street."

"Good, we'll walk down later, but I'd love a little wine and cheese now. Don't trouble yourself," he added when she didn't budge. "I'll just make myself at home." Still carrying the paperweight, he headed for the bedroom.

"The kitchen's back here," Margo began, panicked.

His mouth turned grim. He knew exactly where her kitchen was. He knew where everything was in her flat, and whoever

101

was in the bedroom was going to discover that Joshua Templeton had staked prior claim.

"Damn it." She caught at his arm and was dragged along with him. "I'll get you a glass of wine. Just stay out of—"

But it was too late. She let out a frustrated groan as he strode over the threshold and stopped dead.

Looking at the scene now, she could hardly believe it herself. Clothes were in a stream from closet to bed, sequins piled on denim, cashmere heaped on cotton. Jewelry was spread in a sparkling lake on the rug. It looked, she realized, like some bad-tempered child had thrown a tantrum. But Josh's observation was closer to the mark.

"It looks like Armani and Cartier went to war."

One of those tricky bubbles of laughter tickled her throat. She nearly managed to clear it away, but her voice stuttered dangerously. "I was just . . . sort of . . . organizing."

The look he sent her was so dry and bland, she lost her slippery hold on control. Holding her stomach, she stumbled to the chest and collapsed onto it in a wild explosion of laughter. Casually, Josh reached down to pick up a slate-blue jacket, fingered the material.

"The man is a god," he said, before tossing the Armani onto the bed.

That sent her off into fresh peals. "Joshua." She managed to hitch in enough breath to speak. "You have to be the only living soul I know who could look at this and not run for the butterfly net." Because she loved him for it, she held out a hand to invite him to sit beside her. "It was a temporary episode," she said and let her head tilt against his shoulder. "I think I'm over it."

With an arm draped around her, he surveyed the chaos. "This is all your stuff?"

"Oh, no." She chuckled. "I have a closet in the second bedroom, too. It's packed."

"Of course it is." He pressed a kiss to the top of her head, frowned at the scattered gems. "Duchess, how many earrings do you figure you own?"

"I haven't the foggiest. I didn't get into the costume stuff yet." Feeling better, she sighed. "Earrings are like orgasms. You can never have too many."

"I never thought about it quite that way."

"Well, you're a man." She gave his knee a friendly pat. "Why don't I get that wine?"

She was wearing nothing under the robe, and his fingertips were beginning to tingle against the thin silk. "Why don't I get it?" Distance, he told himself, was the key. The last thing she needed him to do just then was to lose his mind and start to slobber.

"The kitchen—"

"I know where the kitchen is." He flashed a grin at her narrow-eyed stare. "I was hoping to come in here and intimidate your lover."

"I don't have a lover at the moment."

"That's handy, isn't it?" He strolled out, certain that he'd given her something to mull over. When he came back, pleased to have found an excellent Barola in her wine rack, she was kneeling on the floor, carefully putting jewelry back in boxes.

The robe was flirting off her shoulder again. Josh was tempted to tug the sash tight himself, double-knot it so the fabric wouldn't continue to slip and slide so devastatingly.

When she saw him and rose, he couldn't avoid seeing the flash of long, slim leg. Every muscle in his body groaned.

The worst of it was she wasn't trying to drive him to his knees. If she had been, he could have, without qualm, tossed her onto the bed and finally fulfilled his fantasies.

But that careless sexuality was pure Margo.

She took the glass he held out, smiled at him. "I suppose

103

I have to thank you for interrupting the insanity.''

"Want to tell me what started the insanity?''

"Just a stupid idea.'' She walked to the doors of the bedroom terrace, threw them open. Night poured in, full of sound and scent. She drew it in as she drew in the wine. "I really love Milan. Almost as much as . . .''

"As?''

Annoyed with herself, she shook her head. "Doesn't matter. I'm working on ways to stay here, with some level of comfort. Going home to Templeton House isn't an option.''

"You're going to let Peter lock you out?''

She bristled at that, turning. The fairy lights on the terrace twinkled around her and dazzled through the thin silk of her robe. "I don't give a gold-plated shit about Peter Ridgeway, but I'm not going to complicate things for Laura.''

"Laura can manage. She doesn't let Peter dust her around the way she used to. If you had bothered to hang around, you'd have seen that for yourself.''

She felt her hackles rise again. Damn him. But she spoke smoothly: "Regardless, she's got a marriage to worry about. For some ridiculous reason, marriage is what matters to her. Christ knows why she wants to be tied down to one man, especially a pompous jerk like Peter.''

Josh took a contemplative sip. "Weren't you planning on marrying Alain, the slick, lying drug smuggler?''

She tried for dignity. "I didn't know he was a smuggler.''

"Just a slick liar.''

"All right, fine. You can say that experience gave me a fresh viewpoint on and a general dislike for the institution. The point is, Laura is married and I'm not going to make it more difficult for her.''

"It's your home too, Margo.''

Now her heart swelled, and broke just a little. "He can't

change that. But you can't always go home. Besides, I've been happy here, and I can be again."

He moved closer, wanting to read her eyes. "Kate says you're considering selling your flat."

Her eyes were simple to read. They were filled with annoyance. "Kate talks too much." She turned around to study those last gilding lights. He turned her back again.

"She's worried about you. So am I."

"You don't have to be. I'm working on a plan."

"Why don't I take you to dinner? You can tell me about it."

"I'm not sure I'm up to the telling stage, but I could probably eat. We don't have to go out. The trattoria will deliver."

"And that way you don't risk bumping into anyone who knows you," he concluded and shook his head. "Don't be a coward."

"I like being a coward."

"Then you'd better get dressed." Deliberately, he skimmed his fingertip over the bare skin of her shoulder, up her throat. And watched her eyes go dark and wary. "Because you're asking for trouble right here."

She nearly tugged her robe into place before she stopped herself. Odd how the skin could tingle. "You've already seen me naked."

"You were ten." He slid the robe into place himself, gratified when he felt her quick shiver. "It doesn't count." To test her reaction, he hooked his fingers in the belt of the robe, gave one gentle tug. "Want to risk it, Margo?"

Danger had snapped into the air, abruptly, unexpectedly, fascinatingly. Struggling to be cautious, she stepped back. "I'll get dressed. We'll go out."

"Safe choice."

But she didn't feel safe when he walked out and closed the door behind him. She felt . . . stirred.

105

                    *   *   *

He'd done it to push her into going out. That was the simple, rational conclusion Margo came to. It seemed the only conclusion when he settled into the busy little restaurant and dived into his first-course selection of *antipasto di funghi crudi* with exuberance.

"Try one." He held a marinated mushroom to her lips, nudged it through. "Nobody does vegetables like the Italians."

"Nobody does anything edible like the Italians." But she toyed with her salad of tomato and mozzarella. She'd grown so accustomed to denying herself full meals that eating heartily still felt like cheating.

"You need a good five pounds, Margo," he said. "Ten wouldn't hurt."

"Ten and I'd have a whopping bill from the dressmaker for alterations in my wardrobe."

"Eat. Live dangerously."

She nibbled on cheese. "You're sort of a businessman," she began and made him laugh.

"Oh, if you stretch the point."

"That wasn't meant to be an insult. It's hard for me to picture you as an executive, making corporate decisions. Your father's always had this aura of power. You're more—"

"Feckless?" he suggested.

"No. Relaxed." Impatient with herself, she huffed out a breath. "I'm really not trying to insult you, Josh. What I should say is that whatever it is you do, you make it seem easy. Take Peter."

"No, thanks."

"In comparison," she continued. "He's tense and driven. 'Successful yet ambitious corporate man' is etched onto his face."

"And I, on the other hand, the scion of the Templeton fortune, am relaxed, was it? And carefree, jetting my way around the world's hot spots, seducing women in between squash matches. Or is it playing squash in between seducing women?"

"I'm not entirely sure," Margo said evenly, "but that's beside the point."

"And the point of this deathless observation is . . . ?"

"I have insulted you." Too used to him to be concerned, she shrugged. "You have to have some talent for business because your parents aren't fools. However much they love you, they wouldn't give you free rein to poke into the hotels. They'd just let you drain your trust fund and be a wastrel."

"Your confidence in me is touching." With a sneer, he topped off their glasses. "I think I need another drink."

"And you have that law degree."

"Yes, the one they gave me after I'd finished racketing around Harvard."

"Don't be so sensitive." She patted his hand. "It occurs to me that you must know something about managing . . . things. I've had a few interesting offers," she began. "The most lucrative and least complicated is from *Playboy*."

His eyes went so sharp, so flinty, it surprised her that they didn't strike sparks off the silverware. "I see."

"I've posed naked before—or the next thing to it." Wary of his enigmatic response, she sliced off a bit of cheese. "European magazines aren't as puritanical as American ones."

"And you consider an arty ad in Italian *Vogue* on the same level as a centerfold in a skin magazine?" There were murderous thoughts rocketing through his head, making him feel ridiculously like the cuckolded lover.

No, she didn't, and felt incredibly foolish. "Same body," she said with a careless shrug. "The point is, I've made my living in front of the camera in varying stages of dress and undress. This is a way to continue to do so. A one-shot deal, anyway, that would put some distance between me and the creditors. With what they're offering me I could get back on my feet. Well, one foot anyway.''

His eyes never left her face. Nearby, a waiter dropped a tray of dishes with a resounding crash, and Josh didn't so much as blink. ''Are you asking me to look over the offer?''

It had been her thought, but she reconsidered, and reconsidered quickly, at the razor-edged tone in the question. ''No, I was simply mentioning one of my alternatives.''

''Is that what you want to be, Margo? Some sweaty-palmed adolescent's wet dream? This month's pinup in the auto mechanic shop, a visual aid at the fertility clinic?''

''I think that's in very poor taste,'' she said stiffly.

''That's in poor taste?'' The way he exploded with it had several diners jerking their heads around and murmuring.

''Don't shout at me,'' she said under her breath. ''You've never had any respect for what I do. I don't know why I thought you might have some sensible comment about this.''

''You want a sensible comment. Terrific.'' He gulped down wine to force the bile back down his throat. ''Go right ahead and do it, duchess. Take the money and run. Don't worry about embarrassing your family. Why should you care? So they snicker the next time your mother's standing in line at the supermarket. If the kids tease Ali at school, it's not your problem. Just make sure you're well paid.''

''That's enough,'' she said quietly.

''Is it?'' he tossed back. ''I'm just warming up.''

''I said it was an option. I didn't say I was going to accept.'' With impatient fingers she rubbed at a headache brewing at her left temple. ''Goddamn it, it's just a body. My body.''

''You're connected to people. I'd hoped you'd begun to realize that what you do affects them.''

''I have.'' Wearily she let her hand drop. ''All right, I have. Judging from your reaction, it wouldn't go over very well.''

Inch by inch he reeled in his temper and studied her. "Is that what this was about? Testing the waters with me?"

She managed a smile. "Yes. Bad idea." Sighing, she pushed her plate away. "On to the next. We won't bother with the German producer who's offering a considerable pile of marks if I let him showcase me in his latest adult film."

"Jesus Christ, Margo—"

"I said we wouldn't bother with that. So what do you do when you decide to redecorate one of your hotels?"

He rubbed a hand over his face. "While I'm trying to make that leap of thought, we'll order the pasta course." He signaled the waiter, ordered tagliolini for himself and risotto for Margo.

Bracing her chin on her palm, she began to think through that next option. "Your Italian's much better than mine. That might be helpful, too."

"Margo darling, don't go off on another tangent until I've caught up." His blood was still hot at the idea of her being spread out in full, glorious color for any man with pocket change to drool over. "Are you asking me for decorating advice?"

"No. No, of course not." The very idea made her snicker. The headache and unsteady stomach his temper had caused began to ease. "I'm curious about what you do with the furnishings when you redo suites."

"You want furniture?"

"Josh, just answer the question. What do you do when you change the decor?"

"Okay, fine. We rarely do that in one of our established hotels, as the clientele appreciates the tradition." What the hell was going through that fascinating mind of hers now? he wondered, but shrugged. It wouldn't take long to find out. "However, when we buy out another hotel, we will usually revamp the rooms in the Templeton style, using the locale for inspiration. We'll keep whatever is suitable or up to our standards, sometimes shipping pieces off to another location. What doesn't suit is normally sold at auction, which is where the decorator and buyer would pick up replacements. We also buy at antique shops and through estate sales.''

"Auction," she murmured. "It might be best. Simplest. Auctions, antique shops, estate sales. They're all really just secondhand stores, aren't they? I mean, everything there has been owned before, used before. Sometimes people value things more if they've belonged to someone else.''

She beamed up at the waiter, nearly causing him to jostle the plates as his blood pressure spiked. "Grazie, Mario. Ho molta fame.''

"Prego, signorina. Mia piacere. Buona appetite.'' He bowed away from the table, narrowly avoiding a collision with a busboy.

"Your Italian's fine," Josh said dryly. "You don't even need words.''

"He's a sweetheart. He has a lovely wife who presents him with a bambina every year. And he never looks down my blouse.'' She paused, considered. "Well, hardly ever. Anyway,'' she said, digging into the risotto with genuine enthusiasm, "speaking of secondhand shops.''

"Were we?''

"Yes. What sort of percentage of the value is customary when you sell?''

"It would depend on several factors.''

"What are they?''

Deciding he'd been patient and informative long enough, he shook his head. "No, you first. Why do you want to know?''

"I'm thinking of—what's the term?—downsizing.'' She speared a shrimp from his plate.

"Actually, rightsizing has become the more politically correct term.''

"Okay. I like that better anyway. Rightsizing." She chuckled over the idea. "I've been collecting things for ten years. I thought I might unload some of them. My apartment's entirely too crowded, and I've never taken the time to weed out my wardrobe. Since I've got some free time, I thought . . ."

She trailed off. He hadn't said a word, but she knew he understood she was scrambling for pride. "I need the money," she said flatly. "It's stupid of me to pretend otherwise. Kate thinks liquidation is the best option." She tried to smile again. "And since *Playboy* is out . . ."

"You don't want me to offer you a loan," he murmured. "You just want me to sit back and do nothing while you sell your shoes for grocery money."

"And my bags, and my porcelain boxes, and my candlesticks." He wasn't going to feel sorry for her, she determined. By God, no one was going to feel sorry for her. "Look, Streisand did it a couple years ago, didn't she? Not that she needed the money, but what's the difference? She sold things she'd collected over the years, and I doubt she turned up her nose at the money. It doesn't appear that I'm going to be able to sell my face for the foreseeable future, and I don't intend to sell my body, so I've whittled the options down to my things."

She didn't want sympathy, he determined. So he wouldn't offer it. "Is that what you were doing tonight when I came by? Inventory?"

"In an impulsive, semihysterical sort of way. But now I'm calm and rational, and I see that the plan—actually Kate's plan—has value." She covered his hand with hers. "Josh, when you saw me back home, you asked if I needed help. I'm telling you I do. I'm asking you for it."

He looked down at her hand, the glint of sapphire and diamonds against creamy white skin. "What do you want me to do?"

"First, keep this between us for now."

111

He turned his hand over, linked his fingers with hers. "All right. What else?"

"If you could help me figure out how and where to sell what I have to sell. How to get the best price. I haven't managed my money well. Hell, I haven't done such a hot job with my life either, but I'm going to start now. I don't want to get fleeced because I'm not sure what something's worth, or because I'm in too much of a hurry."

He picked up his wine with his free hand, considered. Not just what she was asking, but what it meant, and what could be done. "I can help you, if you're sure it's what you want."

"I'm sure."

"You've got a couple of choices, as I see it. You can get an agent." Keeping his eyes on hers, he topped off their wine. "I know an outfit here in Milan that's very trustworthy. They'll come in, appraise what you've selected, give you around forty percent."

"Forty? But that's terrible."

"It's actually a bit on the high side, but we do a lot of business with them and you'd probably get it."

Grimly, she set her teeth. "What are my other choices?"

"You could try one of the auction houses. You could go with an appraiser and then contact some of the antique or collectible shops and see what you'd get there." He leaned closer, watching her face. "But, if you ask me, you should sell yourself."

"Excuse me?"

"Margo Sullivan can sell anything. What else have you been doing for the last ten years but hawking someone else's products? Sell yourself, Margo."

Baffled, she sat back. "Excuse me. Aren't you the one who just finished rapping my knuckles for mentioning doing just that?"

"Not your picture. You. Open a shop, stock it with your own possessions. Advertise it. Flaunt it."

"Open a shop?" Her laugh bubbled out as she reached for her glass. "I can't open a shop."

"Why not?"

"Because I . . . I don't know why," she murmured and deliberately pushed her glass aside. "I've had too much wine if I don't know why."

"Your flat's already a small-scale department store."

"There are dozens of reasons why it wouldn't work." Her head spun just thinking about it. "I don't know anything about running a business, keeping books."

"Learn," he said simply.

"There's taxes, and fees. Licenses. Rent, for Christ's sake." Flummoxed, she began to run her fingers up and down the jeweled chain she wore. "I'm trying to eliminate bills, not make more of them. I'd need money."

"An investor, someone who would be willing to pump in the startup money."

"Who'd be stupid enough to do that?"

He lifted his glass. "I would."

Chapter Seven

She spent most of the night picking the idea apart, tossing in bed and reciting all the sane objections she should have thought of in the first place.

It was a ridiculous notion. Reckless and foolish. And it had come along just when she was trying so hard to stop being ridiculous and reckless and foolish.

When tossing in bed frustrated her enough, she rose to pace in the dark. Obviously Josh knew little more about business than she did, or he would never have suggested such a preposterous plan.

She wasn't a shopkeeper, for God's sake. Appreciating lovely things only meant she had expensive taste. It didn't mean she could turn herself into a merchant. And maybe she did know how to sell, but being the Bella Donna Woman and urging some tourist to write a traveler's check for a Daum goldfish were two entirely different matters.

Certainly people would come, at first. Out of curiosity, out of glee to see the once famous, now notorious Margo Sullivan hawking her wares. She would probably make a few sales too, initially. And some society matron with too many face-lifts could gesture to her curio cabinet to point out the antique snuff bottle she'd bought from that poor model who'd fallen on hard times.

Margo set her teeth. Well, she'd have that snooty matron's money in her pocket, wouldn't she?

Catching herself, she shook her head. No, it was an impossible idea. Starting a business was simply too complicated, and maintaining one would be beyond her. She would only be setting herself up for another failure.

Coward.

"Just shut up, Josh. It wouldn't be your butt on the line. Just your money."

And she wasn't going to take his money anyway. The idea of being indebted to him was more than her pride could stand. Even if she swallowed her pride, she didn't think her nerves could handle working with him. He'd undoubtedly be popping up even more than usual, checking on her, checking on his investment.

Looking at her the way he looked at her. Absently she rubbed a hand between her breasts. Had he always looked at her that way? Had she just begun to notice? She recognized hunger in a man's eyes when she saw it. Was used to seeing it. There was no reason for her mouth to go dry and her pulse to start jittering because they were Josh's eyes.

His eyes were as familiar to her as her own. She'd known those eyes, known him, all of her life. It had to be her imagination—imagination skewed by her emotional upheaval. It was just that she'd been feeling so unwanted, she'd mistaken kindness and concern from an old friend for desire.

That was it, of course.

But she knew she hadn't mistaken her own reaction when he touched her, when his fingers skimmed over her shoulder. Flesh to flesh. And for an instant, just a quick flash, she'd actually fantasized that his fingers would dip lower, part her robe, cup her breasts and . . .

And she had to be skirting madness to wind an erotic daydream around Josh Templeton.

He was a friend, practically family. And at the moment, the least of her worries.

She had to concentrate on practicalities, not sexual intrigues. After Alain she'd decided that sex, romance, even the whisper of relationship were going to the bottom of her priority list. The most reasonable thing for her to do would be to contact Josh in the morning and ask him for the name of the agent he'd mentioned. She would cull out everything she didn't need for basic survival, take the forty percent, and go on.

She'd sell the car as well. And her furs. Her standing twice-monthly appointment at Sergio Valente in Rome was out, as was her biannual jaunt to Les Pres et les Sources in France. There would be no more strolling down the Montenapoliane with careless forays into Valentino and Armani.

She would make do with what she had, or what she had left, and find a job.

Damn him for making her too ashamed to snatch up a quick six figures for one harmless photo shoot.

Besides, what kind of shop would it be? she asked herself as her mind stubbornly circled back. People didn't go into a store expecting to buy a Gucci bag and a Steuben bird in the same place. It wouldn't be secondhand clothing, or curios, or leather goods. It would be a hodgepodge; confusing, unfocused.

It would be unique.

It would be hers.

With her hands pressed to her mouth, Margo let herself imagine it. Busy shelves with an elegant yet friendly clutter of pretty, useless things. Glass cabinets gleaming with jewelry. Tables and chairs and fussy ottomans. For relaxing, and all for sale. A room fashioned like a huge walk-in closet for clothes. Another little seating area where she would serve tea and flutes of champagne. China and crystal also priced to sell.

It could work. Not only could it work, it could be fun. An adventure. The hell with the details, the fine print, the sanity. She'd figure it out somehow.

With a reckless laugh, she dashed into the bedroom and threw on some clothes.

Josh was dreaming, and dreaming well. He could even smell her, that straight-to-the-glands fragrance that always seeped through her pores. She was murmuring his name, almost sighing it as he stroked his hands over her. God, her skin was like satin, smooth and white, that glorious, generous goddess body growing damp as she clung to him.

Arched back, trembling and—

"Ow. Goddamn it." Pinched him.

He opened his eyes, blinked at the dark. He would have sworn his shoulder ached where fingers had dug. And he could swear that her scent was in the air.

"Sorry. You were sleeping like the dead."

"Margo? Are you crazy? What time is it? What are you doing here? Jesus!" He continued to swear, viciously, as the light she turned on speared into his eyes. "Turn that goddamn thing off or I'll kill you."

"I'd forgotten how surly you are when you wake up." Too

cheerful to take offense, she switched off the light, then moved to the drapes, opening them to the lovely muted glow of sunrise. "Now, to answer your questions: I think I may be. It's about quarter after dawn. I'm here to thank you."

She smiled at him as he stared groggily at the coffered ceiling. The bed was a lake of rumpled linen sheets and the slick royal blue satin of the spread. The headboard was a fantasy of cherubs and fruit, all carved and gilded. Rather than looking ridiculous tucked in all that splendor, he looked just right.

"Gosh, you're cute, all heavy-eyed and grumpy, and that sexy stubble." She leaned over to give it a teasing rub, then squealed when he yanked her onto the bed with him. Before she could gather the next breath, she was pinned under a long, hard male body.

A fully aroused male body. There was no possible way to attribute that to imagination this time. Her hips arched in response before she could prevent it. And his eyes went opaque. Instinctively she pried a hand free and slapped it to his chest.

"I didn't come to wrestle."

"Then why are you here, and how'd you get into the suite?"

"They know me downstairs." Good God, she was out of breath, and shaky. And hot. "I just said you were expecting me, and said you might be in the shower, so . . . the front desk gave me a key." His gaze lingered on her mouth, made her burn. "Ah, listen, I seem to have interrupted one of your prurient dreams, so I can just wait in the parlor until . . ."

She trailed off, deciding it was best not to continue the thought, when he caught her wrist and pulled her arm back over her head.

"Until?"

"Whenever." His mouth was close. She could almost feel it on hers. Hard and hungry. "I wanted to talk to you, but obviously I should have waited. Until."

118

"You're trembling," he murmured. And her eyes were delicately shadowed from lack of sleep. Her hair, those sexy miles of it, spread wildly over the tumbled sheets. "Nervous?"

She could hear her own labored breaths, knew no one could mistake the desire in the sound. "Not exactly."

He lowered his head, scraped his teeth lightly over her jaw. When she moaned, he hoped he was making her suffer for even one of the nights he'd burned for her. "Curious?"

"Yes."

He cruised up to her ear, and her eyes crossed with lust. "Ever wonder why we haven't ended up like this before?"

She was having a hard time keeping a coherent thought in her head as he nibbled along her neck. "Maybe, once or twice."

He lifted his head. The light from the rising sun showered over him. With his hair tousled, his eyes dark, his face shadowed, he looked rough and reckless, dangerously and delectably male.

"Don't." She didn't know where the denial came from when every nerve in her body was primed to beg for more.

"Don't what?"

"Don't kiss me." She let out a shaky breath, drew in another. "If you do, we're going to have sex. I'm just turned inside out enough to jump in without giving a damn about an hour from now."

"You don't have to give a damn about an hour from now." His mouth skimmed along her temple, teased the corner of her lips. "This is going to take longer. A lot longer."

"Please. A few hours ago . . . Jesus, Josh . . . you convinced me that what I do affects other people."

"Believe me," he murmured, "I'm affected."

Her heart drummed in her ears, insistently. "I can't afford to ruin another part of my life. I need a friend. I need you to be my friend."

119

Cursing her, he rolled off. "No offense, Margo, but go to hell."

"No offense taken." She didn't touch him. She was certain that if she did one or both of them would go off like a rocket. For a moment they lay there on the rumpled satin spread in silence, not moving, barely breathing. "I'm just saving us both a lot of trouble."

His gaze shifted, pinned hers. "You're only postponing it. We'll get back to this."

"I've been choosing my own bedmates for some time."

He moved fast, snagging her wrist and hauling her against him. "You want to be careful, duchess, about throwing your lovers in my face just now."

It was exactly what she needed to break the spell. Her chin angled. "Don't get pushy. I'll let you know if and when I want to play." She saw the change in his eyes and flashed her own. "Try it, just try it, and I'll shred the skin from your bones. You aren't the first man who thought he could shove me on my back and make me enjoy it."

He let her go because it was a wiser course than strangling her. "Don't compare me to the wimps and washouts you've wasted your time with."

Knowing her temper was ready to snap, she got off the bed. "I didn't come here to tear up the sheets with you, or to fight. I'm here to discuss business."

"Next time make an appointment." No longer worried about the niceties, he tossed back the sheets. Her eyes didn't flicker as he strode naked into the adjoining bath. "Since you're here, order up some breakfast."

She waited until she heard the shower running before she let out a long, relieved breath. Another minute, she admitted, and she might have eaten him alive. With a hand pressed to her jumpy stomach, she told herself they were both lucky she'd forced them to avoid that mistake.

120

But as she glanced back at the bed, she didn't feel lucky. Only deprived.

While Josh dressed, Margo enjoyed the first cup of coffee and picked over the silver basket of baked goods on the linen-decked table in the window nook of the dining area. She relaxed with the view of the piazza, the statues of gods and winged horses in white marble.

As did any suite in any Templeton, it offered a sumptuous interior as well as the view. A massive Oriental carpet spread over a floor of ivory tile. The walls were papered with roses with golden leaves, the fancy work of cornices and textured ceilings added to the opulence. Curvy settees rich with brocade and tasseled pillows, entertainment centers discreetly concealed in intricately carved cabinets, the little touches of statuary, antique lamps, heavy crystal ashtrays, giant urns filled with flowers, the full ebony bar curved in front of a glass wall—all bespoke that distinct Templeton flair.

The Art Nouveau style was just rich enough, just decadent enough to make even the most jaded guest sigh. She sighed herself.

But with Templeton, style went hand in glove with efficiency. A touch of a button on the streamlined white phone in every room of the suite could summon anything from fresh towels to tickets to *La Scala* or a bottle of perfectly chilled Cristal in a silver bucket. There was a basket of fruit on the pond-size coffee table, the grapes plump, the apples glossy. Behind the bar, the mini fridge would be stocked with unblended Scotch, Swiss chocolates, French cheeses.

The flowers, abundant even in the bath and dressing rooms, were fresh, watered and replaced daily by one of the well-trained and always amenable staff.

She sniffed at the pink rose on the breakfast table. It was long-stemmed, fragrant, and just opening. Perfect, she mused, just as anything with the Templeton name was expected to be.

Including, she thought as Josh stepped into the room, the Templeton heir.

Because she was feeling just a little guilty about invading his rooms at dawn, she poured him a cup from the heavy silver pot, adding the generous dollop of cream she knew he preferred.

"Service at Templeton Milan is still the best in the city. So's the coffee." She passed him the cup when he joined her at the table.

"I'll be sure to pass your comments along to the manager—after I fire him for letting you in."

"Don't be cranky, Josh." She slanted her most persuasive smile his way, only slightly annoyed when she saw it didn't make a dent. "I'm sorry I woke you up. I wasn't thinking about the time."

"Not thinking is one of your most highly honed skills."

She plucked a berry from the bowl, popped it into her mouth. "I'm not going to fight with you, and I'm not going to apologize for not sleeping with you just because your ego's bruised."

His smile was thin and sharp as a scalpel. "Duchess, if I'd gotten your clothes off, you not only wouldn't have to apologize, you'd be thanking me."

"Oh, I see I'm mistaken. Your ego's not bruised, it's just painfully swollen. Let's clear the air here, Joshua." She leaned forward, the confidence in her eyes sultry. "I like sex. I think it's an excellent form of entertainment. But I don't have to be entertained every time someone suggests a party. I select the time, the place, and my playmates."

Satisfied, she sat back and lazily chose a tiny cake from the basket. That, she was sure, should settle that.

"You might be able to get away with that." She was right, he thought. The coffee was excellent, and put him in a better mood. "If you hadn't been trembling and moaning under me half an hour ago."

"I was not moaning."

He smiled. "Oh, yes. You were." Yes, indeed, he was feeling much, much better. "And on the verge of writhing."

"I never writhe."

"You will."

She bit neatly into the cake. "Every boy should have his dreams. Now if we're finished jousting over sex—"

"Darling, I haven't even picked up my lance."

"That's a very weak double entendre."

She had him there. "It's early. Why don't you tell me why I'm having breakfast with you."

"I was up all night."

The comment that occurred to him was not only weak, but crude. He let it pass. "And?"

"I couldn't sleep. I was thinking about the spot I'm in, the options you'd suggested. The first seems the most sensible. Having an agent come in and make me an offer on the furnishings, my jewelry. It would probably be the quickest solution, and the least complicated."

"Agreed."

She pushed away from the table, rubbing her hands together as she paced. Her soft suede boots were as soundless on the tile as they were on the thick carpet. "It's probably time I learned to be sensible. I'm twenty-eight, unemployed, with the wolf snarling at the door. I was feeling sorry for myself at first, but now I realize I had an incredible run of luck. I got to go places and do things, be things that I'd always dreamed of. And why?"

She stopped in the center of the room, turned a slow circle under the ornate gold and crystal chandelier. In tight jodhpur-style pants and a drapey white blouse, she looked voluptuous and vibrant.

"Why?"

"Because I have a face and a body that translate well through the camera. That's all. A good face, a killer body. Not that I didn't have to work hard, be clever and stubborn. But the core of it, Josh, is luck. The luck of the draw from the gene pool. Now, through circumstances that may or may not have been beyond my control, that's done. I'm through whining about it."

"You've never been a whiner, Margo."

"I could give lessons. It's time for me to grow up, take responsibility, be sensible."

"Talk to life insurance salesmen," Josh said dryly. "Apply for a library card. Clip coupons."

She looked down her nose. "Spoken like a man born with not only a silver spoon but the whole place setting stuck in his arrogant little mouth."

"I happen to have several library cards," he muttered. "Somewhere."

"Do you mind?"

"Sorry." He waved her on, but he was worried. She looked eager and happy, but she wasn't talking like Margo. Not his delightfully reckless Margo. "Keep going."

"Okay, I can probably weather this, eventually I could wrangle some shoots, get a spot on the catwalk in Paris or New York. It would take time, but I could come around." Struggling to think clearly, she traced a finger down a candlestick in the form of a maiden in flowing robes flanked by twin cups holding gold tapers. "There are other ways to make money modeling. I could go back to catalogs, where I started."

"Selling teddies for Victoria's Secret?"

She whirled, fire in her eyes. "What's wrong with that?"

"Nothing." He broke open a small roll. "I appreciate a well-sold teddy as much as the next guy."

She took a slow breath. He would not annoy her, not now. "It wouldn't be easy in my current situation to get bookings. But I did it before."

"You were ten years younger," he pointed out helpfully.

"Thank you so much for reminding me," she said between her teeth. "Look at Cindy Crawford, Christie Brinkley, Lauren Hutton, for God's sake. They're not teenagers. And as far as your brilliant solution, the idea of opening a shop is ludicrous. I thought of half a dozen valid reasons against it last night. Over and above the fact that I don't have a clue how to run a business is the larger fact that if I was crazy enough to try I could very well make my situation—a very unstable situation—worse. It's more than likely I'd be bankrupt within six months, faced with yet another public humiliation and forced to sell myself on street corners to traveling salesmen looking for cheap thrills."

"You're right. It's out of the question."

"Absolutely."

"So when do you want to start?"

"Today." With a jubilant laugh, she dashed to him, threw her arms around his neck. "Do you know what's better than having someone who knows you inside out?"

"What?"

"Nothing." She gave him a noisy kiss on the cheek. "If you're going to go down—"

"Go down swinging." He caught her hair in his hand and pulled her laughing mouth to his.

It wasn't a laughing matter. She discovered that very quickly. His lips were hot and clever and had hers parting in sighing response. The lazy sweep of his tongue sent shock waves of need vibrating out to her fingertips.

It should have been familiar. She'd kissed him before, tasted him before. But those casual brotherly embraces hadn't prepared her for the instant, undeniable jolt of pure animal lust.

125

Part of her mind tried to draw back, to remember that this was Josh. Josh who had scorned her prized collection of dolls when she was six. Who had dared her to scramble with him on the cliffs when she was eight, then had carried her back to the house when she gashed her leg on a rock.

Josh who had smirked at her adolescent crushes on his friends, who had patiently taught her to handle a five-speed. Josh who had always been somewhere right around the corner wherever she had gone in her life.

But this was like kissing someone new. Someone dangerously exciting. Painfully tempting.

He'd been expecting it. Hadn't he dreamed, hundreds of times, of tasting her like this? Of having her go taut in his arms, her mouth answering his with a kind of banked fury?

He'd been willing to wait, just as he'd been willing to dream. Because he knew she would be his. He knew she needed to be.

But he wasn't going to make it easy.

He drew back, pleased that when her lashes slowly lifted her eyes were dark and clouded. He hoped to God the same jittery desire that was churning in his gut was churning in hers.

"You're awfully good at that," she managed. "I'd heard rumors." She realized she was in his lap but wasn't sure if he'd pulled her there or if she'd simply crawled onto him. "I believe they might have been understated. Actually I did sneak outside one night and watch you put the moves on Babs Carstairs out by the pool. I was impressed."

Nothing she could have said could have been more perfectly designed to make desire wilt. "You spied on me and Babs?"

"Just once. Or twice. Hell, Josh, I was thirteen. Curious."

"Jesus." He remembered exactly how far things had gone with Babs out by the pool on one pretty summer night. "Did you see— No, I don't want to know."

126

"Laura and Kate and I all agreed she was over-mammaried."

"Over—" Before he could laugh at the term, he winced. "You *and* Laura *and* Kate. Why didn't you just sell tickets?"

"I believe it's perfectly natural for a younger sister to spy on her older brother."

His eyes glinted. "I'm not your brother."

"From where I'm sitting, I'd say that fact saves our immortal souls."

The glint turned into a grin. "You may be right. I want you, Margo. There are all manner of incredible, nasty, unspeakable things I want to do to you."

"Well." She let out a breath she hadn't realized she'd been holding. "So much for our immortal souls. Listen, I have to say this change is a little abrupt for me."

"You haven't been paying attention."

"Obviously not." She couldn't take her eyes off his. It would be wiser to, she knew. She had survived all the games men and women play by always, without exception, staying in control. Those eyes, gray and cool and confident, warned her that that wouldn't be an option with him. Not for long. "I'm paying attention now, but I'm not ready for the starting gun."

"It went off years ago." His hands skimmed up her sides, brushed her breasts. "I'm way ahead of you."

"I have to decide if I want to catch up." She laughed and scrambled off his lap. "It's just too weird, the whole concept of you and me and sex." Then she rubbed a hand over her heart because it was plunging like a mare in heat. "And it's surprisingly tempting. There was a time, not that long ago, I'd have said what the hell, it'll be fun, and raced you to the bed."

When he rose, she laughed again and put the table between them. "I'm not being coy. I don't believe in it."

"What are you being?"

127

"Cautious, for once in my life." Suddenly, her eyes were sober, her mouth soft instead of teasing. "You matter too much. And I've just figured out that I matter, too. Not just out here," she said, gesturing toward her face. "Inside. I've got to straighten out my life. I've got to do something with it I can be proud of. I have all these new plans, all these new dreams. I want to make them work. No." She closed her eyes a moment. "I *have* to make them work. To do that I need to take time and effort. Sex is distracting if you do it right." She smiled again. "We would."

He tucked his thumbs in his pockets. "What are you going to do? Take a vow of celibacy?"

Her smile spread slowly. "That's an excellent idea. I can always count on you for a viable solution."

His jaw dropped. "You're kidding."

"I'm perfectly serious." Delighted with both of them, she walked over and patted his cheek. "Okay, I'm celibate until my life is in order and my business is up and running. Thanks for thinking of it."

He circled her throat with his hand, but was more inclined to throttle himself. "I could seduce you in thirty seconds flat."

Now he was getting cocky. "If I let you," she said silkily. "But it's not going to happen until I'm ready."

"And I'm supposed to enter a monastery until you're ready?"

"Your life's your own. You can have anyone you want." She turned to wander back toward the cakes, looked over her shoulder. "Except me."

But the idea didn't sit very well. Nibbling on the cake, she contemplated. "Unless, of course, you'd like to make it a kind of bet."

She was licking those crumbs off her bottom lip on purpose, he thought. He knew when a woman was trying to drive him crazy. "What kind of bet?"

128

"That I can abstain longer than you. That I can make an adult commitment to control my hormones and seriously pursue a career."

His face bland, he added hot coffee to his cup, then hers. Inside he was snickering. She hadn't a clue how long it would take to open the doors to this shop she was planning. It could be months. She would never last that long, he mused as he lifted his cup, watched her over the rim. He'd see to it.

"How much?"

"Your new car."

He choked on coffee. "My car? My Jag?"

"That's right. I have to sell my car and I don't know when I'll be able to replace it. You succumb first, I get the Jag. Clear title. You ship it to Italy."

"And if you succumb first?" When she gestured, dismissing the possibility, he grinned. "I get your art."

"My street scenes." Her heart actually fluttered at the thought. "All of them?"

"Every last one. Unless you're afraid to risk it."

She lifted her chin, held out a hand. "Done."

He closed his hand over hers, then brought it up, brushed his lips over her wrist, nibbled lightly to her palm.

"Nice try," she murmured, and shook free. "Now I've got business to tend to. I'm going to go sell my car."

"You're not going to take it to a dealer," he objected as she grabbed her bag and jacket. "They'll scalp you."

"Oh, no." She paused at the door, her smile sly and irresistible. "No, they won't."

Chapter Eight

It amazed Margo how quickly she got into the spirit. She'd never realized how much fun, how simply exhilarating wheeling and dealing could be. The car started it all.

It hadn't shamed her a bit to use every ounce of charm, all of her sex appeal and generous dollops of femininity, not merely as bargaining chips, but as weapons, God-given and well honed. She was at war.

After choosing the car dealer, she had ambushed her quarry with flattery and smiles, fencing expertly with claims of her inexperience in business dealings, her trust in his judgment. She batted her eyes, looked helpless, and slowly, sweetly annihilated him.

And had squeezed lire out of him until he was gasping for breath.

The jeweler, being a woman, had been more of a challenge.

Margo had selected two of her best and most expensive pieces, and after sizing up her opponent as a clever, hardheaded, unsentimental businesswoman, she had adopted the same pose.

It had been, she thought, *mano a mano*, female style. They'd negotiated, argued, scorned each other's offers, insulted one another, then come to terms each of them could live with.

Now, adding the take from her furs, she had enough ready cash to hold her more impatient creditors off for a few weeks.

With the breathing room, she buckled down and completed a tentative cataloging of her possessions, and began to pack them up, knowing the sooner she thought of them as inventory, the easier it would be. No longer were they her personal possessions. Now they were business assets.

Each morning she studied the paper for available space to rent. The prices made her wince and worry and eventually concede that she wouldn't be able to afford a prime location. Nor would she be able to advertise by conventional means if she wanted her money to last. Which left her a second-rate location that she would have to make work, and unconventional means.

Comfortable in leggings and a T-shirt, she stretched out in a chair and surveyed her living space. Tables had been ruthlessly cleared off. A good many of them were stacked alongside packing boxes and crates. Her paintings remained on the walls. A symbol, she thought, of what she was risking in so many areas of her life just now.

She'd gone to work elsewhere in the flat as well. Her wardrobe had been cut down to a quarter of its original size. The other seventy-five percent was carefully packed away. She'd been merciless in her selections, with an eye to her new lifestyle rather than sentiment. Not that she intended to dress down as a merchant. She would dress as she would run her business. With flair and style and bold pride.

With luck, one of the three locations she had arranged to

view that afternoon would be just the one she was looking for.

She was anxious to begin before the press got a firm hold on her situation. There were already dribbles in the papers about La Margo selling her jewelry to pay her mounting debts. She'd taken to sneaking out of the service entrance to avoid the reporters and paparazzi who so often ambushed her outside the building.

She'd begun to wonder if she should just give up the flat after all. Kate had been right—trying to keep it was whittling her already meager resources to nothing. If she found a good location for the shop, she could simply move in there. Temporarily.

At least, she thought with a laugh, that way she would have her things around her.

She wished she had Josh to play the idea off of. But he was in Paris. No, she remembered, by now it was Berlin, and after that Stockholm. There was no telling when she would hear from him again, much less see him.

The few days they'd spent together in Milan, that jarring and exciting morning in his suite, were more like a dream now than a memory. She might have wondered if she'd actually ached when he'd kissed her, but whenever she thought of it, she ached again.

He was probably nibbling some Fräulein's ear right now, Margo thought and kicked at the corner of the sofa as she rose. He'd never be able to keep those clever hands of his off a willing female. The jerk.

At least she was going to get a car out of the whole mess. If nothing else, Josh Templeton was a man of his word.

She didn't have time to think about him—swilling beer and tickling some statuesque German goddess. She had to change for her appointments, adopt the appropriate image. As she dressed she practiced the technique she would employ with the realtor. Picky, she mused, braiding her hair. No enthusiasm.

"Questa camera . . ." A dismissive look, a gesture of the hand. "Piccola." Or, it would be too large to suit her needs. She would make unhappy noises as she wandered around and let the realtor try to convince her. Of course, she would remain unconvinced. She would say the rent was absurd. She would ask to see something else, say she had another appointment in an hour.

She stepped back, studied herself. Yes, the black suit was businesslike but had the flair the Italian eye recognized and appreciated. The smooth French braid was feminine, flattering but not fussy, and the oversized Bandalino bag was tailored like a briefcase.

Odds were, her opponent—and she thought of everyone on the other side of her business deals as opponents now—would have recognized her name. He would certainly recognize her face. So much the better. In all likelihood he'd assume he was meeting a flighty, empty-headed bimbo. And that would give her not only the advantage but the sizzling satisfaction of proving him wrong.

Drawing a long breath, she stared at herself. Margo Sullivan was not a bimbo, she insisted to the reflection. Margo Sullivan was a businesswoman, with brains, ambition, plans, goals, and determination. Margo Sullivan was not a loser. She was a survivor.

She closed her eyes for a moment, struggling to absorb the self-administered pep talk, needing to believe it. Doesn't matter, she thought with an inner quaver, as long as I can make everyone else believe it.

Damned if she wouldn't.

The phone was ringing as she shouldered her bag and headed out. "Just leave your name and a brief message," she told the insistent two-toned bell, "and I won't get back to you."

It was Kate's impatient voice that stopped her.

"Damn it all to hell and back, Margo. Are you ever going to answer this thing? I know you're there. I know you're standing right there sneering at the phone. Pick it up, will you? It's important."

"It's always important," Margo muttered and kept right on sneering.

"Goddamn it, Margo. It's about Laura."

Margo pounced on the phone, jerking the receiver to her ear. "Is she hurt? What's wrong? Was there an accident?"

"No, she's not hurt. Take off your earring, it's clinking on the phone."

Disgusted, Margo worked it off. "If you're yanking my chain just to get me to talk to you—"

"Like I've got nothing better to do at five A.M. on April fifteenth than make crank phone calls. Listen, pal, I haven't slept in twenty-six hours and I've burned off most of my stomach lining with caffeine. Don't start with me."

"You called me, remember? I'm on my way out the door."

"And Laura's on her way to see a lawyer."

"A lawyer? At five A.M.? You said there wasn't an accident."

"She's not literally on her way. She has an appointment at ten. I wouldn't have even known about it, but her lawyer's a client of the firm and he thought I knew. He said he was sorry she was upset, and—"

"Just nail it down, Kate."

"Sorry, I'm strung out. She's divorcing Peter."

"Divorcing?" Since the chair that had been by the phone was now in the inventory section, she sat down abruptly on the floor. "Oh, Christ, Kate, it's not because they fought over me?"

"The world doesn't revolve around you, Margo. Hell, sorry. It's not your fault," she said more gently. "I didn't get much out of her when I went over, but the deciding factor seemed to be that she walked in on him and his secretary. And he wasn't dictating a letter."

"You're kidding. That's so . . ."

"Ordinary?" Kate suggested dryly. "Trite? Disgusting?"

"Yes."

"Well, that sums it up. If it's happened before, she's not saying. But I can tell you she's not giving him another turn at bat. She's dead serious."

"Is she all right?"

"She seems very calm, very civilized. I'm so bogged down here, Margo, I can't work on her. You know how she is when she's really upset."

"Sucks it all in," Margo murmured, jiggling the earring impatiently in her hand. "The kids?"

"I just don't know. If I could get out of here I would. But I've got another nineteen hours before flash point. I'll corner her then."

"I'll be there inside of ten."

"That's what I was hoping you'd say. I'll see you at home."

"I don't know why I'm surprised you'd fly six thousand miles for something like this, Margo." Laura competently sewed stars onto Ali's tutu for her daughter's ballet recital. "It's just like you."

"I want to know how you are, Laura. I want to know what's going on."

Margo stopped pacing the sitting room and slapped her hands on her hips. She was past exhaustion and into the floaty stage of endless travel. Ten hours had been typically optimistic. It had taken her closer to fifteen to manage all the connections and layovers. Now, she was cross-eyed with fatigue, and Laura just sat there calmly plying needle and thread.

"Would you put that silly thing down for a minute and talk to me?"

"Ali would be crushed if she heard you call her fairy tutu silly." But her daughter was in bed, Laura thought. Safe and innocent. For the moment. "Sit down, Margo, before you collapse."

"I don't want to sit." If she did, she was certain she would simply fade away.

"I didn't expect you to be so upset. You were hardly fond of Peter."

"I'm fond of you. And I know you, Laura. You're not chucking a ten-year marriage without hurting."

"I'm not hurting. I'm numb. I'm going to stay numb as long as I possibly can." Gently she smoothed a hand over the net of the ballet skirt. "There are two little girls down the hall who need someone in their life to be strong and stable. Margo . . ." She looked up then with baffled eyes. "I don't think he loves them. I don't think he cares at all. I could handle him not loving me. But they're his children." She stroked the tulle again, as if it were her daughter's cheek. "He wanted sons. Ridgeways. Boys to become men and carry on the family name. Well"—she set the skirt aside—"he got daughters."

Margo lighted a cigarette with a quick jerk, made herself sit. "Tell me what happened."

"He stopped loving me. I'm not sure he ever did, really. He wanted an important wife." She moved her shoulders. "He thought he got one. In the past couple of years we began to disagree over quite a lot of things. Or I began to disagree with him out loud. He didn't care for that. Oh, it's no use going over all the details." She waved her hands with self-directed impatience. "Basically we grew apart. He began to spend more time away from home. I thought he was having an affair,

136

but he was so uncharacteristically furious when I accused him, I believed I was wrong.''

''But you weren't.''

''I'm not sure, about then. It doesn't matter.'' Laura jerked a shoulder, picked up the tulle again to give herself something to do with her hands. ''He hasn't touched me in more than a year.''

''A year.'' It was, perhaps, foolish to be shocked at the idea of marriage without intimacy, but Margo was shocked nonetheless.

''At first, I wanted us to go to a counselor, but he was appalled by the idea. Then I thought I should try some therapy, and he was beyond appalled.'' Laura managed a quick, thin smile. ''It would get out, and then what would people think, what would they say?''

No sex. None. For a year. Margo fought her way past the block and concentrated. ''That's just ridiculous.''

''Maybe. But I stopped caring. It was easier to stop caring and concentrate on my children, the house. My life.''

What life? Margo wanted to ask, but held her tongue.

''But I could see in the last few weeks that it was affecting the children. Ali in particular.'' Gently, she replaced the tutu, folded her hands in her lap to keep them still. ''After you left, I decided we had to straighten things out. We had to fix what was wrong. I went to the penthouse. I thought it would be best if we talked there, away from the children. I was willing to do whatever had to be done to put things back together.''

''You were willing,'' Margo interrupted, leaping up and puffing out an angry stream of smoke. ''It sounds to me like—''

''It doesn't matter what it sounds like,'' Laura said quietly. ''It's what is. Anyway, it was late. I'd put the girls to bed first. All the way over I practiced this little speech about how we'd had a decade together, a family, a history.''

It made her laugh to think of it now. She rose, deciding she could indulge in a short brandy. As she poured two snifters, she related the rest. "The penthouse was locked, but I have a key. He wasn't in the office." Calmly she handed Margo a glass, sat down again with her own. "I was annoyed at first, thinking he'd gone out for a late dinner meeting or some such thing and I'd geared myself up for nothing. Then I noticed the light under the bedroom door. I nearly knocked. Can you imagine how pathetic the situation was, Margo, that I nearly knocked? Instead, I just opened the door." She took a sip of brandy. "He was having a dinner meeting, all right."

"His secretary?"

Laura gave a snorting laugh. "Like a bad French farce. We have the philandering husband sprawled over the bed with his jazzy redheaded secretary and a bowl of chilled shrimp."

Barely, Margo managed to strangle a giggle. "Shrimp?"

"And what appeared to be a spiced-honey sauce, with a bottle of Dom to wash it down. Enter the unsuspecting, neglected society wife. The tableau freezes. No one speaks, only the strains of *Bolero* can be heard."

"*Bolero*. Oh, Jesus." Her breath hitching, Margo dropped into a chair. "I'm sorry. I'm sorry, I can't help it. I'm too tired to fight back."

"Go ahead and laugh." Laura felt a smile breaking through herself. "It is laughable. Pitifully. The wife says, with incredible and foolish dignity, 'I'm terribly sorry to interrupt your dinner meeting.' "

It was an effort, but Margo managed to wheeze in a breath. "You did not."

"I did. They just goggled at me. I've never seen Peter goggle before. It was almost worth it. The fresh young secretary began to squeak and try to cover herself, and in her rush for modesty upended the shrimp sauce on Peter's crotch."

"Oh. Oh, God."

"It was a moment." Laura heaved a sigh, wondering which of the three of them had felt more ridiculous. "I told them not to get up, I would see myself out. And I left."

"Just like that?"

"Just like that."

"But what does he say? How is he handling it?"

"I have no idea." Those soft gray eyes hardened into a look that was pure Templeton—tough, hot, and stubborn. "I'm not taking his calls. That stupid electric gate of his has finally paid off." As her gentle mouth hardened as well, Margo thought it was like watching silk turn to steel. "He can't get in because I've instructed the staff not to admit him. In any case, he's only tried once."

"You're not going to even talk to him?"

"There's nothing to talk about. I could and did tolerate indifference. I could and did tolerate his utter lack of affection and respect for me and my feelings. But I won't tolerate, not for an instant, his lying and his lack of fidelity. He might think that boinking his secretary is simply his *droit de signor*. He's going to find out different."

"Are you sure it's what you want?"

"It's the way it's going to be. My marriage is over." She looked down into her brandy, saw nothing. "And that's that."

The stubborn streak was classic Templeton, Margo thought. Carefully, she tapped out her cigarette, touched a hand to Laura's rigid one. "Honey, you know it won't be that easy— legally or emotionally."

"I'll do whatever I have to do, but I won't play the easily deceived society wife any longer."

"And the girls?"

"I'll make it up to them." Somehow. Some way. "I'll make it right for them." Little tongues of fear licked at her, and she ignored them. "I can't do anything else."

"All right. I'm behind you all the way. Look, I'm going to

go down and scare up some food. Kate's going to be starving when she gets here.''

"Kate's not coming here tonight. She always falls into bed for twenty-four hours after the tax deadline.''

"She'll be here,'' Margo promised.

"You'd think I was on my deathbed,'' Laura muttered. "All right, I'll make sure her room's ready. And yours. We'll put some sandwiches together.''

"I'll put some sandwiches together. You worry about the rooms.'' Which would, Margo thought as she hurried out, give her enough time to pump her mother for information.

She found Ann exactly where she'd expected to, in the kitchen, already arranging cold cuts and raw vegetables.

"I don't have much time,'' Margo began and headed directly for the coffeepot. "She'll be down in a minute. She's not really all right, is she?''

"She's coping. She won't talk about it, hasn't yet contacted her parents.''

"The scum, the slime.'' Her legs wobbled with fatigue and made it hard to storm around the kitchen, but Margo gave it her best shot. "And that little slut of a secretary putting in overtime.'' She broke off when she caught her mother's eye. "All right, I wasn't much better when it came to Alain. And maybe believing he was working out a divorce isn't any excuse, but at least his wife's family wasn't cutting my paychecks.'' She drank the coffee black to fuel her system. "You can lecture me on my sins later. Right now I'm concerned about Laura.''

A mother's sharp eye noted the signs of exhaustion and worry. "I'm not going to lecture you. It never did any good when you were a child and it would hardly do any good now. You go your own way, Margo, you always did. But your way has brought you here when a friend needs you.''

140

"Does she? She was always the strong one. The good one," she added with a wry smile. "The kind one."

"Do you think you're the only one who feels despair when the world falls apart around you? Who wants to pull the covers over her head instead of facing tomorrow?"

A quick flare of temper made Ann slam down the loaf of bread. Oh, she was tired, and heartsick, and her emotions were bouncing like a rubber ball from joy that her daughter was home, misery for Laura, and frustration at not knowing what to do for either of them.

"She's afraid and full of guilt and worry. It's only going to get worse for her." She pressed her lips together but couldn't settle herself. "Her home is broken, and whether you can see it or not, so is her heart. It's time you paid back some of what she's always given to you, and help her mend it."

"Why do you think I'm here?" Margo tossed back. "I dropped everything I was doing and flew six thousand miles to help her."

"A noble gesture." Ann's sharp, accusing eyes pinned her daughter. "You've always had a knack for the grand gesture, Margo, but holding fast takes something more. How long will you stay this time? A day, a week? How long before you're too restless to stick it out? Before the effort of caring for someone else becomes an inconvenience? Before you rush back to your glamorous life, where you don't have to think about anyone but yourself?"

"Well." Because her hand was unsteady, Margo set the cup down. "Why don't you get the rest of it out, Mum? Sounds like you've stored plenty."

"Oh, it's easy for you, isn't it, to come and go on a whim? Sending postcards and presents, as if that made up for your turning your back on everything real you've been given."

Ann's own worries acted as an impetus for resentments harbored for years. They spewed out before she could stop them, splattering them both with bitterness.

"You grew up in this house pretending you weren't the daughter of a servant, and Miss Laura treated you always as a sister. Who sent you money after you'd run off? Who used her influence to get you your first photo shoot? Who was there for you, always?" she demanded, stacking slices of bread like a irate cardsharp. "But have you been there for her? These past few years when she's been struggling to hold her family together, when she's been lonely and sad, were you there for her?"

"How could I have known?"

"Because Miss Kate would have told you. And if you hadn't been so wrapped up in Margo Sullivan, you'd have listened."

"I've never been what you wanted," Margo said wearily. "I've never been Laura. And I can't be."

Now guilt layered onto weariness and worry. "No one's asked you to be someone you're not."

"Haven't you, Mum? If I could have been kinder, more generous like Laura, more sensible, more practical like Kate. Do you think I didn't know that, didn't feel that from you every day of my life?"

Shocked and baffled, Ann shook her head. "Maybe if you'd been more satisfied with what you had and what you were, instead of running away from it, you'd have been happier."

"Maybe if you'd ever looked at me and been satisfied with what I was, I wouldn't have run so far, and so fast."

"I won't take the blame for how you've lived your life, Margo."

"No, I'll take it." Why not? she thought. There was so much on her debit side already, a little more would hardly matter. "I'll take the blame and the glory. That way I don't need your approval."

142

"I've never known you to ask for it." Ann strode out of the room and left Margo to stew.

She gave it three days. It was odd. They had never actually lived together in the house as adults. At eighteen Laura had gotten married, Margo had run to Hollywood, and Kate, always struggling to leap over that single year's age difference, had graduated early and bolted to Harvard.

Now they settled in. Kate used the excuse that she didn't have the energy to drive back to her apartment in Monterey, and Margo claimed to be marking time. She decided her mother had been right about some things. Laura was coping. But the difficult situation was only going to get worse. Already visitors were dropping by. Mostly the country club set, Margo noted, sniffing for gossip on the breakup of the Templeton-Ridgeway merger.

One night Margo found Kayla camped outside Laura's bedroom door because she was afraid her mama might go away too.

That was when she stopped believing it would settle down and she would go back to Milan. Her mother was right about something more, she'd decided. It was time for Margo Sullivan to hold fast and to pay back what had been given to her. She called Josh.

"It's six o'clock in the morning," he complained when she tracked him down at Templeton Stockholm. "Don't tell me you've become that monster of civilized society, Margo—the morning person."

"Listen up. I'm at Templeton House."

"That's all right then. It's the shank of the evening there. What do you mean you're at Templeton House?" he demanded when his brain cleared. "What the hell are you doing in California? You're supposed to be putting a business together in Milan."

She took a moment. It would be, she realized, the first time she'd said it aloud. The first time she would acknowledge the loss of one part of her life.

"I'm not going back to Milan. At least not anytime soon." As his voice exploded in her ear with questions, accusations, she watched one dream fade away. She hoped she could replace it with another. "Just be quiet a minute, would you?" she ordered with a snap. "I need you to do something, whatever it is that needs to be done, to have my things shipped here."

"Your things?"

"Most of it's boxed up anyway, but the rest will have to be packed. Templeton must have a service for that kind of thing."

"Sure, but—"

"I'll pay you back, Josh, but I don't know who to call and I just can't handle the extra expense just now. The plane fare cut into my resources."

Typical, Josh thought and jammed a pillow behind his back. Just typical. "Then why the hell did you buy a plane ticket to California?"

"Because Peter was diddling his secretary and Laura's divorcing him."

"You can't just go flying off whenever— What the hell did you say?"

"You heard me. She's filed for divorce. I don't think he's going to fight it, but I can't imagine the whole thing is going to be friendly, either. She's trying to handle too much of it on her own, and I've decided I'm not going to let her."

"Let me talk to her. Put her on."

"She's asleep." If Laura had been wide awake and standing by her side, she wouldn't have handed the phone over. The icy violence in Josh's voice stabbed over the line. "She had another session with the lawyer today, and it upset her. The

144

best solution all around is for me to stay here. I'm going to ask her to help me find the right location for the shop. It'll take some of this off her mind. Laura's always better at worrying about someone else than she is at worrying about herself."

"You're going to stay in California?"

"I won't have to worry about the VAT tax or Italian law, will I?" She felt hateful tears of self-pity sting her eyes and ruthlessly blinked them back. To ensure that her voice remained brisk and steady, she set her teeth. "Speaking of law, can I give you power of attorney, or whatever it's called? I need you to sell my flat, transfer funds, all those little legal details."

Details of what she was planning ran through and boggled his mind. Had he thought *typical*? he mused. Nothing about Margo was ever typical. "I'll draft one up and fax it there. You can sign it, fax it back to me at Templeton Milan. Where the hell is Ridgeway?"

"Rumor is he's still at the penthouse."

"We'll soon fix that."

Personally, she appreciated the cold viciousness in his voice, but . . . "Josh, I'm not sure Laura would want you rousting him out at this point."

"I outrank Laura in the Templeton feeding chain. I'll take care of the shipment as soon as I can. Are there any surprises I should be prepared for?"

Her American Express bill had arrived just before she'd left. She decided he didn't need another shock just then. "No, nothing worth mentioning. I'm sorry to dump this on you, Josh. I mean that, but I don't know how else to stay here with Laura and get this shop up and running before I'm shipped off to debtors' prison."

"Don't worry about it. Chaos is my business." He imagined her leaving everything in that chaos to rush off to support a friend. Loyalty, he thought, was and always had been her most admirable quality. "How are you holding up?"

"I'm good. And still untouched," she added. "Are you alone in that bed?"

"Except for the six members of the all-girl Swedish volleyball team. Helga's got a hell of a spike. Aren't you going to ask what I'm wearing?"

"Black Speedos, sweat, and a big smile."

"How'd you guess? So, what are you wearing?"

Slowly, she ran her tongue around her teeth. "Oh, just this little . . . very little . . . white lace teddy."

"And stiletto heels."

"Naturally. With a pair of sheer hose. They have little pink roses around the tops. It matches the one I'm tucking between my breasts right now. I should add I've just gotten out of the tub. I'm still a little . . . wet."

"Jesus. You're too good at this. I'm hanging up."

Her response was a long, throaty laugh. "I'm going to love driving that Jag. Let me know when to expect the shipment."

When the phone clicked in her ear, she laughed again, turned, and found herself nearly face to face with Kate. "How long have you been standing there?"

"Long enough to be confused. Were you just having phone sex with Josh? Our Josh?"

Carelessly, Margo brushed her hair behind her ear. "It was more foreplay really. Why?"

"Okay." She'd have to give that one some thought. "Now what is this about getting a shop up and running?"

"My, my, you do have big ears, don't you?" Margo tugged on them hard enough to make Kate yelp. "Well, sit down. I might as well tell you the master plan."

Kate listened, her only comments the occasional grunt, snort, or mutter. "I suppose you've calculated start-up costs?"

"Ah—"

"Right. And you've looked into licenses, fees, applied for a tax number."

"I have a few details to iron out," Margo muttered. "And it's just like you to toss cold water in my face."

"Gee, and here I thought it was cool common sense."

"Why shouldn't I make a business out of selling my things?" Margo demanded. "What's wrong with turning humiliation into an adventure? Just because I hadn't thought about applying for some stupid tax number doesn't mean I can't pull this off."

Sitting back, Kate tapped her fingertips together. It wasn't an entirely insane idea, she mused. In fact, it had some solid financial merit. Liquidation of assets tied to old-fashioned free enterprise. Kate decided she could help iron out some of the details if Margo was truly set on giving capitalism a try. It would be risky, certainly, but then Margo had always been one for taking risks.

"You're going to be a shopkeeper?"

Eyes bland, Margo studied her manicure. "I'm thinking of it more as a consultant position."

"Margo Sullivan," Kate marveled, "selling used clothes and knickknacks."

"Objets d'art."

"Whatever." Amused, Kate stretched out her legs, crossed them at the ankles. "It looks like hell has finally frozen over."

Chapter Nine

Margo stood in front of the storefront on busy Cannery Row and knew this one was it. The wide display window glinted in the sun and was protected from the elements by a charming little covered veranda. Its door was beveled glass decorated with an etched bouquet of lilies. Old-fashioned brass fittings gleamed. The peaked roof was topped by rows of Spanish tile softened to pink by time and weather.

She could hear the tinny tune from a carousel, the harsh cry of gulls, and the busy chatter of tourists. Scents of cooking from the stands and open-air restaurants of Fisherman's Wharf carried on the strong breeze flying off the water. Bicycles built for two clattered by.

Street traffic was a constant snarl, cars desperately seeking a parking spot they were unlikely to find in this busy tourist haven. Pedestrians strolled along the sidewalks, many with

children who were either all eyes and grins or whining crank-
ily.

There was movement everywhere. People and noise and action. The little shops lining the street, the restaurants and at-
tractions, drew them day after day, month after month.

All the other buildings, the narrow storefronts, the empty
storage rooms she'd viewed had just been steps, she thought,
leading to this.

"It's perfect," she murmured.

"You haven't even been inside," Kate pointed out.

"I know it's perfect. It's mine."

Kate exchanged a look with Laura. She had a pretty good
idea what property rented for in this location. If you're going
to dream, she thought, dream big. But then, Margo always had.

"The realtor's probably inside by now." Arriving late was
part of Margo's strategy. She didn't want to appear too eager.
"Just let me do the talking."

"Let her do the talking," Kate muttered and rolled her eyes
at Laura. "We're going to have lunch after this one, right?"
She could smell the frying fish and spicy sauces, aromas waft-
ing down from Fisherman's Wharf. Dull, nagging hunger
pangs attacked her stomach. "This is the last one before
lunch."

"This is the only one." Shoulders squared for battle, Margo
stepped up to the door. She had to force herself not to snatch
the For Rent sign away. Little frissons of possession were
already sprinting along her spine. She didn't question them,
or the fact that she had certainly walked past this building
countless times before and felt nothing.

She felt it now, and that was enough.

The main room was wide and empty. Scars were dug into
the hardwood floor where counters and display cases had been
ripped out. The paint had faded from white to something re-

sembling old paste and was pocked with small holes where the previous tenant had hung wares.

But she saw only a lovely archway leading into an adjoining space, the charm of a set of iron tightwinder stairs spiraling toward the second level, the airy, circling balcony. She recognized the signs in herself, the quickening of her pulse, the sharpening of vision. She often felt the same when she walked into Cartier and saw something that seemed to be waiting just for her.

Sensing trouble, Laura put a hand on her arm. "Margo."

"Can't you see it? Can't you just see it?"

"I see it needs a ton of manual labor." Kate wrinkled her nose. The air smelled of . . . incense? Pot? Old candles? "And fumigating."

Ignoring her, Margo walked over to a peeling door and opened it. Inside was a tiny bathroom with an aging pedestal sink and chipped tile. It thrilled her.

"Hello?" The voice echoed down from the second floor, following by the quick tap of high heels on wood. Laura winced.

"Oh, God, not Louisa. Margo, you said your appointment was with a Mr. Newman."

"Well, it was."

The voice called out again, and if there had been anywhere to dive for cover, Laura would have used it.

"Ms. Sullivan, is that you?" The woman appeared at the top of the stairs. She was all in pink from her flowing swing jacket to her clicking heels. Her hair was the careful ash blond that hairdressers often chose to hold off gray, and it was styled ruthlessly into a helmet that curved around pink cheeks. Gold rattled on her wrists, and an enormous sunburst pin exploded over her left breast.

Mid-fifties, Margo estimated with an experienced eye, and holding desperately on to forty. Very decent face-lift, she

150

mused, smiling politely as the woman picked her way down the circling stairs, chattering all the way. Regular aerobic classes to keep her in shape, possibly aided by a tummy tuck and lipo.

". . . just refreshing my memory," Louisa continued, bubbling like a brook. "I haven't been in here for several weeks. Dear Johnny was supposed to show you through, but he had a teeny little accident with his car this morning." When she reached the bottom, slightly out of breath, she offered a hand. "So delighted to meet you. I'm Louisa Metcalf."

"Margo Sullivan."

"Yes, of course you are." Her raisin-colored eyes glinted with interest and carefully applied bronze shadow. "I recognized you right away. I had no idea my one o'clock was *the* Margo Sullivan. And you're just as lovely as all your photographs. They're so often touched up, aren't they? Then you meet someone whose face you've seen just hundreds of times and it's such a disappointment. You've led such an interesting life, haven't you?"

"And it's not over yet," Margo said and had Louisa tittering with laughter.

"Oh, no, indeed. How fortunate to be so young and lovely. I'm sure you can overcome any little setback. You've been in Greece, haven't you?"

"Hello, Louisa."

She turned, laying a hand over her heart. "Why, Laura dear. I didn't see you there. What a delightful surprise."

Knowing the routine, Laura met her halfway and the women exchanged quick air kisses "You look wonderful."

"Oh, my professional mode." Louisa smoothed her jacket, under which her bosom was heaving happily in anticipation of gossip. "I so enjoy dabbling a few days a week in my little hobby. Real estate takes you into such interesting places, and you meet so many people. With Benedict so busy with his

151

practice and the children grown, I have to have something to do with my time.'' Those glinting eyes sharpened. ''I don't know how you manage, dear, with those two lovely children, all your charity work, the social whirl. I was just telling Barbara—you remember my daughter, Barbara—how amazing I thought you were. Managing all those committees and functions, raising two children. Especially now that you're going through such a trial. Divorce.'' She whispered it as though it were a dirty word. ''Such a heartbreak for everyone involved, isn't it? How are you bearing up, dear?''

''I'm fine.'' More out of desperation than manners, Laura tugged Kate forward. ''This is Kate Powell.''

''Nice to meet you.''

Kate didn't bother to tell her that they'd met at least half a dozen times before. Women like Louisa Metcalf never remembered her.

''Are you interested in the building, Laura?'' she continued. ''I understood that the caller was looking to rent, but if you're wanting an investment now that you're on your own, so to speak, this would be perfect for you. A woman alone needs to think about her future, don't you agree? The owner is willing to sell.''

''Actually, it's Margo who—''

''Oh, of course. I do beg your pardon.'' She pivoted toward Margo like a cannon bearing to aim from the top of a tank. ''Seeing an old friend again, you understand. And the two of you have been friends for years, haven't you? So nice you can be close by during our Laura's time of trouble. It's a wonderful building, isn't it? A clever location. You wouldn't have the least trouble finding a suitable tenant. And I can recommend a very reliable management company.''

Buy it? To own it. Margo had to swallow the saliva that pooled in her mouth. Afraid that Louisa might see the territorial light in her eyes, she turned away and wandered. ''I

152

haven't actually decided whether to rent or buy.'' She rolled her eyes gleefully at Kate and Laura. ''Who were the last tenants?''

''Oh, well, that was a bit unfortunate. Which is why the owner is considering selling out. It was a New Age shop. I don't understand that business myself, do you? Crystals and odd music and gongs. It came out that they were also selling drugs.'' She whispered the last word, as if saying it might addict her. ''Marijuana. Oh, my dear, I hope that doesn't upset you, with your recent troubles.''

Margo sent her an arch look. ''Not at all. Perhaps I could see upstairs.''

''Certainly. It's quite roomy. It's been used as a little apartment and has the most adorable doll's house of a kitchen, and of course the view.''

She picked her way back up, chattering about the delights of the building while the others trailed after her.

''You can't be serious,'' Kate hissed, grabbing Margo's arm. ''You couldn't afford the rent in this location, much less the purchase price.''

''Just shut up. I'm thinking.''

It was hard to think with Louisa's incessant chirping, so Margo shut it out. Shut out everything but sheer delight. It was roomy, surprisingly so. And if the banister circling the second level was shaky, so what? And the pentagram painted on the floor could be removed.

Maybe it was hot as a furnace, and the kitchen alcove was only big enough for one of the Seven Dwarfs. But there were quaint eyebrow windows peeking out, offering teasing glimpses of the sea.

''It has wonderful potential,'' Louisa went on. ''A bit of cosmetic work, some pretty paper or paint. Of course you know that property in this area rents by the square foot.'' She opened the briefcase she'd left on the narrow kitchen counter,

153

took out a file. "This building has six hundred and twenty-eight." She offered papers to Margo. "The owner has kept the rent very reasonable, considering. Of course, the utility fees are the responsibility of the tenant."

Kate turned on the tap, watched gray water sputter out. "And the repairs?"

"Oh, I'm sure something can be worked out there." Louisa dismissed Kate with a wave of her hand and a jangle of bracelets. "You'll want to look over the lease, of course. I don't want to pressure you, but I feel obliged to let you know we have another interested party coming through tomorrow. And once it's officially known that the building's for sale, well . . ." She let that lay, smiling. "I believe the asking price is only two hundred seventy-five thousand."

Margo felt her dream pop—an overinflated red balloon. "That's good to know." She managed a shrug, though her shoulders felt weighted. "As I said, I'm not sure if it's just what I'm looking for. I have several properties I'm considering."

Scanning the lease, she saw that Kate—damn her—had been right. Even the rent was well out of her reach. There had to be a way, she thought.

"I'll be in touch within a day or two." She smiled again, politely and dismissively. "Thank you so much, Mrs. Metcalf, for your time."

"Oh, no trouble at all. I so enjoy showing off places. Homes are more fun, of course. You've been living in Europe, haven't you? Terribly exciting for you. If you're thinking of buying a second home here in the area, I have the most fabulous ten-bedroom on Seventeen Mile. An absolute steal. The owners are in the middle of a vicious divorce, and . . . oh." She looked around to make a tittering apology to Laura, but her eyes continued to gleam. "She must have gone back downstairs. I wouldn't want to upset her by talking about divorce. Such a shame about her and Peter, isn't it?''

"Not really," Margo said dryly. "I think he's scum."

"Oh." Her color fluctuated. "You're just being loyal to your old friend, aren't you? Actually, no one could have been more surprised than I was when I heard they had separated. Just the most charming couple. He's so well mannered, so attractive and gentlemanly."

"Well, you know what they say about appearances? They lie. I think I'll just poke around for a bit longer, if you don't mind, Mrs. Metcalf." Firmly, Margo took her arm to lead her back to the stairs. "It might help me make up my mind if I spend a little time alone."

"Of course. Take all the time you like. Just lock the door behind you. I have the key. Oh, and let me give you my card. You be sure to call if you want to breeze through again, or if you'd like to see that wonderful house on Seventeen Mile."

"I certainly will." Margo didn't see either Kate or Laura on the first floor and kept marching Louisa toward the door.

"Oh, do tell Laura good-bye for me, won't you? And her young friend. I'm sure I'll see you and Laura at the club soon."

"Absolutely. 'Bye now. Thank you so much." Margo closed the door with a quick rattle. "And do be a stranger," she muttered. "Okay, where are you two hiding?"

"We're up here," Kate called out. "In the bathroom."

"Jesus, it's really tacky for two grown women to hide in a bathroom." Once she'd climbed the steps again, she found them. Laura sat on the edge of the old clawfoot tub with Kate facing her from her perch on the john. In any other setting, Margo would have said they were deep in some intense and serious discussion. "I really appreciate you leaving me alone with that nosy magpie."

"You wanted to do the talking," Kate reminded her.

"Nothing really to talk about." Discouraged, Margo joined Laura on the edge of the tub. "I could probably squeeze out the rent, if I didn't eat for the next six months. Which isn't that much of a problem. But I wouldn't have enough left over to handle the start-up costs. I want to buy it," she said with a sigh. "It's exactly what I'm looking for. There's just something about it that tells me I could be happy here."

"Maybe it's the leftover aroma of stale pot."

Margo sent Kate a withering look. "I only smoked it once when I was sixteen. And you had several hits yourself on that memorable evening."

"I didn't inhale," she said with a grin. "That's my story and I'm sticking to it."

"Then explain why you claimed you were doing a *pas de deux* with Baryshnikov."

"I have no recollection of that event—and he told me to call him Misha."

"It's a damn good thing I only wheedled two joints out of Biff." Margo blew out a breath. "Well, this, unfortunately, is reality. I can't afford this place."

"I can," Laura said.

"What do you mean, you can?"

"I mean I can buy it, and I can rent it to you, and we'll be in business."

Margo nearly threw her arms around Laura before sanity, and pride, prevailed. "Oh, no. I'm not starting off this next section of my life that way." She dug in her bag for a cigarette, lighted it with a violent flick. "You're not bailing me out. No one's bailing me out. Not this time."

"Tell her what you told me, Kate, when I suggested it."

"Okay. First I asked her if she was out of her mind. Not that I don't think you couldn't pull off this plan of yours, Margo, but I don't think you can pull it off."

Eyes narrowed, Margo huffed out smoke. "Thanks so much."

"It's an admirable idea," Kate soothed. "But starting a new business is a risky venture at any time, with anyone. The vast majority go tits up in the first year. Basic economics, even if the people have some training and education in retail. Not to mention that Monterey and Carmel are already lousy with gift shops and boutiques. But," Kate continued, holding up a hand before Margo could snarl at her, "some succeed, even thrive. Now, putting your part of it aside for the moment, we look at Laura's current situation. Having been married at the ridiculous age of eighteen, she's never invested on her own. There is the Templeton organization, of course, in which she shares. But she has no personal, individual stocks, bonds, or property beyond her interest in Templeton. As she's just filed for divorce, and is solvent financially, it makes good economic sense for her to seek investments."

"I've never bought anything on my own," Laura interrupted. "Never owned anything that wasn't through the family or with Peter. And when I was looking around this place, I thought, why not? Why shouldn't I buy it? Why shouldn't I take a gamble on myself? On us."

"Because if I screw it up—"

"You won't. You've got something to prove here, don't you, Margo?"

"All right, yes, but it doesn't include taking you down with me."

"Listen to me." Eyes serious and soft, Laura laid a hand on Margo's knee. "All my life I've done what I was told, taken the quiet, well-tended path. Now I'm going to do something just for the hell of it." She felt a giddy little thrill at the thought. "I'm buying this building, Margo, whether you want a piece of it or not."

Margo took a deep gulp, discovered it wasn't pride she was

swallowing. It was excitement. "So, how much are you going to gouge out of me for rent?"

The first shock came at the bank. A cashier's check for ten percent of the asking price was Kate's advice, not only to nail down a contract but to help negotiate that price down by twenty-five thousand.

The money wasn't there.

"There must be some mistake. I should have at least twice this amount liquid."

"Just a moment, please, Mrs. Ridgeway." The teller hurried off while Laura tapped her fingers.

As a sick feeling began to stir in her gut, Margo laid a hand on her shoulder. "Laura, this is a joint account with Peter?"

"Sure. We use it primarily as a checking account, to run the household. I'm taking out less than half, so there shouldn't be a problem. We're a community property state. My lawyer explained all of that."

The vice president of the bank came out into the lobby, shook her hand. "Laura, would you come back to my office for a moment."

"Frank, I'm in kind of a hurry. I just need a cashier's check."

"Just for a moment." He slipped an arm around her shoulders.

Margo gritted her teeth as Laura was guided away. "You know what that bastard did?"

"Yeah. Yeah, I do." Furious, Kate pressed her fingers to her eyes. "I should have thought of it. Christ, I should have known. It's all happened so fast."

"They'd have money scattered around, wouldn't they? In another bank. Stocks, bonds, a portfolio through a broker."

"They'd have to. Laura might have let Peter take over the finances, but neither of them is foolish enough to put all their

158

eggs in one basket. And there's the insurance limit on funds in a bank. This is a drop in the bucket.'' But she had a sick feeling. "Shit. He never let me near their books. Here she comes," Kate muttered. "Goddamn it, it's all over her face."

"Peter cleaned out the account." Face pale, eyes dazed, Laura headed for the doors. "The morning after I found him in bed with his secretary, he came in here and took out all but a couple of thousand." She had to stop, press a hand to her stomach. "We had started little savings accounts for the girls, so they could put money in themselves. He took that, too. He took their money."

"Let's find a place to sit down," Margo murmured.

"No. No, I have to make calls. I have to contact the broker. I don't even know his name." She covered her face with her hands and tried to breathe. "So stupid. So stupid."

"You're not stupid," Kate said furiously. "We're going home. We'll find the numbers and we'll call. We'll arrange to have the rest of your assets frozen."

There wasn't much to freeze.

"Fifty thousand." Kate sat back, slipped off her reading glasses, and rubbed her eyes. "Well, it was damn generous of him to leave you that much. From what I can figure, that's about five percent of your joint holdings." Thoughtfully, she unrolled her package of Tums. "The good news is he wasn't able to touch your stock in Templeton and he doesn't have any claim on the house."

"Their college funds," Laura said weakly. "He closed Ali's and Kayla's college funds. How could money have meant so much to him?"

"Money's probably only part of it. He's teaching you a lesson." Margo poured another glass of wine. It might help them all to be a little drunk. "And he got away with it because you'd never have thought of doing the same thing. I would

159

have, but I wasn't thinking at all. Maybe your lawyer can get some of it back.''

"Odds are it's all tucked away in the Caymans by now." Kate shook her head in disgust. "The way it looks, he's been busily transferring stock and cash and mutuals out of your joint accounts into a personal one for quite a while. He just made a quick final sweep.'' She bit her tongue before she could chastise Laura for signing anything Peter had handed her. ''But you've got the paperwork, copies of the transactions and withdrawals, so you'll be able to fight when you get to court.''

Laura sat back, closed her eyes. "I'm not fighting him for money. He can have it. Every lousy penny.''

"The hell with that,'' Margo erupted.

"No, the hell with him. The divorce is going to be hard enough on the girls without the two of us battling over dollars and cents in court. I've still got fifty thousand cash—which is a lot more than most women start with. He can't touch the house because it's in my parents' name."

She picked up her glass but didn't drink. "I'm the one who was stupid enough to sign whatever he put in front of me without questioning him. I deserved to get fleeced.''

"You've got the Templeton stock,'' Kate reminded her. "You could sell part of your shares."

"I'm not touching the family stock. It's a legacy."

"Laura." To calm her, Kate laid a hand on Laura's. "I'm not saying to put the stock on the market. Either Josh or your parents would buy it, or margin you a loan against it until everything's sorted out.''

"No." Closing her eyes, Laura willed herself to settle down. "I'm not running to them." She drew in a deep breath and opened her eyes again. "And neither is either of you. I made the mistakes, I'll fix the mistakes. Kate, I need you to figure out how to liquidate enough money for the deposit on the building.''

"No way you're going to take more than half of what you have left in cash and buy that place.''

She smiled thinly at Margo. "Yes, I am. Oh, yes, I am. I'm still a Templeton. It's time I started to act like one.'' Before she could change her mind, she picked up the business card Margo had tossed on the table and dialed the phone. "Louisa, it's Laura Templeton. Yes, that's right. I want to make an offer on the building we looked at this afternoon.''

When she hung up, she pulled off her wedding and engagement rings. Guilt and liberation twisted inside her. "You're the expert, Margo. How much can I expect to get for these?''

Margo eyed the five-carat round-cut and the band with sparkling channel-set diamonds. At least, she mused, there was some small justice in the world. "Kate, don't worry about liquidating anything. It looks like we got the down payment out of Peter after all.''

Later that night Margo sat in her room scribbling figures, drawing rough sketches, making lists. She needed to think about paint and paper and plumbing. The shop space had to be remodeled to include a dressing room, and that meant carpenters.

She could move in on the top floor as it was, which would save her the drive down to Monterey every day to check on progress. In fact, she could cut corners if she painted it herself rather than hiring professionals.

How hard could it be to roll paint on a wall?

"Yes, come in,'' she called at the knock on her door and wondered if carpenters charged by the hour or the job.

"Margo?''

Distracted, she glanced up, blinked at her mother. "Oh. I thought it was one of the girls.''

"It's nearly midnight. They're sleeping."

"I lost track of the time." She pushed at the papers scattered over the bed.

"You always did. Daydreaming." Ann skimmed her gaze over the papers, amused at the numbers her daughter had added and subtracted. It had taken bribes and threats and shouts to get Margo to do the simplest arithmetic homework when she was a child. "You forgot to carry the five," Ann said.

"Oh. Well." Margo shoved the paper aside. "I really need one of those little calculators Kate's always got in her pocket."

"I was talking to Miss Kate before she left. She said you're going into business."

"And that's laughable for someone who doesn't remember to carry the five." Margo pushed herself off the bed and picked up the wineglass she'd brought up with her. "Would you like a drink, Mum, or are you still on duty?"

Saying nothing, Ann moved into the adjoining bath and came out with a tumbler. She poured wine. "Miss Kate thinks you've thought it through fairly well, and though the odds are against you, it may work."

"Kate's always so blindly optimistic."

"She's a sensible woman, and she's given me fine financial advice over the years."

"Kate's your accountant?" With a little laugh, Margo sat again. "I should have known."

"You'd be wise to use her services if you go through with this business of yours."

"I'm going through with this business of mine." Prepared to see doubt and derision on her mother's face, Margo flicked her eyes up. "Number one, I don't have many options. Number two, selling things people don't need is what I do best. And number three, Laura's counting on me."

"Those are three good reasons." There was nothing on Ann's face but a small, enigmatic smile. "Miss Laura is footing the bill."

"I didn't ask her," Margo said, stung. "I didn't want her to. She got the idea in her head to buy the building, and there was no shaking it out." When Ann remained silent, Margo crumpled up a sheet of paper and heaved it. "Damn it, I'm putting everything I have into this. Everything I own, everything I worked for. It's not a lot of cash, but it's everything I have."

"Money's not so important as time and effort."

"It's pretty damn important right now. We don't have a lot to start with."

Nodding as she wandered about, looking for something to straighten, Ann considered. "Miss Kate told me what Mr. Ridgeway has done." Ann took a long, deep gulp of wine. "The cold, blackhearted bastard should rot in everlasting hell. Please God."

With a laugh, Margo lifted her glass. "Finally, something we can agree on. I'll drink to it."

"Miss Laura believes in you, and Miss Kate, too, in her fashion."

"But you don't," Margo countered.

"I know you—you'll make some fancy place out of it, where people with no sense at all will come and toss their money around."

"That's the idea. I've even got a name for it. 'Pretenses.' " Margo's laugh was quick and amused. "It suits me, doesn't it?"

"That it does. You're doing this here in California to be with Miss Laura."

"She needs me."

"Yes, she does." Ann looked down into her glass. "I said some things the night you came back that I'm sorry for. I was hard on you, maybe I've always been. But you were wrong when you said I wanted you to be like Miss Laura or Miss Kate. Perhaps I wanted you to be what I could understand, and you couldn't do that.''

"We were both tired and upset." Margo shifted on the bed, not quite sure how to handle an apology from her mother. "I don't expect you to understand this whole idea about a shop, but I hope you'll believe I'm going to try to make something real out of it."

"Your aunt ran a trinket shop in Cork. You've some merchant in your blood." Ann moved her shoulders, her decision made. "It will cost considerable, I imagine."

In agreement, Margo indicated her papers. "I just have to rob Peter to pay Paul for a while. It would help if I could sell my soul. If I still have one to sell."

"I'd feel better if you kept it." Ann reached into the pocket of her skirt, took out an envelope. "Use this instead."

Curious, Margo took the envelope, opened it, then dropped it on the bed as if it had sprouted fangs and bitten her. "It's a brokerage account."

"That's right. Miss Kate recommended the firm. Very conservative investments, as I prefer. But they've done well enough."

"It's almost two hundred thousand dollars. I won't take your savings. I can do this on my own."

"I'm pleased to hear you say so, but it's not my savings in there. It's yours."

"I don't have any savings. Hasn't that been the problem all along?"

"You could never hold on to a penny in a clutched fist. You sent me money, and I banked it for you."

A little amazed, Margo stared down at the brokerage statement. Had she sent so much, had so much to send? It had seemed so little at the time. "I sent the money for you."

"I had no need for it, did I?" Brow arched, Ann angled her head. It pleased her to see the pride in her daughter's face. "I have a good job, a fine roof over my head, enough for a nice vacation twice a year because Miss Laura insists I need it. So the money you sent I banked. And there it is."

Ann took another sip of wine because that wasn't how she'd meant to say it. "Listen to me, Margo, for once. The fact that you did send the money was appreciated. Perhaps I'd have gotten sick and unable to work and needed it. But that didn't happen. Sending it was a loving thing to do."

"No, it wasn't." It shamed her as much to know it as to admit it. "I did it out of pride. I did it to show you I was successful, important. That you were wrong about me."

Understanding, Ann inclined her head. "There's not so much of a difference, and the result's the same. It was your money, and it still is. I had the comfort that you thought to send it, that you had it to send. You'd have frittered it away if you hadn't passed it to me, so we've done each other a favor." She reached out to stroke Margo's hair, then, faintly embarrassed by the show of affection, dropped her hand back to her side. "Now take it and do something with it."

When Margo said nothing, Ann clucked her tongue. She set down her glass, then cupped Margo's chin in her palm. "Why are you so contrary, girl? Did you earn the money with honest work or not?"

"Yes, but—"

"Do what your mum tells you for once. You might be surprised to find she's right. Go into this business venture on equal terms with Miss Laura, and take pride in that. Now clean up this mess you've made before you go to bed."

"Mum." Margo picked up the papers as her mother paused at the door. "Why didn't you send this to me in Milan when you knew I was scraping bottom?"

"Because you weren't ready for it. Be sure you are now."

Chapter Ten

Mine. Holding out her arms, Margo circled the empty main room of the shop on Cannery Row. Technically it wasn't hers quite yet. Settlement was still two weeks away, but the offer had been accepted, the contract signed. And the loan, with the Templeton name behind it, had gone off without a hitch.

She'd already had a contractor in to discuss alterations. It was going to cost big, and in her new frugal fashion she had indeed decided to do the simple cosmetic improvements herself. Research was under way on the rental of floor sanders, the purchase of caulking guns. She'd even looked into something wonderful called a paint sprayer. More coverage, faster. More efficient.

And the building wouldn't actually be hers, she reminded herself. It would be theirs. Hers, Laura's, and the bank's. But in two weeks' time, she would be sleeping in that little room upstairs. In a sleeping bag if need be.

Then by midsummer, the doors of Pretenses would open.

And the rest, she thought with a laugh, would be history.

She turned at the tap on the glass and saw Kate.

"Hey, open up, will you? I'm on my lunch hour. Thought I'd find you here gloating," she said when Margo opened the door. "It still smells," she added after a testing sniff.

"What do you want, Kate? I'm busy."

Kate studied the clipboard and the pocket calculator on the floor. "Did you figure out how to work that thing?"

"You don't have to be a CPA to use a calculator."

"I meant the clipboard."

"Ha ha."

"You know, the place grows on you." Hands tucked in her trouser pockets, Kate wandered. "It's a nice busy area, too. Should pull in some walk-in traffic. And people on vacation are always buying things they don't have any use for. The secondhand clothes, though. Everything's going to be a size eight."

"I've already thought of that. I'm working on some other stock. I know a lot of people who ditch their wardrobes every year."

"Smart people buy classics—seasonless classics—then they don't have to worry."

"How many navy blue blazers do you own, Kate?"

"Half a dozen," she said and grinned, then thumbed a Tums out of the roll in her pocket. Her idea of lunch. "But that's just me. Here's the deal, Margo. I want in."

"In what?"

"In on the building." She popped the antacid, crunched it. "I've got some money to invest, and I don't see why you and Laura should have all the fun."

"We don't need a partner."

"Sure you do. You need someone who knows the difference between black ink and red." Bending down, she scooped up the calculator and began to run figures. "You and Laura put in twelve-five apiece, cash. Now you'll have the settlement costs, points, insurance, taxes. Which should bring it up to somewhere around, oh, eighteen each, which makes it thirty-six." Taking glasses out of her breast pocket, she put them on as she continued to work. "Divide that by three, and it makes twelve each, which is less than you've already shelled out."

She paced as she cleared figures, added more. "Now, you've got repairs, remodeling, maintenance, utilities, business license fees, more taxes, bookkeeping—I can set the books up for you, but I don't have time to take on another client right now so you'll have to hire someone or learn to add."

"I can already add," Margo said, stung.

Kate merely took out a small electronic memo and entered a reminder to herself to earmark time to give Margo a course in basic bookkeeping. The cellular phone in her briefcase rang, and she ignored it. Her service would have to deal with that until her current business was concluded.

"There's the overhead for shopping bags, tissue paper, boxes, cash register tape," she continued. "That'll bump things back up into six figures in no time. You'll have fees to the credit card companies since your clientele will be using primarily plastic." Tipping the glasses down, she peered at Margo over the tops. "You do intend to accept all major credit cards, don't you?"

"I—"

"See, you need me." Satisfied, she bumped up the glasses again. No joint venture between Laura and Margo was going to exclude her, no matter how many funds she had to juggle. "Of course, I'll just be a silent partner, as I'm the only one of the three of us who has a real job."

Margo narrowed her eyes. "How silent?"

"Oh, just a peep now and then." All the practicalities were already ordered in her tidy mind. "You'll have to figure out how and when to replace your stock once it starts to sell, what your markup percentage needs to be to ensure your profit margin. Oh, then there's legal fees. But we can talk Josh into handling that. How did you get him to let you use his Jag? That is his new Jag out front, isn't it?"

Margo's expression turned smug. "You could say I'm test-driving it."

Lifting her brows, Kate slipped her glasses off and back into her pocket. "Are you test-driving him?"

"Not yet."

"Interesting. I'll write you a check for the twelve thousand. We'll have a partnership agreement drawn up."

"A partnership agreement."

"Jesus, you do need me." She caught Margo by the shoulders and kissed her dead on the lips. "The three of us love each other, trust each other. But you've got to make a business legal. Right now the stock is all yours, but—"

"Laura's added to it," Margo interrupted, and wicked humor glinted. "We're selling everything in Peter's office."

"Good start. How's she holding up?"

"Pretty well. She's worried about Ali. The kid took it hard when Peter didn't show up for her ballet recital. Word is he's in Aruba."

"I hope he drowns. Nope, I hope he gets eaten by sharks and then drowns. I'll get over to the house this weekend and spend some time with the girls." She took out a check, already written and signed. "There you go, partner. I've got to get back."

"We haven't cleared this with Laura."

"I did," Kate said breezily, as she opened the door and plowed into Josh. "Hi." She kissed him. "Bye."

"Nice to see you too," he called after her, then cautiously closed the door.

Laura had warned him not to expect much. It was a good thing. "Have you and Kate been smoking grass in here?"

"That's all she ever does on her lunch hour. We really have to get her into a program." Thrilled with herself, Margo spread her arms. "So, what do you think?"

"Uh-huh. It's a building, all right."

"Josh."

"Give me a minute." He walked past her into the adjoining room, came back, looked into the bath, gazed up the pretty, and potentially lethal, staircase. He wiggled the banister, winced. "Want a lawyer?"

"We're going to have that fixed."

"I don't suppose it occurred to you that sometimes dipping your toe in is smarter than diving headfirst."

"It's not as much fun."

"Well, duchess, I'm sure you could have done worse." He walked over, lifted her pouting face to his. "Let's just get this out of the way, shall we? I've been thinking about it across two continents."

He pulled her close, covered her mouth greedily with his. After a moment of token disinterest, she let herself melt into a kiss that tasted of frustrated lust. So unexpected. So thrilling, the way his mouth fit on hers, the way all those hard lines and planes of his body met and meshed so perfectly with the curves of hers.

It didn't give her time to think whether it was simply that she had missed that glorious sensation of being held by a man, or if it was Josh. But because it was Josh, she needed to think.

"I don't know how I missed how potent you were all these years." She drew away, flashed a quick, teasing smile.

His system was straining like an engine revved too high.

"That was just a free sample. Come back here and we'll go for the full treatment."

"I think we'll take it in stages." She walked away, opened her bag, and took out a pack of cigarettes. Her elegant case was already boxed into inventory. "I'm learning to be a cautious woman."

"Cautious." He scanned the room again. "Which is how you got from renting a little shop in Milan to clear your debts and make a reasonable living to buying a building on Cannery Row and adding to those debts."

"Well, I can't change overnight, can I?" She eyed him through a haze of smoke. "You're not going to get all lawyerly on me, are you, Josh?"

"Actually I am." He picked up the briefcase he'd set aside, opened it. "I have some papers for you." He looked around for a place to sit and settled on the bottom step of the staircase. "Come here. Come here," he repeated and patted the narrow space beside him. "I can manage to keep my hands off you."

She picked up a little tin ashtray and joined him. "I'm getting good at papers. I'm thinking of buying a file cabinet."

He didn't sigh. It wouldn't have made any difference. "Is your Italian good enough to wade through this?"

She frowned at the papers he offered. "It's a contract of sale on my flat." Emotions whirled up inside her, regret warring with relief. "You work fast," she murmured.

"It's a very decent offer." He tucked her hair behind her ear. "Are you sure it's what you want?"

"It's the way it is. Reality doesn't always chew well, but I'm trying to acquire a taste." She closed her eyes and leaned her head on his shoulder. "Just let me feel sorry for myself a minute."

"You're entitled."

"Self-pity's a bad habit of mine. It's hard to shake. Damn it, Josh, I loved that place. Sometimes I'd just stand on the

171

terrace and think: Look where you are, Margo. Look who you are.''

"Well, now you're someplace else.'' It wasn't sympathy she needed, he decided, but a good boot in the butt. "And you look the same to me.''

"It's not the same. It's never going to be the same again.''

"Toughen up, Margo. You're starting to wallow in it.''

She jerked up. "Easy for you to say. Joshua Conway Templeton, the bright star of the Templeton empire. You never lost anything. You never groped your way sweating to get a grip on something everyone told you you couldn't have. No one ever told you you couldn't have anything and everything you wanted.''

"That's the breaks, isn't it?'' he said easily. "You played, duchess, and you lost. Whining about it isn't going to change a thing, and it's very unattractive.''

"Thanks so much for your support.'' Fuming, she snatched the contract out of his hand. "When do I get the money?''

"There's time, and there's Italian time. If you're lucky, you may have it settled in sixty days. The bottom line's on the next page.''

He watched her flip it over. Her eyes were hot as they skimmed down, the heat clouded with distress. "That's it?''

"You didn't have a lot of equity built up. The bank gets theirs first, then the government takes its share.''

"It's better than a stick in the eye,'' she muttered. "Barely.''

"I drew on your account to square your American Express bill. I don't suppose it occurred to you to fly back here coach.'' When she only stared coolly, he shook his head. "I don't know why I said that. You're back under the max on your Visa card, but I'd go easy on it. After you distribute the net from the sale of the flat, you'll only be about a hundred and fifty thousand in the hole, excluding interest and penalties.''

172

"Pin money," she said dryly.

"You shouldn't plan on buying any pins for a while. Now, as your representative, I'm willing to clear your debts, and assist you in dealing with any you incur while initiating your business. You got a name for this place yet?"

"Pretenses," she said between her teeth as he flipped out more papers.

"Perfect. I've drawn up the necessary agreements."

"Have you?" she said slowly. "In triplicate?"

Warned by the tone, he looked up, met her icy stare equally. "Naturally."

"And just what would I be agreeing to, Counselor Templeton?"

"To pay back this personal loan in regular installments beginning six months after the date of signing. That gives you some breathing space. You also agree to live within your means during the term of the loan."

"I see. And what are my means, in your legal opinion?"

"I've worked up a budget for personal expenses. Food, lodging, medical."

"A budget?"

He'd expected an explosion. Even, perversely, hoped for one. Margo's tantrums were always so . . . stimulating. It didn't appear that he was going to be disappointed.

"A budget?" she repeated, storming to him. "Of all the unbelievable, bloody nerve. You arrogant son of a bitch. Do you think I'm going to stand here and let you treat me like some sort of brainless bimbo who needs to be told how much she can spend on face powder?"

"Face powder." Deliberately, he scanned the papers, took a pen out of his pocket, and made a quick note. "That would come under 'Miscellaneous Luxuries.' I think I've been very generous there. Now, as to your clothing allowance—"

"Allowance!" She used both hands to shove him back a

173

step. "Just let me tell you what you can do with your fucking allowance."

"Careful, duchess." He brushed the front of his shirt. "Turnbill and Asser."

The strangled sound in her throat was the best she could do. If there had been anything, anything at all to throw, she'd have heaved it at his head. "I'd rather be picked apart, alive, by vultures than let you handle my money."

"You don't have any money," he began, but she barreled on as she whirled around the room. Watching her, he all but salivated.

"I'd rather be gang-raped by midgets, staked naked to a wasp nest, be force-fed garden slugs."

"Go three weeks without a manicure?" he put in and watched her hands curl into claws. "You go after my face with those, I'll have to hurt you."

"Oh, I hate you."

"No, you don't." He moved very fast. One instant he was leaning lazily on the wobbly banister and the next he'd flashed out, grabbed her. He took a moment to enjoy the dark fury on her face, the lethal glint in her eyes, before he crushed her snarling mouth under his. It was like kissing a lightning bolt— that heat, the jolt of deadly power, the sizzling sting of fury.

He knew that when he finally got her into bed, it would be a full-blown storm.

She didn't resist. That would have given him too much satisfaction. Instead, she met him force for force and pleased herself. Until they both stepped back, gasping.

"I can enjoy that and still hate you." She tossed her hair back. "And I can make you pay for it."

Maybe she could. There were women in the world who had the innate gift of knowing just how to make a man suffer and burn and beg. All of them could have taken lessons from Margo Sullivan. But he wasn't fool enough to let her know it. He walked back to the stairs, picked up the papers.

"Just so we know where we stand, darling."

"I'll tell you just where we stand, *darling*. I don't need your insulting offer. I'm running my life my way."

"And that's been such a rousing success so far."

"I know what I'm doing. Take that ridiculous smirk off your face."

"I can't. It sticks there every time you say you know what you're doing." But he tucked all the papers back in his brief-case, closed it. "I'll say this, I don't think it's an entirely moronic idea—this place."

"Well, I'll sleep easy now, knowing I have your approval."

"Approval's a little strong. It's more like hopeful resignation." He gave the banister a last wiggle. "But I believe in you, Margo."

Temper died into confusion. "Damn you, Josh. I can't keep up with you."

"Good." He strolled over, flicked a finger down her cheek. "I think you're going to make something out of this shop that'll surprise everyone. Especially you." He leaned down, and when he kissed her this time it was light and friendly. "Got cab fare?"

"Excuse me?"

Grinning, he pulled keys out of his pocket. "Fortunately, I had a spare set to the Jag. Don't work too late, duchess."

She didn't smile until he was well out of sight. Then she gathered up her bag, her clipboard. She was going to put her newly healed Visa card to use and buy a paint sprayer.

It took Josh less than two weeks at Templeton Monterey to fine-tune his strategy for dealing with Peter Ridgeway. He had already made it clear with a single phone call from Stockholm that it would be best for his brother-in-law, personally and professionally, to take a brief leave of absence from Templeton.

175

Until, as he'd put it, all reason and bonhomie, they'd gotten this little domestic matter ironed out.

He had always steered clear of his sister's marriage. As a bachelor, he hardly felt that he qualified to hand out marital advice. And as he adored his sister, and had mildly despised her husband, he'd also had to consider the indisputable fact that his advice would have been heavily one-sided.

Since Peter had always performed well as a Templeton executive, there'd been no cause for complaint there. He was, perhaps, a bit rigid in his view of hotel management, more than a bit distant from the staff and the day-to-day problems and triumphs, but he'd had a fine hand with the corporate groups and foreign businesses that poured money into Templeton coffers.

Still, there came a time when professional efficiency had to be weighed against personal disgust. Because nobody, but nobody, messed with Joshua Templeton's family and walked away whole.

He'd considered taking the corporate route, simply amputating Peter from any connection with Templeton hotels and using his connections and influence to see to it that the son of a bitch never managed so much as a roadside motel in Kansas.

But that was so easy, so . . . bloodless.

He agreed with Kate that the sensible route, and the most straightforward, was to—in Kate's words—drag Ridgeway's sorry flat ass into court. Josh knew a half a dozen top family lawyers who would rub their hands together in glee at the prospect of nailing the greedy, adulterous husband who had cleaned out his own daughters' little savings accounts.

Oh, that would be sweet, Josh mused as he drew in the early-morning scents of sea and oleander blossoms. But it would also be a painful and public humiliation for Laura. And again, he thought, bloodless.

Still, such matters were best handled in a civilized fashion.

Josh decided the most civilized place to balance the scales was the country club. So he waited, patient as a cat, for Peter to return to California.

Peter accepted his invitation for a morning set of tennis without hesitation. Josh had expected no less. He imagined Peter calculated that being seen exchanging lobs with his brother-in-law would quell some of the rumors over Peter's position with Templeton.

Josh was happy to oblige him.

Golf was Peter's game, but he considered himself a fair hand at the net. He'd dressed for the match in spotless whites, his shorts pressed with lethal pleats. Josh wore a similar uniform, if slightly less formal, with the addition of a Dodgers fielder's cap to shade his eyes from the dazzling morning sun.

Later, Minn Whiley and DeLoris Solmes, who'd been playing their regular Tuesday morning set on the adjoining court, would sip after-match mimosas and comment on what a picture the men had made, golden and bronzed and fit, muscular legs pumping as they thwacked the bright yellow ball back and forth.

Of course, Minn would tell Sarah Metzenbaugh after she joined them for a steam, that had been before The Incident.

"I don't take time to do this often enough," Peter commented as they unzipped their rackets. "Eighteen holes of golf twice a week is all I can squeeze in."

"All work and no play," Josh said affably, and didn't miss Peter's smirk of disdain. He knew exactly what Ridgeway thought of him. The pampered golden boy who spent all his time jetting from party to party. "I feel deprived if I don't get at least one decent set in every morning."

Taking his time, Josh set out a bottle of Evian. "I'm glad you could manage to meet me. I'm sure that between us we can straighten this uncomfortable business out. You're staying at the resort now that you're back from Aruba?"

177

"It seemed best. I'd hoped that if I gave Laura a little time and space she'd see reason. Women." He spread his elegant hands, uncluttered now by the gold band of his marriage. "Difficult creatures."

"Tell me about it. Let's warm up." Josh took his place behind the line, waited for Peter to set. "Volley for serve," he called out and hit the ball easily. "How was Aruba?"

"Restful." Peter returned, pacing himself. "Our hotel there has a few kinks. It should be looked into."

"Really?" Josh had done a complete check on it less than eight months before and knew it ran brilliantly. "I'll make a note of that." Deliberately he fumbled a backhand, sending it wide of the line. "Rusty," he said with a shake of his head. "Your serve. Tell me, Peter, do you plan to contest the divorce?"

"If Laura insists on going through with it, I hardly see the point. It would only add fuel to the gossip. She's dissatisfied with my responsibilities to Templeton. A woman like Laura doesn't understand the demands of business."

"Or a man's relationship with his secretary." Teeth flashing in a feral grin, Josh sent the ball whizzing by Peter's ear.

"She misinterpreted a situation. My point." Testing a fresh ball, Peter shook his head. "Frankly, Josh, she'd become unreasonably jealous over the time it was necessary for me to spend at the office. I'm sure you're aware of the recent influx of conventions, and the ten-day visit last month of Lord and Lady Wilhelm. They took two floors and the presidential suite. We couldn't offer them less than perfection."

"Naturally not. And Laura didn't understand the pressure you were under to deliver." She'd only been nursed at the breast of the grande dame of hoteliers.

"Exactly." Puffing a little as Josh mercilessly worked him cross court, Peter missed the return. "It only got worse when that ridiculous, foulmouthed Margo showed up on the doorstep. Naturally, Laura would take her in without a thought to the consequences.''

''Softhearted, our Laura,'' Josh said easily, and let the conversation lag until he'd taken the first set 5–3.

''It wasn't exactly gallant, old man, cleaning out the bank accounts.''

Peter's lips hardened. He'd expected Laura to have more pride than to go whining to her brother. ''On my lawyer's advice. Simple self-preservation, as she had no sense about finances. The move has certainly been justified now that she's proved her lack of sense by going into partnership with Margo Sullivan. Shopkeepers, for God's sake.''

''As bad as innkeepers,'' Josh murmured.

''What was that?''

''I said who knows what puts ideas in a woman's head.''

''She'll have lost her capital within six months—if Margo doesn't abscond with it before that. You should have tried to talk her out of the whole insane notion.''

''Oh, who listens to me?'' He thought about letting Peter win the second set, then decided he was bored and wanted it over. He played it out for a while and, just to make it interesting, allowed Peter to break his serve.

''Bad luck.'' The pleasure of beating his brother-in-law at his own game pumped through Peter's blood like fine wine. ''You'll have to work on your backhand.''

''Mmm.'' Josh jogged to the sideline, mopped his face, glugged down Evian. As he recapped the bottle, he flashed a smile toward the women in the next court. He was darkly pleased at the idea of an audience for the show he had in mind. ''Oh, before I forget, I've been doing some spot-checking at the hotel. There's been an unusual number of staff turnovers in the last eighteen months.''

Peter arched a brow. ''It isn't necessary for you to involve yourself with Templeton Monterey, or the resort. That's my territory.''

''Oh, don't mean to trespass, but I was here, and you weren't.'' He tossed his towel aside, plunked the plastic bottle onto it, then went back behind the net. ''It's odd, though. Templeton has a tradition of long-term employee loyalty.''

Interfering bastard, pampered fool, Peter thought, carefully controlling his temper as he walked in the opposite direction. ''As you can see if you read the reports, lower management made several errors of judgment in hiring. Weeding out was necessary to continue our standard of service and appearance.''

''I'm sure you're right.''

''I'll be back at the helm tomorrow, so there's no need to concern yourself.''

''Not concerned at all. Just curious. Your serve, isn't it?'' Josh's smile was as lazy as a nap in a hammock.

They resumed play. Peter faulted his first serve, then bore down on his irritation and slammed the next cleanly. Biding his time, Josh entertained himself by bouncing Peter back and forth across the court, forcing him to dig and pump. Barely winded himself, he kept up a steady flow of conversation as he took the next game, forty-love.

''I noticed a few other things while I was fiddling around. Your expense account, for instance. Seventy-five thousand in the last five months for client entertainment.''

Sweat dripped into Peter's eyes, infuriating him. ''My expense account records have never been questioned in the fifteen years I've worked for Templeton.''

''Of course not.'' All easy smiles, Josh gathered balls in preparation for the next game. ''You've been married to my sister for two-thirds of that time. Oh, and there was that bonus to your secretary.'' Idly, he bounced a ball on the heart of his racket. ''The one you were fucking. Ten thousand's very gen-

180

erous. She must make a hell of a cup of coffee.''

Stopping, bending with his hands on his knees to catch his breath, Peter squinted over the net. ''Bonuses and financial incentives are Templeton policy. And I don't appreciate your innuendos.''

''That wasn't an innuendo, Peter. Listen up. It was a statement.''

''And a pathetically hypocritical one coming from you. Everyone knows how you spend your time, and the family money. Cars and women and gambling.''

''You're right about that.'' With a friendly smile, Josh stepped behind the serving line, bounced the ball lightly. ''And you could say it was hypocritical of me even to mention it.'' He tossed the ball up as if to serve, then caught it, scratched his head. ''Except for one little detail. No, no, it would be two really minor details. One, it's my money, and two, I'm not married.''

He tossed the ball up, swung and served an ace. Straight into Peter's nose. As Peter dropped to his knees, blood gushing out from between his fingers, Josh strolled over, twirling his racket.

''And three, it's my sister you're fucking with.''

''You son of a bitch.'' Peter's voice was muffled and thick and breathless with pain. ''You crazy bastard, you've broken my nose.''

''Be grateful I didn't aim for your balls.'' Crouching down, Josh jerked Peter up by the collar of his blood-splattered Polo. ''Now listen to me,'' he murmured while the women on the next court squealed and shouted for the tennis pro. ''And listen carefully because I'm only going to say this once.''

There were stars wheeling in front of Peter's eyes, nausea welling in his stomach. ''Get your damn hands off of me.''

''You're not listening,'' Josh said quietly. ''And you really want to pay close attention here. Don't you even speak my sister's name in public. If I decide you've so much as had a thought about her I don't like, you'll pay with more than your nose. And if you ever talk about Margo again the way you've talked about her to me, I'll twist off your nuts and feed them to you."

"I'll sue you, you bastard." Pain radiated through his face like sunbursts; humiliation darted after it. "I'll sue you for assault."

"Oh, please do. Meanwhile, I suggest you take another trip. Go back to Aruba, or try St. Bart's, or go to hell. But I don't want to see you anywhere near me or mine." He let Peter go in disgust and as an afterthought wiped his blood-smeared hand on the front of Peter's shirt. "Oh, and by the way, you're fired. That's game, set, and fucking match."

Well satisfied with the morning's work, he decided to treat himself to a steam.

Chapter Eleven

Miracles could happen, Margo thought. They only took six weeks, aching muscles, and somewhere in the neighborhood of three hundred and fifty thousand dollars to create.

Six weeks before, she had become the official one-third owner of the empty building on Cannery Row. Immediately after glasses of Templeton sparkling wine had been passed around, she'd rolled up her sleeves.

It was a new experience, dealing with contractors, surrounding herself with the sounds of saws and hammers and men with tool belts. She spent nearly every waking moment of those weeks in the shop or on shop business. The clerks at the supply stores began to weep with joy when she walked through the door. Her carpenters learned to tolerate her.

She debated paint samples with Laura, agonized over the choice between Dusty Rose and Desert Mauve until the slight variance in shades became a decision of monumental proportion. Recessed lighting became an obsession for days. She learned the joy and terror of hardware, spending hours picking through hinges and drawer pulls the way she had once perused the jewelry displays at Tiffany's.

She painted, learning to love and despise the eccentricities of her variable-speed Sears-brand paint sprayer. Growing neurotically possessive, she refused to allow Kate or Laura to try their hand with it. And once after a particularly long session, she jumped at the reflection in the mirror.

Margo Sullivan, the face that launched a million bottles of alpha hydroxy, stared back, her glorious hair bundled messily under a dirty white cap, her cheeks flecked with deep-rose freckles, her eyes naked and a little wild.

She didn't know whether to shudder or scream.

But the shock sent her straight into the clawfoot tub for a hot, frothy soak in sea salts and urged her to give herself a full treatment—facial, hot oil, manicure, just to prove she hadn't completely lost her mind.

Now, after six weeks of insanity, she had begun to believe that dreams could be made. The floors gleamed, sanded smooth and slicked with three satiny coats of varnish. The walls, her personal pride and joy, were a soft, warm rose. Windows she'd washed herself in her mother's secret solution that relied heavily on vinegar and elbow grease, sparkled in their frame of new trim. The iron stairs and circling banisters had been securely bolted and shimmered with fresh gilt.

Tiles in both bathrooms had been regrouted and ruthlessly scrubbed and were now accented with fancy fingertip towels with lace edging.

Everything was rose and gold and fresh.

"It's like Dorian Gray," Margo commented. She and Laura were huddled in the sitting area of the main showroom, struggling to price the contents of a crate.

184

"It is?"

"Yeah. The shop keeps getting prettier and shinier." She pinched her tired cheeks and laughed. "And I'm the picture in the closet."

"Oh, that explains those warts."

"Warts?" Instant panic. "What warts?"

"Easy." It was Laura's first good laugh in days. "Just joking."

"Christ, next time just shoot me in the head." As her blood pressure returned to normal, Margo held up a faience vase painted with stylized flowers. "What do you think? It's Doulton."

It was no use asking Margo what she'd paid for it, Laura knew. She wouldn't have a clue. Following routine, Laura glanced at the stack of price guides and catalogs they'd collected. "Did you look it up?"

"Sort of." Over the past weeks, Margo had developed a love-hate relationship with price guides. She loved the idea of marking prices, hated the knowledge that so much money had already slipped through her fingers. "I think a hundred fifty."

"Go for it."

Tongue caught between her teeth, Margo slowly tapped the keys on the laptop Kate had insisted they couldn't live without. "Stock number 481 . . . G for glassware or C for collectibles?"

"Um, G. Kate's not here to argue the point."

"481-G. Damn it, I said G." She deleted, tried again. "One hundred fifty." Though it was probably inefficient, which Kate would have pointed out, Margo tagged the vase, rose to carry it to the glass étagère that was already filling up, then came back to light a cigarette. "What the hell are we doing, Laura?"

"Having fun. What made you buy something like this?"

Smoking contemplatively, Margo eyed an undoubtedly ugly urn with wing handles. "I must have been having a bad day."

"Well, it's Stinton, and signed, so maybe . . ." She flipped busily through a price book. "About forty-five hundred."

"Really?" Had she really once been in the position to pay so much for so little? She nudged the laptop toward Laura. "They're coming to paint the sign on the window tomorrow. And the crew from *Entertainment Tonight* is supposed to be here by two."

"Are you sure you want to do that?"

"Are you kidding? All that free publicity?" Margo stretched her arms up. Her shoulders were aching, a sensation she'd gotten used to. "Besides, it'll give me a chance to deck myself out, get in front of the camera. I'm thinking the sage green Armani or the blue Valentino."

"We've already tagged the Armani."

"Right. Valentino it is."

"As long as it doesn't make you uncomfortable."

"Valentino never makes me uncomfortable."

"You know what I mean." Laura hefted the urn, decided it looked slightly less unattractive on the corner shelf. "All those questions about your private life."

"I don't have a private life at the moment. You've got to learn to shrug off the gossip, honey." She tapped out her cigarette and knelt to explore the crate. "If you let every whisper and snicker about you and Peter sting, the wasps will know and they'll keep after you."

"He came back to town last week."

Her head jerked up. "Is he hassling you?"

"No, but . . . Josh had an incident with him a few days ago. I didn't hear about it until this morning."

"An incident?" Amused, Margo studied a little Limoges box replicating a French flower stall. Christ, she loved these little bits of nonsense. "What did they do, draw their Mont Blancs and duel?"

"Josh broke Peter's nose."

"What?" Staggered between shock and glory, she nearly bobbled the box. "Josh *punched* him?"

"He broke it with a tennis ball." When Margo collapsed into hoots of laughter, Laura scowled. "There were people in the next court. It's all over the club. Peter had to be taken to the hospital, and he might very well file charges."

"What, assault with a forehand lob? Oh, Laura, it's too delicious. I haven't given Josh enough credit." She pressed a hand on her stomach as her ribs began to ache.

"It had to be deliberate."

"Well, of course it was deliberate. Josh can bean a speeding car at fifty yards with his backhand. He could have played center court if he'd taken himself seriously. Damn, I wish I'd seen it." Wicked delight sparkled in her eyes. "Did he bleed a lot?"

"Profusely, I'm told." It was wrong, Laura had to continually remind herself, it was wrong to enjoy the image of bright red blood geysering out of Peter's aristocratic nose. "He's gone to Maui to recuperate. Margo, I don't want my brother smashing tennis balls into the face of the father of my children."

"Oh, let him have his fun." Without remembering to tag or log it, Margo placed the Limoges in a curved-front cabinet where a dozen others were already displayed. "Ah, is Josh seeing anyone?"

"Seeing anyone?"

"You know, as in dating, escorting, having hot sex with?"

Baffled, Laura rubbed at her tired eyes. "Not that I know of. But then, he stopped bragging about having hot sex around me years ago."

"But you'd know." As if it were vital to world peace, Margo rubbed at a smudge on the display glass. "You'd have heard, or sensed."

"He's awfully busy just now, so I'd say probably not. Why?"

"Oh." She turned back, smiling widely. "Just a little wager we have going. I'm starving," she realized abruptly. "Are you starving? I think we should order something in. If Kate comes by after work and we're not done with this shipment, she's going to lecture us on time management again."

"I don't have time for lectures on time. I'm sorry. I have to pick up the girls. It's Friday," she explained. "I promised them dinner and a movie. Why don't you come with us?"

"And leave all this luxury?" Margo spread her arms wide to encompass boxes, heaps of packing material, half-empty cups of cold coffee. "Besides, I have to practice my gift wrapping. Everything I do still looks like it was wrapped up by a slow-witted three-year-old. I don't mind, really—"

She broke off as the door swung open and Kayla burst through. "Mama! We came to visit." With a beaming smile, she launched herself into Laura's arms, clung just a little too hard.

"Hello, baby." Laura squeezed back, worrying how long these small reassurances would be necessary. "How did you get here?"

"Uncle Josh picked us up. He said we could come and look at the shop 'cause we should take an interest in our legacy."

"Your legacy, huh?" Laughing now, Laura set Kayla down and watched her older daughter come more cautiously, less happily into the room. "Well, Ali, what do you think?"

"It looks different than it did before." She walked unerringly to the jewelry case.

"A girl after my own heart," Margo declared and wrapped an arm around Ali's shoulder.

"They're so beautiful. It's like a treasure chest."

"It is. Not Seraphina's dowry this time, but mine."

"We got pizza," Kayla called out. "Uncle Josh bought lots

and lots of pizza so we can eat here instead of in a restaurant. Can we, Mama?''

"If you like. Do you want to, Ali?''

Ali shrugged, continued to stare at the bracelets and pins. "It doesn't matter.''

"And here's the man of the hour.'' Margo crossed the room as Josh elbowed the door open, his arms loaded with pizza boxes. She leaned over them and gave him a smacking kiss on the mouth.

"Just for pizza? Hell, I could've gone for the bucket of chicken.''

"Actually, that was a reward for your tennis prowess.''

She kept her voice low, and at the answering gleam in his eyes, she took the boxes from him. "Still sleeping alone, darling?''

"Don't remind me.'' He arched a brow. "You?''

She grinned and trailed a finger down his cheek. "I've been much too busy for sports of any kind. Ali, I think there's a bottle of Pepsi in the refrigerator upstairs.''

"Got that covered, too,'' he said, torturing himself with the scent of her perfume. "Can you handle getting the drinks out of the car, Ali Cat?''

"Me, too.'' Kayla bulleted for the door. "I can help. Come on, Ali.''

"Well, well.'' Josh tucked his hands in his pockets and scanned the room as his nieces slammed the door. "You have been busy.'' He wandered toward the adjoining room, had to smile. It looked very much like Margo's closet back in Milan, except that all the clothes were now discreetly tagged.

"Lingerie and nightclothes are upstairs,'' Margo told him. "In the boudoir.''

"Naturally.'' Idly, he picked up a gray suede pump, turned it over. The sole was barely scraped and the price was ninety-two fifty.

"How are you pricing?"

"Oh, we have our little system."

He set the shoe back, glanced at his sister. "I didn't think you'd mind if I brought the girls by."

"No, not at all. What I do mind is you taking it upon yourself to fight with Peter."

He didn't bother to look contrite. "Heard about that, did you?"

"Of course I heard about it. Everyone from Big Sur to Monterey's heard about it by now." She refused to warm when he walked over and kissed her. "I can deal with my marital problems myself."

"Sure you can. That ball just got away from me."

"Like hell," Margo muttered.

"Actually, I was aiming for his caps. Listen, Laura," he continued when she bristled under his hands, "we'll talk about it later, okay?"

She had little choice, since at that moment her daughters came back, carrying bags from the car.

He'd thought of paper plates as well, and napkins and silly party cups for soda and a good red Bordeaux. There seemed to be very little, Margo mused as they spread the makeshift picnic on the floor, that Josh Templeton didn't think of.

It was a little lowering to realize she had underestimated him all these years. He would be a formidable foe, which he'd proved by one swing of the racket. And she was certain he would be a memorable lover.

Josh caught her staring and passed her a plate. "Problem, duchess?"

"More than likely."

But she enjoyed herself, listening to the children. Ali seemed to brighten shade by shade under Josh's teasing and attention. Poor thing wants a father, Margo mused. She understood the need, the empty ache of it. It had been Thomas

Templeton who had helped fill that void for her, and who at the same time, simply by being kind and caring, had made her constantly aware that he was not hers.

She had never had her own—or had had him so briefly she couldn't remember him. Her mother had always been so closemouthed about the man she had married and lost that Margo had been afraid to ask questions. Afraid, she realized, that there had been nothing there, for any of them.

No love, she mused. Certainly no passion.

One more tepid marriage in the world hardly made a difference to anyone. Even those, she thought, involved in it. A good Irish Catholic girl married and had children, as was expected of her. Then accepted God's will with a bowed head. Ann Sullivan wouldn't have mourned and tossed herself, cursing God, into the sea as Seraphina had done. Ann Sullivan had picked herself up, moved on, and forgotten.

And so easily, Margo mused, that there had likely been little to remember. It was as if she had never had a father at all.

And hadn't she sought to fill that lifetime gap with men? Often older men, like Alain, men who were successful and established and always safely beyond commitment. Married men, or oft-married men, or loosely married men with wives who turned a blind eye to an affair as long as their husbands turned a blind eye to theirs.

There had always been a cozy cushion with men who looked at her as a lovely prize to be pampered and fussed over. Displayed. Men who would never stay, which of course only made them more attractive, only more forbidden.

Her stomach shuddered, and she gulped wine to steady it. What a horrible realization, she thought. What a pathetic one.

"Are you all right?" Concerned, Laura laid a hand on her arm. "You've gone pale."

"It's nothing. Just a little headache. I'm going to take something." She rose and used every ounce of control she had to walk up the stairs rather than run.

In the bathroom she riffled through the medicine bottles. Her fingers rested on tranquilizers before she shifted them firmly to aspirin. Too easy, she told herself as she ran the water cold. Too easy to pop a pill and make it all go away.

"Margo." Josh came up behind her, took hold of her shoulders. "What's got you?"

"Demon dreams." She shook her head, swallowed aspirin. "It's nothing, just a nasty little epiphany."

She would have turned, but he held her firm so that their faces reflected back at them. "Nervous about opening the shop next week?"

"Terrified."

"Whatever happens, you've already accomplished something important. You've taken this place and made it shine. It's beautiful and elegant and unique. Very much like you."

"And filled with pretenses, priced to sell?"

"So what?"

She closed her eyes. "So what. Be a friend, Josh, and hold on to me for a minute."

He turned her, gathered her close. He heard her loose a long, shuddering breath, and he stroked her hair. "Do you remember that winter when you went on a search for Seraphina's dowry?"

"Umm. I dug up the rose garden and part of the south lawn. Mum was furious and mortified and threatened to ship me off to my aunt Bridgett in Cork." She sighed a little, comforted by the feel of him, the scent of him. "But your father laughed and laughed. He thought it was a great joke and that I showed an adventurous spirit."

"You were looking for something you wanted, and you went after it." His lips brushed her hair to soothe. "That's what you've always done."

"And I've always wanted the unattainable?"

"No." He eased back, tipped up her chin. "The interesting. I'd hate to think you'd stop digging up rosebushes, duchess."

Sighing again, she snuggled her head on his shoulder. "I really hate to admit this, but you're good for me, Josh."

"I know." And he thought it was long past time that she figured that out.

She hadn't expected to be nervous. There'd been so much to do in the past three months—appointments, meetings, decisions to make, stock to sort through. The decorating, the planning. Even the choice of shopping bags and boxes had prompted hours of debate.

There'd been so much to learn. Inventory, profit-and-loss ratios, tax forms. Sales tax, business tax, property tax.

Interviews to give. The spread in *People* had just hit the stands, and *Entertainment Weekly* had run a blurb on her and her shop. A snide blurb, but it was print.

It was all falling into place, so she had expected the actual opening to be rather anticlimactic. The attack of nerves twenty-four hours before Pretenses' grand opening was both unexpected and unwelcome.

Over the years, Margo had taken various courses to deal with nerves. A glass of wine, shopping, a pill, sex. None of those seemed a viable option now, nor did they fit in with the new direction her life was taking.

She was giving sweat a try instead.

The exercise facilities at the country club were, she supposed, top of the line. She had through her career played with free weights and pranced through a few aerobic classes. But she'd been blessed with a killer metabolism, long legs, long torso, and generous breasts that weren't echoed in hips, and she had smugly scorned the fitness craze.

Now she struggled through the programming of a Stair-

Master, wondering how anyone could get excited about climbing steps to nowhere. She could only hope it would turn her busy mind to mush—and keep the weight she'd put back on properly distributed.

The huge room was ringed with windows that offered views of the golf course or the pool. For those who weren't interested in the great outdoors, there were individual television sets affixed above treadmills, so one could walk or trot to health while watching Katie and Bryant or CNN. Various pieces of what she considered rather terrifying equipment were placed here and there.

Beside her, a woman in red Spandex doggedly climbed flight after flight while reading the latest Danielle Steele. Margo struggled to get her rhythm and focus on the bobbing print of the business section of the *Los Angeles Times*.

But she couldn't concentrate. This was a whole new world, she realized. One that had been bumping, jogging, and grunting along while she'd been wrapped up in her own. A man with a gorgeous body and biceps like bricks watched himself carefully in a mirror while lifting brutal-looking weights. A bevy of women, trim or pudgy, pumped on stationary bikes. Some of them chattered together, others rode to the tune on headsets.

People crunched, twisted, bent, and punished their bodies, mopped sweat from their faces, glugged down mineral water, then went back for more.

It was, to her, amazing.

For her, this was a lark, a momentary diversion. But for them, all these damp, straining bodies, it was a serious lifestyle choice.

Perhaps they were all slightly insane.

Still . . . weren't these the very people she would need to appeal to? The businesspeople, the clever rich. The women who worked out in hundred-dollar bike shorts and two-hundred-dollar shoes. After straining and stretching their bodies, wouldn't they enjoy a bit of pampering? Beyond the Swedish massages, the Turkish baths, the whirlpools, surely they would enjoy strolling into a classy shop to browse, be offered a cup of cappuccino, a glass of chilled champagne, while an attractive woman helped them select the perfect bauble or a tasteful gift.

Of course, the challenge would be to convince them that the fact that the bauble or gift was secondhand only made it more interesting and unique.

Calculating, she slanted a look at the woman beside her. "Do you do this every day?"

"Hmm?"

"I was wondering if you do this every day." With a friendly smile, Margo sized up her companion. Mid-thirties, carefully groomed. The channel-set diamonds on her wedding band were excellent quality and weighed in at about three carats. "I've just started."

"Three days a week. It's really all you need to maintain." Obviously willing to be distracted, she skimmed a glance over Margo. "Losing weight isn't your goal."

"I've gained seven pounds in the last three months."

With a laugh, the woman lifted the towel she'd slung over the bar and blotted her throat. Margo noted the watch was a slim Rolex. "We should all be able to say that and look like you. I've lost thirty-three over the last year."

"You're kidding."

"If I put it back on, I'll kill myself. So now I'm on maintenance. I'm back to a size eight, and by God, I'm staying there."

"You look wonderful." Size eight, she thought. Perfect. "Do you like working out?"

The woman smiled grimly as her stepper pumped up the pace. "I hate every fucking minute of it."

"Thank God," Margo said sincerely as her calves began to burn. "Sanity. I'm Margo Sullivan. I'd offer my hand, but I'm afraid I'd fall off."

"Judy Prentice. Margo Sullivan," she repeated. "I thought you looked familiar. I used to hate you."

"Oh?"

"When I was cruising toward a size sixteen, and I'd flip through a magazine. There'd you'd be, curvy and perfect. I'd head straight for the Godivas." She offered a quick grin. "It's rewarding to know you sweat just like a human being."

Deciding Judy was likable as well as a potential customer, Margo grinned back. "Isn't there supposed to be something about endorphins?"

"Oh, that's a lie. I think Jane Fonda started it. You grew up here, didn't you?"

"Big Sur," Margo confirmed, puffing now. "I'm back. I have a shop in Monterey. Pretenses, on Cannery Row. We're having our grand opening tomorrow. You should drop in, look around." She gritted her teeth. "I'll make sure we have Godivas."

"Bitch," Judy said with a quick laugh. "I might just do that. Well, that's my twenty minutes of hell. Fifteen with the free weights and a short session on the Nautilus torture chamber and I'm out of here." She grabbed her towel, glanced toward the entrance. "Oh, here comes the diva."

"Candy Litchfield," Margo muttered as she spotted the redhead in a floral unitard.

"Know her?"

"Too well."

"Hmm. If you have the good taste to loathe her, I might just check out that shop of yours. Oops, she's heading this way, and she's all yours."

"Listen, don't—" But it was too late. Candy let out a squeal that had every head swiveling.

"Margo! Margo Sullivan! I just can't believe it."

"Hello, Candy." To Margo's despair, Candy bounced up to the stepper.

Candy bounced everywhere. It was just one of the many reasons to despise her. She was bandbox pretty, all perky features and tumbling red hair. In their high school days, Candy had been head cheerleader, and head pain in the ass. She'd married well—twice—had two perfect children, one from each marriage, and spent her days, as far as Margo knew, planning perfect tea parties and indulging in discreet affairs.

Under the surface, past the perky face and well-toned body, was the heart of a viper. To Candy, other women weren't simply members of the same sex and species. They were the enemy.

"I heard you were back, of course." With a perfect pink nail she tapped in her choice of time and program on the machine Judy had vacated. "I've been meaning to call, but I've been so busy." The diamond studs in her ears winked as she smiled at Margo. "How are you, Margo? You look wonderful. No one would ever know."

"Wouldn't they?"

"All those terrible stories." Delighted malice flitted around her Kewpie-doll lips. "Why it must have been just dreadful for you. I just can't imagine the terror of being arrested—and in a foreign country, too." Her voice was just loud enough to catch the interest of several morning athletes.

"Neither can I." Margo struggled not to puff and wished violently for a cigarette. "I wasn't arrested. I was questioned."

"Well, I was sure the stories were exaggerated." Her tone was a bright brew of sympathy laced with doubt. "All those horrible things they said about you. Why, when I heard, I told several of the girls over lunch that it was just nonsense. But the stories just kept coming. The press is so heartless. You were wise to get out of Europe until the scandal dies down.

It's so like Laura to overlook all the talk and take you in."

There was nothing to say to that but "Yes."

"It's such a shame about Bella Donna. I'm sure your replacement won't be nearly as effective. You're so much more photogenic than Tessa Cesare." Bouncing perkily, Candy sharpened her lance. "Of course, she's younger, but she doesn't have your . . . experience."

It was a shaft to the heart, well aimed and well honed. Margo's fingers tightened on the bar, but she kept her voice easy. "Tessa's a beautiful woman."

"Oh, of course. And very exotic. That golden skin, those wonderful black eyes. I'm sure the company felt they had to go with a contrast." Her smile was calculatedly tinged with amused disdain. "You'll make a comeback, Margo. Don't you worry."

"Not if I'm serving time for murder," she said under her breath.

"So, tell me everything. I heard the most hilarious story about you going into retail."

"I laugh about it all the time. We open tomorrow."

"No! Really?" Her eyes popped wide on a titter. "Then poor Laura Ridgeway did buy you a building. That's so touching."

"Laura, Kate Powell, and I bought the building together."

"The three of you always did stick together." Candy's smile turned sharp. She'd always detested them for their unshakable friendship. "I'm sure it'll be great fun for you, and poor Laura certainly needs a distraction just now. There can't be anything more painful and distressing than seeing your marriage fail."

"Unless it's seeing your second marriage fail," Margo returned with a cheery smile. "Is the divorce final, Candy?"

"Next month. You never did marry any of those . . . men, did you, Margo?"

"No, I just had sex with them. Most of them were already married anyway."

"You've always had such a European attitude. I suppose I'm just too American. I don't think I could ever be comfortable being a mistress."

Temper shot little lights of red in front of Margo's eyes. "Darling," she drawled, "it's blissfully comfortable. Believe me. But then, you're probably right. You're not suited for it. No alimony."

She stepped off the machine, grateful that her session with Candy had taken her mind off nerves and screaming muscles. Maybe her legs felt like limp strings of linguini, but she wouldn't give Candy the satisfaction of seeing them buckle. Instead, she carefully wiped off the machine as she had seen Judy do.

"Do come by the shop, Candy. We're having our grand opening tomorrow. You've always wanted what I had. This is your chance to get it. For a price."

As Margo flounced out, Candy drew a breath up her pert, tip-tilted nose and turned to the interested woman puffing behind her. "Margo Sullivan always pretended to be something she wasn't. Why, if it wasn't for the Templetons, she wouldn't be allowed through the front gates of this club."

The woman blinked the sweat out of her eyes. She'd admired Margo's style. And her sapphire tennis bracelet. "What was the name of her shop?"

Chapter Twelve

Nine-forty-five, July twenty-eighth. Fifteen minutes to zero hour and Margo was sitting on the bed in the ladies' boudoir. The bed she had once slept in, made love in. Dreamed in. Now she was perched on the edge of it, holding her stomach and praying for the nausea to pass.

What if no one came? What if absolutely no one so much as stepped through those freshly washed glass doors? She would spend the next eight hours trembling, staring out the display window now so painstakingly arranged with her charcoal silk taffeta St. Laurent—worn only last year to the Cannes film festival—its skirts draped over a Louis XIV hall chair. That flowing skirt was surrounded by once prized possessions. A Baccarat perfume bottle, rhinestone-studded evening slippers, sapphire drop earrings, a black satin purse with a jeweled clasp in the shape of a panther. The Meissen candlestick, the

Waterford champagne flute, a display of her favorite trinket boxes, and the silver-backed dresser set that had been a gift from an old lover.

She'd placed every piece personally, as a kind of ritual, and now she feared that those things she had once owned and loved would draw no more than scorn from passersby.

What had she done?

Stripped herself. Stripped herself raw, and in public. She thought she could handle that, live through that. But she had dragged the people she cared about most into the morass with her.

Wasn't Laura downstairs right now waiting for that first customer? And Kate would dash over on her lunch hour, eager to see a sale rung up on the vintage cash register she'd hauled in from an antique shop in Carmel.

And Josh would probably swing by toward evening, strolling in with a smile on his face to congratulate them on their first day's success.

How could she possibly face them with failure? When the failure was all hers?

What she wanted most at that moment was to bolt downstairs and out the door. And just keep running.

"Stage fright."

With one arm still wrapped around her queasy stomach, she glanced up. Josh was in the doorway. "You talked me into this. If I could stand up right now, I'd kill you."

"Lucky for me those gorgeous legs of yours aren't steady." He gave her a quick, appraising look. She'd chosen a simple and perfectly tailored suit in power red with a short, snug skirt that gave those stunning, unsteady legs plenty of exposure to do their work. Her hair was braided, with just a few tendrils calculatingly free to frame her face. Pale as marble now, eyes glassy with fear.

"You disappoint me, duchess. I figured to find you downstairs revved up to kick ass. Instead you're up here shaking like a virgin on her wedding night.''

"I want to go back to Milan."

"Well, you can't, can you?" His tone was hard as he crossed the room, took her by the arm. "Stand up, get a grip on yourself." Those big blue eyes were swimming, and he was afraid that if the first tear fell, he would break and carry her off anywhere she wanted to go. "It's a damn store, for Christ's sake, not a capital trial. It's just like you to blow it out of proportion."

"It's not just a store." Her voice hitched, mortifying her. "It's all I've got."

"Then go down and do something about it."

"I don't want to go down. What if no one comes? Or if they only come to stare and snicker."

"What if they don't? What if they do? There are plenty of people who'll be interested enough to breeze by just to see you fall on your face. Keep this up and that's all they're going to see."

"I shouldn't have started out so big."

"Since that applies to every aspect of your life, I don't see why you're complaining now." He studied her face, angry with her for letting him see the fear, angry with himself for wanting to protect her. "Look, you've got five minutes, and you'll make up your own mind. I've got my own problems to deal with." He brought out the single red rose he'd held behind his back and curled her fingers around the stem. "Let me know how you deal with yours."

He closed his lips over hers impatiently and didn't wait for her reaction.

He could have offered a little sympathy, she fumed and stalked into the bathroom to retouch her makeup. Just a little understanding and support. No, not Josh. She slammed her blusher back into the cabinet. All she got from him was insults and surly remarks. Well, that was fine. That was good. It reminded her that she had no one to lean on but herself.

Five minutes later, she made herself walk downstairs. Laura was beaming at the big, ornate cash register as its bells chimed.

"You've got to stop playing with that thing."

"I'm not playing." Face flushed with excitement, she turned to Margo. "I've just rung up our first sale."

"But we're not open."

"Josh bought the little Deco lamp before he left. He said to box it up and ship it." Reaching across the counter, she grabbed Margo's hands and squeezed. "Box it up and ship it, Margo. It's our first box it up and ship it. You can always depend on Josh."

Margo let out a shaky laugh. Damn him, it was just like him. "Yeah, you can, can't you?" The mantel clock behind the counter chimed the hour. Zero hour. "Well, I guess we'd better . . . Laura, I'm—"

"Me, too." Laura drew a long, cleansing breath. "Let's open for business, partner."

"Yeah." Margo straightened her shoulders and angled her chin as she crossed to the door. "And fuck them if they can't take a joke."

Two hours later, she wasn't sure if she was thrilled or punch-drunk. She couldn't claim they were jammed with customers, particularly of the paying variety. But they'd enjoyed a small, steady stream almost from the first minute. She had, with her own trembling hands, rung up the second sale of the day barely fifteen minutes after opening the doors. Both she and the tourist from Tulsa had agreed that the silver cuff bracelet was an excellent buy.

With some amazement and no little admiration, she'd watched Laura steer a trio of browsers toward the wardrobe room like a veteran shop clerk and flatter them into reaching for their credit cards.

When Kate arrived at twelve-thirty, Margo was closing the sapphire earrings from the display window into one of the bright gold boxes with silver lettering that she'd chosen for the shop's trademark.

"I know your wife's going to love them," she said as she slipped the box into a tiny gold bag. Her hands weren't trembling, but they wanted to. "I did. And happy anniversary."

The minute the customer stepped away from the counter, she snagged Kate's hand and pulled her into the powder room. "That was fifteen hundred and seventy-five dollars, plus tax." Grabbing Kate around the waist, she led her into a quick, clattering dance. "We're selling things, Kate."

"That was the idea." It had killed her not to be there, with Laura and Margo, to open the doors for the first time. But responsibility at Bittle took priority. "You own a store, you sell things."

"No, we're really selling them. Liz Carstairs was in and bought the set of Tiffany wineglasses for her daughter's shower gift, and this couple from Connecticut bought the gateleg table. We're shipping it. And, oh, more. We're not going to be paying that storage bill for the rest of the stock much longer."

"Are you logging the sales?"

"Yeah—well, I might have made a couple of mistakes, but we'll fix that. Come on, you can ring something up." She paused with a hand on the door. "It's sort of like sex. There's this attraction, and you build on it, then there's foreplay, little thrills of anticipation, then there's this big bang."

"Want a cigarette?"

"I'm dying for one."

"You're really getting into this, aren't you?"

204

"I had no idea that sales could be so . . . stimulating. Give it a shot."

Kate glanced at her watch. "I've only got forty-five minutes, but, hey, I'm all for cheap thrills."

Margo snagged her wrist, studied the clean lines of the practical Timex. "You know, we could get a good price for this."

"Control yourself, Margo."

She tried. But every now and again throughout the day she had to find some quiet corner and simply gloat. Maybe her emotions were swinging high and wide like a batter too eager to score, but she just didn't care. If there was a pang now and then when one of her treasured trinkets slipped away in a gold-and-silver box, there was also a sense of triumph.

People had come. And for every one who snickered there was another who admired, and another who bought.

By three, when there was a lull, she poured two cups of the tea they'd offered to customers throughout the morning. "I'm not hallucinating, am I?"

"Not unless we both are." Laura winced as she wriggled her toes. "And my feet hurt too much for this to be a dream. Margo, I think we've actually done it."

"Let's not say that yet. We could jinx it." Carrying her cup, she walked over to straighten a vase of roses. "I mean, maybe this is just fate's way of sneering at us. Giving us a few hours of success. We're open for three more hours, and . . . the hell with that." She whirled around. "We're a hit. We're a smash!"

"I wish you'd be more enthusiastic—and I wish I could stay and ride the next wave with you." Wincing, Laura looked at her watch. "But the girls have dance class. I'll wash out the cups before I go."

"No, I'll take care of them."

The door opened, letting in a group of teenage girls who made a beeline for the jewelry counter.

205

"We have customers," Laura murmured and gathered up the cups herself. "We have customers," she repeated, grinning. "I'll try to be here tomorrow by one." There were so many obligations to juggle, and she worried about how long it would be before she started dropping balls. "Are you sure you can handle working the shop by yourself?"

"We agreed from the start that you'd have to be part time. I'm going to learn how to handle it. Get going."

"As soon as I wash these." She stopped, turned. "Margo, I don't know the last time I had this much fun."

Nor did she, Margo thought. As she measured her young customers, a smile began to bloom. Teenage girls who wore designer shoes had generous allowances—and parents with gold cards. She crossed to the counter, took her place behind it.

"Hello, ladies. Can I show you something?"

Josh didn't mind long hours. He could handle being chained to a desk and being buried under paperwork. Though it wasn't as appealing as zipping across continents to fine-tune the workings of a busy hotel chain and its subsidiaries, he could deal with it cheerfully enough.

But what really pissed him off was being played for a fool.

The longer he remained in the penthouse and studied the files generated from the California Templetons, the more certain he was that Peter Ridgeway had done just that.

He'd done his job. There was no way to accuse him, legally, of mishandling funds or staff, of cutting corners. Though he had done precisely those things, Peter had documented it all, in terms of his rationale, his position, and the increase in profit that his alterations had generated.

But Templeton had never been an organization that was motivated exclusively by profit. It was a family-owned operation steeped in two hundred years of innkeeping tradition that prided itself on its humanity, on its commitment to the people who worked in it and for it.

Yes, Ridgeway had increased profits, but he had done so by changing staff, cutting back on full-time employees in favor of part-time ones. And thereby squeezing people out of benefits and slicing their pay stubs.

He'd negotiated a new deal with wholesalers, produce distributors, and as a result had lowered the quality in the staff kitchens. Employee discounts in reservations and in Templeton hotel boutiques had been cut back, reducing the incentive that had always been traditional for Templeton people to use Templeton services.

In the meantime, his own expense account had increased. His bills for meals, laundry, entertainment, flowers, travel, had steadily grown. He'd even had the gall to charge his trip to Aruba to Templeton as a business expense.

It gave Josh great pleasure to cancel Peter's corporate credit cards. Even if he did consider it too little, too late.

Should have aimed for his balls after all, he thought, and leaned back to rub his tired eyes.

It would take months to rebuild trust among the staff. A huge bonus and a mountain of flattery would be necessary to lure back the head chef who had quit in a huff at Ridgeway's interference. Added to that was the resignation from the longtime concierge at Templeton San Francisco that he'd found buried in Peter's files. There were others as well. Some could be lured back, others were lost to competitors.

None of them had come to him, Josh mused, or to his parents. Because they'd believed, justifiably, that Peter Ridgeway was a trusted, highly placed member of the Templeton group.

He tugged at his tie, trying not to think about the amount of work that still lay before him. Someone was going to have to take over his responsibilities in Europe, at least temporarily. He wasn't going anywhere.

Already the penthouse suite was more his than Ridgeway's. The fussy furniture had been replaced with Josh's preference for the traditional. American and Spanish antiques, with deeply cushioned, generous chairs were more in keeping with the scheme of Templeton Monterey. After all, the hotel and its decor followed the history of the area. The resort was more truly of California Spanish design, but the hotel echoed it in the ornate facade, the musical fountains, and lush gardens. The lobby was done in deep reds and golds, offering heavy chairs, long, high tables, winking brass, and glossy tiled floors.

There were potted palms, like the one he'd chosen for the corner of his office, in a huge hand-thrown clay pot that took two men with beefy arms to lift.

He'd always thought Templeton Paris more feminine, with its mix of the airy and the ornate, and Templeton London more distinguished, so British with its two-level lobby and cozy tearoom.

But Monterey was perhaps closest to his heart after all. Not that he'd ever pictured himself settling behind a desk here, even if it was a Duncan Phyfe, with an eye-blurring view of the coast he loved only a head's turn away.

It didn't bother him for outsiders to consider him the globe-trotting trust fund baby. Because he knew better. The Templeton name wasn't simply a legacy, it was a responsibility. He'd worked long and hard to meet that responsibility, to learn the craft of not simply owning but managing and expanding a complex organization. He'd been expected to learn hotels from the ground up, and he had done just that. By doing so he'd developed respect and admiration for the people who worked in the kitchens, picked up wet towels from bathroom floors, calmed the tired and frazzled incoming guests at the front desks.

He appreciated the hours that went into public relations and sales and the frustrations of dealing with oversized conventions and harried conventioneers.

But there was a bottom line, and that line was Templeton. Whatever went wrong, whatever needed to be fixed, smoothed over, or polished up was up to him. And there was a great deal of fixing, smoothing over, and polishing up to be done in California.

He thought about getting up and brewing coffee, or just calling down to room service. But he didn't have the energy for either. He'd sent the temp home because she'd gotten on his nerves, scrambling around like an eager puppy desperate to please.

If he was going to be stuck behind a desk for the foreseeable future, he would need an executive assistant who could match his pace and not go wide-eyed with terror every time he gave an order. He was going to have to toss the temp back into the pool and go fishing.

But for now he was on his own.

He swiveled to his keyboard and began to compose a memo to all department heads, with a copy to his parents and the rest of the board of directors. It took him thirty minutes to perfect it. He faxed a copy, with the addition of a personal note, to his parents, printed out the others, and arranged for them to be messengered or overnighted.

Seeing no reason to waste time, he set up a full staff meeting at the hotel for eleven A.M., another at the resort at two. Though it was already after six, he contacted legal and left a message on voice mail outlining the urgency of a meeting and setting it up for nine sharp in his penthouse office.

It was highly probable that Ridgeway would sue over his abrupt termination. Josh wanted his bases covered.

Shifting back to the keyboard, he began another memo, reinstating the previous employee discounts. That, he thought, was something they would be able to see immediately, and, hopefully, it would build morale.

Standing in the open doorway, Margo watched him. It was a delightful shock to discover that watching him work made her juices flow. The loosened tie, the hair disarrayed by restless fingers, the dark and focused intensity of his eyes had her all but vibrating.

Odd, she'd never thought of Josh taking work of any kind seriously. And she had never realized that a serious man at work could be quite so arousing.

Maybe it was the months of self-imposed celibacy, or the heady success of the day. Maybe it was Josh himself—and had been all along. She didn't, at the moment, give a damn. She'd come here for one thing—a good, hot, sweaty bout of sex. She wasn't leaving without it.

Quietly, she closed the doors at her back, flipped the locks. "Well, well," she murmured, her pulse leaping when his head shot up like a wolf scenting his mate. "The scion at work. Quite a picture."

Knowing exactly the kind of picture she made—God knew she'd worked on it—she swaggered to his desk. After setting a frosty bottle of Cristal on the blotter, she eased a hip onto the edge. "Am I interrupting?"

His mind had gone blank the moment she'd stepped toward him. He did his best to snap it back. "Yeah, but don't let that stop you." He glanced down at the bottle, back into her glowing face. "So, how was your day?"

"Oh, nothing worth mentioning." She leaned over the desk, all but slithered over it, and gave him a tantalizing glimpse of pearly lace and cleavage. "Just fifteen thousand dollars in sales." She screamed, reaching out to tug his hair. "Fifteen thousand, six hundred and seventy-four dollars, eighteen cents in sales."

She sprang back off the desk, whirled in a giddy circle. "Do you know how I felt the first time I saw my face on the cover of *Vogue*?''

"No.''

"Just like this. Insane. I closed the doors at six, and there was half a bottle of champagne left. I drank it all myself, right from the damn bottle. Then I realized I didn't want to drink alone. Open the bottle, Josh. Let's get drunk and crazy.''

He rose, began to rip the foil. He should have known that gleam in her eye had been helped along by bubbly. "From what you've just said, you're already there.''

"I'm only half drunk.''

The cork popped celebrationally. "This should fix that.'' He went to the kitchen, setting the bottle on the counter of granite-colored tile and reaching into a glass-front oak cabinet for glasses.

"That's what you do, isn't it? Fix things. You fixed me, Josh. I owe you.''

"No.'' That was one thing he didn't want. "You did it yourself.''

"Made a start on it. I'm not finished yet.'' She clinked her glass to his. "But, oh, it's a hell of a start.''

"To Pretenses, then.''

"You bet your adorable ass. I know it won't be like this every day. It can't be.'' Fueled with energy, she prowled back into the office. "Kate says we can expect sales to dip, then level off. But I don't care. I watched this incredibly ugly woman waltz out with one of my Armanis, and I just didn't care.''

"Good for you.''

"And I—'' Her voice hitched, strangled, and he set his glass down in pure panic.

"Don't do that. Don't cry. I'm begging you.''

"It's not what you think.''

"Don't give me that shit about happy tears. They're all the

211

same to me. They're wet and make me feel like slime."

"I can't get hold of myself." As a defense, she gulped down more champagne, sniffled. "I've been like this all day. Dancing on the ceiling one minute, bawling in the bathroom the next. I'm selling my life away, and it makes me so sad. And people are buying it, and that makes me so happy."

"Jesus." Frustrated, he rubbed his hands over his face. "Let's trade in the champagne for some coffee, shall we?"

"Oh, no." Spurting up again, she danced away from him. "I'm celebrating."

"Okay." When she folded, he would pour her drunk, sexy body into his car and drive her to Templeton House. But for now, she had the right to celebrate, to gloat and be ridiculous. He sat on the desk, picked up his glass again. "To ugly women in secondhand Armani."

She tossed back the champagne and let it fizz down her throat. "To teenage girls with rich, indulgent parents."

"God love them."

"And tourists from Tulsa."

"Salt of the earth."

"And hawk-eyed old men who appreciate long legs in a short skirt." When he only frowned into his glass, she laughed and poured them both more. "And who plunk down cash for Meissen tea sets and harmless flirtation."

Before she could drink again, he caught her wrist. "How harmless?"

"I let him cluck my chin. If he'd bought the raku vase, he could have pinched any and all of my cheeks. It's such a rush."

"The clucking."

"No." She giggled happily. "The selling. I had no idea I'd find it so exciting. So . . . arousing." She spun back, sprinkling them both with champagne before he could pluck the glass from her hand and set it safely aside. "That's why I came to find you."

"You came to find me," he repeated, too cautious to move forward, too needy to move back.

With a low laugh she slid her hands up his shirt front, over his shoulders, into his hair. "I thought you could finish the job."

She was more than half drunk, he calculated, and told himself to remember the rules. He just couldn't think of them. "What do you want me to sell?"

She laughed again, dragged his mouth to hers for a steamy kiss. "Whatever it is, I'm ready to buy it."

He came up for air, tried for reason. "You've got champagne on your brain, duchess. This might not be the time to do business."

She made quick work of his tie, slinging it over her shoulder while her mouth went to war with his. "It's the perfect time. I could eat you alive, in great . . . big . . . bites."

"Jesus." It was hard to focus on reason when all the blood was draining out of his head. "In about ten seconds . . ." His mouth clashed with hers again as she dragged his shirt clear of his waistband. "I'm not going to give a damn if you're drunk or sober."

"I told you I'm only half drunk." She tossed her head back so that he could see her eyes. They were filled with laughter and desire. "I know exactly what I'm doing and who I'm going to do it with. What would you say if I suggested we consider that little bet of ours a draw?"

He was busy tugging her buttons free before he realized his hands had moved. "How about 'Thank you, God'?"

"It's probably a mistake." She attacked his throat with her teeth. "A terrible, terrible mistake. Jesus, put your hands on me."

"I'm trying." He managed to drag her jacket off while they stumbled toward the bedroom.

"Try harder." She wriggled out of her shoes, tripped, and sent them both crashing into the wall. When his hands streaked under her skirt, hiking it high as they greedily cupped her bottom, she arched back. "Don't stop," she panted, "whatever you do, don't stop."

"Who's stopping?" Desperate, he lifted her off her feet so that his mouth could close over her lace-covered breast.

She moaned once, grasping his hair for balance. "This could ruin our friendship."

He mumbled, his mouth busy with soft, hot flesh. "I don't want to be friends anymore."

"Me either," she managed as they fell onto the bed.

She'd always thought of sex as one of the quirky bonuses life had to offer, with the act itself rarely measuring up to the anticipation. There was certainly nothing dignified about two people panting like dogs and groping each other frantically. It was, if you discounted all the fripperies, a laughable, if temporarily satisfying, experience.

But she'd never made love with Josh Templeton.

There was panting, plenty of groping, even some laughter. But she was about to discover that reality could occasionally outdistance anticipation.

The minute her body was pinned under his, it shifted into overdrive. She was wild for him, wild to feel strong male hands stroke over her, to taste the heat and reckless lust of a hungry mouth, to hear that animal sound of flesh slapping against flesh.

The light from the office slanted in, cut across the bed so that they rolled from brightness to shadow and back again. But there was nothing innocent in the wrestling. It was ripe with purpose, desperation, and edgy greed. She could see the dark intensity of his eyes, the restless smoke of them focused on hers. She could feel the taut muscles of his shoulders under her hands before she tore his shirt aside and reared up to taste.

When he tugged her skirt impatiently down her hips, she thought, now. Thank God, now, and arched to meet him. But he dragged her to her knees and battered her senses with mouth on mouth.

Hot, voracious kisses lashed with tongue and teeth, the frantic strain of torso against torso with one thin layer of silk between dampening flesh. She rocked against him, sizzling, as those clever hands soothed, abraded, tormented her skin. She thought she might burn from the inside out and fumbled desperately at his waistband.

Then he cupped her, fingers streaking under silk, plunging inside velvet fire to drive her hard and mercilessly over the edge. She came like a geyser, release spurting out of her, shooting out shock waves that made her nails bite viciously into his back.

Before she could gulp in air, he shoved her on her back to devour.

He'd wanted her like this—just like this—mindless and frantic and burning for him. He'd dreamed of it, the way she would move under him, the sounds she would make, even the scent of her skin as desire shot to quivering need.

Now he had it, and even that wasn't enough.

He wanted to unravel her inch by inch, to watch her come apart. To hear her scream for him. His own needs were brutal, unreasonable, pumping through his blood like fiery little demons on their way to hell.

She clutched at him, wrapped those glorious long arms and legs around him, and slammed him through the wall of his own sanity.

He yanked her chemise down, baring her breasts for ravenous mouth and bruising hands, and filled himself with her.

It was a war now, fought with moans and gasps and needs

215

that clashed like swords. She rolled, slithered, tearing at his slacks until with a cry of triumph she wrapped long, smooth fingers around him.

His vision grayed. He feared for a moment that he might simply erupt like a novice at that first jolt of pleasure. Then he focused on her face, saw that slow, sly smile, and was damned if he'd let her win.

"I want you inside me." She all but purred it, even though her pulse was pounding like a wound. "I want you inside me. Come inside me." Dear God, he was huge, and iron hard, and she wanted, wanted, wanted. Her smile spread as he lowered his mouth to hers.

"Not yet." Even as she drew breath to curse him, he drove her up and over. Climax slapped into climax like battling tidal waves that left her floundering and gasping for air. And as she scrambled frantically toward the next peak, he plunged into her.

Fresh, outrageous energy blasted through him, fired by new, unspeakable greed. A feral snarl vibrated in his throat as he yanked her hips higher, arrowed deeper. In response, she locked her legs around him, arched back like a bow. Each thrust was like a hammer to the heart, battering them both.

He could no longer see her. He desperately wanted to see her face, to watch her face as they met and mated. But the animal had taken over, and it was blind and deaf and insatiable.

He could see nothing but the red haze that was as much fury as passion. Then even that vanished as the vicious climax ripped through him and emptied him.

Chapter Thirteen

She thought she'd seen stars. Of course that had probably been her imagination, some latent romantic streak she hadn't been aware of possessing.

More likely it had been a physical reaction due to near unconsciousness. What they'd done, Margo decided with lazy pleasure, had been to nearly fuck each other to death.

They were sprawled over the bed, two casualties of war, limp and sweaty and scarred. What an intriguing surprise, she mused, running a hand over her damp torso, that Josh should have been the most worthy of opponents.

Stirring up the energy to move, she turned her head and smiled affectionately at him. He was stretched out flat on his stomach, facedown. He hadn't moved since he'd groaned, rolled off her, and plopped there like a landed trout.

Probably asleep, snoring any minute, she decided. Men were

so predictable. But then, she was feeling much too lazy and satisfied to be irked. After all, she wasn't the kind of woman men cuddled, particularly after sex. Draining them of all signs of life was just one of her little skills.

She grinned, stretched. Still, he'd surprised her. She'd never had a man come so close to making her beg. The rough, reckless sex had left her feeling very much like a cat with a mouthful of cream-drenched feathers, but there had been a few moments there—perhaps more than a few—when she'd been almost frightened of what he was able to pull out of her.

Good old Josh, she thought. Then her gaze skimmed down his long, naked body and her pulse went to fast shuffle. Gorgeous, sexy, fascinating Josh. Time to move on, she told herself, before she got wound up for something he wouldn't be able to deliver.

She sat up, gave him a friendly slap on the butt, then let out a squealing laugh as his arm snaked out and tumbled her back.

"I'm finished with you, pal." She pressed a kiss to his shoulder. "Gotta go."

"Uh-uh." To her surprise, he pulled her close, shifting until she was curled against him. "I'm getting sensation back in my toes again. Who knows what could be next?"

"We're lucky we lived through it." He nuzzled her hair, moving her in new and lovely ways. After a brief hesitation, she curled an arm over his chest. "Your heart's still pounding."

"Thank Christ. I was afraid it had stopped." Lazily he stroked a hand up her leg, down again. "Margo?"

Her eyes were nearly closed. It was so sweet to be held, to be murmured to. "Hmm?"

"You definitely writhed."

She opened one eye balefully and found him grinning down

at her. "I didn't want to hurt your feelings. It seemed so important to you."

"Uh-huh. Not that I was counting . . ." He twirled her tumbled hair around his finger. "But you came five times."

"Only five?" She patted his cheek. "Don't blame yourself, I've had a long day."

He rolled on top of her, watched surprise flicker into her eyes. "Oh, I can do better."

"Think so?" Lips curved, she linked her arms around his neck. "I dare you to try."

"You know the Templetons." He nipped that curved bottom lip. "We can't resist a dare."

When she woke, the room was dark and she was alone. It surprised her that he was out of bed. They hadn't let loose of each other for more than five minutes all night. When she glanced over and saw the red glow of the alarm clock, she realized she hadn't been asleep much longer than that. It was barely after six, and the last time they'd collapsed it had been quarter to.

Whatever the press gleefully reported on her exploits, she'd never actually made love all night before. She hadn't believed it was physically possible. As she shifted to sit up and every muscle of her body wept, she realized it was certainly possible but not necessarily wise.

Because she had to crawl out of bed, literally, she was grateful not to have an audience. Josh would surely have made some snide remark—then jumped her.

As lowering as it was, she was ready to toss in the towel. Another orgasm might kill her.

And she was a businesswoman now. Time to put fun and games aside and get ready to face the day. She heard herself moan as she limped across the room. A press of a button had the drapes swinging open to admit a dazzling view of the coast, the curve of beach, the rocky inclines. The milky dawn light flowed in—and saved her from a painful encounter with a ficus tree planted in a toe-bruising copper pot.

There were two of them, she noted, a little bleary-eyed. Two delicate-leaved trees flanking the wide window, adding a homey touch to the sheen of the framed elbow chairs done in ivory brocade. The high gloss of oak tables reflected back the little pieces of him. Cuff links, loose change, keys.

He'd tossed a comb on the bureau, she noted. Beside it stood a bottle of men's cologne and a thick black appointment book. She imagined there were women's names and numbers from every time zone around the globe noted in it.

She caught a glimpse of herself in the mirror, naked, still glowing from the aftermath of good sex. Well, she mused, she was here now, wasn't she? And they weren't.

Her gritty eyes popped wide as she noticed the bed reflected behind her. How could she have been so involved with Josh that she hadn't noticed the bed? They had made love throughout the night on a lake-sized mattress framed with glinting brass head- and footboards, subtly curved to embrace jade green sheets.

But then, the elegant simplicity of the jade-and-white room, the shining touches of brass and copper, suited Templeton. The man, and the hotel.

She found one of the plushy white robes the hotel provided in the closet and wrapped it around her. The thought of a long, hot shower almost made her whimper, but curiosity drew her to the door first, and she cracked it open.

Josh was wearing nothing but wrinkled slacks that he hadn't bothered to fasten. He'd opened the shades so the fragile light crept into the room, and he held a portable phone to one ear while he paced the room in his bare feet.

He was speaking French.

God, he was gorgeous, she thought. Not just that wonderful

gold-tipped hair, the long, lithe body, the elegant, surprisingly capable hands. It was the way he moved, the timbre of his voice, that aura of power around him that she'd always been too close to see.

Her French was spotty at best, so she understood little of what he said. It didn't matter. It was the way he said it, the warm, liquid sounds, the hand gestures he unconsciously added to emphasize.

She watched those smoke gray eyes narrow—irritation, impatience—before he rattled off what could have been orders or oaths. Then he laughed, and his voice simply creamed over lovely, exotic words.

Suddenly she realized she was holding her breath, that she had a hand pressed to her heart, like some dreamy-eyed teenager over the captain of the football team.

It's just Josh, she reminded herself and deliberately drew in air, firmly dropping her hand to her side. It was a matter of pure ego that made her lean provocatively against the door to wait until he'd finished.

"Ça va, Simone. Oui, oui, oui, c'est bien. Ah, nous parlerons dans trois heures." Pausing, he listened, wandered to the window. "Parce que ils sont les idiots." He chuckled. "Non, non, pas de quoi. Au revoir, Simone."

He clicked the phone off, turned toward the desk, before he spotted her. Tumbled blond hair, witchy blue eyes, and a white robe loosely belted. His glands went on full alert.

"A little loose end I left dangling in Paris."

"Simone." Watching him, Margo ran a hand down the soft lapel of the robe. "Tell me, is she as . . . intriguing as her name?"

"Oh, more so." He walked over, slid his hands inside the robe. "And she's crazy about me."

"Pig," Margo murmured against his mouth.

"And she does whatever I tell her," he added, walking her backward toward the bed.

"Aren't you lucky?" Margo shifted, jabbed her elbow into his gut. When he grunted, she slipped out of his arms, smoothed her hair. "I need a shower."

"Just for that I'm not going to tell you she's fifty-eight, has four grandchildren, and is the associate director of marketing, Templeton Paris."

She shot a look over her shoulder. "I didn't ask. Why don't you order up some breakfast? I want to be in the shop by eight-thirty."

He obliged her, ordering room service to deliver it in an hour. That should give him just enough time, he decided as he joined her in the shower. She frowned at him when he blocked the best part of the spray.

"It's lukewarm," he complained.

"It's better for the skin. And I like privacy when I shower."

"Templeton's a green company." He nudged up the hot water even when she slapped at his hand. Steam began to rise satisfactorily along the glossy black walls of the stall. "As vice president it's my corporate duty to conserve our natural resources." Reaching out, he worked up the lather in the hair she'd just begun to wash.

The shower was large enough for a party of four, she reminded herself. There was no reason for her to feel crowded. "You're just in here because you think you can get lucky again."

"God, the woman sees right through me. It's mortifying." When she turned away to finish the job herself, he contented himself with washing her back. "How long does it take to dry all that hair? There's miles of it."

"It's not the length, it's the thickness," she said absently. It was foolish, she knew. He'd already run and rubbed and

222

stroked those hands over every inch of her body. But this . . . cleansing ritual was uncomfortably intimate.

She'd spoken no less than the truth. She didn't bathe with her lovers. She only slept with them in the literal sense, when she chose. It wasn't just a matter of control, though that was part of it. It was a matter of maintaining image and illusion.

Now with Josh she had not only spent the night with him without intending to, but she was sharing the shower with him. It was time, she decided, to lock a few parameters in place.

She tipped her face under the spray, let it stream the suds from her hair. When he handed her the soap and turned his back to her, she stared blankly.

"Your turn," he told her.

Her eyes narrowed, then lighted with wicked purpose. He hissed between his teeth when she slapped lather on his back.

"Oh, sorry. Those scratches must sting some."

Hands braced on the tile, he looked back at her. "It's all right. I've had my shots."

Without realizing it, she gentled her strokes. It was such a nice back, she mused. Muscled, broad at the shoulder, tapering to the waist, with all that smooth, tasty skin between. On impulse, she pressed a light kiss between his shoulder blades before stepping out of the shower.

"You know, Josh, I was only teasing about Simone." Bending at the waist, she turbaned her hair in a towel, then reached for another. "We've both had other relationships, and are free to continue to have them. We're not going to tangle each other up with strings at this point in our lives." After securing the towel between her breasts, she made do with the complimentary body cream in Templeton's spiraled bottle on the counter. Setting a foot on the padded vanity stool, she smoothed fragrant lotion onto her legs. "Neither one of us is looking for complications, and I'd hate for us to ruin a simple affair by making promises we'd never keep."

She slicked cream down her other leg, humming a little. "We have an advantage here that most people don't. We know each other so well, we don't need to play all those games or juggle all the pretenses." She flicked a glance toward the shower, mildly troubled by his lack of response.

He could handle the anger that simmered up to his throat. That was simply a matter of control. But the hurt, the little slashing knives that her careless words had dueling in his gut were another matter. For those, he could have cheerfully murdered her.

He turned off the water with a snap of his wrist, stepped through the double glass doors that separated the shower from the rest of the bath.

"Yeah, we know each other, duchess," he said as he flicked a towel from the heated bar. She was standing front and center of the eight-foot-long bath counter, looking perfect in the stark and sophisticated black-and-white decor, her skin glowing from the lotion she still held in one hand. "Inside and out. What would two shallow sophisticates like us want with mixing romance with our sex?"

She rubbed her arms. Despite the billowing steam, the room seemed abruptly chilly. "That's not entirely what I meant. You're angry."

"See, you do know me. Okay, no strings, no games, no pretenses." He walked over, slapped his hands on the counter, and caged her. "But I've got a hard and fast rule of my own. I don't share. As long as I'm fucking you, no one else is."

She balled her hands at her sides. "Well, that's clear enough. And crude enough."

"Your call. Why cloud the issue with euphemisms?"

"Just because you're angry that I said it first is no reason to—"

"There you go, seeing right through me again."

She took a steadying breath. "There's no reason for either

224

of us to be angry. First, I don't like to fight before I've had at least one cup of coffee. And second, I didn't mean that I would stroll out of here and jump into someone else's bed. Contrary to popular belief, I don't juggle men like flaming swords. I simply meant that when either of us is ready to move on, there won't be any nasty scenes."

"Maybe I like nasty scenes."

"I'm beginning to see that. Have we finished with this one?"

"Not quite." He caught her by the chin. "You know, duchess, this is the only time since you first picked up a mascara wand that I've seen you without makeup." With his free hand, he tugged the towel off her hair so that it tumbled wet and wild over breasts and shoulders. "Without all that sheen and polish."

"Cut it out." She tried to jerk her chin free, furious that he'd reminded her she was without her accustomed shield.

"You're so goddamn beautiful." But there was grim purpose rather than admiration in his eyes. "They'd have burned you at the stake a few hundred years ago. They'd never have believed you'd gotten that face, that body, without seducing the devil."

"Stop it." Was that her voice? she wondered. So weak, ready to melt on words she didn't mean. Her unsteady hands were an instant too late to stop the second towel from sliding to the floor. "If you think I'm going to let you—"

"Let me, hell." He slipped his hand between her legs and felt her hot and wet and ready. "You said no pretenses, Margo. So if you tell me you don't want me, right now . . ." He gripped her hips, braced her as he eased slowly inside her. "If you tell me, I'll believe you."

She felt the avalanche of need carrying her under. Saw by the dark triumph in his eyes that he knew it. "Damn you, Josh."

"Well, that makes two of us."

225

*　　*　　*

She skipped breakfast. She'd simply felt too raw and unsteady to share a civilized meal with him after they'd savaged each other in a steamy bathroom. Still, she'd gotten back to the shop, changed into a fresh suit, and brewed both coffee and tea.

The coffee she attacked herself, drinking half a pot before it was time to open the doors. Revving on nerves and caffeine, she faced her first day alone as a merchant.

By midday, despite several bolstering sales, both her spirits and her energy were flagging. A night without sleep certainly explained the fatigue, and she knew exactly where to point the finger of blame for her sulks. Right at Josh Templeton's calculating heart.

She hated the way he had shrugged and bid her an absent good-bye that morning. Sitting down to his breakfast as if there hadn't been wild sex and angry words between them. It hardly mattered that his attitude was exactly what she had outlined. That didn't stop her from worrying over the nagging certainty that he was playing some game she hadn't been informed of. And he kept shifting the rules to suit himself.

There had been a cold gleam in his eyes as he glanced up from his coffee, she thought. And she was sure she'd seen a calculating smirk on his mouth before she'd shut the door. Well, slammed it—but that was beside the point.

Just what was he up to? She knew him well enough to be sure . . . Damn it, she was beginning to wonder if she knew him at all.

"Miss, I'd like to see this pearl choker."

"Yes, of course." It made her feel brisk and efficient to fetch the keys, unlock the display, spread the gleaming pearls on black velvet. "They're lovely, aren't they? Beautifully matched."

A present, she remembered, from a shipping magnate old

enough to be her grandfather. She'd never slept with him, though the press had beat war drums about their affair. He'd only wanted someone young and attractive to talk to, someone to listen while he spoke of the wife he'd lost to cancer.

He had been, in the two years she had known him, a rare thing in her life. A male friend. The pearls had been nothing more than a gift from a friend who was pining away from a broken heart and who soon died from it.

"Is this clasp eighteen-karat?"

Suddenly Margo wanted to snatch them back, to scream at the woman that she couldn't have them. They were hers, a reminder of one of the few unselfish and loving things she'd ever done in her life.

"Yes." She forced herself to speak through a smile so stiff it ached. "Italian. It's stamped. Would you like to try them on?"

She did, and hemmed, hawed, preened, and stroked. In the end, she handed them back with a shake of her head. Margo locked the pearls into the display like a guilty secret.

Tourists came in, poking through the treasures, carelessly clanking porcelain against glass, china against wood. Margo lost three potential customers when she testily informed them not to handle the merchandise unless they were prepared to buy it.

That cleared the shop long enough for her to run upstairs and pump some aspirin into her system. On her way down again, she caught a glimpse of herself in the mirror.

Her face was set and angry, her eyes deadly. She felt her stomach jitter with repressed temper.

"Want to scare all the customers away, Margo?"

She closed her eyes, breathed deep, visualized a cool white screen. It was a technique she'd often used in modeling when a session had dragged on, with hairstylist and makeup artist poking, photographer waiting, assistants whining.

All she had to do was go away for a minute, remind herself that she could, and would, fill the blank screen with whatever image they wanted.

Calmer, she opened her eyes, watched her face smooth out. If her head still throbbed, no one had to know but herself. She walked downstairs ready to greet the next customer.

She was delighted when Judy Prentice dropped in, bringing a friend with her. She poured them tea, then excused herself to show another customer into a fitting room. At two, she opened the first bottle of complimentary champagne and wondered what was keeping Laura.

By two-thirty, she was feeling frazzled, struggling with the gift wrap she was afraid she would never get the hang of. And Candy breezed in.

"Oh, what an adorable little shop." She clapped her pretty hands together and bounced over to the counter, where Margo was sweating over a tape dispenser. "I'm so sorry I couldn't make it by for your opening, Margo. I just couldn't squeeze it into my day. But I made a special point of coming by today."

Particularly since the shop and its owners had been the hot topic at brunch.

"I'm just going to poke around, but don't you worry, I'll be sure to buy something. Isn't this fun," she said to the woman waiting for the package. "Just like a big yard sale. Oh, what a nice little bowl." She danced over, running her fingers over the frosted glass, looking for chips. "The price is a little high for secondhand." Still holding the bowl, she turned a sharp-edged smile on Margo. "I suppose you inflate it to give your customers room to bargain."

Keep cool, Margo warned herself. Candy was just trying to get her goat, the same way she had in high school. "We consider our merchandise priced to sell."

"Well." With a careless shrug, Candy set the bowl down. "I suppose I don't know very much about cost. I just know what I like." She eyed a pair of enameled candlesticks. "These are . . . unusual, aren't they?"

"You have lovely things," the waiting customer commented as Margo slipped the wrapped box into a bag.

"Thank you." Margo shuffled through her tired mind for the name on the credit slip. "Thank you very much, Mrs. Pendleton. Please come again."

"I certainly will." She accepted the bag, hesitated. "Do you mind if I say I only came in today because I've seen your photograph so many times? I spend a lot of time in Europe. La Margo's face is everywhere."

"Was everywhere. No, I don't mind."

"I switched to the Bella Donna line of skin-care products primarily because of your advertisements."

She winced before she could prevent herself. "I hope you're satisfied with the products."

"It's an excellent line. As I said, I came in because I wanted to see you in person. I'll come back because you have beautiful things imaginatively presented." She slid the bag onto her arm as she stepped back from the counter. "I think you're a very brave and adventurous woman." Mrs. Pendleton flicked a glance toward Candy, who was frowning over a paperweight. "And an admirable one." She leaned back over the counter, her eyes dancing. "Make sure that one doesn't stick something in that Chanel bag of hers. She looks shifty."

Chuckling, Margo waved her now favorite customer off and walked over to deal with Candy. "Champagne?"

"Oh, such a clever idea. I imagine the offer of free drinks lures in a certain type of clientele. Just a tiny glass. How are you managing, darling?"

"Well enough."

"I was just admiring your jewelry." Coveting it. "It must be heartbreaking for you to have to sell it."

"My heart's cold steel, Candy, remember?"

"When it comes to men," Candy said breezily and turned to the jewelry case. "But diamonds? I wouldn't think so. What did you have to do for those earrings?"

"Things better not spoken of in polite company. Would you like to see them? Considering your last divorce settlement, they're within your price range. Unless, of course, dumping a husband doesn't earn a woman what it used to."

"Don't be snide, Margo. You're the one peddling your wares. And no, I'm not interested in secondhand jewelry. In fact, I'm having a hard time finding anything I can use at all. Your taste is more . . . let's say, emancipated than mine."

"Not enough gold leaf? I'll be sure to keep your taste in mind when we restock."

"You're actually planning on keeping this place running?" She sipped her champagne and giggled. "Margo, that's so sweet. Everyone knows you never finish anything. A few of us were having a wonderful time over brunch at the club, speculating on how long you'd last."

The customer, Margo thought, was not always right. "Candy, do you remember that time all your clothes were stolen from gym class and you were shoved into a locker and stayed trapped in there until Mr. Hansen from Maintenance sawed off the lock and got you out, naked and hysterical? You, not Mr. Hansen."

Candy's eyes narrowed to lethal slits. "You. I knew it was you, but I couldn't prove it."

"Actually it was Kate, because I lost the draw. But it was my idea. Except for calling Mr. Hansen. That was Laura's. Now would you like to leave quietly, or should I knock you down, rip off that Laura Ashley blouse—which doesn't suit you, by the way—and send you out of here naked and hysterical?"

"To think I actually felt sorry for you."

"No, you didn't," Margo corrected, nipping the flute out of Candy's hand before it could be hurled.

"You're nothing but a second-rate slut who spent all her life begging for scraps and pretending to be something she never could be," Candy spat out.

"Funny, most people consider me a first-rate slut. Now get the hell out of here before I stop pretending to be what I'm not and rip off the nose your parents bought you when you were twelve."

Candy shrieked, curled her fingers into talons. She might have leaped, but the sound of the door opening stopped her from making a public display.

One brow lifted, Laura assessed the scene. "Hello, Candy, you're looking healthy. Sorry I'm late, Margo, but I brought you a present."

Candy whirled, intending to give Laura a taste of the temper both of her ex-husbands could attest to. But Laura wasn't alone. Candy shuddered back the venom and beamed a delighted smile.

"Mr. and Mrs. Templeton—how wonderful to see you both."

"Ah, Candace Lichfield, isn't it?" said Susan Templeton, knowing full well. "Margo." Easily ignoring Candy's outstretched hand, Susan glided into Margo's open arms. She kissed both of Margo's cheeks lavishly, then winked. "We didn't even take time to unpack. We just couldn't wait to see you."

"I've missed you." She clung hard, enveloped by the familiar scent of Chanel. "Oh, I've missed you. You look wonderful, beautiful."

"Doesn't give me the time of day," Thomas Templeton complained, giving his daughter's shoulder a quick squeeze. He nodded absently to Candy as she stalked out, then grinned as Margo raced across the room. She bounded into his arms. "Now that's more like it."

"I'm so glad to see you. I'm so glad you're here. Oh, I'm so sorry." And she buried her face in his shoulder and wept like a child.

Chapter Fourteen

"Better?"

"Mmm." Leaning over the sink in the upstairs bath, Margo splashed water on her face. "I guess I've been a little on edge."

"Nothing like a good cry to smooth out those edges." Susan offered her a fingertip towel and a quick, supportive rub on the shoulder. "And you always cried well."

"Poor Mr. T." As much for comfort as to dry her skin, Margo buried her face in the towel. "What a greeting. Two seconds and I'm blubbering all over his shoulder."

"He loves having his girls blubber on him. It makes him feel strong. Now—" Susan put her ring-studded hands on Margo's shoulders, turned her around. "Let's have a look." She pursed her pretty mouth, narrowed her pale blue eyes. "A little blush, a couple coats of mascara, and you'll do. Do you have your arsenal up here?''

In answer, Margo opened the mirror cabinet over the sink. Inside were neatly arranged bottles and tubes. ''Emergency kit.''

''That's my girl. Still using Bella Donna,'' she commented when Margo took out a small tube. ''I threw mine out.''

''Oh, Mrs. T.''

''They made me mad.'' Susan jerked an athletic shoulder. She was a small woman, delicate-boned and slim like her daughter. She kept in shape in her own style. She skied like a demon, played a vicious game of tennis, and swam laps as though competing in the Olympics. To fit her lifestyle, her sable-colored hair was cut short and sleek to cap a bright, interesting face that she cared for religiously.

''I screwed up,'' Margo reminded her.

''Which was hardly enough cause to dump you as the Bella Donna Woman. Which is an irritatingly redundant title in the first place. All in all, you're better off without them.''

Margo smiled into the mirror, smoothed on a light base. ''I really have missed you.''

''What I'd like to know is why you didn't contact Tommy and me the minute you found out you were in trouble.'' With her hands on her hips, Susan strode to the tub, then back to the sink. ''It was weeks before we heard a thing. The photographic safari kept us out of touch, but Josh and Laura knew how to reach us.''

''I was ashamed.'' She couldn't explain why she could admit it so easily to Susan. She just could. ''I'd made such bad choices. I was having a seedy affair with a married man, I let him use me. No, worse—I was too stupid to realize he was using me. I ruined my career, destroyed what little reputation I had, and nearly bankrupted myself in the process.''

''Well.'' Susan angled her head. ''That's quite an accomplishment. How busy you must have been to do all that by yourself.''

"I did do it myself." She chose taupe shadow to accent her eyes, brushing it on with a deft and practiced hand.

"This man you were involved with had nothing to do with it, I suppose. Did you love him?"

"I wanted to." Even that was easier to admit now. "I wanted to have someone, to find someone I could build a life with. The kind of life I thought I wanted. Fun, games, and no responsibilities."

"And that's past tense?"

"It is. Has to be." Margo carefully darkened her eyebrows. "Naturally, I chose someone completely inappropriate, someone who could never offer me permanence. That's my system, Mrs. T."

Susan waited a moment, watching as Margo dashed on eyeliner and mascara with the skill of a master. "Do you know what's always worried me about you, Margo? Your self-esteem."

"Mum always said I thought too much of myself."

"No, on that Annie and I have always disagreed, and we disagreed rarely. Your self-worth is too tied up in your looks. You were a beautiful child, dazzlingly beautiful. Life is different for children with dazzling looks. More difficult in some ways, because people tend to judge them by their beauty, and then they begin to judge themselves by that same standard."

"It was my only skill. Kate had the brains, Laura had the heart."

"It makes me sad that you believe that, and that too many people pointed you in that direction."

"You were never one of them." She replaced the makeup carefully, as a master carpenter would store his tools. "I'm trying to go in a new direction now, Mrs. T."

"Well, then." Slipping a bolstering arm around Margo's

waist, Susan led her back into the boudoir. "You're young enough to take a dozen different directions. And smart enough. You've wasted your brains for a while, made foolish mistakes and poorly considered choices."

"Ow." With a sheepish smile, Margo rubbed her heart. "You've always been able to sneak those jabs in."

"I haven't finished. You've worried and disappointed your mother. A woman, I'll add, who deserves not only your love and respect but your admiration. There aren't many who at the tender age of twenty-three and still grieving could leave behind everything familiar and cross an ocean with a small child to build a new life. But that's not the point." Susan waved that away and nudged Margo onto the edge of the bed. "You squandered your money and danced your way to the edge of a very high and dangerous cliff. But," she lifted Margo's chin with a finger, "you didn't jump. Unlike our little Seraphina, you stepped back, you squared your shoulders, and you showed you were willing to face what life had dealt you. That takes more courage, Margo—much more—than leaping into the void."

"I had people to turn to."

"So do we all. It's only fools and egotists who think no one will be there to lend a hand. And bigger fools and bigger egotists who don't reach out." She held out a hand. Without hesitation Margo took it, then pressed it to her cheek.

"Better?" Laura asked in an echo of her mother as she came to the door. It took only an instant to survey the scene and feel relief.

"Much." After a long breath, Margo rose, smoothed down her skirt. "Sorry to leave you in the lurch down there."

"No problem. Actually, Dad's having the time of his life. He's made three sales. And the way he's charming Minn Whiley right now, I think we can count on four."

"Minn's downstairs?" Amused, Susan flicked her fingers

236

through her boyish hair. "I'll go add my charm. She'll walk out loaded down with bags and won't know what hit her." She paused at the doorway to rub a hand over Laura's back. "You girls have a lovely place here. You've made a good choice."

"We're worrying her," Laura murmured when her mother's greeting to Minn floated upstairs. "You and I."

"I know. We'll just have to show her how tough we are. We are tough, aren't we, Laura?"

"Oh, sure. You bet. The disgraced celebrity and the betrayed trophy wife."

Temper snapped into Margo's eyes. "You're nobody's trophy."

"Not anymore. Now, before I forget—why was Candy looking at me as if she was hoping to grind up my liver for pâté?"

"Ah." Remembering the scene put a sneaky smile on her face. "I had to tell her whose idea it was to call Mr. Hansen when she was trapped naked in her locker."

Laura closed her eyes, tried not to think of the next meeting of the Garden Club. She and Candy were co-chairs. "Had to tell her?"

"Really had to." Margo smiled winningly. "She called you 'poor Laura.' Twice."

Laura opened her eyes again, set her teeth. "I see. I wonder how difficult it would be to stuff her bony butt into a locker at the club?"

"For tough babes like you and me? A snap."

"I'll think about it." Automatically she checked her watch. Her life now ran on packets of time. "Meanwhile, we're having a family dinner tonight. A real one this time. Kate's meeting us at the house, and I left a message for Josh."

"Ah, Josh." As they started for the stairs, Margo linked her fingers together, pulled them apart. Wished desperately for a cigarette. "There's probably something I should tell you."

"Mmm-hmm. Look, Margo." Chuckling, she leaned on the rail. "Dad's playing with the cash register and Mama's packing boxes. Aren't they wonderful?"

"The best." How could she tell Laura she'd spent the night ripping up the sheets at Templeton Monterey with her brother? Better left alone, she decided. In any case, the way they had parted, it was unlikely to happen again.

"What did you want to tell me?"

"Um . . . only that I sold your beaded white sheath."

"Good. I never liked it anyway."

Margo felt she'd made the right decision when Josh arrived at Templeton House. He joined the family in the solarium, exchanged warm embraces with both his parents, then helped himself from the hors d'oeuvres tray. He entertained his nieces, argued with Kate over some esoteric point of tax law, and fetched mineral water for Laura.

As for the woman with whom he'd spent the night committing acts that were still illegal in some states, he treated her with the absent, vaguely infuriating affection older brothers reserved for their pesky younger siblings.

She thought about stabbing him in the throat with a shrimp fork.

She restrained herself, even when she was plunked down between him and Kate at the glossy mahogany table at dinner.

It was, after all, a celebration, she reminded herself. A reunion. Even Ann, who considered it a breach of etiquette for servants to sit at the family table, had been cajoled into joining in. Mr. T.'s doing, Margo thought. No one, particularly if it was a female, could say no to him.

Surely part of Josh's problem was that he resembled his father so closely. Thomas Templeton was as tall and lean as he'd been in his youth. The man Margo had frankly adored for twenty-five years had aged magnificently. The lines that unfairly made a woman look worn added class and appeal as they crinkled around his smoky gray eyes. His hair was still thick and full, with the added dash of glints of silver brushed through the bronze.

He had, she knew, a smile that could charm the petals off a rose. And when roused, a flinty, unblinking stare that chilled to the bone. He used both to run his business, and his family, and with them he incited devotion, unswerving love, and just a little healthy fear.

It was rumored that he had cut a wide, successful, and memorable swath through the ladies in his youth, romancing, seducing, and conquering at will. Until thirty, when he'd been introduced to a young Susan Conway. She had, in her own words, hunted him down like a dog and bagged him.

Margo smiled, listening to him build stories for his goggle-eyed granddaughters of herds of elephants and prides of lions.

"We have the *Lion King* video, Granddaddy." Kayla toyed with her Brussels sprouts, hoping a miracle would make them disappear.

"You've watched it a zillion times," Ali said, tossing her hair back in the way she'd seen Margo do.

"Well, we'll have to make it a zillion and one, won't we?" Thomas winked at Kayla. "We'll have ourselves a moviethon. What's your favorite video, Ali?"

"She likes to watch kissy movies." Striking back, Kayla pursed her lips and made smacking noises. "She wants Brandon Reno to kiss her on the mouth."

"I do not." Mortified, Ali flushed scarlet. It proved there was no secret safe with a little sister. "You're just a baby." She dug for her deepest insult. "A baby pig-face."

"Allison, don't call your sister names," Laura said wearily. Her two little angels had been sniping at each other for weeks.

"Oh, and she can say whatever she wants. Just because she's the baby."

"I am not a baby."

"I thought you were my baby." Thomas sighed sadly. "I thought you were both my babies, but I guess if you're all grown up and don't need me anymore . . ."

"I'll be your baby, Granddaddy." Eyes wide and sincere, Kayla gazed up at him. Then she saw, to her delight, that a miracle had happened. The dreaded Brussels sprouts were gone from her plate. They'd made the leap to his. Love swarmed through her. "I'll always be your baby."

"Well, I'm not a baby." Far from ready to surrender, Ali jutted out her chin. But her lip was quivering.

"No, I suppose you're not." Laura cocked a brow at her daughter's mutinous face. "And since you're not, you won't fight with your sister at the table."

"Oh, I don't know." Margo picked up her wineglass. The fairy light of crystal chandeliers and flickering candlelight shot through it in red and gold glints. "I always fought with Kate at the table."

"And you usually started it," Kate added, forking up a bite of lamb.

"You always started it."

"No, I always finished it." Kate peered around Josh to grin. "You always got sent to your room."

"Only because Mum felt sorry for you. You were so outgunned."

"Outgunned, my butt. When it came to a verbal showdown, you were always playing with blanks. Even when I was Ali's age, I could—"

"Isn't it nice to be home, Tommy?" Susan lifted her glass in a toast. "It's so comforting to see that no matter how life goes on, little changes. Annie, dear, how are you managing all our girls without me?"

240

"It's a trial, Mrs. T. Now, my ma, she kept a switch in the kitchen. A good hickory switch."

War forgotten, Ali gaped at Ann. "Your mother hit you with a stick?"

"Once or twice she did indeed, and sitting down after was a punishment itself. Mostly just seeing it there on the peg by the door was enough to keep a civil tongue in your head."

"Your weapon of choice was a wooden spoon." Remembering, Margo shifted in her seat.

"A fine deterrent it was to a sassy mouth, too."

"You walloped me once with it, Annie, remember?" It was Josh who spoke.

"Really?" Intrigued, Susan studied her son. "I never heard about that."

Josh sampled his wine and watched Ann squirm out of the corner of his eye. "Oh, Annie and I decided it would be our little secret."

"And so it has been," Annie muttered. "Until now." She cleared her throat, dropped her hands into her lap. "I beg your pardon, Mrs. T. It was hardly my place to spank the boy."

"What nonsense." Intrigued, Susan leaned forward. "I want to know what he did to deserve it."

"I might have been innocent," Josh objected, to which his mother merely snorted.

"You never had an innocent day in your life. What did he do, Annie?"

"He'd been hounding me." Even after all the years that had passed, Ann could remember the insistence in his voice, the demon in his eye. "I tell you the truth, I've never known a child so tenacious as Master Josh. He could devil you beyond death, and that's the truth."

"Persistence." He grinned at Annie, then glanced at his father. "It's a trait of the Templeton males, right, Dad?"

"And plenty the times I earned a warm rear end because of it," Thomas agreed.

"I'd love to hear about Josh's." Margo tipped back her glass, sent him a smoldering look. "In fact, I'm dying to. How many whacks did you give him, Mum?"

"I didn't count. It was—"

"I did. Five. In rapid and shocking succession." He met Margo's look sneer for sneer. "I still say it was Margo's fault."

"Mine? Oh, that's so typical."

"He was teasing you unmercifully," Ann put in. "And picking on Miss Laura. And as Miss Kate had just come to us, he had a new target there. He was twelve, I believe, and acting like a bully."

"It was just high spirits," Josh claimed. "And I still say Margo—"

"Four years your junior," Ann said in a tone that made him feel twelve again. "And you, who should have known better, daring her and the other girls to clamber down those cliffs looking for that foolish treasure chest. Calling them names, too. And going out there after I'd told you to stay in the yard with them for one blessed hour. One blessed hour," she repeated, shrinking him with a look, "so I could finish the ironing in some peace. But off you went, and if I hadn't caught sight of you, the lot of you might have dashed yourselves on the rocks."

"Oh, that time." Margo smiled. "I'd like to know how that was my fault."

Josh cleared his throat because his tie suddenly felt too tight. Annie, he realized, hadn't lost her touch. "You said you knew where it was. That you'd seen it, and even had a gold doubloon."

"So," she shrugged, "I lied."

"Which would have earned you a swat if I'd known that part of it."

Satisfied, Josh poured more wine. "See?"

"Took it like a man, did you?" Thomas reached over to slap his son on the back. "And didn't drag a lady's name into it."

"He yelped like a scalded dog." Ann's dry comment brought a burst of laughter around the table. "But it hurting me more than him was never truer. I was sure I would be fired on the spot, and rightfully so for spanking the master's son."

"I'd have given you a raise," Susan said easily.

"Nothing like a mother's love," Josh muttered.

"Well, he came up to me about an hour later. Seemed he had thought it through well enough." Now the look Ann sent Josh was full of warmth. "He apologized as neat as you please, then asked if we couldn't keep the matter between us."

"Smart boy." Thomas slapped him on the back again.

Later, when Laura was up putting the children to bed, they lounged in the parlor. It was, Margo realized, moments like this, rooms like this, that had spurred her quest for more.

Soft, rich lights from jewel-hued lamps bathed the glossy walls, played over the dark windows where drapes had been left open wide. The faded colors in the Oriental rugs seemed to highlight the gleam of the wide-planked chestnut floors.

A perfect room in a perfect house, she thought, with the old, heirloom furniture more a statement of permanence than wealth. Fresh flowers lovingly arranged by her mother's hands speared out of china and crystal. Terrace doors, flung open, welcomed a quiet, fragrant night with just the right touch of moonlight.

It was a room that breathed elegance and warmth and welcome. And, she understood now that when she had run from it to make her own, she had focused only on the elegance.

Warmth and welcome had been neglected for too long.

Josh sat at the baby grand improvising blues with Kate. Lazy, blood-stirring music, she mused. That suited him. He didn't play often. Margo had nearly forgotten how clever he was with the keys. She wished it didn't remind her how clever those hands had been last night.

She wished that hearing the companionable way he and Kate laughed together, seeing the intimate way their heads bent close, didn't shoot a burning blast of jealousy through her blood.

Ridiculous reaction, she told herself. Knee-jerk. Which certainly suited the occasion, as he'd been a complete and utter jerk all evening. But he wasn't going to spoil it for her, she decided. She was going to enjoy her time with the Templetons, her evening in the house she'd always loved, and the hell with him.

Couldn't he at least look at her when she was despising him?

She was too wrapped up in her own foul thoughts to notice the tacit look that passed between the Templetons. With a nod, Susan rose. She would go upstairs, corner Laura, and find out exactly how her daughter was feeling.

Thomas poured a brandy, lighted the single cigar his wife now allowed him per day, and sat on the curved settee. Catching Margo's eye, he patted the cushion beside him.

"Aren't you afraid I'll start bawling again?"

"I've got a fresh handkerchief."

She did sit, brushed her fingers over the edge of white in his top pocket. "Irish linen. Mum tricked me into learning to iron with your handkerchiefs. They always felt so soft and smelled so good when they came out of the wash. I never see Irish linen without remembering standing at the ironing board in the laundry room, pressing your handkerchiefs into perfect white squares."

244

"Ironing's becoming a lost art."

"It would have been lost years ago if men had had to do it."

He laughed and patted her knee. "Now tell me about this business you're running."

She'd known he would ask, known she'd fumble for an explanation. "Kate could give you a better, more organized rundown."

"I'll get the fine print and bottom line from our Kate. I want to know what you're looking to get out of it."

"A living. I let the one I had get away."

"You fucked up, girl. No use prettying it up, or moping over it. What are you doing now?"

It was one of the reasons she loved him. No sentimentalizing over mistakes. "Trying to make people buy what I want to sell. I collected a lot of things over the years. It was one of the things I did best. You know, Mr. T., I realized when I was packing up that I might not have deliberately surrounded myself with the interesting or the potentially valuable, but that's what I did. I think I have an eye for buying."

"I won't argue with that. You always had a sense of quality."

"Even when I didn't have any other kind of sense. I tossed my money away on things, and now I've found a way that I don't have to be sorry about it. Buying the building instead of renting was a risk, I know."

"If it hadn't been a good investment, Kate wouldn't have let you do it, and she damn well wouldn't have anted up her own money."

"Including repair, remodeling, and startup, six hundred and thirty-seven dollars a square foot," Kate said over her shoulder. "And some loose change."

"A good price." Thomas puffed on his cigar. "Who did the renovations?"

"Barkley and Sons handled the carpentry and subcontracted out the plumbing and wiring." Margo took his snifter for a sip. "I did most of the painting myself."

"Did you now?" He grinned around his cigar. "Advertising?"

"I'm using my checkered past to get print space with interviews, some television. Kate's going to try to squeeze out time to look things over and see if we can budget in advertising money."

"And how are you going to replace your stock?"

Looking forward made her nervous, but Margo answered briskly. "I'll have to try auctions and estate sales. I thought I could contact some of the models and designers I know, negotiate to buy used clothes that way. But I'll have to expand from that, because we've already gotten a lot of requests for larger sizes."

She scooted around on the settee, curled her legs under her. If anyone would understand the thrill of business dealings, it would be Mr. T. "I know we've only been open for two days, but I really think we can make it work. No one else has anything like it."

She forgot to be worried, and her voice began to bubble with excitement. "At least I don't know of any shop that offers secondhand designer clothes along with fashion and fine jewelry, furniture, glassware, antiques."

"Don't forget kitchen appliances and art," Josh put in.

"My cappuccino maker isn't for sale," she shot back. "And neither are my paintings. But the rest"—she shifted back to Thomas—"hell, I'd sell my underwear for the right price."

"You are selling your underwear," Kate reminded her.

"Pegnoirs," Margo corrected. "Negligees. Laura has already added to the stock. Of course, Kate won't part with a bedroom slipper."

"I'm still wearing them."

"But we're drawing people in, and a lot of them are buying."

"And you're happy."

"I don't know about happy yet, but I'm determined."

"Margo." He patted her knee. "In business that's the same thing. Why don't you have a display set up in the hotel lobby?"

"I—"

"We have half a dozen up for boutiques and jewelry stores, gift shops. Why don't we have one from our own girls?" He jabbed the air with his cigar, spilling ashes that Margo automatically brushed from his knee. "Josh, I'd have expected you to take care of that. Templeton takes care of its own, and it has a policy of supporting small businesses."

"I've already arranged it." Josh continued to noodle out boogie-woogie. "Laura's going to select the pieces for the hotel, and for another display at the resort."

Margo opened her mouth, then set her teeth. "You might have mentioned it to me."

"I might have." He shot a look over his shoulder, his fingers never faltering. "I didn't. Laura knows what works best for Templeton clientele."

"Oh, and I wouldn't know anything about that."

"Here she goes," Kate murmured.

"I know as much as you do about Templeton clientele," Margo fumed, unfolding her legs to get to her feet. "Damn it, I've *been* Templeton clientele. And if you're interested in displaying merchandise from Pretenses, then you talk to me."

"Fine." He stopped playing to glance at his watch. "I've got a tennis match with Mom at seven. I've set up the board meeting for nine-thirty. Does that suit you?"

"Well enough." Thomas settled back with his brandy. "We'll meet at eight-forty-five, to discuss those other matters beforehand."

"Good." Josh flicked his eyes back to Margo. "Annie's got your bag packed by now. Why don't you go up and get it?"

"My bag?" She found herself teetering between unfinished temper and bafflement. "Why do I need a bag?"

"So you won't have to rush back to the shop to change every morning. It makes more sense to have your clothes where you sleep."

Her cheeks flushed, not from embarrassment but from fury. "I sleep here, or at the shop."

"Not anymore." He walked over, took her hand in a firm grip. "Margo's staying with me at the hotel, for the time being."

"Look, you jerk, just because I made the regrettable mistake of sleeping with you once—"

"Neither of us got any sleep," he reminded her. "But we'll have to tonight. I've got a full day coming up. Let's get going."

"Oh, I'll go all right." Her toes bumped into his. "I'll be delighted to go with you so I can have the time and the privacy to tell you exactly what I think of you."

Appreciating good timing, Kate waited until the door had closed behind them before she swiveled on the piano bench. "Okay, Uncle Tommy, which one is going to be found in the morning in a pool of their own blood, and which one will be holding the blunt instrument? My money's on Margo," she decided. "She's vicious when she's cornered."

He sighed, trying to compute the new development. "Have to go with my boy, Katie girl. Never known him to lose a fight unless he wanted to."

Chapter Fifteen

She didn't speak on the drive to the hotel. She had a great deal to say, but she was saving it up. When he carried her garment bag into the bedroom and hung it in the closet, she pounced.

"If you're laboring under some egotistical delusion that I came here to have sex with you—"

"Not tonight, honey." He loosened his tie. "I'm beat."

The only sound she could make was a strangled growl in her throat as she used both hands to shove him back.

"Okay, okay, if you insist. But I won't be at my best."

"Don't you put your hands on me! Don't even think about it." Because her feet were tired, she pulled off her shoes. She kept one handy as a weapon, tapping it restlessly against her palm as she paced. "It wasn't bad enough that you told your

249

family I'd been with you last night, you had the nerve to tell my mother to pack my clothes."

"I asked her," Josh corrected, hanging his jacket over the valet. "I asked if she would mind putting what she thought you'd need for a day or two in a bag. Until you had a chance to take care of the rest yourself."

"And that makes it all right? Because you said please and thank you? Which is certainly more than you said to me."

He flicked open the buttons of his shirt, worked out kinks in his shoulders. "I have no intention of sneaking around the way you did with your last choice of bedmates, duchess. If we're sleeping together, we do it, metaphorically speaking, in the open."

His shoes went next, then socks, while she fumbled through her mind for the right retort. "I haven't decided if I'm going to sleep with you again."

His gaze flicked up to her face, filled with both amusement and challenge. "Well, you should have said so."

It was her good luck that he was sitting on the edge of the bed. So much easier to look down her nose at him. "I didn't care for the way you behaved before I left here this morning."

"That makes us even." He rose, unhooked his trousers, and walked into the bath to turn on the water in the oversized whirlpool tub. "Now that we've settled that, let's stop playing the games you claimed we weren't going to play. We haven't finished with each other yet." Off went his briefs, on went the jets. "Now I want to work out some kinks before I go to bed. You're welcome to join me."

"You think I'm just going to pop into the tub with you? After you spent most of the evening ignoring me?" Men never ignored her, she fumed. Never. He was going to pay for that, if for nothing else. "And the way you were flirting with Kate?"

"Kate?" Genuinely surprised, he blinked at her. "Jesus, Margo, Kate's my sister."

"No more than I am."

Unsure whether he was amused or just plain tired, he stepped down into the tub, lowered himself, and let the hot bubbling water do its job. "You're right, she's not. Let's put it this way. I've always thought of Kate as my sister." His eyes rested on hers before he laid his head back and sank down. "I never thought of you that way. But, if you're jealous . . ." He trailed off with a shrug.

"I'm not jealous." The very idea was appalling to the pride. "I'd have to give two good damns to be jealous. I'm making a statement. Will you open your eyes and pay attention to me?"

"I'm paying attention. I'm too damn tired to open my eyes. Christ, for someone who couldn't wait to throw down warning flags about not getting too serious, not tangling each other up with strings, you're acting more like a nagging wife than a casual lover."

"I am not nagging." Then she closed her mouth, afraid she might have been close to doing so. "And I'm certainly not acting like a wife. From what I've observed about wives, any one of them worth her salt would have booted you out on your pointy head by now."

He merely smiled, dipped down a little lower. "It's my penthouse, baby. If anyone gets booted out on anything pointy, it'll be you."

Her hand clamped down on his head. From the advantage of surprise and leverage, she managed to hold him under the churning water for ten glorious seconds. It was even worth the water splashing out on her white linen suit when he surfaced, sputtering.

"I believe I'll get my bag and check into another room."

He caught her wrist, hard, threw her off balance enough that she had to stoop down to brace on the ledge of the tub. Their eyes met, locked.

"You wouldn't—" She stopped herself before uttering the D word, but already implied, it was too late. He yanked her into the tub and, as she hissed and spat like a cat, wrapped his arms around her and shoved her under.

He contemplated the ceiling for a few seconds as she kicked, hummed a few seconds more as she thrashed. Then pulled her up by the hair.

"You bastard. You goddamn—"

"Whoops, not done yet." He cheerfully dunked her again. The tub was big enough for four, which was handy because she was slippery and he needed room to maneuver. By the time she was gasping and trying to drag her sopping hair out of her eyes, hc'd already dealt with her jacket. He was working on removing the clinging wet blouse.

"What the hell do you think you're doing?"

"I'm getting you naked." He flicked open the front hook of her bra. "I'm not feeling tired anymore."

Eyes narrowed, she shifted quickly so that her knee was pressed dangerously close to his crotch. "Do you have some sort of incredibly lame, essentially male idea that being manhandled arouses me?"

It was a tricky one, he thought. "Yeah—in a manner of speaking."

She increased the pressure. "Whose manner of speaking?"

"Ah . . ." He took a chance, reached out to rub his thumb gently over her nipple. It was pebble hard. "I might have resisted if you hadn't dared me." The pressure eased off slightly, and he figured it was safe to breathe again. "I want you to stay with me, Margo." His voice was soft now, barely a murmur as he stroked a hand up her leg. "If you'd rather book another room until you've thought about it, that's fine. If you're not in the mood for sex, that's fine, too."

For a moment she simply studied him. All innocence, she mused, except for that wicked glint in his eye. All patient reason—except for the challenging quirk at the corner of his mouth.

"Who said I wasn't in the mood?" She pushed back her dripping hair, slanted him that killer look under her lashes. "Are you going to help me out of the rest of these wet clothes, or do I have to do it myself?"

"Oh, allow me."

It was an interesting experience, living with a man. She'd never done so before because she hadn't been willing to share her space or privacy with anyone for longer than a weekend trip to the mountains, a jaunt to the seaside, or perhaps an extended cruise.

But it worked well enough with Josh. Perhaps, she supposed, because they had lived under the same roof for years, and because the one that currently covered their heads was a hotel.

It made it all seem less structured, more like an arrangement than a commitment. They merely shared rooms, she thought, business rooms at that. The flowers were freshened, the furniture polished, the towels replaced by staff rarely seen. That kept it impersonal, almost like an extended holiday.

Fun and games, she decided, was exactly what she and Josh wanted, and expected from each other.

No one in the family questioned her new accommodations. After days stretched into a week, then two, she began to wonder why they didn't.

Her mother at least should have been outraged, or tight-lipped. But she seemed completely unconcerned. Neither of the Templetons so much as lifted an eyebrow. And though she caught Laura watching her with a worried frown now and then, Laura also said nothing.

It was Kate who made the single pithy comment. "Break his heart and I'll break your neck," she said. And it was such a ridiculous statement that Margo had chosen to ignore it rather than rise to the bait.

She had too much to do to worry about Kate's snippy temperament. Echoes of the nastiness that Candy was spreading bounced back to her—the merchandise at Pretenses was inelegant and overpriced, the service lax, rude, and inexperienced. Laura had overextended herself to bail out her reckless, undeserving friend, and they would be bankrupt within the month. The clothing was gray market knockoffs fashioned from inferior materials.

Brooding over Candy's vindictiveness and the inevitable fallout ate into Margo's time. The shop took up at least ten hours a day, six days a week. On the one day she closed it, she struggled with paperwork until she was cross-eyed from trying to learn the fine points of bookkeeping. Though she had resented every minute she'd been forced to sit in a classroom, she now considered signing up for a course on business management.

There she was on a balmy Sunday morning, a cigarette burning in the ashtray beside her, pecking at the keys of the computer—the desktop Kate had insisted they couldn't live without—and struggling to make sense out of a spreadsheet.

Why were there so many bills? she wondered. There were more eating away at her pockets than there had been when she was unemployed. How was anyone supposed to remember how and when and whom to pay and stay sane? Life had been so much simpler when she'd had a manager seeing to all the irritating financial details of life.

"And look where that got you, Margo," she muttered. "Concentrate. Take charge."

"I told you it was serious."

At the sound of the voice, Margo shrieked and jerked back

254

in the chair. The computer manual on her lap went flying.

"I see what you mean," Kate agreed. "I only hope we're not too late."

"Why don't you just shoot me next time?" Margo crossed her hands over her breasts and pressed to keep her heart in place. "What the hell are you doing here?"

"Rescuing you." Laura darted over in time to catch the cigarette before it finished rolling to the floor and igniting the papers spread around Margo's chair. She tapped it out neatly. "Talking to yourself, drinking alone."

"It's coffee."

"Closed up in your little room counting your money like Silas Marner," Laura finished.

"I'm not counting my money—though I have been able to pay off another five thousand, despite Candy Litchfield's plot to see me dragged off in chains—I'm—"

"She'll start gibbering any minute," Kate put in. "Told you we should have brought the nets."

"Such wit." Margo grabbed her cigarettes, lighted a fresh one. "Since you're so bright and sharp, explain all this insurance to me again. How come we have to pay these—what are they?"

"Premiums," Kate said dryly. "They're called premiums, Margo."

"I think they should be called extortion. I mean, look at this. There's fire and theft, there's mortgage insurance, title insurance, earthquake insurance, comprehensive—whatever that means, because it's incomprehensible to me. And this umbrella. Is that some cute insurance-speak for flood protection?"

"Oh, yeah, that's it." Kate rolled her eyes. "Insurance companies are filled with jokers. Those boys are a laugh a minute. You'll see that for yourself the first time you file a claim."

"Look, smart-ass, if you'd just explain how it works again."

"No, no, I'm begging you." Laura grabbed Kate's shoulders. "Please, don't explain how it works again. And don't get into the thing again."

"The thing?" Kate repeated.

"You know the thing."

"Yeah, the thing." Shifting in her chair, Margo jabbed at the air with her cigarette. "I'd like to talk about the thing, actually."

"Oh, that thing." Kate sniffed at Margo's coffee, decided it was probably palatable, and picked up the cup. "Okay, here's the thing. Estimated tax payments are split into quarters—" She broke off, staring blandly at Laura. "That's a very good scream. I see where Kayla gets it." With a sigh, she leaned over and to Margo's distress and envy, batted a few keys and had the screen blinking off. "There, all gone. Feel better now?"

"Much." Laura shuddered. "But it was close."

"Well, the two of you are in a rare mood." Margo snatched her coffee back from Kate. "Now run along and play. Some of us have work to do."

"It's worse than I thought." Laura heaved a sigh. "Okay, Sullivan, come quietly, or we'll have to get tough. It's for your own good."

Margo wasn't sure whether to laugh or call for help when they flanked her and took her arms. "Hey, what's the idea?"

"Shock therapy," Kate said grimly.

An hour later, Margo was naked and sweating. Lying on her back, she let out a long, heartfelt moan. "Oh, God. God. *God.*"

"Just roll with it." Sympathetically, Laura patted her hand. "It'll be better soon."

"Mum? Is that you?"

With a chuckle, Laura leaned back. Steam billowed in clouds and drained some of her own tension away. Maybe she'd come up with the idea of a day in the spa facilities of the resort for Margo's sake, but it wasn't doing her any harm either.

"How do you all just lie here like this?" From her perch on the second-level bench, Kate rolled over, stared down at Margo. "I mean, are we really having fun?"

"I could weep," Margo murmured. "I'd forgotten, actually forgotten what it was like." She reached out to pat Laura's naked knee. "My life for you. I'm getting a facial, and a fango, and a pedicure."

"You know, honey, you're staying right at the hotel. The facilities there aren't as extensive as here, but you could use the sauna, get a massage. And they give very good facials in the beauty salon."

"She's too busy boffing Josh."

Laura winced. "Do you mind? That's an image I'd just as soon not have in my head."

"I kinda like it." Kate peeked over the edge. "It's like something on the Discovery Channel. Two sleek golden animals mating." When Laura moaned, Kate's grin widened. "So is he good, or what? Like on a scale of one to ten."

"We're out of high school. I don't rate men," Margo said primly and rolled onto her stomach. "Twelve," she muttered. "Maybe fourteen."

"Really?" The idea perked Kate up. "Good old Josh. Our Josh."

My Josh. Margo nearly said it before she caught herself. "Ignore the idiot in the balcony," she told Laura. "Does it really bother you? Josh and me?"

"Not bother." Uncomfortable, Laura shifted. "It's just

weird. My brother and one of my closest friends and sex. It's just . . . weird. It's none of my business.''

"She's worried you'll toss him out like an old Ferragamo pump when you're done with him.''

"Shut up, Kate. And I don't throw my shoes out anymore. I sell them. Laura, Josh, and I understand each other. I promise you.''

"I wonder if you do,'' Laura murmured, and whatever else might have been said was interrupted as the door to the steam room opened.

"Look who's here,'' Kate said brightly. "It's Candy Cane.'' Because her teeth threatened to grind together, she set them in a feral smile. "Won't this just be cozy?''

With her turbaned head erect, Candy sat down on the bench opposite Laura. "The three of you still travel in a pack, I see.''

"Like rabid dogs,'' Kate agreed. "And since you're the one who's been trying to steal our bone, be careful we don't bite.''

"I have no idea what you're talking about.''

"Inferior, overpriced merchandise, my ass,'' Kate shot out. "You'd better watch your mouth, Candy, before you find yourself in the middle of a slander suit.''

"Expressing an opinion isn't slander.'' She'd checked with her second husband, the lawyer, to be sure. "It's a matter of taste.'' Proud of the body her first husband, the plastic surgeon, had helped create, Candy spread her towel open. "One might have thought you had more, Laura. But apparently bloodlines and breeding aren't always enough to ensure taste in companions.''

"You know, I was just thinking that.'' Margo sat up. "Both of your exes had such sterling pedigrees. Go figure.''

With some dignity, Candy crossed her naked legs. "I wanted to speak to you, Laura, about the Garden Club. Under the circumstances, I think it would be best if you resigned as co-chair.'' When Laura only lifted a brow, Candy dabbed at her throat with the edge of her towel. "There's gossip brewing, about you and Peter, about your association with . . ." She skimmed her eyes over Margo. "Certain unsuitable elements."

"I'm an unsuitable element," Margo told Kate.

"That's nothing. I'm an undesirable element. Aren't I, Candy?"

"You are simply detestable."

"See?" Grinning, Kate leaned over, staring into Margo's upturned face. "I'm detestable. It's because I'm the poor and distant relation. The Powells were a questionable offshoot of the Templetons, you know."

"I'd heard that."

"And I'm an accountant," Kate went on. "Which is much worse than a shopkeeper. We actually talk about money."

"That's enough," Laura said quietly. "You want the chair to yourself, Candy, it's all yours." She only regretted she wasn't able to break it over Candy's empty head. "That'll give me more time to associate with unsuitable and undesirable elements."

The easy capitulation was disappointing. Candy had so hoped for a fight. "And how is Peter enjoying Hawaii?" she said with a sneer. "I heard he took that clever little secretary of his with him this time. Though now that I think of it, they did take several . . . business trips before. It must be devastating to find yourself replaced by an employee of your own company. She's quite young too, isn't she?"

"Candy likes them young," Kate said, as fury bubbled through her. "How old is the pool boy you're bumping, Candy? Sixteen?"

"He's twenty," she snapped, then seethed at the way she had stepped into the trap. "At least I can get a man. But then, you don't want a man, do you, Kate? Everyone knows you're a lesbian."

Margo snorted, had to slap a hand over her mouth to hold the next one in. "Oh-oh, Kate, secret's out."

"It's a relief." Kate scooted forward on the bench so that she could leer at Candy's body. "I've had my eye on you for years, Sugar Lips, but I was too shy to tell you."

"It's true." Conspiratorially, Margo leaned toward Candy. "She's been afraid of her love for you."

Unsettled, unsure, Candy shifted. "That's not amusing."

"No, it's been painful, wrenching." Kate swung her legs over the bench, slid down. "But now that you know the truth, I can make you mine at last."

"Don't touch me." Squeaking, Candy jumped up, fumbled with her towel. "Don't come near me."

"I think they want to be alone," Laura commented and wrapped her towel over her breasts.

"I hate you. I hate all of you."

"God." Kate gave a quick shudder. "Isn't she the sexiest little thing?"

"You're revolting." Fearing for her life, Candy dashed out of the steam room, leaving her towel behind.

"Pervert," Margo said mildly when Kate collapsed on the bench.

"Careful, you might get me hot. If I was a lesbian, I'm sure you'd be more my type." Catching her breath, she looked over at Laura. "Honey, don't let her get to you."

"Hmm?" Distracted, Laura glanced back. "I was just thinking—how much do you think she paid for that boob job?"

"Not enough." Margo rose and tucked the towel in place. "Come on, let's go stuff her in a locker. For old time's sake."

"I do like men," Kate insisted, fidgeting as her toenails were painted. The salon's cotton-candy-pink and spun-sugar-white decor was designed to put a woman into a relaxed and

260

festive mood. It made Kate itchy. "I just don't have a lot of time for them."

"You won't need time after Candy gets done," Laura said. She sipped her sparkling mineral water and relaxed in the deep cushions of the high-backed swivel chair. "By the time she gets through spreading the word, any man within a hundred-mile radius is going to avoid you like a vasectomy."

"Well, maybe it's a blessing." Kate flipped through the stack of fashion magazines on the table beside her and found nothing of interest. "It might discourage that jerk Bill Pardoe from calling me all the time."

"Bill is a very sweet and decent man."

"Then you go out with him, let him tickle your knee under the table and call you honeybunch."

"She's always been too picky." Margo kept her eyes closed, nearly purring as her feet were massaged. "She'd have had more fun in her life if she'd gone looking for Mr. Goodbar instead of Mr. Perfect."

"I look for more in a date than a fat portfolio and a penis."

"Girls, girls." Laura picked up her mineral water again. "We have to stick together now. If Candy follows through and files charges for assault, it could get sticky."

"But, officer," Margo cooed, batting her lashes. "It was just high-spirited, girlish fun. Shit, she'd never humiliate herself by admitting in public that for the second time in her life she'd been trapped naked in a gym locker. She'll be more subtle than that. I say within a week we all have new identities. The slut, the shrew, and the dyke."

"I might like being the shrew," Laura decided. "Being the wimp gets old fast."

"You were never the wimp," Margo said loyally.

"Oh, yes, I've been a practicing wimp for years. It's going to take some doing to make the leap to shrew. But I might

261

give it a shot. Josh?'' She blinked as her brother walked into the salon, looking hot and harassed.

"Ladies." He plopped down in a vacant chair, picked up Margo's glass of water, and guzzled it down. "Well don't you all look . . ." He paused, skimmed his eyes over three faces packed in green goo. "Hideous. Been having fun?"

"Go away." Living with a man didn't mean he had to see you in a seaweed pack, Margo thought. "This is a girl thing."

He set her empty glass down, picked up Kate's, and guzzled that too. "I was into my second set with Carl Brewster on the courts here. You know Carl Brewster, television journalist, investigative reporter, and anchor on *Informed*, that long-running, highly rated, and revered newsmagazine."

The tone of his voice had Laura biting her lip. "I've heard of it. How is Carl?"

"Oh, fit and sassy, not that I wasn't whipping his ass, but I digress. *Informed* is planning to do a series of reports on the fine hotels of the world, with Templeton, of course, as a highlight. I've spent weeks arranging for various crews to film our hotels, interview staff, certain guests. All to show the viewing public the fine, upstanding, sophisticated, and unrivaled class and hospitality of Templeton, worldwide."

He set aside Kate's glass. Laura wordlessly handed him hers. "I'm sure they got some wonderful footage."

"Oh, they did. Naturally when Carl suggested we get some clips of the two of us playing tennis at our landmark resort here in Monterey, I agreed. A nice, human touch, the VP of Templeton enjoying the pleasant surroundings where his guests are always pampered and satisfied."

He paused, smiled charmingly at the hovering beauticians. "Would you mind giving us a moment?" After they'd moved away a discreet distance, his smile turned to a snarl. "Imagine my surprise, my distress, when one of our regular patrons raced screaming into camera range, her Templeton Spa robe

262

flapping open, her eyes wild as she sputtered accusations about being attacked—bodily attacked—by Laura Templeton Ridgeway and her cohorts.''

"Oh, Josh, I'm so sorry." Laura turned her head away, hoping he'd take it for shame. It would never, never do to laugh.

He showed his teeth. "One snicker, Laura. Just one."

"I'm not snickering." Composed, she turned back. "I'm terribly sorry. It must have been very embarrassing for you."

"And won't it just be a laugh riot when they run that little scene? Of course, they'll beep out most of the dialogue to conform to Standards and Practices, but I think the viewing audience, the millions of people who tune into *Informed* each week will get the gist."

"She started it," Kate said, then winced when he turned flinty eyes on her. "Well, she did."

"I'm sure Mom and Dad will understand that completely."

Even the stalwart Kate could be cowed. "It was Margo's idea."

Margo hissed through her teeth, "Traitor. She called Kate a lesbian."

Shaking his head, Josh covered his face with his hands and rubbed, hard. "Oh, well, then, get the rope."

"I suppose you'd have let her get away with it. She's been trying to damage the shop. She said nasty things to Laura," Margo went on, heating up. "And just the other day she came into the shop and called me a slut. A second-class slut."

"And your answer was to gang up on her, three to one, smack her around, strip her naked, and shove her into a locker?"

"We never smacked her. Not once." Not, Margo thought, that she wouldn't have liked to. "As for the locker business, it was a matter of tradition. We did nothing more than embarrass her, which is no more than she deserved after the way

263

she insulted us. And anyway, a real man would applaud our actions."

"Unlike you, and your idiot sisters here, pitiful insults from crazy women don't bother me. And your timing was rare and perfect." He leaned forward, pleased to be able to pay her back, in spades, for the "real man" comment. "I'd just begun to get Carl to nibble at the idea of doing a sidebar story on the latest innovation of a Templeton heir. Laura Templeton Ridgeway's partnership with old and dear friends Margo Sullivan—yes, *the* Margo Sullivan, and Kate Powell. Smart, savvy women creating and running a smart, savvy business."

"We're going to get air on *Informed*? That's fabulous."

He shot Margo a disgusted look. "Christ, you are an idiot. What you're going to get, unless I can do some fast and sweet talking, is sued and very possibly charged in a criminal action. She's claiming assault, verbal and physical abuse—and now that I know Kate's a lesbian, that explains the sexual abuse she tossed in."

"I am not a lesbian," Kate fumed. "Though the way she said it was an insult to any rational person who supports freedom of sexual preference." From his expression she realized it wasn't the time to get up on any liberal or feminist soapbox. Instead, she shifted, sulked. "And I never touched her in any sexual way. This is completely out of proportion, Josh, and you know it. She gave us grief, and we gave her some back. That's all."

"That's not all. The Templeton Resort isn't second-period gym class. This is the adult world. Didn't any of you remember her second husband was a litigator? A litigator who delights in pursuing and winning just this sort of nuisance suit. She could go after the shop."

Every ounce of blood in Margo's face drained. "That's ridiculous. She'd never get it. No court would take her that seriously."

"Maybe not." His voice was a cold snap, an unmerciful whip. "But the time and expense you'd have to put into fighting her off could go a long way toward draining your capital." He rose, shook his head at the three of them. "If you haven't been paying attention the last decade or so, school's out. So, you sit here and enjoy having your toenails painted while I go back to work and try to save your sorry butts."

"He's really steamed," Kate murmured as he stormed out. "One of us should go talk to him." She looked from Margo to Laura. "One of you should go talk to him."

"I'll go." Laura rose, feeling ridiculous in her little paper slippers and cotton balls.

"No, you'd better warn your parents, tell them we've put our foot in it." Margo sighed, struggled not to be terrified. "I'll do what I can with Josh."

She gave him an hour. It took her nearly that long to put herself together, in any case. When facing a furious man, she thought it wise to look her best.

He was on the phone at the desk in the office when she walked in, and he didn't so much as flick a glance at her. So much, she thought, for a five-hundred-dollar session at the spa. Saying nothing, she crossed to the desk and waited for him to complete his call.

He'd frightened her, he noted. And he'd meant to. Her wild temperament was part of what he found so appealing about her. But in the past weeks, he'd watched her channel that temperament, all that passion and energy into building something for herself. It infuriated him that with one careless tantrum, she'd risked damaging it.

"Yes, I said for a full year. Any and all services. I'll draft a memo to that effect. You'll have it by tomorrow." He hung up the phone, drummed his fingers on the desk.

"Tell me what I have to do," she said quietly. "If an apology will help, I'll go over and apologize to her right now."

"Give me a dollar."

"What?"

"Give me a goddamn dollar."

Baffled, she opened her purse. "I don't have a single. I have a five."

He snatched it out of her fingers. "I'm now your legal counsel, and as such I'm advising you to admit nothing. You're not going to apologize for anything because you didn't do anything. You don't know what she's talking about. Now if you tell me there were six other naked women and three attendants hanging around who saw you shove her into the locker, I'll have to kill you."

"There was nobody else there. We're not idiots." She grimaced. "I know you think we are, but we're not stupid enough to have done it in front of witnesses. Actually, we timed it that way so she'd be stuck in there longer." She smiled weakly. "It seemed like a good idea at the time." When he said nothing, she felt her temper simmer again. "Aren't you the one who broke Peter's nose?"

"I could afford to indulge myself."

"Oh, that's typical. The Templeton heir can behave any way he pleases and damn the consequences."

His eyes flashed, a dangerous, edgy glint. "Let's just say I pick my battles."

She forced herself to stop. Josh's attitude and position were hardly the point. "How much trouble am I in?" she demanded. "I know you're not a trial lawyer, so that five bucks isn't going to do me much good if this actually goes to court."

"It depends on how stubborn she is." With an effort, he calmed himself. Her little jab at his character was nothing new. "Templeton's official stand will be shock and distress that such an incident occurred while she was a guest. We're compensating her for her inconvenience and stress with a year's

266

complementary services at any of our Spa Resorts. That, and the fact that publicizing the incident will be embarrassing for her, might do it.''

He ran the five-dollar bill through his fingers, laid it on the desk blotter. ''She might be satisfied with bad-mouthing you and the shop and using her influence to have her friends boycott. And since she does have a wide range of acquaintances, a boycott will likely sting.''

''We'll get over that.'' Calmer, she pushed her hands through her hair. She'd come to apologize, and intended to do it right. ''I'm sorry. I know the whole thing was—is—embarrassing for you and your family.''

He braced his elbows on the desk, his brow on his fists. ''She came shrieking across the court. I'd just hit a line drive, barely missed beaning her. Cameras rolling, and there I am trying to look my sixth-generational-hotelier best, the athletic yet intelligent, the world-traveled yet dedicated, the dashing yet concerned heir to the Templeton name.''

''You'd be good at that,'' Margo murmured, hoping to placate him.

He didn't even look at her. ''Suddenly I've got my arms full of this half-naked, spitting, swearing, clawing mass who's screaming that my sister, her lesbian companion, and my whore attacked her.'' He pinched the bridge of his nose, hoping to relieve some pressure. ''I figured out right away who my sister was. Though I didn't appreciate the term, I deduced you must be my whore. The lesbian companion might have stumped me, but for process of elimination.'' He lifted his head. ''I was tempted to belt her, but I was too busy trying to keep her from ripping off my face.''

''It's such a nice face, too.'' Hoping to soothe, she walked around the desk and sat on his lap. ''I'm sorry she took it out on you.''

''She scratched me.'' He turned his head to show her the

trio of angry welts on the side of his throat. Dutifully, Margo kissed them. "What am I going to do with you?" he said wearily and rested his cheek on her head. Then he chuckled. "How the hell did you stuff her into one of those skinny lockers?"

"It wasn't easy, but it was fun."

He narrowed his eyes. "You're never going to do it again, no matter what the provocation—unless you sedate her first."

"Deal." Since the crisis seemed to have passed, she slipped a hand under his shirt, stroked it over his chest, watched his brow lift. "I've been waxed and polished. If you're interested."

"Well, just so the day isn't a complete loss." He picked her up and carried her to the bed.

Chapter Sixteen

It didn't take long for the fallout. Sales and traffic fell off sharply during the following week. Sharply enough to have Margo's stomach jittering as she wrote out checks for the monthly bills. Oh, there were still plenty of tourists and walk-ins, but a great many of the ladies who lunch, the very clientele Pretenses required in order to move the high-end merchandise, were giving the shop a wide berth.

If things didn't pick up within the next thirty days, she would have to dip into her dwindling capital just to stay open.

She wasn't panicked, just uneasy. She'd told Josh they could wait it out, and she believed it. The loyalty of Candy's country club pals could be measured in their demitasse cups with room to spare.

But that didn't mean her business didn't need a jolt of adrenaline. She didn't want the shop merely to struggle along, she wanted it to thrive. Perhaps, she realized, she wanted it to be as she had once been. In the spotlight, admired, successful.

As she arranged and rearranged displays, she wracked her brains to come up with a workable concept to turn Pretenses from an intriguing little secondhand shop into a star.

When the door opened, she had a bright—and, she was afraid, desperate—smile waiting. "Mum. What are you doing here?"

"It's my day off, isn't it?" Ann pursed her lips as she scanned the showroom. "And I haven't come by here since the first week you opened. It's awful quiet."

"I'm being punished for my sins. You always said I would be."

"I heard of it." She clucked her tongue. "Grown women behaving like hoydens. Though I never liked that woman, not even when she was a girl. Always with her nose in the air."

"This time I put it out of joint. She's managed to slice a chunk out of sales. Though Kate says it's also part of the natural correction of a new business after its initial opening weeks." Margo scowled at an amber globe. "You know how she talks when she's wearing her accountant hat."

"I do, yes. More often than not I listen to her when she's going on about my investments, and just nod soberly without a clue as to what the devil she's talking about."

For the first time all day, Margo indulged in a long laugh. "I'm glad you came in. There haven't been many friendly faces in here today."

"Well, you'll have to do something about that." Out of habit, Ann checked for dust on a table, nodded in approval when she found the surface smooth and glossy. "Have a sale, give away prizes, hire a marching band."

"A marching band—good one, Mum."

"Well, what do I know about shopkeeping? It's getting people in that's the trick, isn't it?"

Absently, Ann picked up a pretty glass bottle. Not to put things in, she mused, perplexed as always with fripperies. Just to sit about the house.

"Your uncle Johnny Ryan back in Cork had himself a pub," she continued. "He would hire musicians now and then—the Yanks liked it especially and would come in to hear the music and buy pints while they did."

"I don't think an Irish jug band is the answer to traffic flow in here."

The dismissive tone was an insult as far as Ann was concerned. "I'm speaking of fine, traditional music. You've never respected your heritage."

"You never gave me the chance to," Margo shot back. "What you've told me about Ireland and my family there could fit into one paragraph."

It was true enough. Ann tightened her lips. "So, you couldn't pick up a book, I suppose, or take a bit of a detour on your gallivanting through Europe?"

"I've been to Cork twice," Margo said and had the satisfaction of seeing Ann's mouth fall open. "Surprise. And to Dublin and Galway and Clare." She shrugged her shoulders, annoyed with herself for admitting she had once gone searching for her roots. "It's a pretty country, but I'm more interested in the one I'm living in now."

"No one wrote me, told me you'd gone to see them."

"I didn't see anyone when I was there. What would have been the point? Even if I'd gone around digging up Ryans and Sullivans, we wouldn't have known each other."

Ann started to speak, then shook her head. "No, I suppose you're right."

For a moment she thought she saw regret in her mother's eyes, and was sorry for it. "I have problems now, ambitions now," she said briskly, "that have to be dealt with now. Reminiscing about pennywhistles and pints of Guiness won't help get the business moving the way I want it to move.''

"Music and drink appeal to more than the Irish," Ann pointed out. "What's wrong with offering a bit of entertainment?"

"I need customers," Margo insisted. "I need a hook to lure the platinum-card set in past Candy's boycott and set a standard for Pretenses."

"So, you'll have a sale." Suddenly Ann wanted badly to help. "You've pretty things in here, Margo. People want pretty things. You've only to get them in the door."

"Exactly my point. What I need is . . . Wait."

Margo pressed a hand to her head as an idea tried to form. "Music. A harpist, maybe. An Irish harpist, maybe, in traditional dress. Music and drink. A reception. Champagne and little trays of canapés like at a gallery opening. Prizes."

She grabbed her mother's shoulders, surprising Ann with the quick hug. "A prize, just one. It's more alluring to have just one. No, no, no, not a prize," Margo continued, circling the shop. "An auction, on one piece. The diamond brooch. No, no, the pearl choker. Proceeds to charity. What's a good charity? Oh, Laura will know. A charity reception, Mum, it'll get them in here."

The girl's mind whirled like a dervish, Ann thought, running and spinning from one point to the next. That, she saw, hadn't changed a wit. "Well, then, you'd better get to it."

She got to it with a vengeance. Within a week, invitations to the charity reception and auction benefiting Wednesday's Child, a program for handicapped and underprivileged children, were being printed. Laura was delegated to handle interviews, and Margo went to work trying to charm liquor distributors into donating cases of champagne.

She auditioned harpists, begged Josh to select waiters from

272

Templeton staff to serve, and flattered Mrs. Williamson into making the canapés.

It was just the beginning.

When Josh came back to the penthouse after a long day trip to San Francisco, he found his lover in bed. But she wasn't alone.

"What the hell is this?"

Margo tossed back her hair, turned on a smile. Creamy curves of white breasts rose above glossy red-satin sheets. Those same slick sheets were artfully twisted to showcase a long, shapely leg.

The camera flashed.

"Hello, darling. We're nearly done here."

"Hold the sheet between your breasts," the photographer ordered, crouching at the foot of the bed on which Margo was sprawled seductively. "A little lower. Now tilt your head. That's it, that's it. You're still the best, baby. Let's sell the goods."

Josh set down his briefcase, stepped over a cable, and earned a mutter from the photographer's assistant. "What are you wearing?"

"Pearls." She skimmed her fingers down them, ran her tongue invitingly over her lips as the camera clicked. "The choker we're auctioning off. I thought photos would help bump up the bids."

Since she appeared to be wearing nothing else, Josh had to agree with her.

"Just a couple more. Give me the look. Oh, yeah, that's the one. Got it." He stood, an agile, sharp-eyed man with a flowing red ponytail. "Great working with you again, Margo."

"I owe you, Zack."

"Not a thing." He handed off his camera to his assistant, then leaned over the bed to kiss Margo warmly. "I've missed seeing that billion-dollar face in my viewfinder. Glad I could

273

help.'' He glanced at Josh. "Be out of your way in a shake."

"Josh, be a doll and get Zack and Bob a couple of beers." Without a flicker, she dropped the sheet, then reached for a robe to cover her lovely breasts.

"A couple of beers." His smile was quick and feral. "Sure, why not?"

"We met before." Leaving his assistant to pack up, Zack followed Josh back into the office. "In Paris—no, no, Rome. You dropped by one of Margo's shoots."

The green lights of jealousy faded a bit. It was hard to forget a man with a foot-long red ponytail. "Yeah. I think she was dressed at the time."

Zack took the beer. "Just to clear the air here, I've seen more naked women than a bouncer in a strip joint. It's just part of the job."

"Not that you enjoy it."

"I'm willing to sacrifice for my art." He grinned winningly. "Pal, I fucking love it. But it's still part of the job. If you want a professional's opinion, you've got yourself the top of the line. Some women you have to know how to shoot, what angle, what lighting, so the camera'll love them. Doesn't matter if they're beautiful—the camera's fickle, and it's picky." He took a long, satisfying gulp of beer. "It don't matter a damn how you shoot Margo Sullivan. It just don't matter a damn. The camera fucking worships her."

He looked toward the bedroom as her warm, throaty laugh flowed out. "And I'll tell you, if she wasn't set on running this store of hers, I'd talk her into coming back to L.A. with me and giving fashion photography a try."

"Then I'd have to break all the bones in your fingers."

Zack nodded. "I thought you might. And since you're bigger than me, I think I'll take Bob his beer to go."

"Good choice." Josh decided a beer might go down well

and was just tipping a bottle back when Margo came into the room.

"God, it was good to see Zack again. Is there a split of champagne in there? I'm parched. I'd forgotten how hot you get under the lights."

Her face was glowing as she tilted her head back and ran her fingers through her hair. She'd done something curling and sexy with it, he noted, so that it spiraled wildly.

"And how much I love it," she went on. "There's just something about the whole process. Looking into the camera, the way it looks at you. The lights, the sound of the shutter."

When she let her hair fall and opened her eyes, he was staring at her in a way that made her heart stutter. "What is it?"

"Nothing." His eyes never left hers as he held out the glass of wine he'd poured. "I didn't realize you were thinking of going back to it."

"I'm not." But she sipped, knowing that for a moment it had been a tantalizing thought. "I don't mean I'd never pose again or take an intriguing offer, but the shop's my priority now and making it a success is number one on my list."

"Number one." Had he carried this mood back with him from San Francisco, he wondered, or had it dropped on him like a cloud when he'd walked into the suite and seen her? "Tell me, duchess, just what position do you and I rate on that list?"

"I don't know what you mean."

"Simple question. Are we five, seven? Have we even made it to the list yet?"

She looked into her glass, watched the wine bubble like dreams. "Are you asking me for something?"

"I think it's about time I did. And that, I imagine, is your cue to exit stage right." When she said nothing, he set down his beer. "Why don't we try something different? You stay and I'll go."

"Don't." She still didn't look at him, but kept staring at the bubbles rising and dancing in her glass. "Please don't. I know you don't think much of me. You care about me, but you don't think much of me. And maybe I deserve that."

"We're even there, aren't we? You don't think much of me either."

How could she answer when she wasn't at all sure just what she thought of Joshua Templeton? She turned then. He was waiting, and she was grateful for that. Halfway across the room, but waiting.

"You're important to me," she told him. "More important than I expected or wanted you to be. Isn't that enough?"

"I don't know, Margo. I just don't know."

Why was her hand shaking? It was civilized, wasn't it? Just as it was supposed to be. "If you're . . . if this has run its course for you, I'll understand." She set her glass down. "But I don't want to lose you altogether. I don't know what I'd do if you weren't in my life."

This wasn't what he wanted, this calm, gentle understanding. He wanted her to rage, to throw the wine at his head, to scream at him for having the nerve to think he could walk out on her.

"So if I walk out, we'll be friends again?"

"Yes." She squeezed her eyes shut as her heart contracted. "No."

Relieved, he crossed back to her. "You'll hate me if I go." Gathering her hair in his hand, he drew her head back until their eyes met. "You need me. I want to hear you say it."

"I'll hate you if you go." She reached up, framed his face with her hands. "I need you." She pulled his mouth to hers. "Come to bed." It was the best way to show him, the only way.

276

"The easy answer," he murmured.

"Yes, it should be easy. Let's make it easy." The moment he lifted her into his arms, she tugged at his jacket, whispered hot promises in his ear.

But he didn't intend to make it easy this time, for either of them. He stood her next to the bed, let her undress him with quick, eager hands. When she would have pulled him down with her to the sheets still warm from the lights and her body, he gathered her close and began his assault.

One long, lazy meeting of lips that spun out and trembled and shimmered with something new. Simple tenderness. He took her hands, drew them down to her side, behind her back, and cuffed them there so that his free hand could stroke over her face, down her throat, into her hair while his mouth continued to seduce.

"Josh." Her heartbeat echoed slow and thick in her head. "Touch me."

"I am." He feathered kisses over her cheeks, her jaw. "Maybe for the first time I'm touching you. It's hard to feel when there's only heat. But you're feeling now, aren't you?" When her head fell weakly back, he nuzzled her throat. "No one's ever made you feel what I'm going to make you feel."

It was frightening, this weakness weighing down her limbs, clouding her brain. She wanted the flash, the fire. There was simplicity in that. And even in dangerous heat, safety. But mixed with the fear was the dark, dizzying thrill of being taken slowly, so slowly that each touch, each brush of lips lasted eons.

He could swear he felt her bones melting inside that sleek, pampered flesh. The drum of her turgid pulse thudded against his fingers. Low, baffled whimpers sounded in her throat where pearls glowed against her skin. He slid the robe aside so she wore nothing but them, luminous white orbs circling a long, slim neck.

"Lie down with me." She lifted her arm to take him. "Lie down on me."

Her voice alone, that husky flow of it, could have brought a man to his knees. And had, he thought, too often. He stroked his hands down her back, up, a teasing fingertip caress that had her shuddering, had her lips parting on what might have been a plea before his closed over them and swallowed it.

When she was limp against him, when her hands slid weakly back to her sides, he lay her on the bed, on the slick, slippery satin. But he didn't cover her. Again, he braceleted her wrists, lifted them above her head. Sigh layered over sigh as he began a slow, thorough trail down her body.

She thought the air had turned gold. How else could every breath she took be so rich? His mouth was so gentle, yet it exploited weaknesses she hadn't known were hidden inside her. His hands were impossibly tender and patient, yet they made her burn. And they made her weep.

It was more than pleasure. She had no words for it. It was soft, stronger than lust, and lovelier than any dream she'd ever held in her heart. Her body simply wasn't hers any longer, not hers alone.

He could feel her opening for him, that pliant surrender that was beyond passion and more exciting. Her skin hummed as his tongue teased over it, her muscles tensed in anticipation of climax. Lazily he backed off and left them quivering.

And when he met her lips with his again, emotions poured like wine. He slipped inside her like a wish.

"No." He used his weight to pin her as she moved restlessly. "It won't be fast this time." Even as the blood pounded in his brain, he nipped at her mouth in small, torturous bites. "It's me who's filling you, Margo. As no one else has. No one else could." He moved in her, long, slow strokes. Shattering.

She could see nothing but his face, feel nothing but that

glorious friction. Then the gradual, the delicious, the aching build of luxurious orgasm.

Her hands slid bonelessly off his shoulders.

"No one knows you like I do. No one can love you like I do."

But she was beyond words.

She was afraid of him. It was a staggering realization, especially in the middle of the night when she lay wakeful beside him. He'd changed something between them, Margo thought. Shifted the balance so that she felt vulnerable.

And he'd done it by showing her what it was like to feel cherished.

Cautious and quiet, she slipped out of bed, left him sleeping. The champagne was still on the table. Flat now, but she drank it just the same. She found a cigarette, lit it, and told herself to calm down.

She was terrified.

It had been a risk, certainly, to sleep with him. But one she'd been willing to take. But she'd never counted on falling in love with him. That was a dare she would have turned down cold.

Still could, she assured herself and drew deep on the cigarette. Her emotions were still her own. No matter how often or how quickly her life seemed to be changing, she was still in charge of her emotions.

She wasn't going to be in love with anyone, most particularly Josh. She didn't know anything about love, not this kind. And didn't want to.

Pressing a hand to her head, she let out a quiet laugh. Of course—that was it. She didn't know anything about love, so why was she so sure that was what she was feeling? More than likely it was just surprise that he could be so sweet and that she could be so susceptible to sweetness.

And it was the first time she'd been involved with a man she'd cared for as deeply as she did Josh. The closely twined history they shared, the memories, the affection.

It was easy, and foolish of her, to twist that all up inside and come out with love. More settled, she crushed out the cigarette, took a deep breath.

"Can't sleep?"

She jumped like a cat, made him laugh.

"Sorry, didn't mean to startle you." The light from the bedroom pooled behind him as he stepped closer. She stepped back. "Problem?"

"No."

He cocked his head and, as his eyes adjusted, got a good look at her face. His smile spread, arrogant and male. "Nervous?"

"Of course not."

"I'm making you nervous."

"I don't like being stalked when I'm trying to think." She stepped aside, evading him. "I've got a lot on my mind with the reception and . . ." She trailed off, going blank when his hand skimmed down her arm.

"You're tense," he murmured. "Jittery. I like it."

"You would. I need a clear mind and a good night's sleep. I'm going to take a sleeping pill."

"Let's try something else." He shook his head when she eyed him balefully. "Can't you think of anything but sex? I'm going to rub your back."

Doubt mixed with interest. "You are?"

"Guaranteed to beat off tension and chase away insomnia," he promised as he led her back to the bed. "Lie down on your stomach, duchess, close your eyes, and leave it to me."

Wary, she twisted her head to look at him. "Just my back?"

"Neck and shoulders, too. That's a girl." He eased her down, straddled her, and grinned when all those long lovely

280

muscles bunched into wires. He pressed the heels of his hands just at the base of her neck. "What's worrying you, baby?"

"Things."

"Name one."

You was the first answer on her tongue, but she bit that one off. "Those quarterly tax things are almost due, and sales are down."

"How down?"

"We've never matched the sales from the first two weeks. Kate says Candy hasn't done that much damage—it's just the natural leveling off of a new business. But I'm afraid I might have made a mistake funneling money into this reception when I should be using it for day-to-day expenses. God, you have wonderful hands."

"That's what they all say."

"The necklace I'm contributing was priced at eighty-five hundred. It's a big chunk out of inventory."

"It'll also be an excellent deduction."

"That's what Kate said." Her voice thickened as he stroked the tension out of her shoulders. "I'm tired of being afraid, Josh."

"I know."

"I never used to be afraid of anything. Now everything scares me."

"Including me."

"Hmm." She was drifting off, too tired to deny it. "I don't want to mess things up again."

"I'm not going to let you." He leaned down to touch his lips to her shoulder. "Go to sleep, Margo. Everything's on the right track."

"Don't go away," she managed before she sank.

"When have I ever?"

Chapter Seventeen

It had to be perfect. Margo was determined that every detail of the night would go off flawlessly. It took hours of rearranging stock before she was satisfied that she had achieved just the right presentation, the best traffic pattern, the most attractive corner for the harpist, who was even now tuning up.

She had redressed the window, highlighting the pearl choker with just a few carefully selected bottles and trinket boxes and silk scarves to add color.

The gilded banister that ringed the second floor was sparkling with fairy lights. Vases and decorative urns were filled with fall flowers and hothouse roses, culled from the Templeton gardens and greenhouse and elegantly arranged by her mother. On the tiny veranda, still more flowers bloomed lusciously out of copper pots and glazed pottery.

She had personally buffed, polished, and scrubbed every surface of the shop until it shined.

It was just a matter of controlling every detail, she told herself as she puffed manically on a cigarette. Of making sure everything was first class and overlooking nothing.

Had she overlooked something?

Turning, she studied herself in the wall of decorative mirrors. She wore the little black dress she'd chosen for her first dinner back at Templeton House. The neckline, that low square, was the perfect canvas for the choker. It had seemed a smart sales pitch to remove it from the window and display it against soft, female flesh. And she realized she'd chosen well when she'd selected that piece to auction.

Not just because it was elegant and lovely, she mused. Because it reminded her of a time of her life that would never come again. And a lonely old man she had had enough heart to care for.

So rare, she thought, for Margo Sullivan to have heart, to do something out of kindness rather than calculation.

Dozens of Margos, she mused. It had taken her almost twenty-nine years to realize that there were dozens of Margos. One who would throw caution to the winds, another who would worry endlessly. There was the Margo who knew how to hot-wax an antique table and the one who could laze away the day with a fashion magazine. The one who understood the rich pleasure of buying an art nouveau bottle for no more reason than seeing it sit on a shelf. And the one who'd learned to thrill at selling it. The one who could flash a smile and turn men to jelly, no matter what their age.

And the one who was suddenly able to think of only one man.

Where was he? Sick with nerves, she lit yet another cigarette. It was nearly time, nearly zero hour. He should have been there. This was a crisis point in her life. Josh was always there at the crisis points.

Always there, she thought, with a dull jolt of surprise. How odd that he should always be there at her turning points.

"Why don't you just chew that pack up, swallow it, and get it over with?" Kate suggested as she came through the door.

"What?"

"If you're going to eat that cigarette, you might as well use your teeth. Traffic's murder out there," she added. "I had to park three blocks away, and I don't appreciate the hike in these stupid shoes you made me buy." Shrugging out of her practical coat, she lifted her arms. "Well, am I going to pass the audition?"

"Let's have a look." Margo crushed out the cigarette and with lips pursed circled her finger so Kate would turn around. The long sweep of the simple black velvet suited the angular frame, and the flirty scoop-necked bodice added softness. The back dipped alluringly.

"I knew it would be perfect for you. Despite being all skin and bones and flat-chested, you look almost elegant."

"I feel like an impostor, and I'm going to freeze." Kate didn't mind the critique of her body nearly as much as the inconvenience of bare shoulders. "I don't see why I couldn't wear my own clothes. That dinner suit I have is fine."

"That dinner suit is fine for the next accountant convention you go to." Margo knit her well-shaped eyebrows. "Those earrings."

"What?" Protectively, Kate closed her hands over earlobes decorated with simple gold swirls. "They're my best ones."

"And so department store. How could we have been raised in the same house?" Margo wondered and marched over to the jewelry display. After sober study, she chose jaw-length swings of rhinestones.

"I'm not wearing those chandeliers. I'll look ridiculous."

"Don't argue with the expert. Put them on like a good girl."

"Oh, I hate playing dress-up." Bad-temperedly, Kate strode to a mirror and made the exchange. She hated more that Margo was right. They added dash.

"Kitchen's under control." Laura started down the winding steps balancing a silver tray with three flutes of champagne. "I thought we'd have our own private toast before—" She paused at the bottom, grinned. "Wow! Don't we look fabulous?"

Margo studied Laura's slim black evening suit, trimmed in satin, winking with buttons of rhinestone and pearl. "Don't we just?"

"I don't see why we all had to wear black," Kate complained.

"We're making a statement." Margo took her glass, lifted it. "To partners." After one sip, she pressed a hand to her stomach. "My system's gone haywire."

"Want a Tums?" Kate asked.

"No. Unlike you, I don't consider antacids a member of the four major food groups."

"Oh, yeah, you'd rather hit the Xanax, chase it with a little Prozac."

"I am not taking tranquilizers." But she had one in her bag, just in case. No need to mention it. "Now take that thing you call a coat into the back room before it scares off the guests. You sure I shouldn't check upstairs?" she asked Laura.

"Everything's fine. Don't worry so much."

"I'm not worried. This little party's only costing us about ten thousand dollars. Why should I be worried? Did I overdo it with the fairy lights?"

"They look charming. Get a grip, Margo."

"I'm getting one. But maybe a little Xanax wouldn't hurt.

No, no.'' She tugged another cigarette out of the pack on the counter. ''I'm handling this without chemical assistance.'' She caught Laura's bland look at the wine and tobacco and hissed out a breath. ''Don't expect miracles.''

But she made herself put the cigarette back. ''I know I'm obsessing.''

''Well,'' Laura said with a bland smile, ''as long as you know.''

''What I don't know is how this event got to be worse than the opening. Maybe it's because your parents put off going back to Europe to stay for it.''

''And because rubbing Candy's nose in a bust-out success wouldn't hurt,'' Kate added as she came back from the store-room.

''There is that,'' Margo agreed and found some comfort in it. ''Bottom line, the shop isn't a means to an end the way I expected it to be. And I'm not just worried that we'll all lose what we put into it. It's gotten to be more important than money.'' She glanced around at the setting where what had been hers was offered. ''And I'm feeling a little guilty, I re-alize, that I've dragged this charity, this children's charity into it just so I can keep the doors open.''

''That's just plain dumb,'' Kate said flatly. ''The charity is going to benefit. Without fundraisers and patrons eyeing the tax deduction, it would have to close its doors.''

''Be sure to tell me that whenever I get a greedy gleam in my eye.'' And she had one now. ''Damn, I want to empty some deep pockets tonight.''

''That's more like it.'' Kate lifted her glass in approval. ''You were starting to worry me.'' She looked around as the door opened. ''Oh, God, my heart.'' She patted her hand against her chest. ''There's nothing like a man in a monkey suit to start it fluttering.''

''You look nice, too.'' Josh, sleeked into black tie, held out

286

three white roses. "Actually, the three of you would knock the breath out of the Seventh Fleet."

"Let's get this charming man some champagne, Kate." Taking her friend firmly by the hand, Laura tugged her toward the steps.

"It doesn't take two of us."

"Get a clue."

Kate glanced back, noted the way Josh and Margo were staring at each other, and shook her head. "Jesus, isn't knowing they're sleeping together enough without having to watch them smolder? People should have some control."

"You have enough for everybody," Laura murmured and pulled her up the rest of the way.

"I was afraid you wouldn't be here in time."

Josh lifted Margo's hand to his lips, then angled his wrist to look at his watch. "Fifteen minutes to spare. I figured if I made a fashionably late entrance, you'd kill me in my sleep."

"Good guess. What do you think? Does everything look right?"

"You really expect me to look at anything but you?"

She laughed even as her pulse jittered. "Boy, I must be in bad shape when a shopworn line like that hits the mark."

"I mean it," he said and watched her smile fade. "I adore looking at you." Laying a hand on her cheek, he leaned down and buckled her knees with a long, slow, thorough kiss. "Beautiful Margo. Mine."

"Well, you're certainly taking my mind off my . . . kiss me again."

"Glad to."

Deeper this time, longer, until everything but him drained from her mind. When she eased away, his hand remained gentle on her cheek. "It's different," she managed.

"You're catching on."

287

"It's not supposed to be." New nerves, different nerves, jittered. "I don't know if it can be."

"Too late," he murmured.

There was the panic again, spurting up through mists of pleasure. "I have to—" She nearly shuddered with relief when the door opened.

"Thought we'd beat the rush," Thomas claimed. "Take your hands off the girl, Josh, and give someone else a chance." When Margo rushed into his arms, he wiggled his brows teasingly at his son. "She was mine first."

First didn't mean a damn, Josh thought as he leaned negligently on the counter. Last was what counted.

At least, he was trying to believe that.

By ten, two hours after the doors opened for Pretenses' First Annual Reception and Charity Auction, Margo was in her element. This was something she understood—beautifully dressed people chatting, bumping silk-covered elbows as they sipped wine or designer water.

It was a world she had focused her life on entering. And this time, they'd come to her.

"We thought a week or two in Palm Springs would do the trick."

"I don't know how she continues to turn a blind eye to his affairs. They're so blatant."

"I haven't seen him since the last time we were in Paris."

Small talk among the privileged, Margo thought, and she knew how to chat right back. Entertaining had been one of her hobbies in Milan. She knew how to juggle three conversations, keep an eye on the roving waiters, and pretend she had nothing on her mind but the next sip of champagne.

She also knew how to ignore, when necessary, the catty and sly snippets that came to her ears.

"Imagine having to sell everything. I mean, darling, even your shoes."

". . . just last week that Peter asked her to file for the divorce so that she could save face. The poor thing's frigid. The doctors haven't been able to help her."

Margo wouldn't have ignored that one, if she could have found the source, but before she could ease away and try to locate it, there was more.

"So clever, the way it's all set up like some interesting European flat. And I simply adore the collection of compacts. I must have the little elephant."

"There's a Valentino in the other room, darling, that just screamed your name. You really should see it."

Let them talk as much as they wanted, Margo decided and pasted a smile back on her face. And let them buy.

"Great party." Judy Prentice slipped up to Margo's side.

"Thanks."

"I guess Candy had a prior commitment."

Matching the gleam in Judy's eye, Margo smiled. "She wasn't invited."

"Really?" Judy leaned closer to Margo's ear. "That'll burn her ass."

"I do like you."

"In that case, you won't mind putting that flora minaudière aside for me until I can get in to pick it up?"

"The Judith Leiber? Consider it yours. There's a matching lipstick case, and a compact too. It makes a really fabulous set."

"Your middle name's Satan, right?" Judy tossed up a hand. "Put them all aside for me. I'll be in next week."

"We appreciate your patronage." She laid a hand on Judy's shoulder as she eased by. "Oh, and don't forget to save something to bid on the choker. I heard it screaming your name."

"You are the devil."

With a laugh, Margo moved on to the next group. "So nice to see you. What a gorgeous bracelet."

"She's a natural, isn't she?" Susan murmured to her son. "No one would know there's a nerve in her body."

"See the way she's running her fingers up the stem of her glass. She can't keep her hands still when she's tense. But she's pulling it off."

"So well that I just had Laura put aside two jackets, a bag, and a jeweled snuff bottle for me." Tucking her arm through Josh's, Susan laughed at herself. "They were Laura's jackets, for God's sake. I'm buying my own daughter's castoffs."

"She comes by her excellent taste honestly. Except in men."

Susan patted his hand. "She was too young to know any better, too much in love to be stopped." Laura was older now, Susan thought, and hurting. "You'll keep your eye on her and the girls once your father and I leave, won't you?"

"I guess I haven't been doing my brotherly duty very well lately."

"You've been distracted, and you've earned your own life." Her eyes, sharp and maternal, scanned the room until they found Laura. "I'm a little worried that she's holding up too well."

"You'd rather she fell to pieces."

"I'd rather be sure that if and when she does, someone's there for her." Then she smiled, watching Kate and Margo grab a quick moment with Laura. "They will be."

"We've got to make some sort of list," Margo whispered. "Otherwise, we're going to be promising the same things to different people. I'll never keep it all in my head."

"I told you to keep the cash register open," Kate grumbled. "It would be tacky."

She sent Margo a withering look. "It's a store, pal."

290

"Margo's right—you don't go ringing up sales and making change at an affair like this."

"God save me from delicate tastes." Kate blew out a breath that fluttered her bangs. "I'll duck into the storeroom and log the promised merchandise. What the hell was it you said, a minatoe?"

"A minaudière," Margo said with a superior smirk. "Just put down 'jeweled evening bag.' I'll know what it is. And don't start playing with the computer. You have to mingle."

"I'm mingled out. Except there's this one guy. He's kind of cute." She craned her head, zeroed in. "There, the one with the moustache and shoulders. See him?"

"Lincoln Howard." Laura identified him easily. "Married."

"Figures." Muttering, Kate walked off.

"You ought to make her keep that dress," Laura commented. "I've never seen her look better."

"She'd look better yet if she didn't walk as though she was late for an audit." Margo caught herself before she pressed a hand to her jumpy stomach again. "We're going to have to start the auction, Laura." She gripped her friend's hand. "Christ, I need a cigarette."

"Make it fast, then. The rep from Wednesday's Child has been giving me the high sign for ten minutes."

"No, I'll suck it in and make another pass so people can cast avaricious looks at the pearls. Then I'll work my way over to Mr. T., and tell him to start the auction."

She started the glide, pausing here and there to touch someone's arm, share a quick laugh, to note who needed a refill of champagne. The minute she saw Kate come back out of the storeroom, she stepped up to Thomas.

"It's showtime. I want to thank you again for helping us out."

"It's a good cause, and good business." He patted her head affectionately. "Let's hose 'em."

"Damn right." She kept her hand in his as they stepped to the front of the room. She knew the murmurs would grow as people turned their heads to study them, knew how to let them play out as she, in turn, sized up the room. From close by, she caught a curious whisper.

"I don't know what Candy was talking about. She doesn't look debilitated or desperate."

"Tommy Templeton wouldn't have let things go so far with his son if she was the conniving whore Candy claims she is."

"Darling, if men recognized conniving whores when they saw them, it wouldn't be the oldest profession."

She felt Thomas's hand tense in hers and looked up at him with an easy smile and hot eyes. "Don't worry." Rising on her toes, she kissed his cheek. "They got the conniving part right, after all."

"If I wasn't a man, I'd punch that jealous cat in the nose." His eyes lit up. "I'll get Susie to do it."

"Maybe later." She gave his hand another squeeze, turned to the crowd. "Ladies and gentlemen, if I could interrupt for a moment." She waited while conversations ebbed, flowed, then politely tapered off. "I'd like to thank you all for coming to Pretenses' first reception."

The speech had been in her head, the one she and Laura and Kate had fine-tuned, but it was slipping away. Using her nerve, she skimmed her gaze over faces.

"We'd especially like to thank you for staying even after you'd had your fill of champagne. Most of you are aware of my . . . checkered career, the way it ended with the kind of delectable little scandal we all love to read about."

She caught Laura's eye and the concern in it. Just smiled. "When I left Europe and came back here, it wasn't because I was thinking of America as the land of opportunity and free

292

enterprise. I came back because home is where you go when you're broken. And I was lucky, because the door was open." She picked her mother out in the crowd, kept her eyes on Ann's. "I don't have anyone to blame for the mistakes I made. I had family who loved me, cared for me, watched over me. That isn't the case with the children who so desperately need what Wednesday's Child offers. They're broken because they weren't loved and cared for and watched over. Because they weren't given the same chances as those of us in this room. Tonight, with my partners, Laura Templeton and Kate Powell, I'd like to take a small step toward giving a few of those children a chance."

She reached back, unclasped the choker, and let it slide through her fingers. " 'Bye, baby," she murmured. "I hope you'll bid generously. Remember, it's only money." After draping the pearls over a velvet stand, she turned to Thomas. "Mr. Templeton."

"Miss Sullivan." He took her hand, kissed it. "You're a good girl. Now, then." He turned a cagey eye on the audience as Margo slipped to the rear of the room. His voice boomed out, challenging as he described the single item up for bid, and ordering the bidders, many of whom he called by name, to keep their wallets open.

"That was better than the script," Laura murmured.

"Much better." In agreement, Kate slipped an arm around Margo's waist. "Let's hope it inspires some of these tight-wads."

"All right," Thomas called out. "Who's going to get this ball rolling and open the bid?"

"Five hundred."

"Five hundred." Thomas's brows lowered. "Jesus, Pick-erling, that's pitiful. If it wasn't against the rules I'd pretend I didn't hear that."

"Seven-fifty."

He huffed and shook his head. "We have a miserly seven-fifty. Do I hear a thousand?" He nodded at a raised hand. "There's a thousand, now let's get serious."

The bidding continued, some called out, others signaled—a lift of the finger, a sober nod, a careless wave. Margo began to relax as they slipped over five thousand. "That's better," she murmured. "I'm going to try to think of anything else as gravy."

"It's making me nuts." Kate fumbled in her bag for her roll of Tums.

"We have six thousand two," Thomas continued. "Madam, you have the throat of a swan. These pearls might have been made for you."

His quarry laughed. "Tommy, you devil. Six-five."

"How much did you say those were worth?" Kate wanted to know.

"Retail at Tiffany's? Maybe twelve-five." Delighted, Margo tried to see through the crowd as hands went up. "They're still getting a bargain."

When the bidding topped nine thousand, she wanted to dance. When it hit ten, she wished she had a chair so she could see the bidders. "I never expected it to go this high. I underestimated their generosity."

"And their competitive spirit." Kate balanced on her toes. "It seems to be between two or three people, but I can't see."

"And it's serious now," Margo murmured. "No called bids."

"That's twelve thousand, looking for twelve-five." His sharp eyes darting back and forth, Thomas guided the bidding. "Twelve-five is bid. Thirteen?" At the head shake response, he zeroed in on another bidder. "Thirteen? Yes, we have thirteen. Thirteen is bid, will you bid thirteen-five? The call is for thirteen thousand five hundred. And we have it. Thirteen-five. Will you go fourteen? There's a man who knows his mind.

Fourteen is bid. Calling fourteen-five. Fourteen is the bid on the floor. That's fourteen thousand going once, and going twice. Sold for fourteen thousand to the man with exquisite taste and an eye for value.''

There was polite applause, pleasant laughter. Margo was too busy trying to see through the now milling crowd to notice the looks aimed her way. "We should go congratulate the winner. Make sure the paper gets a picture. Whoever gets up there first, make sure to hold on to him.''

"Margo, dear.''

She hadn't made it two steps before her arm was snagged. Staring into the woman's face, Margo searched desperately for a name, then settled on the usual out. "Darling, how wonderful to see you.''

"I've had the best time. Such a delightful affair, and a charming little shop. I would have been in weeks ago, but I was so . . . swamped. If I'm asked to serve on another committee, I'll simply slit my wrists.''

One of Candy's friends, Margo remembered. Terri, Merri . . . Sherri. "I'm delighted you were able to shuffle us into your schedule.''

"Oh, so am I. I've had a wonderful evening. And I've got my heart set on those darling earrings. The little ruby-and-pearl ones. They're just so sweet. Can you tell me how much you're selling them for? I'm going to insist that Lance buy them for me since he lost the choker to Josh.''

"I'll have to check the— To Josh.'' Her mind stopped searching for price tags and went blank. "Josh bought the choker?''

"As if you didn't know.'' Sherri's eyes glittered as she tapped Margo's arm again. "So clever of you to have him buy it back for you.''

"Yes, wasn't it? I'll put a hold on the earrings, Sherri.

Come in anytime next week during business hours and take a look at them. You'll have to excuse me."

She worked her way through the crowd, bid good night to dozens while struggling to keep that bright, careless smile on her face. She found Josh flirting ruthlessly with the teenage daughter of one of his board members.

"Josh, I have to steal you away for a minute," she began as the girl went automatically to a pout. "If you could just help me with this little thing in the storeroom." She all but shoved him inside, shut the door. "What have you done?"

"Just giving the kid something to dream about tonight." All innocence, he lifted his hands, palms out. "Never laid a hand on her. I have witnesses."

"I'm not talking about your pathetic flirtation with a child young enough to be your daughter."

"She's seventeen. Give me a break. And I was letting her flirt with me. Just target practice."

"I said I wasn't talking about that, though you should be ashamed of yourself. What do you mean buying the choker?"

"Oh, that."

"Oh, that," she repeated. "Do you know what it looks like?"

"Yeah, it's three strands, beautifully matched pearls with a bow-shaped pavé diamond clasp on eighteen-karat."

She made a sound like expelling steam. "I know what the damn choker looks like."

"Then why did you ask?"

"Don't play lawyer games with me."

"It's really more politics than law."

Now she held up her hands, closing her eyes until she thought she had a shaky hold on her temper. "It looks as though I wheedled you into buying it—and paying more than it's worth on the retail market—just so I could have my cake and eat it too."

He decided that telling her she hadn't served any cake would not result in an amused chuckle. "I was under the impression that the proceeds went to charity."

"The proceeds do, but the necklace—"

"Was offered to the highest bidder."

"People think that I asked you to buy it."

Interested, he angled his head. Yes, her face was definitely flushed, he noted. Her eyes bright and hot. Embarrassment was a new, and not unattractive, look on her. "Since when do you care what people think?"

"I'm trying to learn to care."

He considered. "Why?"

"Because . . ." She closed her eyes again. "I have no idea. I have no earthly idea."

"All right, then." He slipped the pearls out of his pocket, running them through his hand as he studied them. "Just grains of sand, hunks of carbon, tricked into something lovely by time and nature."

"Spoken like a man."

His gaze lifted, locked on hers, made her stomach tremble. "I made up my mind to buy it when I was inside you, and this was all you were wearing, and you looked at me as if nothing else existed but us. That's spoken like a man, too. A man who loves you, Margo. And always has."

Terrified and thrilled, she stared at him. "I can't breathe."

"I know the feeling."

"No, I really can't breathe." Quickly, she dropped into a chair and put her spinning head between her knees.

"Well, that's quite a reaction to a declaration of love." He slid the pearls back into his pocket so he could rub her back. "Is it your usual?"

"No."

His grim mouth curved a little. "That's something, then."

"I'm not ready." She drew in air slowly, tried to let it out molecule by molecule. "I'm just not ready for this. For you. I love you too, but I'm not ready."

Of all the scenarios he'd imagined when she would finally tell him she loved him, none of them had included her saying the words with her head between her knees.

"Would you mind sitting up and telling me that again. Just the 'I love you' part."

Cautious, she lifted her head. "I do love you, but— No, don't touch me now."

"The hell with that." He hauled her out of the chair and crushed his mouth to hers with more impatience than finesse.

Chapter Eighteen

Kate opened the door of the storeroom and let out a long, windy sigh at the sight of Josh and Margo locked in a passionate embrace. Maybe it did warm her heart, but there was no reason to let them know that.

"Do you two mind putting your glands on hold so we can finish out the evening with some sense of decorum?"

Josh tore his mouth from Margo's long enough to suck in a breath. "Scram," he ordered and got back to business.

"I will not scram. There are still over a dozen people out there who expect to be bid a fond farewell by the owners. All three owners. And that includes the woman you're currently performing an emergency tonsillectomy on."

Josh gave her a brief glance over the top of Margo's head. "Kate, you're such a romantic fool."

"I know, it's a weakness of mine." She stepped up and

pried them apart. "I'm sure the two of you can remember where you left off. Come on, partner. Oh, and Josh, you might want to stay in here until you're a little more . . . presentable."

He damned near blushed. "Sisters aren't supposed to notice that sort of thing."

"This one sees all, knows all." She whisked Margo through the door. "What's the matter with you?" she muttered. "You look like you've been poleaxed."

"I have been. Give me one of those damn Tums you're so crazy about."

"Soon as I can get to my purse." Concerned, she rubbed her hand over Margo's back. "Tell me what's wrong, honey?"

"I can't now. Tomorrow." And because she understood her job, she curved her lips into a bright smile and held out both hands to the woman approaching them. "So glad you could come. I hope you enjoyed the evening."

She repeated those sentiments, with variation, for nearly an hour before the last lingerer trickled out. Necessity, along with aspirin and antacids, kept her functioning. She wanted a quiet room, a moment to herself to sort out all the emotions whirling through her, but she was swept along when the Templetons insisted on taking the family out to celebrate.

It was nearly one before she walked into the penthouse with Josh. She should have had it all figured out by now, she thought. She should know exactly what to say and do. But when the door closed behind them and they were alone, she didn't have a clue.

"I'm going to miss them—your parents—when they go back to Europe."

"So am I." There was an easy smile on his face. His formal tie was loose now, as were the studs on his tuxedo shirt. Margo thought he looked like an elegantly male ad for an outrageously expensive and sexy cologne. "You've been quiet."

300

"I know. I've been trying to think, to figure out what to say when we talk about this."

"You shouldn't have to think that hard." He stepped toward her, began to slide the pins from her hair. "I've been thinking about being alone with you. Finally." As her hair tumbled free, he tossed the pins on the dresser. "It didn't take much effort."

"One of us has to be sensible."

"Why?"

At any other time, she would have laughed. "I'm not sure why, I just know one of us has to be. And it doesn't look as though it's going to be you. Josh, I'm not sure either of us knows how to handle this."

"I've got a pretty good idea how to start." His arms slipped around her, raced up her back to cup her shoulders and pull her into him.

"This part's easy, maybe too easy for both of us. I don't think we want that to change."

"Why should it?" He skimmed his mouth along her jaw. And the taste of her was warm and silky.

"Because we've muddied up the waters." How did he expect her to think when he was sampling her as if she was a delicacy he'd chosen from under glinting crystal? "Because I've never really been in love before, and I don't think you have either." Her pulse was already stuttering. "We don't know what we're doing."

"So, we'll improvise." His mood was soaring too high and too free to let her sudden attack of logic dampen it. He tugged on the zipper at the back of her dress, and when the silk parted, he slid his hands along her skin.

"Are you saying things don't have to change?" Bubbles of relief warred against flickers of need as her dress slipped down.

He wanted to tell her everything had already done so. But

301

he knew her so well, understood that if he spoke of change, of commitment, of forever, she'd balk or evade, or simply bolt. "Nothing that we don't want to change. This, for instance," he murmured, skimming his thumbs along the soft white swell of her breasts. They rose, full and white, out of the strapless lace of a black body skimmer. Her stockings stopped high on the thigh, another seductive contrast of black against white. He let his fingers trail from stocking to flesh to lace, and thrilled at each sharply defined texture. All the while, his eyes stayed on hers.

"The minute you touch me, I want you. It's something I can't seem to control." And it worried her, worried her enough that she purposely pushed all rational thought aside and eased open his stark white shirt to caress the pale gold tint of the flesh beneath. "I've never had a lover who stirred me up so much just by being in the same room. How long can that last?"

"Let's find out." He eased her onto the bed—pale hair spilling, milk-white skin against black silk and lace. She was all promising scents and luscious curves, long, limber limbs that reached out to enfold.

She held him against her, reveling in the feel of his weight pinning her, imprisoning sex under sex with slow friction. All she had to know, for this moment, was that she wanted him. And her mouth sought his eagerly for that dreamy mating of tongues.

When had she come to need the flavor of him, the scent and texture of his skin? After so many years, how had friendship and family shot into passion and longing? And why, when their bodies meshed so perfectly, should it matter?

Her skin hummed under his hands, those long, gliding strokes that shifted in a pulsebeat to rough and possessive. What spurted to life inside of her was too layered and complex to analyze. She let the heat take her.

302

He felt every shift and sigh, knew when nerves had melted into acceptance. Here, in this big, soft bed, there were no questions. She was, and always had been, everything he wanted.

Long, lean limbs, sumptuous curves, sleek, perfumed skin. Her body had been designed to take and give pleasure. And no one else, he thought as his mouth fused to hers, would take it from or give it to her again. No one else understood her heart, her mind, and her dreams as he did.

No one else.

Her heart leapt, then stuttered as his mood turned urgent. Desperate hands, a ravenous mouth raced over her. Sighs deepened into moans as she matched him beat for beat, flame for flame.

How delicious was madness.

She rolled over, her hands as quick and fast as his, to drive him as he was driving her. Dangerous heights. Pleasure that was a shuddering kin to pain. She rose up. In the shadowed lights her skin gleamed like damp silk. Her eyes, wildly blue, locked on his. One heartbeat. Two.

Now. The demand seemed to shimmer in the air around them. In answer he gripped her hips, fingers digging in. In one fluid move, she took him deep, deep, holding there, holding them both trembling. On a long, feline moan, she arched back, skimming her hands over her own body, from center over torso to breast, where she felt her heart thundering. Slow, very slow, acutely aware of every tremor of her body, acutely aware that his eyes were following her movements, she trailed her hands down until they covered, caressed that mating of bodies.

Glorying in every breath, she sleeked her hands up again, lifted her hair. And began to ride.

The pace she set was hard and fast and merciless. He watched as she drove herself to the peak, shuddered over it. Sensations battered him like an avalanche, blurring his vision.

But he knew he'd never seen anything more glorious than Margo lost in her own passion.

When she cried out, flinging herself forward, her hands braced on his shoulders, her hair curtaining his face, he had no choice but to lose himself with her.

"Why do I always feel as if I've dived off a mountain whenever I make love with you?" Margo didn't really expect an answer. She thought Josh was asleep, or at least comatose, but he shifted, his lips brushing over the curve of one breast, then the other.

"Because you and I together, duchess, are a dangerous pair. And I want you again already." He nibbled his way up to her throat, found her warm, swollen mouth.

She was ready to float again, her arms light and limber as they lifted to circle him. "It's never been like this for me before." Through the daze of sensations building fresh, she felt the change. And understood the reason for it. "I know how that sounds."

"It doesn't matter." He didn't want to think about it. Only wanted to have her, to hold her.

"It does. To both of us." Suddenly unsure here, where she had always felt so confident, she cupped his face in her hands to raise it. His eyes were heavy with desire, a hint of irritation now working through. "I think we have to talk about it."

"Neither one of us took a vow of chastity."

That was true enough. She also knew that though she had taken lovers before, the press had gifted her with a libido and a trail of broken hearts that was well beyond reality.

"We need to talk about it," she repeated.

"I haven't asked you any questions, Margo. Whoever, how many ever, have been in your life before, there's only one now. There's only me."

The cool, possessive tone might have annoyed her under

304

other circumstances. It was so Joshua Templeton—I see, I want, I take. But they were still linked, still warm from each other. "There haven't been as many as you might think. Josh, I didn't sleep with every man I dated."

"Fine. I didn't sleep with every woman I took to dinner." He snapped it out as he turned over on his back to drag the hair off his face. "It's now that matters, in any case. Are we straight about this?"

She wanted them to be. It was his anger, the cold control of it, that told her differently. "Josh, my reputation's never really mattered to me before. In fact, it only added to my bank account. But now . . . it matters now." Suddenly chilled, she sat up, wrapped her arms around herself. "It matters now because you matter now. And I don't know how to handle it. I don't know how either of us is going to handle it. When it was just sex—"

"It was never just sex for me."

"I didn't know that," she said quietly. "I didn't know how you felt, or how I felt, until it was just there. And it's so big, so important. So scary."

It surprised him, not just what she said but the way she said it. Nerves, regrets, confusion. All those things were so rare in Margo when it came to the games men and women played.

"You're scared?"

"Terrified." She hissed out a breath and rose to yank a robe out of the closet. "And I'm not happy about it."

"So am I."

With the beginnings of temper simmering in her eyes, she looked at him over her shoulder. A long, lean male animal, she mused, his hands tucked behind his head now, the start of a smirk on that gorgeous mouth. She wasn't sure whether to slug him or jump on him.

"So are you what?"

"Terrified, and not happy about it."

305

She tugged the belt on the robe, kept her hands in place as she turned. "Really?"

"You know what I figure, duchess?"

"No." It was the smirk that drew her, had her going back to sit on the side of the bed. "What is it that you figure?"

"It's all been so easy for us before. Too easy."

"And this isn't going to be."

He took her hand, linking fingers casually. "Doesn't look like it. Maybe I've got a little problem, a hitch, when it comes to other men. After all, the woman I'm in love with has been engaged five times."

"Three." She jerked her hand free, aware that her past was constantly going to sneak up and slap her in the face. "The other two were products of an overeager press. And the three were . . . quickly rectified mistakes."

"The point being," he said, with what he considered admirable patience, "that none of my relationships ever progressed that far."

"Which could be taken as a fear of commitment on your part."

"Could be," he murmured. "But the simple fact is I've been in love with you nearly half my life. Nearly half my life," he said again, sitting up so that his eyes, dark as shadows, were level with hers. "Every woman I touched was a substitute for you."

"Josh." She only shook her head. There was nothing she could say, nothing that could rise above the wave of emotion that swamped her.

"It's demoralizing, Margo, to watch the woman, the only woman you really want, turn to anyone but you. To wait and to watch."

It was thrilling, and panicking, to think it. To know it. "But why did you wait?"

"A man has to use what advantage he has. Mine was time."

306

"Time?"

"I know you, Margo." He skimmed a finger down the curve of her cheek. "Sooner or later you were going to get in over your head, or just get bored with the high life."

"And you'd be right there to pick up the pieces."

"It worked," he said lightly and snagged her wrist before she could jump out of the bed. "No reason to get frosted."

"It's a perfect reason. You arrogant, egotistical son of a bitch. Just wait till Margo fucks up and then step in." She'd have taken a swing at him if he hadn't anticipated her and grabbed her other wrist.

"I wouldn't have put it exactly that way, but . . ." He smiled winningly. "You did fuck up."

"I know what I did." She tugged her arms outward and only succeeded in performing a warped rendition of patty-cake. "I also got out of that mess with Alain on my own." It was the flicker in his eyes that stopped her. It was there and gone quickly, but she knew every nuance of his face. "Didn't I?"

"Sure you did, but the point is—"

"What did you do?" Incensed, she batted her trapped hands against his chest. "You weren't in Greece. I'd have known if you were. How did you fix it?"

"I didn't fix it. Exactly." Hell. "Look, I made a few calls, pulled in a few markers. Christ, Margo, did you expect me to sit around on the beach while they were toying with tossing your butt in jail?"

"No." She spoke quietly because she was afraid she might scream. "No. I have a crisis, you ride to the rescue. Let go of my hands."

"I don't think so," he said, judging the temper in her eyes. "Listen, all I did was make it go away faster. They didn't have anything on you, didn't want to have anything on you. But there wasn't any point in you cooling your heels in custody longer than necessary. All you'd done was have the bad taste and poor sense to hook up with some slick con artist who was using you for cover.''

"Thank you very much.''

"Don't mention it.''

"And since you have mentioned it, yet again, I'll admit that I've had plenty of experience with bad taste and poor sense.'' She jerked her arms, fuming when he held firm. "But I'm over it now. I took charge of my own life, damn you. And I put it back together, piece by piece. Which is something you've never had to do. I took the risk, I did the work, I—''

"I'm proud of you.'' Deflating her completely, he brought her fisted hands to his lips.

"Don't try to turn this around.''

"Proud of the way you faced what had to be done and turned it all into something unique and exciting.'' He opened her fingers, pressed his lips to her palm. "And moved by you. By the way you stood there tonight, by the things you said.''

"Damn you, Josh.''

"I love you, Margo.'' His lips curved. "Maybe it was my poor sense that made me love you before. But I'm even more in love with the woman I'm with now.''

Defeated, she rested her brow against his. "How do you do this, wind me up, spin me out? I can't remember why I was mad at you.''

"Just come here.'' He drew her into his arms. "Let's see what else we can forget.''

Later when she lay curled beside him, the weight of his arm around her, the sound of his heart beating slow and steady under her ear, she remembered it all. They had, she realized, resolved nothing. She wondered if two people who had known each other so long and so well could understand each other's hearts so little.

Until tonight, she'd never been ashamed of the men she had let into her life. Fun, excitement, romance had been everything she'd looked for, dreamed of. Most women had viewed her as competition. Even as a child she had had few female friends other than Laura and Kate.

But men . . .

She sighed and closed her eyes.

She understood men, had at an early age deduced the power that beauty and sex could wield. She'd enjoyed wielding it. Never to hurt, she thought. She had never played the game with the risk of genuine pain on either side. No, she'd always been careful to choose game partners who understood the rules. Older men, experienced men, men with smooth manners, hefty wallets, and guarded hearts.

None of them would interfere with her career, her ambitions, because the rules were simple and always followed.

Fun, excitement, romance. With no spills, no tangles, no hard feelings when she moved on.

No feelings at all. But plenty of poor judgment.

Now there was Josh. With him her power was different, her dreams were different. The rules were different. Oh, the fun was there, and the excitement, and the romance. But there had already been spills and tangles.

Didn't it follow that someone was going to get hurt?

However much he loved her, she hadn't yet earned his trust. And inches behind trust, she thought, was his respect.

He loved the woman he was with now, she remembered. But she wondered if he was waiting to see whether she would stay or run. And she wondered, deep down wondered, if she was waiting too.

After all, he'd been born to a life of privilege, had the in-the-blood advantage of being able to choose and discard anything—and anyone—at his leisure. If it was true that he'd

309

wanted her for so long, he'd waited and watched, and, being Josh, he'd reveled in the challenge.

Now that the challenge had been met . . .

"I'll hate you for it," she murmured and pressed her lips to his shoulder. "Whoever does the hurting, I'll hate you for it." She curled closer, wishing he would wake, wake and make her mindless again so she wouldn't have to worry and wonder.

"I love you, Josh." She laid her palm over his heart and counted the beats until hers matched them. "God help both of us."

Chapter Nineteen

The cliffs were always the place Margo went for thinking. All of her major decisions had been made there. Who should be invited to her birthday party? Did she really want to cut her hair? Should she go to the homecoming dance with Biff or Marcus?

Those decisions had seemed so monumental at the time. The crash of waves, the smell of the sea and wildflowers, the jagged sweep of rocks from dizzying heights had both soothed and aroused her. The emotions she felt here went into all those decisions.

It was here she had come the day before she ran away to Hollywood. Just after Laura's wedding, she thought now. She was eighteen and so certain that life with all its mysteries was passing her by. She was desperate to see what was out there, to see what she could make of it. Make from it.

How many arguments had she had with her mother during those last weeks? she wondered. Too many to count, she thought now.

You've got to go to college, girl, if you want to make something out of yourself.

It's boring. It's useless. There's nothing for me there. I want more.

So you always have. More what this time?

More everything.

And she'd found it, hadn't she? Margo mused. More excitement, more attention, more money. More men.

Now that she had come full circle, what did she have? A new chance. Something of her own. And Josh.

She threw her head back, watched a gull swoop, skim the air, and bullet out to sea. Far out on the diamond-blue water a boat glided, glossy and white, the sun just catching the brasswork to wink and flash. The wind swirled up and spun like a dancer, teasing her hair, whipping at the draping silk of her white tunic.

She felt shockingly alone there, small and insignificant on the high, spearing cliffs, with destruction or glory only a few small steps away.

A metaphor for love? she thought, amused at herself. Deep thoughts had never been her forte. She was alone without him, solitary. If commitment to Josh was like a leap from a cliff, would a woman like her fly up or tumble and crash?

If it was a risk she was willing to take, what would it do to him? Would he trust her? Could he? Would he believe in her, stand with her? Would he, most of all, be willing to hold through all the ups and downs of a life together?

And how, in God's name, had she leaped from love to marriage? Jesus, she was actually thinking of marriage.

She had to sit down.

Shaky, she eased down onto a rock, waited for her breath

to come back. Marriage had never been a goal in her life. The engagements had simply been a lark, a tease, no more serious to her than a wink and a smile.

Marriage meant promises that couldn't be broken with a shrug. It meant a lifetime, a sharing of everything. Even children. She shivered once, pressed her hand to her stomach. She wasn't the motherly type. No, no, white picket fences and car pools were light-years out of her realm.

No—she nearly laughed at herself—it wasn't even to be considered. She would live with him. The situation as it was now was perfect. Naturally, it was the way he wanted it as well. She couldn't understand why she'd gotten so worked up over it. The penthouse suite suited their needs, their lifestyles, gave them each a chance to fly off, together or separately, when the whim struck.

Nothing permanent, nothing that hinted at obligation. Of course, that had been the answer all along. Hotel life was in his blood, and it was part of her choice of living. Tired of looking at the same view? Pack up your clothes and find another.

Of course that was what he would want. And what she would be comfortable with.

Then she turned and looked up, higher still, at the house with its rock-solid permanence, its strength and its beauty. Towers added by new generations, colorful tiles set by the old. She knew that memories made there lasted forever. Dreams dreamt there never really faded away. Love spoken there bloomed as free and as wild as the tangled vines of bougainvillea.

But it wasn't hers. A home of her own was something that had always eluded her. She turned away again, looked out to sea, surprised that her eyes were stinging.

What do you want, Margo? What in God's name do you want?

More. More everything.

"Figured you'd be here." Kate dropped down on the rocks beside her. "Good day for sea gazing."

"You must be feeling jazzed this morning." Laura laid a hand on her shoulder. "Last night was a smash, beginning to end."

"She's brooding." Kate rolled her eyes at Laura. "Never satisfied."

"I'm in love with Josh." Margo stared straight ahead when she said it, as if speaking to the wind.

Kate pressed her lips together, considered. Because she couldn't see Margo's eyes behind the shaded lenses, she tipped them down on Margo's nose. "Lowercase or uppercase 'l'?"

"Kate, it's not high school," Laura murmured.

"It's still a relevant question. What's the answer?"

"I'm in love with Josh," Margo repeated. "And he's in love with me. We've lost our minds."

"You mean it," Kate said slowly and shifted her gaze from Margo's eyes to Laura's. "She means it."

"I've got to walk." Margo rose quickly and began to follow the curving line of the cliffs. "I've got all this energy I don't know what to do with. And all these nerves that keep circling around from my head to my gut and back again."

"That doesn't have to be a bad thing," Laura told her.

"You were in love with Peter, weren't you?"

Laura looked down at her feet, told herself it was necessary to watch her step. "Yes. Yes, I was. Once."

"There's my point. You were in love with him, started a life together, and then it all fell apart. Do you have any idea how many relationships I've watched unravel or just rip? I couldn't count them. Nothing lasts forever."

"My parents?"

"Are the shining example of an exception to the rule."

"Wait a minute. Wait a minute." Kate grabbed at her arm.

314

"Are you and Josh thinking of getting married?"

"No. Good God, no. Absolutely not. Neither of us is the 'till death do us part' type." Needing to be closer to the sea, Margo picked her way down some rocks.

"Do you want to be in love with him?"

At Kate's question she looked over, annoyed, impatient. "It's not a choice."

"Of course it is." Kate didn't believe that love, or any other emotion, was uncontrollable.

"Love isn't a spring suit," Laura put in, "that you try on for size."

Kate merely moved her shoulders and scrambled agilely down to the ledge. "If it doesn't fit, you put it aside, as far as I'm concerned. So, Margo, does it fit or not?"

"I don't know. But I'm wearing it."

"Maybe you'll grow into it." Or, Laura worried, grow out of it.

It was the tone that made Margo stop. Concern was a layer over doubt. "I really do love him," she said quietly. "I don't know exactly how to handle it yet, but I do. We don't seem to be able to talk it through sensibly. I know, I can see that part of him is hung up on the way I've lived. The men I've been with."

"Oh, right. Like he's been in a monastery copying scripture for the last ten years." Kate squared her shoulders, her feminist flag waving high. "It's none of his damn business if you've taken on the Fifth, Six, and Seventh fleets. A woman has just as much right as a man to be stupidly and irresponsibly promiscuous."

Margo opened her mouth, but for a moment she could only laugh at the cleverly insulting support. "Thank you so much, Sister Immaculata."

"Anytime, Sister Slut."

"My point is," Margo continued dryly, "that it's not just

315

garden-variety jealousy with Josh. I could overlook that, or be annoyed by that. In this case, he has cause to doubt, and I'm not sure how long it will take to prove to both of us that that part of my life is over.''

"I think you're being too easy on him,'' Kate muttered.

"And too hard on myself?''

Kate smiled cheerfully. "I didn't say that.''

"Then I will,'' Laura said with an elbow jab to Kate's ribs.

"It's more than the men.'' Staring out to sea, Margo tried to make sense of it all. "That's just a kind of symptom, I suppose. He says he's proud of me, what I've done to put my life back in order. I'd say he's more surprised than anything else. And because of that,'' she said slowly, "I realize that it's unlikely he really expects me to follow it all the way through, to stand and to stay. Why should he?'' she murmured, remembering his sharp reaction to her recent photo shoot. "He's waiting for me to take off again, to run to something bigger, easier.''

"I'd say you don't have enough faith in him.'' Frowning, Kate studied Margo's face. "Are you planning to run?''

"No.'' It was something, at last, that she could be absolutely certain of. "I've finished running. But with my track record—''

"The two of you better start concentrating on now,'' Laura interrupted. "Where you are now and what you feel for each other now. All the rest, well, that just brought you to where you're standing, and who you're standing with.''

It sounded so simple, so clean. Margo struggled to believe it. "Okay. I think it's best if we take it one step at a time,'' Margo decided. "Like a recovery program, in reverse.'' Reaching down, she picked up a pebble, tossed it out to sea. "Meanwhile, we're in meanwhile. It might be fun.''

"Love's supposed to be.'' Laura smiled. "When it's not hell.''

"You're the only one of the three of us who's been there."
Margo glanced at Kate for confirmation.

"Affirmative."

"If it doesn't bother you, would you mind telling me how
you came out the other side. I mean how did you fall out?"

It did bother her. It scraped her raw inside and left her a
failure. But she would never admit it. "It was gradual, like
water against rock gradually wears it down. It wasn't a flash,
like waking up one morning and realizing I wasn't in love
with my husband. It was a slow, nasty process, a kind of
calcifying of emotions. In the end, I felt nothing for him at
all."

A terrifying thought, Margo decided. Not to feel anything
for Josh. She was sure she'd rather hate him than feel nothing
for him. Or worse, much worse, she realized, to have him feel
nothing for her. "Could you have stopped it?"

"No. We might have been able to stop it, but I couldn't.
Not alone. He never loved me." And oh, that stung. "That
makes it entirely different than you and Josh."

"I'm sorry, Laura."

"Don't be." Easier, Laura leaned against Margo's supporting arm. "I have two beautiful daughters. That's a pretty good
deal all around. And you have a chance for something special,
and uniquely yours."

"I might take that chance." She plucked another pebble,
tossed it.

"Well, if you're looking to start a love nest, an account I
have is unloading a property about half a mile south of here."
Getting into the spirit, Kate scooped up pebbles herself. "A
beauty, too. California Spanish."

"We're perfectly happy in the suite." Safe in the suite, a
small voice whispered in her head. In limbo.

"Whatever works for you," Kate shrugged. She believed
strongly in the investment value of real estate. A home was

317

one thing—it couldn't be measured in terms of short- or long-term capital gains. But property, well chosen, was a necessary addition to any well-rounded portfolio. "But it's got a killer view."

"How would you know?"

"I delivered some forms there once." She caught Margo's smirk. "Gutter mind. The client is female. She got the house in the divorce settlement and wants to sell it and buy something smaller, lower-maintenance."

"Is that Lily Farmer's house?" Laura asked.

"One and the same."

"Oh, it's beautiful. Two stories. Stucco and tile. They had it completely restored about two years ago."

"Yep. Finished it up just in time to say 'adios.' He got the boat, the BMW, the Labrador retriever, and the coin collection. She got the house, the Land Rover, and the Siamese cat." Kate grinned. "There are no secrets from your CPA."

"That's just the sort of thing I'm talking about, and why I don't want a house, a four-wheel-drive, or a dog." The very idea made Margo's stomach hurt. "I've simplified my life. Streamlined it, anyway, and I'll be damned if I'm going to fuck it up again." She had a handful of stones now and was shooting them over the edge like bullets. "What was it my mother always said? Begin as you mean to go on? Well, that's just what I'm doing. Begin simple, keep it simple. Josh doesn't want all those responsibilities any more than I do. We'll leave it—"

"Wait!" Laura grabbed her wrist before she could heave the next stone. "What is that? It's not a rock."

Frowning, Margo began to rub it with her thumb. "Someone must have dropped some change. I didn't notice. It's just a . . . Oh, my Jesus."

As she brushed off the dirt and sand, it gleamed at her, a small disk nestled in the palm of her hand.

318

"It's gold." Kate closed her hand over Laura's, and the three of them were linked. "It's a doubloon. Holy God, it's a gold doubloon."

"No, no." Breathless, Margo shook her head. "It's got to be one of those fake tokens they give away at the arcade in town." But it had weight. And such a fine gleam. "Doesn't it?"

"Look at the date," Laura managed. "1845."

"Seraphina." Margo pressed a hand to her head as it revolved like a carousel. "Seraphina's dowry. Could it be?"

"It has to be," Kate insisted.

"But it was just lying there. We've walked along here hundreds of times. We even searched here when we were kids. We never found anything."

"I guess we never looked in the right place." Kate's eyes danced with excitement as she leaned up to give Margo a hard, smacking kiss. "Let's look now."

As laughingly eager as the girls they had once been, they crawled over the dirt and rocks, ruining manicures, nicking fingers.

"Maybe she didn't leave it hidden after all," Margo suggested. "Maybe when he didn't come back and she decided she wouldn't live without him, she just chucked it all. Scattering coins into the sea."

"Bite your tongue." Kate wiped sweat from her brow with a dusty forearm. "The three of us always swore we'd find it, and now that we've actually got a piece, you want to have her taking the treasure into the sea with her!"

"I don't think she'd do that." Muffling a yelp as she scraped a knuckle on rock, Laura sat back on her heels. "The dowry wasn't important to her anymore. Nothing was. Poor thing, she was just a child." She blew hair out of her eyes. "And speaking of children . . . look at us."

It wasn't the order that made Kate and Margo stop. It was

the laughter that rolled out of her. Such a rare sound these days, Laura's low, gurgling laugh.

And getting a good look at one of society's most respected matrons with her hair flying, her face streaked with dirt, her once well-pressed cotton shirt soiled with sweat and grime, Margo laughed with her.

Then she clutched her stomach and pointed at Kate, who was on her hands and knees staring at them. She managed to clutch a rock before the next spurt of laughter rolled her off the cliff.

"Jesus, Kate! Jesus, even your eyebrows are dirty."

"You're not exactly bandbox-fresh yourself, pal. Only you would go treasure hunting in white silk."

"Oh, shit, I forgot." Wincing, Margo looked down at herself. The once spotless and fluid tunic was now filthy and stuck to her skin. She let out a low moan. "This used to be an Ungaro."

"Now it's a rag," Kate said smartly. "Next time try jeans and a T-shirt like the rest of the peasants." Kate rose and brushed the dirt off her denim. "We're never going to find anything this way. We need to organize. We need a metal detector."

"That's actually a good idea," Margo decided. "Where do we get one?"

By the time Margo got back to the penthouse it was dark. She limped through the front door and began stripping as she aimed directly for the whirlpool.

Josh halted in the act of pouring a glass of Poully Fuisse. "What in God's name have you been doing?" Glass cracked against wood as he rushed to her. "Was there an accident? Are you hurt?"

"No accident, and I hurt everywhere." She whimpered as she reached to turn on the hot water. Her fingers cramped

320

painfully. "Josh, if you really do love me, you'll get me a glass of whatever you were pouring and you won't, no matter how much you want to, laugh at me."

He couldn't spot any blood as she eased her body into the water. Relieved, he went back and brought two glasses filled with pale gold wine. "Tell me this—did you fall off a cliff?"

"Not exactly." She took a glass from him and downed the wine in a few greedy swallows. She took a breath, handed him the empty glass, then took the full one. "Thanks."

He only lifted a brow, then went back for the bottle. "I know, you took the girls to the beach and let them bury you in your clothes."

She leaned back, groaned. "I work out regularly now. How can there still be muscles I haven't been using? How can they hurt this much? Can you order me a massage?"

"I'll give you one myself if we can stop playing guess what."

She opened her eyes. She wanted to see if he laughed. If she spotted so much as a quiver, he'd have to die. "I was with Laura and Kate."

"And?"

"And we were treasure hunting."

"You were . . ." He ran his tongue around his teeth. "Hmm."

"Was that a chuckle?"

"No, it was a hmm. You spent the afternoon and a good part of the evening treasure hunting?"

"On the cliffs. We got a metal detector."

"You got a—" He tried manfully to disguise the laugh with a cough, but her eyes narrowed. "Did you figure out how to work it?"

"I'm not an idiot." But she pouted and, as the water level rose, hit the button for jets. "Kate did. And before you make any other smart comments, go check the pocket of my slacks

321

out there." She sank deeper, sipped wine, and felt as though she might live after all. "Then you can apologize."

Willing to play along, he set his glass down on the ledge of the tub and sauntered into the other room. Her slacks were near the door, less than a foot in front of where she'd stepped out of her shoes. And they were filthy enough to have him lifting them gingerly with two fingertips.

"You're going to need a new treasure-hunting outfit, honey. This one's shot."

"Shut up, Josh. Look in the pocket."

"Probably found a diamond that fell out of somebody's ring," he muttered. "Thinks she's hit the mother lode."

But his fingers closed over the coin. With a puzzled frown he drew it out. Spanish coin, more than a century old and bright as summer.

"I don't hear any laughing out there," she called out. "Or any apology, either." She began to hum to herself as the churning water loosened her muscles. Sensing him in the doorway, she flicked him a glance from under her lashes. "You don't have to grovel. A simple 'Please forgive me, Margo. I was a fool' will do nicely."

He flipped the coin and caught it neatly before sitting on the ledge. "One doubloon does not a treasure make."

"Rudyard Kipling?"

He had to grin. "J. C. Templeton."

"Oh, him." She closed her eyes. "I always thought he was cynical and overblown."

"Take a breath, darling," he warned, and dunked her.

When she surfaced, sputtering, he turned the coin over in his hand. "I admit it's intriguing. Where exactly did you find it?"

She was pouting and blinking water out of her eyes. "I don't see why I should tell you. Seraphina's dowry is a girl thing."

"Okay." He shrugged and picked up his wine. "So, what else did you do today?"

"At least you could wheedle," she said in disgust.

"I've cut way back on my wheedling." He passed her the soap. "You really need this."

"Oh, all right, then." One long, gorgeous leg shot out of the water. She soaped it lavishly. "It was on the cliffs in front of the house. Kate put a pile of stones up to mark the spot. But we searched there for hours after I found the coin and didn't find so much as a plug nickel."

"And what exactly is a plug nickel? Just a rhetorical question," he said when she hissed at him. "Look, duchess, I'm not going to spoil your fun. You've got yourself a nice little prize here. And the date's right. Who knows?"

"I know. And Kate and Laura know." She dragged her fingers through her wet hair. "And I'll tell you something else. It meant something to Laura. She lost that look in her eyes, that wounded look that always seems to be there if she doesn't know you're watching."

When his face went grim, she was sorry she'd said it. She covered his hand with hers. "I love her too."

"Firing the bastard wasn't enough."

"You broke his nose."

"There was that. I don't want her hurting. I don't know anyone who deserves it less than Laura."

"Or who seems to handle it better," she added, giving his hand a quick squeeze. "You should have seen her today. She was laughing and excited. We even got the girls in on it. I haven't seen Ali smile like that in weeks. It was so much fun. Just the anticipation of what might be there."

He eyed the coin again before setting it down to gleam on the ledge. "So when are you going back?"

"We decided to make it a regular Sunday outing." She wrinkled her nose at the water. "I might as well be taking a mud bath.'' And pulled the plug. ''I'm starved. Do you mind eating in tonight? I have to shower off and wash my hair.''

He watched her rise up, water sluicing off creamy skin in streams. ''Can we eat naked?''

''Depends.'' She laughed as she padded toward the shower. ''What's on the menu?''

The next morning, loose with love, she stretched as Josh maneuvered through traffic. ''You didn't have to drive me in,'' she told him, ''but I appreciate it.''

''I want to drop by the resort anyway. Check on a few things.''

''You haven't mentioned any travel coming up.''

''Things are covered.''

She glanced out the window, as if engrossed in the passing scenery. ''Once you replace Peter you'll have to go back to Europe, I imagine.''

''Eventually. I'm handling things from here well enough for now.''

''Is that what you want?'' She needed to keep the question easy, for both of them. ''To stay here?''

He was as cautious as she. ''Why do you ask?''

''You've never stayed in one place for long.''

''There was never a reason to.''

Her lips curved. ''That's nice. But I don't want you to feel tied down. Both of us have to understand that the other's business has demands. If Pretenses continues to do well, I'll have to start making buying trips.''

He'd considered that, had already begun working on a solution. ''Where did you have in mind?''

''I'm not sure. Local estate sales won't do. And for the clothing end of it, I want to try my contacts first. I could probably pitch a better ball in person. L.A. certainly, and New

York, Chicago. And if it all keeps rolling, back to Milan, London, Paris."

"Is that what you want?"

"I want the shop to shine. Sometimes I miss Milan, the being there, the feeling of being in the center of something. Of having it all buzzing around me." She sighed a little. "It's hard to let go completely. I'm hoping that if I can visit there a couple of times a year, do business there now and again, it'll be enough. Don't you miss it too?" She turned to face him. "The people, the parties?"

"Some." He'd been too busy changing his life, and hers, to think about it. But now that he did think, he could admit that the whirl was in his blood. "There's no reason we couldn't coordinate your buying trips with my business. Just takes a little planning."

"I'm getting better at planning." When he pulled to the curb in front of Pretenses, she leaned over to kiss him. "It's good, isn't it? This is good."

"Yeah." He cupped her neck to linger over the kiss. "It's very good."

All they had to do, she thought, was keep it that way. "I'll take a cab back. No, I mean it." She kissed him again before he could protest. "I should be there by seven, so try not to work too late. I'd love to go somewhere fabulous for dinner and neck over champagne cocktails."

"I think I can arrange that."

"I've never known you to fail."

He caught her hand as she started to alight. "I do love you, Margo."

She tossed him a brilliant smile. "I know."

Chapter Twenty

It was a smug feeling, spending the day in her own shop, among her own things, reaping the rewards of her first successful reception. And so she told her mother when Ann dropped by in the middle of the day with a box of Margo's old favorite. Chocolate chip cookies.

"I just can't believe it all happened," Margo said over a greedy bite. "People have been coming in all day. This is the first break I could manage. Mum, I really think I have a business. I mean I wanted to believe it all along. I nearly believed it after the first day went so well. But Saturday night." She closed her eyes and shoved the rest of the cookie into her mouth. "Saturday night I really believed it."

"You did a good job." Ann sipped the tea she'd brewed in the upstairs kitchen. Though she raised an eyebrow at Margo's choice of champagne—champagne at lunchtime!—she didn't comment. "You've done a good job. All these years . . ."

"All these years I've squandered my life, my time, my resources." Margo shrugged her shoulder. "The old ant and grasshopper story again, Mum?"

Despite herself Ann felt a smile tug at her lips. "You never listened to that story, never stored your larder for winter. Or so I thought." She rose to walk to the doorway, glanced into the tastefully decorated boudoir. "It looks as if you've been storing up after all."

"No. That's a different adage. Necessity being the mother of invention. Or maybe it's desperation." Since she was working hard on honesty in the new Margo, she might as well start here. "I didn't plan it this way, Mum. Or want it this way."

Ann turned back, studied the woman who sat on the fussy ice cream chair with its hot-pink cushion. Softer than she'd been, Ann thought. Around the eyes and mouth. She wondered that Margo, who had always been so aware of every inch of her own face, didn't seem to notice the change.

"So you didn't," Ann said at length. "And now?"

"Now I'm going to make it work. No, that's wrong." She picked up another cookie, tapped it against her glass like a toast. "I'm going to make it fabulous. Pretenses is going to grow. In another year or two, I'll open a branch in Carmel. Then—who knows? A tastefully elegant little storefront in San Francisco, a funky shop in L.A."

"Still dreaming, Margo?"

"Yes, that's right. Still dreaming. Still going places. Just different places." She tossed her hair back and smiled, but there was an edge to it. "Under it all, I'm still the same Margo."

"No, you're not." Ann crossed over, cupped her daughter's chin in her hand. "You're not, but there's enough of the little girl I raised that I recognize you. Where did you come from?" she murmured. "Your grandfathers caught fish to live. Your grandmothers scrubbed floors and hung out the wash with wooden pegs in high winds.'' She picked up Margo's hand, studied the long, narrow palm, the tapering fingers accented with pretty rings. ''My mother's hand would have made two of yours. Big and hard and capable it was. Like mine.''

She saw the surprise in Margo's eyes that she should speak so freely, so casually of people she had never spoken of at all. From selfishness, Ann had come to realize. Because if she didn't speak of them, it didn't hurt so deeply to be without them.

Oh, she'd made mistakes, Ann berated herself. Big and bad mistakes with the one child God had given her. If it stung to try to fix them, it was only just.

''My mother's name was Margaret.'' She had to clear her throat. ''I didn't mention that to you before because she died a few months after I left Ireland. And I felt guilty about leaving her when she was ailing, and about being unable to go back and say good-bye. I didn't talk to you of her, or to anyone. She would have been sad to know that.''

''I'm sorry'' was all Margo could say. ''I'm sorry, Mum.''

''So am I—for that and for not telling you sooner how she doted on you in the little time she had with you.''

''What—'' The question was there, but Margo was afraid to ask it, afraid it would be brushed off again.

''What was she like?'' Ann's lips curved in a quiet smile. ''You used to badger me with questions like that when you were a small thing. Then you stopped asking, because I never answered. I should have.''

She turned away, crossed to the pretty eyebrow windows that offered the sounds and sights of busy streets. Her sin, she realized, had been one of cowardice, and self-indulgence. If the penance was the pain of remembering, it was little enough.

''Before I answer, I want to tell you that I never did before because I told myself not to look back.'' With a small sound

328

of regret, she turned and walked to her daughter. "That it was more important to raise you up right than to fill your head with people who were gone. Your head was always filled with so much anyway."

Margo touched the back of her mother's hand briefly. "What was she like?"

"She was a good woman. Hardworking, but not hard. She loved to sing, and she sang when she worked. She loved her flowers and could grow anything. She taught us to take pride in our home, and in ourselves. She wouldn't take any nonsense from us, and she doled out whacks and hugs in equal measure. She'd wait for my father to come home from the sea with a look in her eye I didn't understand until I was grown."

"My grandfather? What was he like?"

"A big man with a big voice. He liked to swear so that my mother would scold him." A smile ghosted around Ann's mouth. "He'd come home from the sea smelling of fish and water and tobacco, and he'd tell us stories. Grand stories he could tell."

Ann steadied herself, brushed a few crumbs from the table. "I named you for my mother. My father called her Margo when he was teasing with her. Though I can't see her in you, nor much of myself when it comes to it. The eyes sometimes," she continued while Margo sat silently staring. "Not the color of them, but the shape and that stubborn look that comes into them. That's me right enough. But the color's your father's. He had eyes a woman could drown in. And the light of them, sweet Jesus, such a light in them it could blind you."

"You never speak of him."

"It hurt me to." Ann dropped her hand and sat again, tiredly. "It hurt, so I didn't, then I got out of the habit, and robbed you of him. It was wrong of me not to share him with you, Margo. What I did was keep him for myself," she said in an unsteady voice. "All for myself. I didn't give you your father."

Margo took a shaky breath. It felt as though a huge, hard weight was pressing on her chest. "I didn't think you loved him."

"Didn't love him?" Shock came first, followed by a long, rolling laugh. "Mother of God, girl, not love him? I had such a love for him my heart couldn't hold it. Every time I looked at him it flopped around like one of the fish he'd toss on the table after a catch. And when he'd sweep me up as he liked to do and swing me around, I wouldn't be dizzy from the spinning, but just from the smell of him. I can still smell him. Wet wool and fish and man."

She tried to picture it, her mother young and laughing, caught up in strong arms and wildly in love. "I thought . . . I assumed that you'd married him because you had to."

"Well, of course I had to," Ann began, then stopped, eyes wide. "Oh, *had* to. Why, my father would have thrashed him within an inch of his mortal life. Not that he didn't try, my Johnny," she added with a quick smile. "He was a man, after all, and had his ways. But I had mine, as well, and went to my wedding bed a proper, if eager virgin."

"I wasn't—" Margo picked up her glass, took a bracing sip. "I wasn't the reason he married you?"

"*I* was the reason he married me," Ann said with a lilt of pride in her voice. "And I'm sorrier than I can say that you had that thought planted in your head, that I didn't realize it until this very moment."

"I thought—I wondered . . ." How to put it, Margo wondered, when there were so many emotions spinning? "You were so young," she began again. "And in a strange country with a child to raise on your own."

"You were never a burden to me, Margo. A trial many a time," she added with a wry curve of her lips. "But never once a burden. Nor were you a mistake, so get that idea out of your head for good. We had to get married, Margo, because we loved each other. We were desperate in love. Sweet and desperate and so young, and it was all that sweet and desperate love that made you.''

"Oh, Mum, I'm so sorry."

"Sorry? I had more in those four years God gave us than a less fortunate woman could pack into two lifetimes."

"But you lost him."

"Yes, I lost him. And so did you. You didn't have much time with him, but he was a good father, and, God, he adored every inch of you. He used to watch you sleeping and touch your face with his fingertip, as if he was afraid he'd break you. And he'd smile so it seemed his face would split open with it.'' She pressed a hand to her mouth because she could picture it too well, still. Feel it too well, still. ''I'm sorry I never told you that.''

"It's all right." The weight was off her chest now, but it welled full of tears. "It's all right, Mum. You've told me now."

Ann closed her eyes a moment. How could she explain that grief and love and joy could carry in a heart for a lifetime? "He loved us both, Margo, and he was a fine man, a kind one, full of dreams for us, for the other children we were going to have.'' She fumbled in her pocket for a tissue and wiped away her tears. "Silly to cry over it now. Twenty-five years."

"It's not silly." To Margo it was a revelation, a beautiful, wrenching one. If there was grief after a quarter of a century, then there had been love. Sweet and desperate. And more, enduring. "We don't have to talk about it anymore."

But Ann shook her head, blinked her eyes dry. She would finish and give her child, her Johnny's child, what should have been her birthright. "When they came back that night in the storm. Oh, God, what a storm it was, wailing and blowing and

331

the lightning breaking the sky into pieces." She opened her eyes then, met her daughter's. "I knew—I didn't want to believe but I knew he was lost before they told me. Because something was gone. In here." She pressed a hand to her heart. "Just gone, and I knew he'd taken that part of my heart with him. I didn't think I could live without him. Knew I didn't want to live without him."

Ann linked her fingers together tight, for the next would be harder still to speak of. "I was almost three months along with another baby."

"You—" Margo wiped at tears. "You were pregnant?"

"I wanted a son for Johnny. He said that would be fine because we already had the most beautiful daughter in all the world. He kissed us good-bye that morning. You, then me, then he laid his hand on me where the baby was growing. And smiled. He never came back. They never found him so I could look at him again. One last time to look at him. I lost the baby that night, in the storm and the grief and the pain. Lost Johnny and the baby, and there was only you."

How did anyone face that and manage to go on? Margo wondered. What kind of strength did it take? "I wish I had known." She took her mother's clasped hands in hers. "I wish I had known, Mum. I would have tried to be . . . better."

"No, that's nonsense." After all these years, Ann realized, she was still doing it wrong. "I'm not telling you enough of the good things. There wasn't only grief and sorrow. The truth is I had him in my life for so many years. I first set my eyes on him when I was six, and he was nine. A fine, strapping boy he was then, Johnny Sullivan, with a devil's laugh and an angel's eyes. And I wanted him. So I went after him, putting myself in his face."

"You?" Margo sniffled. "You flirted with him?"

"Shamelessly. And by the time I was seventeen, I'd broken him down, and I snapped up his proposal of marriage before he could finish the words." She sighed once, long and deep. "Understand and believe this. I loved him, Margo, greedily. And when he died, and the baby died inside me, I wanted to die too, and might have, but for you. You needed me. And I needed you."

"Why did you leave Ireland? Your family was there. You must have needed them."

She could still look back to that, to rocky cliffs and tempestuous seas. "I'd lost something I'd thought I would have forever. Something I loved, something I'd wanted all my life. I couldn't bear even the air there without him. I couldn't breathe it. It was time for a fresh start. Something new."

"Were you frightened?"

"Only to death." Her lips curved again, and suddenly she had an urge for a taste of champagne herself. She took her daughter's glass, sipped. "I made it work. So maybe there's more of me in you than I thought. I've been hard on you, Margo. I haven't understood how hard until just recently. I've done some praying over it. You were a frighteningly beautiful child, and willful with it. A dangerous combination. There was a part of me that was afraid of loving you too much because . . . well, to love so full again was like tempting God. I couldn't show you, didn't think I could dare, because if I lost you I'd never have been able to go on."

"I always thought . . ." Margo trailed off, shook her head.

"No, say it. You should say what's inside you."

"I thought I wasn't good enough for you."

"That's my fault." Ann pressed her lips together and wondered how she could have let so many years slip away with that between them. "It was never a matter of that, Margo. I was afraid of and for you. I could never understand why you wanted so much. And I worried that you were growing up in a place where there was so much, and all of it belonging to others. And maybe I don't understand you even now, but I

333

love you. I should have told you more often.''

''It's not always easy to say it, or to feel it. But I always knew you loved me.''

''But you haven't known that I'm proud of you.'' Ann sighed. It was her own pride, after all, that had kept her silent. ''I was proud the first time I saw your face in a magazine. And every time after.'' She drank again, prepared to confess. ''I saved them.''

Margo blinked. ''Saved them?''

''All your pictures. Mr. Josh sent them to me and I put them in a book. Well, books,'' she corrected. ''Because there got to be so many.'' She smiled foolishly at the empty glass. ''I believe I'm just a little tipsy.''

Without thinking, Margo rose to get the bottle from the refrigerator, took off the silver cap, and poured her mother more. ''You saved my photos and put them in scrapbooks?''

''And the articles, too, the little snips of gossip.'' She gestured with her glass. ''I wasn't always proud of those, I'll tell you, and I have a feeling that boy held back the worst of them.''

Margo understood that Josh was ''that boy,'' and smiled. ''He would only have been thinking of you.''

''No, he's always thought of you.'' Ann inclined her head. ''There's a man blind in love if ever there was one. What are you made of, Margo? Are you as smart as your mother to latch on to a strong, handsome man who'll make you dizzy in bed and out?'' She caught herself when Margo snorted, and she struggled for dignity. ''It's the drink. It's sinful to be drinking in the middle of the day.''

''Have another and take a cab home.''

''Maybe I will, at that. Well, what's your answer then? Are you going to leave the man dangling or reel him in proper?''

Dangling had seemed a fine idea, the best idea. And now

334

she wasn't sure. "I'm going to have to give that some thought. Mum, thank you for giving my father to me."

"I should have—"

"No." A little surprised at herself, Margo shook her head. "No, let's not worry about 'should haves.' We'll be here all day pitching them back and forth between us. Let's start with now."

Ann had to use her tissue again. "I did a better job with you than I've given either one of us credit for. I have a fine daughter."

Touched, Margo pressed her lips to her mother's cheek. "Let's say you still have a work in progress. And speaking of work," she added, knowing both of them were about to start weeping again, "you enjoy the rest of your wine. My lunch break's over, and I have to go down and open up."

"I have photographs." Ann swallowed hard. "I'd like to show you sometime."

"I'd like to see them. Very much like to see them." Margo walked to the doorway, paused. "Mum, I'm proud of you, too, and what you've made of your life."

Josh heard the sound of girlish laughter as he circled the east terrace toward the pool. The squeals and splashing lightened his heart. As the curved sweep of water came into view, he grinned. A race was on.

Obviously Laura was holding back, keeping her strokes small and slow. When she was serious about her pace, no one could beat her. It used to infuriate him, having his little sister outdistance him. But then as captain of her swim team, she'd gone All-State and had even flirted with the Olympics.

Now she was letting her daughters overtake her, all but crawling to the edge as Ali put on a furious burst of speed.

"I won!" Ali bounced in the water. "I beat you to the side." Then her bottom lip poked out. "You let me."

335

"I gave you a handicap." Laura ran a hand over Ali's slicked-back hair, then smiled as Kayla surfaced, her mouth working like a guppy's. "Just like you gave your sister a handicap because you're bigger and faster and stronger."

"I want to win on my own."

"The way you're going, you will." She bent to kiss Kayla between the eyes. "Both of you swim like mermaids."

The thought of that made the mutiny die out of Ali's eyes and Kayla swim backward with a dreamy smile. "I'm a mermaid," Kayla claimed. "I swim all day with the dolphins."

"I'm still faster." Ali started to push off, then caught a movement out of the corner of her eye. She saw a man, tall, the suit, the glint of hair. Her heart speared up. But when she blinked her eyes clear of water, she saw it wasn't her father after all. "Uncle Josh!"

"Uncle Josh! Uncle Josh is here." Kayla kicked her feet to send water flying. "Come in and swim with us. We're mermaids."

"Anyone could see that. I'm afraid I'm not dressed to play with mermaids. But they're fun to watch."

To entertain him, Kayla did handstands, somersaults. Not to be outdone, Ali rushed to the board to show him how her diving had improved. He whistled and applauded, offered advice as Laura climbed out and toweled off.

She'd lost weight. Even a brother could see that. He had to concentrate on keeping his smile in place for the girls and not allowing his teeth to grind together.

"Got a minute?" he asked her when she'd bundled into a terry-cloth robe.

"Sure. Girls, shallow end." That brought groans and complaints, but both of them paddled in. "Is there a problem at work?"

"Not precisely. You mentioned you wanted to take a more active part." The frown came as he wandered toward a gardenia bush. He wanted to be out of the girls' hearing. "You've got a lot on your plate, Laura."

"I don't want your job, Josh." She smiled and combed her fingers through hair that the water had curling wildly. "I just think it's time I paid attention. I let things slide by me before. It's never going to happen again."

"You'll piss me off if you start blaming yourself."

"It takes two people to make a marriage." Laura sighed, making sure she kept her daughters in view as they walked along the edge of the garden. In the distance were the stables, the lovely old stucco and dark-beamed building, tucked behind the slope of the uneven land. She wished there were horses inside, or frisking in the paddock. She wished she had the time to tend to them as she did when she was a girl.

"I'm not taking it on, Josh. What Peter did was inexcusable. It was bad enough that he ignored his children, but then to take what was theirs—"

"And yours," he reminded her.

"Yes, and mine. I'm going to make it back. It's going to take a while, but I'm going to make it back."

"Honey, you know if you need money—"

"No." She shook her head. "No, I'm not taking money from you or Mom and Dad, I'm not using Templeton money I haven't earned to pay for my life. Not as long as the girls aren't doing without." She smiled a little, running a hand over his arm as they walked. "Let's be realistic, Josh. The three of us have a beautiful home, food on the table. Their tuition's paid. There are plenty of women who find themselves in my position and have nothing left."

"It doesn't make your situation any less rotten. How long are you going to be able to pay the servants, Laura, and the tuition if you're determined to use only your share of profits from the shop?"

She'd worried about the servants. How could she let them

go when most of them had been at Templeton House for years? What would Mrs. Williamson or old Joe the gardener do if she had to cut the staff?

"Pretenses is bringing in money, and I have the dividends from Templeton stock—which I intend to start earning. I've got time on my hands, Josh, and I'm tired of filling it up with committees and lunches and fundraisers. That was Peter's lifestyle."

"You want a job?"

"Actually, I thought I might be able to work part time. It's not that I'm destitute, it's that it's long past time that I started to make my own way. I look at Kate and the way she's always worked toward what she wanted. And Margo. Then I look at me."

"Just stop it."

"I've got something to prove," she said evenly. "And I'm damn well going to do it. You're not the only Templeton in this generation who knows hotels. I know about putting events together, catering, entertainment. I'd have to juggle time with the shop and the girls, of course."

"When can you start?"

She stopped dead. "Do you mean it?"

"Laura, you have just as much interest in Templeton as I do."

"I've never done anything for it, or about it. Not for years, anyway."

"Why?"

She grimaced. "Because Peter didn't want me to. My job, as he told me often, was being Mrs. Peter Ridgeway." It would, she understood, always humiliate her to admit it. "You know what finally occurred to me a year or so ago, Josh? My name was nowhere in there. I was nowhere in there."

Uncomfortable, he looked over toward the pool where his nieces were having a contest to see who could hold her breath longer. "I guess marriage is a loss of identity."

"No, it isn't. It shouldn't be." It was salt in a raw wound to admit it, but . . . "I let it be. I always wanted to be perfect. Perfect daughter, perfect wife, perfect mother. It's been a hard slap in the face to realize I couldn't be any of those things."

He laid his hands on her shoulders and gave her a little shake. "How about perfect sister? You won't hear any complaints from me."

Touched, she rested her hands on top of his. "If I were the perfect sister, I'd be asking you why you haven't asked Margo to marry you." She tightened her grip when he would have slipped his hands away. "You love each other, understand each other. I'd say you have more in common than any two people I know, including fear of taking the next step."

"Maybe I like the step I'm on."

"Is it enough, Josh? Really enough for you, or for Margo?"

"Damn, you're pushy."

"That's only one required element of the perfect sister."

Restless, he moved away, stopped to toy with a pale pink rosebud. "I've thought about it. Marriage, kids, the whole package. Pretty big package," he murmured. "Lots of surprises inside."

"You used to like surprises."

"Yeah. But one thing Margo and I have in common is an appreciation for being able to pick up and move whenever we like. I've lived in hotels for the last dozen years because I like the transience, the convenience. Hell." He broke off the bloom, handed it absently to Laura. "I've been waiting for her all my life. I always figured after the wait was over, I'd bide my time. A year or two of fun and games—which is exactly what she expects of me. How she thinks of me. Then I'd sneak the idea of marriage in on her."

With a half laugh, Laura shook her head. "Is this a chess game or a relationship, Josh?"

"It's been a chess game until recently. Move and counter-move. I finessed her into falling in love with me."

"Do you really think so?" Laura clucked her tongue and slid the rosebud into the lapel of his jacket. "Men are such boobs." She rose on her toes to kiss him lightly. "Ask her. I dare you."

He had to wince. "I wish you hadn't put it like that."

"One more element of the perfect sister is knowing her brother's deepest weakness."

Blissfully ignorant of the plans afoot, Margo watched a satisfied customer walk out the door. The way her feet were aching she was relieved that Laura would be putting in a half day tomorrow. As it was five-forty-five, she considered cashing out for the day, maybe nipping out just a few minutes early to go back to the suite and make herself beautiful for the fabulous dinner Josh had promised her.

The advantages to her new life were just piling up, she decided as she swung around the counter and slipped out of her shoes. Not only was she proving that she had a brain as well as a body, but she had discovered a whole new aspect of her background to explore.

Her parents had loved each other. Perhaps it was foolish for a grown woman to find such comfort and joy in that. But she knew it had opened something in her heart. Some things do last forever, she thought. Love held.

And tonight, she was going to tell Josh what she knew, what she believed, and what she wanted. A real life, a full life.

A married life.

It made her laugh to imagine his face when she proposed to him. She would have to be clever in her phrasing, she mused while she transferred cash out of the till into the bag for deposit. A subtle challenge, she decided. But not too subtle.

340

She would make him happy. They would travel the world together, go to all those exciting places they both loved. And always come back here. Because here was home for both of them.

It had taken her much too long to accept that.

She glanced up as the door opened, pushed back impatience with a shopkeeper's smile. Then squealed.

"Claudio!" She was around the counter in a dash, her hands flung out toward the tall, handsomely distinguished man. "This is wonderful." She kissed both of his cheeks before drawing back to arm's length to beam at him.

He was, of course, as stunning as ever. Silver wings flew back from his temples into thick black hair. His face was smooth and tanned, set off by his long Roman nose and the light in his chocolate-brown eyes.

"*Bella.*" He brought both of her hands to his lips. "*Molta bella.* I was set to be angry with you, Margo *mia*, but now, seeing you, I'm weak."

Appreciating him, she laughed. "What is Italy's most successful film producer doing in my little corner of the world?"

"Looking for you, my own true love."

"Ah." That was nonsense, of course. But they had always understood each other perfectly. "Now you've found me, Claudio."

"So I have." And he could see immediately that he need not have worried. She was glowing. "And the rumors and buzzing I heard when I returned from location were true after all. La Margo is running a shop."

With a challenging gleam in her eye, she lifted her chin. "So?"

"So?" He spread his hands expressively. "So."

"Let me get you a glass of champagne, darling, and you can tell me what you're really doing in Monterey."

"I tell you I come to search for my lost love." But he

341

winked at her as he accepted the glass. "I had a bit of business in Los Angeles. How could I come so close without seeing you?"

"It was sweet of you. And I am glad to see you."

"You should have called me when there was trouble for you."

It seemed a lifetime ago. She only shrugged. "I got through it."

"That Alain. He's a pig." Claudio stalked around the shop in the long, limber strides he used to stalk a soundstage. His burst of gutter Italian termed Alain as a great deal more, and less, than a mere pig.

"I cannot but agree," Margo said when he had run down.

"If you had called my offices, the studio, they would have gotten word to me. I would have swept down on my winged charger and saved you."

She could picture it. Claudio was one of the few men who wouldn't look foolish on a winged charger. "I saved myself, but thanks."

"You lost Bella Donna. I'm sorry for it."

"So was I. But now I have this."

His head angled, his mouth quirked. "A shopkeeper, Margo *mia*."

"A shopkeeper, Claudio."

"Come." He took her hand again, and though his voice was teasing, his eyes were serious. "Let me whisk you away from this. To Roma, with me. I have a new project to begin in a few months. There's a part perfect for you, *cara*. She's strong, sexy, glamorous. Heartless."

She laughed delightedly. "Claudio, you flatter me. Six months ago I'd have snapped it up, without worrying that I'm not an actress. Now I have a business."

"So, let someone else see to it. Come with me. I'll take care of you." He reached out, toyed with her hair, but his eyes

342

were serious. "We'll have that affair we always meant to have."

"We never got around to that, did we? That's why we still like each other. No, Claudio, though I am very, very touched and very, very grateful."

"I don't understand you." He began to prowl again. "You weren't meant to make change and box trinkets. This is not the— *Dio*! These are your dishes." He stopped at a shelf and gawked. "You have served me pasta on these plates."

"Good eye," she murmured.

That eye was dazed as he turned back, began to recognize other things he had admired as a guest in her home in Milan. "I thought it was a joke, a poor one, that you were selling your possessions. Margo, it should not have come to this."

"You make it sound as though I'm living out of a shopping cart in an alley."

"It's humiliating," he said between his teeth.

"No, it's not." She bristled, then calmed herself. He was only thinking of her. Or the woman he had known. She, Margo realized, would have been humiliated. "It's not. I thought it would be, but I was wrong. Do you want to know what it is, Claudio?"

He swore again, ripely, and gave serious thought to hauling her over his shoulder and carrying her off. "Yes, I want to know what it is."

She came close to him, until they were eye to eye. "It's fun."

He nearly choked. "Fun?"

"Great, wonderful, giddy fun. And do you know what else? I'm good at it. Really good at it."

"You mean this? You're content?"

"No, I'm not content. I'm happy. It's mine. I sanded the floors. I painted the walls."

He paled a little, pressed a hand to his chest. "Please, my heart."

"I scrubbed the bathrooms." She laughed and gave him a bracing kiss. "And I loved it."

He tried to nod, but couldn't quite pull it off. "I'd have some more wine, if you please."

"All right, but then you have to browse." She filled his glass and her own before tucking her arm through his. "And while we're browsing, I'll tell you what you can do for me."

"Anything."

"You know a lot of people." Her mind was working quickly as she led him toward the stairs. "People who grow tired of last year's fashions or the trinkets they bought. You could give them my name. I'd like first shot at the discards."

"Jesus" was all he could say as they climbed the stairs.

The first thing Josh noted when he walked into the shop was the deposit bag. He shook his head at her carelessness, then locked the door. Going behind the counter, he tucked the bag back into the till—and noticed her shoes.

He was going to have a little talk with her about basic precautions, but it could wait. In his pocket was his grandmother's ring. He was still rolling with the excitement he'd felt when he'd lifted it out of the safety deposit box. The square-cut Russian white diamond might have been fashioned with Margo in mind. It was sleek and glamorous and full of cold fire.

He was going to dazzle her with it. He would even go so far as to get down on one knee—after he had plied her with a little champagne. A man needed an edge with Margo.

She would probably balk at the idea of marriage, but he would sweet-talk her into it. Seduce her into it if necessary. It wouldn't be such a sacrifice. The image of her wearing nothing but his ring was alluring enough to calm the nerves in the pit of his stomach.

Enough fun and games, he told himself. Time for serious business.

He started up the steps, nearly called out to her when he heard her laughter drift out like smoke. Nearly smiled before he heard the low male chuckle that followed.

A customer, he told himself, furious at the instant knee jerk of jealousy. But when he walked to the doorway of the boudoir, the knee jerk jolted into a full, vicious kick.

She was locked in a man's arms, and the kiss had enough smolder to singe him where he stood.

He thought of murder, bloody, bone-breaking, brain-splattering murder. His hands clenched into ready fists, the snarl already in his throat. But pride was nearly as violent an emotion as vengeance. It iced over him in a gale wind as Margo drew back.

"Claudio." Her voice was a silky purr. "I'm so glad you came. I hope we can—" She spotted Josh then, and myriad emotions flickered over her face. Surprise, pleasure, guilt, amusement. The amusement didn't last. His eyes were hard and cold and much too easy to read. "Josh."

"I wasn't expected," he said coolly. "I know. But I don't think an apology for the interruption's in order."

"This is a friend from Rome," she began, but he cut off her explanation with a look that sliced to the bone.

"Save the introductions, Margo. I won't keep you from entertaining your friend."

"Josh." He was halfway down the stairs before she reached the landing. "Wait."

He shot her one last, lethal look as he flipped open the lock on the front door. "Stay healthy, Margo. Stay away from me."

"*Cara.*" Claudio laid a hand on Margo's shoulder where

she stood shivering at the base of the stairs. "I'm surprised he let us live."

"I have to fix it. I have to make him listen. Do you have a car?"

"Yes, of course. But if I could suggest giving him a little time to calm—"

"It doesn't work that way with Josh." Her hand was shaking as she reached for her purse, forgetting her shoes. "Please, Claudio. I need a ride."

Chapter Twenty-one

She'd worked up a fine head of steam by the time she burst into the penthouse. Being angry, being furious was better than being terrified.

And she had been terrified when she'd read that cold disgust in his eyes, heard the icy dismissal in his voice. She wasn't going to tolerate that. No, sir, not for one New York minute. He was going to have to crawl.

"Josh Templeton, you bastard!" She slammed the door at her back and darted toward the bedroom in bare feet. "How dare you walk out on me that way! How dare you embarrass me in front of my friend!"

Her breath caught with a jerk of a heartbeat when she saw him at the closet calmly transferring clothes into a garment bag. "What are you doing?"

"Packing. I have to make a run to Barcelona."

"The hell with that. You're not just walking out." She'd taken two strides forward with the intent of ripping the clothes free when he whirled on her.

"Don't do it" was all he said, and it shocked her anger back to fear.

"This is childish," she began, but her teeth chattered as panic shot frozen fingers up her spine. "You don't even deserve an explanation, but I'm willing to overlook your filthy attitude and give you one. Claudio and I—"

"I didn't ask for an explanation." In quick jerks, he zipped the bag.

"No," she said slowly. "You've already made up your mind what you saw, what it meant. What I am."

"I'll tell you what I saw." He dipped his hands into his pockets to keep them off her throat. But his fingers brushed the velvet box he carried and doubled his fury and pain. "I saw you in the bedroom, a couple of glasses of champagne, nice soft light coming in through the lace curtains. A very romantic setting. You had your mouth on another man—your usual type, too, if I'm not mistaken. Fiftyish, rich, foreign."

He lifted the bag from the hanger, folded it. "What it meant, Margo, is that I walked in on the first act. You should be able to figure out what that makes you."

She would rather he'd used his fists on her. Surely there would have been less pain in that. "You believe that?"

He hesitated. How could she sound so hurt? How dare she sound hurt after she'd ripped out his heart and stomped on it while it was still beating. "You've sold sex your whole life, duchess. Why should you change?"

What little color that was left in her cheeks drained. "I suppose that's true. It looks like my mistake was giving it to you for free."

"Nothing's free." He bit off the words like stringy meat. "And you had your fun as well. I fit most of the requirements,

348

didn't I? I'm not old enough to be your father, but I qualify for the rest. Rich, restless, irresponsible. Just another social piranha living off the family fortune.''

''That's not true,'' she said, furious with panic. ''I don't think—''

''We know what we think of each other, Margo.'' He spoke calmly now, had to speak calmly. ''You've never had any more respect for me than you do for yourself. I thought I could live with that. I was wrong. I told you in the beginning I don't share, and I don't want a woman who thinks I'm stupid enough, or shallow enough, to overlook her old friends.''

''Josh.'' She stepped forward, but he slung the bag over his arm.

''I'd like you out by the end of the week.''

''Of course.'' She stood where she was as he brushed by her. She didn't cry, not even when she heard the door close. She simply sank to the floor and rocked.

''Byron De Witt agreed to take over Ridgeway's position. He'll be ready to make the move to California in six to eight weeks.''

''That's fine.'' Thomas sipped his after-dinner coffee and exchanged a look with his wife as their son prowled the drawing room of their villa. ''He's a good man. Sharp. Tough-minded.''

''You'll go back.'' Susan crossed her legs. ''Through the transitional period.''

''It's not really necessary. Things are again in running order. I wasn't able to lure our old chef back.'' He flashed a fleeting grin. ''But the one I stole from the BHH is working out well.''

''Hmm.'' He needed to go back, Susan thought, but she would work on that. ''How's Laura doing in Conventions?''

''She's a Templeton.'' He started toward the brandy, reminded himself that was too easy, and settled for coffee. "She's got a knack for handling people."

Susan lifted a brow, a signal that she was tossing the ball back into her husband's court. He picked it up smoothly.

"And she's putting in time at the shop? Not overdoing, is she?"

"Kate says not. She's a reliable source."

"I'd feel better if one of us could keep an eye on her for a while yet. She's in a rough patch."

"Dad, she's handling it. I can't go play baby-sitter."

"You look tired," Susan said mildly. "That's probably why you're so cranky. Remember, Tommy, how he'd squall if he missed his nap?"

"Jesus. I'm not cranky. I'm trying to get business settled. I have to be in Glasgow tomorrow afternoon. I don't have time to . . ." He caught himself as his parents watched him indulgently. There was nothing worse than being smiled at like a fretful child. Unless it was being a fretful child. "Sorry."

"Don't give it a thought." Thomas rose, slapped him on the back. "What you need's a drink, a cigar, and a nice game of billiards."

Josh rubbed his tired eyes. When was the last time he'd slept, really slept? Two weeks? Three? "It couldn't hurt," he decided.

"You go ahead, Tommy, and set things up for your man hour." She patted the cushion beside her. "I want Josh to keep me company for a few more minutes."

Understanding, Tommy strolled off. "Fifty bucks a ball," he called out.

"He'll trounce me," Josh muttered as he sat. "He always does."

"We all have our game." She patted his knee. Hers was a deft and merciless knack for interrogation. "Now, are you going to tell me what happened between you and Margo?"

350

"Hasn't Kate given you a full report?"

She ignored the annoyance in his tone, was sorry for the bitterness underneath it. "Reports are spotty. Apparently Margo is being stubbornly closemouthed. All Kate can drag out of her is that the two of you decided to call it a day."

"Well, then."

"And you expect me to believe it's as simple as that when you're sitting here looking mean and miserable?"

"I caught her with another man."

"Joshua." Susan set her cup down with a snap. "No," she said positively, "you didn't."

"I walked into the goddamn bedroom, and there they were."

She hurt for him, couldn't help but hurt for him. Still, she shook her head. "You misinterpreted something."

"What the hell is there to misinterpret?" he shot back and sprang up to pace again. "I walked in and she was kissing another man. Fucking Claudio."

"Josh!" She wasn't so much shocked by the word, but she had taken his statement literally. "I don't believe that."

"No, I didn't mean—" Frustrated, he dragged both hands through his hair. "It hadn't gotten that far yet. I meant, she called him Claudio."

"Oh." Her heart settled a little. "Well, what was her explanation?"

He stopped his pacing to stare at her. "Do you really think I waited around for explanations?"

On a long sigh, she picked up her coffee again. "No, of course you didn't. You stormed out, wishing them both to go to hell. I'm surprised you didn't toss him out the window on your way."

"I thought about it," he said with relish. "I thought about tossing both of them. It seemed . . . more civilized to leave."

"More pigheaded," she corrected. "Oh, sit down, Joshua.

351

You're making me tired just watching you. You know you should have given her a chance to explain.''

"I didn't—don't—want excuses and explanations. Damn it, I overlooked the hordes of men from before, but—''

"Ah,'' Susan said with a satisfied nod. Now they had nailed it. "Did you now? Did you really?''

"I was working on it.'' He found he did want a brandy after all and poured a generous snifter before he obeyed her command to sit. "When I came home and found her posing naked in our bed, I took it in stride.'' He caught his mother's eye. "Pretty much in stride. That was business. And when we go out to a restaurant or to the club and every man within half a mile has drool running down the side of his chin, I shrug it off. Mostly.''

"Shame on me. I've raised a jealous fool.''

"Thanks for your support.''

"You listen to me. I understand it must be difficult on one level to love a woman who looks like Margo. The kind of woman who attracts men, inspires fantasies.''

"Good.'' He gulped at the brandy. "I feel better now.''

"The point is, that's the woman you fell in love with. Now, let me ask you. Did you fall in love with her because she has a beautiful face and a stunning body? Is that all you see when you look at her?''

"It's the sort of thing that drills between the eyes.'' But he sighed, surrendered. "No, that's not all I see. That's not why I fell in love with her. She's warm and reckless and stubborn. She's got more guts and brains than she realizes. She's generous and she's loyal.''

"Ah, loyal.'' Susan smiled smugly. "I'd hoped you wouldn't overlook that. It's one of her most admirable traits. And a woman with Margo's sense of loyalty would not have done what you accused her of doing. Go home, Josh, and deal with this.''

352

He set the snifter down, closed his eyes. "It wasn't just the men. It was seeing her that way and realizing when I did what we had together, and didn't have. Telling her I loved her didn't seem to be enough. Showing her didn't seem to be enough. She doesn't want what I want, and she'd be shocked speechless if she knew what I wanted."

"What do you want?" She smiled and brushed at his hair. "I won't be shocked speechless."

"Everything," he murmured. "Usually Margo understands everything just fine, but not this time. She doesn't see marriage and family and commitment when she looks at me. She sees a pampered idiot who's more interested in fine-tuning his backhand than in making a contribution to his legacy or building a life."

"I think you're underestimating both of you. But if you're right, you only proved her point by walking away before you sorted it out."

"I'd have killed her if I'd stayed. I didn't know she could hurt me like this. I didn't know anyone could."

"I know. I'm sorry. When you were little and you were hurt, I could make it better by sitting you in my lap and holding on."

He looked at her, loved her. "Let's try this." He lifted her into his lap and held on. "I think it'll work."

Kate sauntered into the shop at midafternoon. She'd had to take an hour off, but she loved being the messenger. "How's it going, troops?"

Laura glanced up as she slid the credit card machine back under the counter. Automatically she glanced at her watch to be certain she hadn't lost a couple of hours. The girls had to be picked up from dance class at six-thirty sharp.

"It's going pretty good. What are you doing here this time of day?"

"Taking a break. Where's Margo?"

"She's in the wardrobe room with a couple of customers. Kate . . ." Lowering her voice, Laura leaned over the counter. "We sold my rubies."

Kate's mind shuffled back. "The necklace. Oh, but Laura, you loved that necklace."

She only shrugged. "Peter gave it to me for our fifth anniversary—bought it, naturally, with my money. I'm glad it's gone." And her share would go a long way toward paying next year's tuition for her daughters. "And there's more. My supervisor called me in this morning and gave me a raise."

Kate waited a beat. "The daughter of the owners has a supervisor and gets a raise. I don't understand life."

"I wanted to start at an entry position. It's only fair."

"Okay. Okay." Kate held up a hand to hold her off. She understood the need to prove oneself, had been scrambling to do just that all her life. "Congratulations, pal. So I guess everybody's happy."

Laura had to sigh as she glanced back toward the wardrobe room. "Not everybody."

"She still being stoic and stubborn?"

"I could shake her," Laura said fiercely. "She flits around here all day as if nothing in the world is wrong. And as if a couple of layers of polished ivory base coat can hide the shadows under her eyes."

"Still refusing to move back into the house?"

"The resort has everything she needs. She loves it there." Laura sucked air through her nose. "I'm going to hit her the next time she says that. And she's already making excuses for skipping the treasure hunt this weekend. Sunday's the only time she can squeeze in for a manicure. It's such bullshit."

"Ooh, you are pissed. Good, you're going to love what happens when I get hold of her."

With surprising speed and strength, Laura reached across

the counter and grabbed Kate's hand. "What's up? What do you have? Can we double-team her?"

"That's a thought. Listen, I— Whoops, here she comes. Just follow my lead."

Margo spotted Kate, gave her a raised-eyebrow look even as she continued to chat up her customers. "I don't think you could have found anything more perfect for you. That red St. Laurent is going to draw every eye."

The woman currently clutching it gnawed on her lip. "Still, it's a little early to be shopping for holiday parties."

Margo only smiled, and Laura caught the steel in her eyes. "It's never too early. Not for something that special."

"It is a wonderful price." As she laid it on the counter, she ran a loving hand over the satin skirt. "I've never owned a designer anything."

"Then you're overdue. And that's just what Pretenses is for. To give everyone a chance to feel lush."

"You can't waffle," the woman's companion ordered, giving her friend an encouraging nudge. "You couldn't pry this green velvet away from me with a crowbar." She laughed as she handed it to Margo. "Well, just ring it up and box it. But don't seal the box," she ordered. "I'm going to have to drool over it in the car."

"That's the spirit." Margo took the plastic card, and her eyes softened. "It really did look fabulous on you. I'm sorry we didn't have any shoes that worked."

"I'll find some—or go barefoot." Flushed with the pleasure of the hunt, the woman elbowed her friend. "Give her your credit card, Mary Kay, and live a little."

"Okay, okay. The kids can always get new shoes next month." When Margo snatched back her hand, appalled, Mary Kay let out a long, cheerful laugh. "Only kidding. But if you want to take an extra ten percent off . . ."

"Not on your life." She rang up both sales while Laura

355

competently wrapped and boxed the gowns. "I ought to charge you an extra ten for making my heart stop."

"How about we call it even and I tell you I love it in here. When my conscience is clear again, I'm coming back for that silver evening bag shaped like an elephant."

"Buy it now and take the ten percent."

"I—" Mary Kay's mouth worked for a moment, then she shut her eyes tight. "Ring it up. Go ahead, but I can't watch."

A few minutes later, Margo watched the door close, then dusted her hands together. "Another satisfied victim—I mean customer."

"Right, killer." Laura filed the credit slips. "You gave her a hell of a deal."

"Yeah, but they'll both be back—and the formal wear is slow to move. What's going on, Kate? Did you run out of red ink?"

"Oh, I can always find a fresh supply. Actually I had a couple of errands to run, so I slipped out a little early. And I like to check up on my investment."

"Going to audit the books?"

"Not until the first of the year," she said blithely. "How much is my partner's discount on those wineglasses there, the ones rimmed with gold? My boss's grandson is getting married."

Margo decided to sneak a cigarette. "You pay the full shot and get your share out of the profits."

"God, you're tough. Well, box them up pretty, but I want Laura to wrap them. You still screw it up."

Margo smiled sweetly. "Sorry, I'm on my break. Box them yourself."

"Can't get decent help anymore," Kate muttered. But she ran her tongue around her teeth as she took the box Laura handed her and carefully began to pack the glasses. "Oh, guess who called the office right before I left?"

"Donald Trump, looking for a new accountant."

"I wish." She glanced casually at Margo and brought the box to the counter. "Josh."

Out of the corner of her eye she watched Margo's hand freeze on the way to her lips, jerk, then continue. Smoke billowed out in a shaky stream. "I'd better straighten up the other clothes Mary Kay and her pal tried on." She started to crush out her cigarette in nervous taps, and Kate continued.

"He's back in town."

"Back?" The cigarette kept smoldering as Margo's hand dropped away. "Here?"

"Well, at the hotel. I want the silver bells, Laura, with a silver ribbon. He said he had some business to finish up." She smiled sweetly at Margo. "Something he left . . . hanging."

"And you just had to rush right over here to rub my face in it."

"Nope. I rushed right over here to slap your face in it."

"A rude but effective wake-up call," Laura commented and earned a shocked stare.

"I expected better from you."

"You shouldn't have." Hands brisk and competent, she affixed a shiny silver bow to the box. "If you don't want to tell us what happened between you and Josh, fine. But you can't expect us to sit around quietly while you mope."

"I have not been moping."

"We've been cleaning up the blood spilling out of your heart for weeks." Kate passed Laura her credit card. "Face it, pal, you're just no fun anymore."

"And that's all this friendship is about? Fun? I thought I might get a little support, a little sympathy, a little compassion."

"Sorry," Laura imprinted the card with a steady sweep. "Fresh out."

357

"Well, the hell with you." She snatched up her purse. "The hell with both of you."

"We love you, Margo."

That stopped her. She whirled back to glare at Kate. "That's a lousy thing to say. Bitch." When Kate grinned, she tried to grin back. Instead she dropped her purse back behind the counter and burst into tears.

"Oh, shit." Shocked, Kate leaped forward to gather her close. "Oh, hell. Oh, shit. Lock the door, Laura. I'm sorry, Margo. I'm sorry. Bad plan. I thought you'd just get mad and go tearing off to fix his butt. What did the bastard do to you, honey? I'll fix his butt for you."

"He dumped me." Thoroughly ashamed, she sobbed wretchedly on Kate's shoulder. "He hates me. I wish he were dead. I wish I had slept with Claudio."

"Wait. Whoa." Firmly, Kate drew her back while Laura brought over a cup of tea. "Who's Claudio and when didn't you sleep with him?"

"He's a friend, just a friend. And I never slept with him." The tears were so hot it felt as though her eyes were on fire. "Especially not when Josh found us in the bedroom."

"Uh-oh." Kate rolled her eyes at Laura. "Is it a French farce or a Greek tragedy? You be the judge."

"Shut up, Kate. Come on, Margo. Let's sit down. This time you tell us everything."

"Christ, I feel like a fool." Now that everything had poured out, she felt not only foolish but empty.

"He's the fool," Laura corrected. "For jumping to conclusions."

"Give the guy a break." Kate handed Margo another tissue. "The evidence was pretty damning. Not that he should have taken off before he listened," she added quickly when Margo sniffled. "But you have to look at it from his side a little."

"I have looked at it from his side." And she was finished weeping. "I really can't blame him."

"I wouldn't go that far," Kate began.

"No, I can't. The history was there. Why should he trust me?"

"Because he loves you," Laura put in. "Because he knows you."

"That's what I told myself when I was busy hating him. But now, saying it all out loud, it's hard for me to believe me. He thinks I look at him and the whole relationship as one more exciting amusement. And it's probably better that it happened before I . . ."

"Before you . . . ?" Kate prompted.

"Before I asked him to marry me." Suddenly she covered her face with her hands, but this time it was laughter that poured out. "Can you believe it? I was going to propose. I was going to set the scene—candlelight, wine, music—and when I had him wrapped around my finger, I was going to pop the question. What a brainstorm!"

"I think it's wonderful! I think it's perfect." This time it was Laura's eyes that overflowed.

Kate tugged a tissue free for herself. "And I think you should go get him."

"Go get him." Margo snorted. "He can't even look at me."

"Pal, you go fix your face, get yourself back in gear, and he won't have a chance."

It was such a huge risk. Margo told herself he wouldn't even come, and if he did he wouldn't listen. But she was willing to dream, one more time. Fingering the gold coin in her pocket, she wandered the sloped lawn in front of the house.

It was everything Kate had said, a magnificent example of California Spanish at its best, with the elegant arched windows, the dull red of hand-rolled tile on the roof. The recessed doorway of the entrance tower was framed in floral tiles. Bougainvillea climbed riotously.

And the view. She turned to it, drew in a long, greedy breath. All sea and cliffs beyond the sweeping road. Perhaps Seraphina had stood there, walked there, mourning her lost love. But Margo wanted to believe she had walked there with him, when hope and dreams were still vivid. She needed that hope now as she saw Josh's car zip down the road and swing up the snaking drive.

Oh, God, just one more chance. All or nothing now.

Her heart was pounding like the surf when he stepped out of his car. The wind blew through his hair, the sun shot light off the dark glasses he wore. And she couldn't see his eyes. But his mouth was set and cold.

"I wasn't sure you'd come."

"I said I would." He was still reeling from her call, one that had come even as he'd cursed himself and reached for the receiver to call her. "These your new digs?"

"No, I haven't risen back up in the world quite that much. It belongs to a client of Kate's. She's moved out. It's empty." Her breath was almost steady, and she was pleased with the easy, measured tone. "I thought neutral ground would be best."

"Fine." He wanted to touch her, just touch her, so badly his hands ached with it. "Do we start with small talk? How are you? How's business?"

"No." It was easier to walk than to look at him looking at her. She could already feel the humiliation, and she accepted it. She'd already lost him once. She could live through anything now. "I'll just say this straight out so we can get it done with. I didn't sleep with Claudio. In fact, I never slept with him. He's one of those rare finds. A true male friend. I'm not telling you this to put things back the way they were. I don't want them the way they were. But I don't want you believing I was unfaithful.''

"I apologize," he said stiffly. He still wanted to touch her, if only to wrap his hands around her throat. He'd come knowing he would beg her to take him back, to forgive him for being a jealous, insensitive idiot, and she was already telling him she didn't want him.

"And I don't want an apology. I might have reacted the same way if the situation had been reversed." She turned her head toward him and smiled. "After I'd torn her eyes out and stomped on your throat."

"It was a close call," he said, struggling to match her light tone.

"I know." Her smile warmed. "I've known you long enough to recognize murder in your eyes when I see it." She only wished she could see his eyes now. "And I think I understand that you left the way you did before you did something or said something neither of us could live with."

"I said more than I should have, certainly more than was warranted. I'll apologize for that, too."

"Then I'll say I'm sorry for kissing Claudio, even though it was a kiss of friendship and gratitude. He'd come to offer me his help, and a part in his next movie."

It took him only a moment. "Oh, that Claudio." Emotions swirled and tightened and threatened to strangle him. "Well, that's a break for you."

"Could be," she said with a careless shrug and started walking again. "In any case, in retrospect, I can see just how it looked and why you reacted the way you did."

He swore lightly. "Just how guilty do you want me to be?"

"That's probably guilty enough." She turned, and this time she laid a hand on his arm. "But I need to tell you that you were wrong about something else. I don't think about you the way you seem to believe. I know you're not spoiled and careless. Maybe I used to think that, and maybe I once resented the fact that you were born to all the advantages I thought I wanted. Hell, I did want them," she corrected with a quick smile. "It used to irritate me that you didn't have to fight for them."

"You always made that clear."

"I suppose I did. But what I haven't made clear is how much I admire the man you've made of yourself. I know how important you are to Templeton, and how important Templeton is to you. I've come to understand just how much responsibility you have, and how seriously you take it since we— well, since we've been together. It's important to me that you believe that."

"You make me feel like an idiot." He had to walk away from her, crossing the tiled terrace to look out to the cliffs. "It matters," he managed. "What you think of me matters." He turned back. "I was fascinated, and often irritated by the girl you were, Margo."

She cocked a brow. "*You* always made that clear."

"I still am, fascinated and often irritated, but I admire the woman you've made of yourself, Margo. I admire her a great deal."

So there was hope, she thought, closing her eyes briefly. And where there was hope, there could be trust and respect, and certainly love. "I want us to be friends again, Josh. You're too important to my life to do without. We managed to be friends before. I want us to be friends again."

"Friends." It threatened to choke him.

"I think both of us forgot that part of our history along the way. I wouldn't want that to happen again."

She was smiling at him, the wind making a sexy mess of of her fancy braid, the sun slanting in her eyes as it drifted lazily down in the west. "You can stand there and tell me you think friendship is the answer."

"It's one of them. An important one."

He couldn't start all over again. It would kill him. The rage of love inside him would never settle for something as patient as friendship. Slowly, he crossed back to her. "One of us has lost his or her mind."

"Let's give it some time. We can start with you giving me some friendly advice." Smooth as silk, she tucked her hand through his arm and guided him around the side of the house. "Isn't this place fabulous? Wait until you see the fountain in the back. It's charming. Of course, I think it should have a pool. There's enough land for a small free-form. And the view from that upper balcony—that must be the master suite, don't you think? It's got to be incredible. I guess there's at least two fireplaces. I haven't been inside yet, but I'm hoping there's one in the master bedroom."

"Wait a minute. Hold on." His mind was spinning. Her perfume was clouding his brain, and her words jammed into his consciousness.

"And look at this bougainvillea. It really should be cut back, but I love it wild. The terrace is perfect for entertaining, isn't it? And the location couldn't be better. Just up the coast from the shop and all but next door to Templeton House."

"I said, hold it." He turned her around, took a firm grip on her shoulders. "Are you thinking of buying this place?"

"It's a once-in-a-lifetime chance." Her only chance. "Kate says it's a fabulous deal, a solid investment, and you know how pessimistic she is. It isn't even going on the market until next week—there was some problem with clearing the deed—so it's ground floor."

"Jesus, duchess, you never change."

Her heart lightened a bit at the amused exasperation in his tone. "Should I?"

"Listen, this place has got to run at least three hundred K."

"Three hundred fifty, but Kate thinks three hundred will close it."

"Dream on," he muttered.

"I am."

"You've been in business less than a year, a month before that you were sniffing at bankruptcy. There isn't a bank on the planet that's going to approve a loan of this size. Margo, you just can't afford it."

"I know." She aimed her best smile, the one that had earned her fleeting fame and fortune. "But you can."

He did choke. "You want me to buy a damn house for you?"

"Sort of." She toyed with the button of his shirt, shot a look up from under her lashes. "I thought if you bought it, and married me, we could both live here."

He couldn't get a word out. When his vision hazed, he realized he wasn't breathing either. "I have to sit down."

"I know how you feel." She linked her hands together, found them damp, as he lowered himself to a bench.

"You want me to buy a house and marry you so you can live in it?"

"So we can live in it," she corrected. "Together. When we're not traveling."

"You just got finished telling me you didn't want things back the way they were."

"I don't. It was too easy before. Too easy to dive in, too easy to walk. I want to make it hard. I want to make it very, very hard. I love you." Because her eyes were filling, she turned away. "I love you so much. I can live without you. You don't have to worry that I'll jump off a cliff like Seraphina if you walk. But I don't want to live without you. I want to be married to you, have a family with you, build something here with you. That's all I have to say."

"That's all you have to say," he repeated. His heart had

settled back in place, but it seemed to be taking up too much room. So much that it hurt his chest. Just as the grin was so wide it hurt his face. "I guess it's my turn to say something."

"I'd never cheat on you."

"Shut up, Margo. You lost your chance to see me crawl over that one. I was wrong, I was stupid and I was careless with you, and it won't happen again. And I'm going to add that I always thought a hell of a lot more of you than you thought of yourself. That's all I have to say."

"All right, then." She struggled to find a dignified exit. But he laid a hand on her shoulder and put what he had in his hand under her nose.

The ring caught fire and light and promise. She covered her mouth with her hand as it shot out dreams that dazzled her eyes. "Oh, my God."

"Grandmother Templeton's engagement ring. You remember her."

"I— Yes. Yes."

"It came to me. I got it out of the safe deposit box, had it in my pocket the day I walked in on you and your Italian friend."

"Oh. Oh."

"No, you're not going to sit down." He jerked her upright and into his arms. "I want your knees weak. I wouldn't mind if you babbled too, since you've spoiled my romantic plans of giving you this on one knee in candlelight."

"Oh." She dropped her head on his chest. "Oh."

"Don't cry. I can't stand it when you cry."

"I'm not." To prove it, she lifted her face and showed him she was laughing. "I was going to ask you."

"Ask me what?"

"Jesus, why can't we keep up with each other?" She mopped at tears with her fingers. "That night, I was going to ask you to marry me. I figured it was going to take a lot of work and flare to talk you into it. So I had it all planned. I was going to dare you.''

"You're kidding.''

"Take off those damn glasses.'' She snatched them off herself, tossed them recklessly over her shoulder, heard them shatter on the terra-cotta. "I still beat you to it. I still asked you first.'' Before he could move, she snatched the ring out of his hand. "And you said yes. This proves it.''

"I didn't say anything yet,'' he corrected and made a grab for her. "Damn it, Margo, come here. If I don't get my hands on you, I'll explode.''

"Say yes.'' She danced out of reach, holding the ring aloft like a torch. "Say yes first.''

"All right, yes. What the hell. I'll take you on.''

He caught her on the fly, whirled her around. And she felt something swirl inside her. No, it's not the spinning, Mum, she thought. It is the man.

His mouth was on hers before her feet touched the ground. "For life,'' he murmured, cupping her face.

"No. Forever.'' She tipped her mouth to his again. "I want forever.''

He took her hand, holding her gaze as he slipped the ring on her finger. It fit like a dream. "Done,'' he said.

Turn the page for an exclusive preview of
the second novel in the Dream *trilogy*

Holding the Dream

Available now from Piatkus

Her childhood had been a lie.

Her father had been a thief.

Her mind struggled to absorb those two facts, to absorb, analyze, and accept. Kate Powell had trained herself to be a practical woman, one who worked hard toward goals, earned them step by careful step. Wavering was not permitted. Short-cuts were not taken. Rewards were earned with sweat, planning, and effort.

That, she had always believed, was who she was, a product of her heredity, her upbringing, and her own stringent standards for self.

When a child was orphaned at an early age, when she lived with the loss, when she had, essentially, watched her parents die, there seemed little else that could be so wrenching.

But there could be, Kate realized as she sat—still shell-shocked—behind her tidy desk in her tidy office at Bittle and Associates.

Out of that early tragedy had come enormous blessings. Her family had been taken away, but she had been given another. The distant kinship hadn't mattered to Thomas and Susan Templeton. They had taken her in, raised her, given her a home and love. They had given her everything, without question.

And they must have known, she realized. They must have always known.

They had known when they had taken her from the hospital after the accident. When they'd comforted her and had given her the gift of belonging, they had known.

They'd taken her across the continent to California. To the sweeping cliffs and beauty of Big Sur. To Templeton House.

There, in that grand home, as gracious and welcoming as any of the glamorous Templeton hotels, they had made her part of the whole.

They'd given her Laura and Josh, their children, as siblings. They'd given her Margo Sullivan, the housekeeper's daughter, who had been accepted as part of the family even before Kate.

They had given her clothes and food, education, advantages. They had given her rules and discipline and the encouragement to pursue her dreams. And most of all, they had given her love and family and pride.

Yet they had known from the beginning what she had— twenty years later—just discovered.

Her father had been a thief, a man under indictment for embezzlement. Caught skimming from his own clients' accounts, he had died facing shame, ruin, prison.

She had never known, might never have known, if not for a capricious twist of fate, which had brought an old friend of Lincoln Powell's into her office that morning.

He'd been so delighted to see her, had remembered her as a child. It had warmed her to be remembered, to realize that he had come to her with his business because of the old tie with her parents. She'd taken the time to chat with him, though she had little to spare during those last weeks before the April fifteenth tax deadline.

And he had sat just there, in the chair on the other side of the desk, reminiscing. He'd bounced her on his knee, he'd said, had worked in the same ad firm as her father. Which was why, he'd told her, since he'd relocated to California and now had his own firm, he wanted her as his accountant. She'd thanked him, had mixed her questions about his business and his financial requirements with ones about her parents.

Then she had said nothing, could say nothing when he had so casually spoken of the accusations, the charges, and the sorrow he felt that her father had died before he could make restitution.

"He'd never intended to steal, just borrow. Oh, it was wrong, God knows. I always felt partially responsible because I was the one who told him about the real estate deal, encouraged him to invest. I didn't know he'd already lost most of his capital in a couple of deals that went sour. He'd have put the money back. Linc would have found a way, always did. He was always a little resentful that his cousin rode so high while he barely scraped by."

And the man—God, she couldn't remember his name, couldn't remember anything but the words—had smiled at her. The whole time he'd spoken, made excuses, added his explanations, she had simply sat, nodding, while this stranger who'd known her father destroyed her foundation.

"He had a sore spot where Tommy Templeton was concerned. Funny, when you think it turned out that he was the one to raise you after it all. But Linc never meant any harm, Katie. He was just reckless. Never had a chance to prove himself, and that's the real crime if you ask me."

The real crime, Kate thought as her stomach churned and knotted. He had stolen, because he had been desperate for money and had taken the easy way. Because he'd been a thief, she thought now. A cheat, and had cheated the justice system by hitting an icy patch of road and crashing his car. Killing himself and his wife, and leaving his daughter an orphan.

And fate had given her as a father the very man her own father had been so envious of. Through his death, she had, in essence, become a Templeton.

Had it been deliberate? she wondered. Had he been so desperate, so reckless, so angry that he'd chosen death? She could barely remember him, a thin, pale, nervous man who was quick to temper.

A man with big plans, she thought now. A man who had spun those plans into delightful fantasies for his child. Visions of big houses, fine cars, fun-packed trips to Disney World.

And all the while they had lived in a tiny house so like all the other tiny houses on the block, with an old sedan that rattled and no trips to anywhere.

So he had stolen, and he had been caught. And he had died.

What had her mother done? Kate wondered. What had she felt? Was this why Kate remembered her best as a woman with worry in her eyes and a tight smile?

Had he stolen before? The idea made her cold inside. Had he stolen before and somehow gotten away with it? A little here, a little there, until he'd become careless.

She remembered arguments, often over money. And worse, the silence that followed them. The silence that night. That heavy, hurting silence in the car between her parents before the awful spin, the screams and pain.

Shuddering, she closed her eyes, fisted her hands tight and fought back the drumming headache.

Oh, God, she had loved them. Loved the memory of them. Couldn't bear to have it smeared and spoiled. And couldn't face, she realized with horrid shame, being the daughter of a cheat.

She wouldn't believe it. Not yet. She took slow breaths,

turned to her computer. With mechanical efficiency she accessed the library in New Hampshire where she'd been born and had lived for the first eight years of her life.

It took time, and determination, but she ordered copies of newspapers for the year before the accident, requested faxes of any article having to do with Lincoln Powell. While she waited, she contacted the lawyer back east who had handled the disposition of her parents' estate.

She was a creature comfortable with technology. Within an hour she had all she needed. She could read the details in black and white, details that cemented what facts the lawyers had given her.

The accusations, the criminal charges, the scandal. A scandal, she realized, that had earned print space because of Lincoln Powell's family connection to the Templetons. And the missing funds, replaced in full after her parents were buried. Replaced, Kate was certain, by the people who had raised her as one of their own.

The Templetons, she thought, who had been drawn into the ugliness, had quietly taken the responsibility, and the child. Had protected, always, the child.

There in her quiet office, alone, she laid her head on the desk and wept. And wept. And when the weeping was done, she shook out pills for the headache, and more for the burning in her stomach. When she gathered her briefcase, she told herself she would bury it. Just bury it. As she had buried her parents.

It could not be changed, could not be fixed. She was the same, she assured herself, the same woman she had been that morning. Yet she found she couldn't open her office door, couldn't face the possibility of running into a colleague in the corridors. Instead, she sat again, closed her eyes, sought comfort in old memories. A picture, she thought, of family and tradition. Of who she was, what she had been given, and what she had been raised to become.

STOP HERE

Visit **www.facebook.com/ norarobertsjdrobb**

Discover Nora Roberts' latest news
Connect with Nora Roberts' readers
Sign up to Nora Roberts' newsletter
Enter exclusive competitions

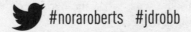 #noraroberts   #jdrobb